ROYAL
Baby

TRISH MOREY

LYNN RAYE HARRIS

SABRINA PHILIPS

MILLS
BOON

Mills & Boon, an imprint of Harlequin (UK) Limited, Eton House, 18-24 Paradise Road, Richmond, Surrey TW9 1SR

ROYAL BABY © Harlequin Enterprises II B.V./S.à.r.l. 2012

Forced Wife, Royal Love-Child © Trish Morey 2009
Cavelli's Lost Heir © Lynn Raye Harris 2009
Prince of Montéz, Pregnant Mistress © Sabrina Philips 2009

ISBN: 978 0 263 89780 7

012-0613

Forced Wife, Royal Love-Child

TRISH MOREY

Trish Morey wrote her first book at age eleven for a children's book-week competition. Entitled *Island Dreamer*, it told the story of an orphaned girl and her life on a small island at the mouth of South Australia's Murray River. *Island Dreamer* also proved to be her first rejection—her entry was disqualified unread and, shattered and broken, she turned to a life where she could combine her love of fiction with her need for creativity—and became a chartered accountant. Life wasn't all dull though, as she embarked on a skydiving course, completing three jumps before deciding that she'd given her fear of heights a run for its money.

Meanwhile, she fell in love and married a handsome guy who cut computer code and later penned her second book—the totally riveting *A Guide to Departmental Budgeting*—whilst working for the New Zealand Treasury.

Back home in Australia after the birth of their second daughter, Trish spied an article saying that Mills & Boon® was actively seeking new authors. It was one of those "Eureka!" moments—Trish was going to be one of those authors! Eleven years after reading that fateful article (actually on 18th June, 2003, at 6:32 p.m!) the magical phone call came and Trish finally realized her dream.

According to Trish, writing and selling a book is a major life achievement that ranks up there with jumping out of an airplane and motherhood. All three take commitment, determination and sheer guts, but the effort is so very, very worthwhile.

Trish now lives with her husband and four young daughters in a special part of South Australia, surrounded by orchards and bushland and visited by the occasional koala and kangaroo.

You can visit Trish at her website at www.trishmorey.com or drop her a line at trish@trishmorey.com.

For Gavin, with much love.
Thanks for your endless support over the years,
for all the good times and the laughs, and thanks,
more than anything, for just being there.
Happy anniversary, honey.

CHAPTER ONE

THE sex was good.

Surprisingly good.

With a growl Rafe gave himself up to the inevitable and hauled her naked body against his own, drinking deeply of the sleepy scent of her skin, enjoying the way the last remnants of her perfume mingled with the lingering muskiness of passion, and feeling a corresponding tightening in his loins. He'd barely dozed but again he was ready for her and he wasn't about to waste a minute of their first night together. Not after it taking the best part of a week to get her into his bed.

He couldn't remember the last time that had happened.

Through the filmy curtains of his apartment the lights of Paris still glowed, even as the night sky slowly peeled away and the soft light of dawn turned her skin lustrous. He pressed his lips to her neck and suckled at the tender flesh below her ear, and was instantly rewarded with a sound like a purr. His lips curled into a smile on her skin. There was a price for making him wait so long and he'd enjoyed every last minute of exacting his payment.

She stirred into life then, rolling towards him and reaching out, a low sigh vibrating through her as her Titian hair moved across her pillow like a curtain rising on the next act.

How appropriate, he thought, already anticipating it. He raised himself over her, settling between her legs. A week it had taken to get her here. A week they had wasted. He wasn't wasting a moment more.

He lowered his head and captured one ripe nipple between his lips, drawing it in deep, circling the tightening bud with his tongue. She arched under him, made another of those little mewing sounds and clung on, her fingers tangling in his hair.

He loved her breasts, loved their shape and the feel of them in his hands, and he loved the contrast in textures, from their satin-soft skin to their pebbled circles to their bullet-like peaks when she was aroused. Loved making them so. She tasted of woman and salt and sex and he couldn't get enough. And when she lifted her hips and teased her curls against the throbbing length of him, he couldn't see the point of waiting any longer.

Rearing up, he grabbed a packet from the side table, jammed it between his teeth and reefed off the top.

'Let me,' she said, a raw huskiness edging her voice, and a hunger in her hazel eyes that reflected his own desperate need fed into it and ramped it up tenfold. He allowed himself a smile as she took it from him, lifting herself higher on the bed and applying it almost reverentially. He raised his eyes to the ceiling at that first, delicate touch. So much for the woman who just last night had seemed almost nervous about sex. The prospect of the next few weeks was looking better all the time.

And then anticipation turned to agony, his smile morphing into a grimace when she took her own sweet time rolling the damn thing on. He grabbed her hand, finished the job and pushed her down in one fell movement, her gasp of surprise changing to one of delight as he plunged deep into her exquisite depths.

The act of fusion shorted his thought processes, until there was room for just one spark of awareness, barely a thought, more an acknowledgement that seeped through his sex-fogged senses.

Not just good.

The sex was perfect.

That couldn't be her face in the mirror. Sienna Wainwright stopped dead in her tracks and looked hard. The stranger stared back at her, wide-eyed despite the lack of sleep, her lips plump and pink from his attention, and her usually restrained hair coiled and wild with abandon. She looked wanton, thoroughly ravished and a million miles away from who Sienna Wainwright was supposed to be.

Had been!

Until last night. Until the final unravelling of her defences.

Tentatively, almost experimentally, she put the fingers of one hand to her lips, felt their still tender flesh, traced the now blurred line where they melded into the rest of her face.

Rafe had touched her like this, the pads of his fingers tender on her skin, tracing every line and curve of her lips, almost as if worshipping them, before he'd dipped his mouth and kissed her. Kissed her so sweetly it had taken her breath away. Kissed her so passionately it had made her forget all about the insanity of letting him have his way with her.

And before she'd let him have his way with her all over again.

She squeezed her eyes shut and dragged in a breath, her breathing coming in short bursts with the fresh memories of his amazing lovemaking still sparking off thrills in her body like tiny aftershocks.

Rafe Lombardi, international financier and self-made billionaire, and no wonder, given his knack for pulling back businesses from the brink of failure and turning them into global success stories—only the most marriageable and least-attainable man on earth, if you believed what gossip rags world-wide suggested. Sienna had had no reason to disbelieve them or the reports of the long list of one-time partners left ship-wrecked in his wake. It was half the reason she'd wanted to keep her distance, if not run a mile in the opposite direction.

She wasn't in Rafe's league and she knew it, economically, socially or sexually, her experience with men up until now limited and frankly disappointing in the bedroom department.

Whereas Rafe Lombardi moved in the highest circles, mixing with the crème de la crème of society, power brokers and tycoons and with the designer women who clung to them like accessories. What would a man like him see in her, a woman who had to work for her living and so far down the social scale as not to register, other than just another chance encounter, another notch in his belt?

So she'd tried to hold him off as long as she could, thinking he'd give up and move on to greener pastures. Expecting he would as soon as she'd told him no the first time.

But he hadn't. Instead of abandoning the chase, he'd pur-sued her with a single-minded determination that had simul-taneously terrified and secretly thrilled her.

Rafe Lombardi was clearly a man used to getting his own way.

She turned on the shower and adjusted the temperature, stepping in and turning her face into the spray, eyes closed as the liquid massage worked its magic on her newly sensitised skin, caressing places where just so recently Rafe had worked his own unique brand of magic and where he no doubt would again as soon as he kept his promise to join her in the shower.

Her body hummed in anticipation. Rafe, that body and water. That would make for one lethal combination.

A bubble of laughter welled up unexpectedly. She'd turned him down how many times these last few days? She must have been mad. For it was clear after just one night with him that any woman in her right senses would take Rafe Lombardi and whatever he offered and hang onto him as long as she possibly could, and to hell with the consequences.

Besides, she'd been working hard these few months, getting herself established back in Europe, with a new home and a new job. She deserved a bit of rest and recreation.

There would be consequences, nothing surer, but for now she hugged the knowledge that he'd asked to see her again like a secret treasure.

She spun around, letting the water pound the back of her neck as she soaped her hair, half a mind anticipating his arrival, the other half employed on working out what it was that made him so different to every other man she'd ever met. His tall, dark good looks, the designer stubble and thick wavy hair that coiled at his collar just a shade too long to be considered conservative were enough in themselves to set him apart from the crowd.

But he was so much more than the superficial. There was a confidence in the way he carried himself and in the masterful way he handled people and situations. He wore power as easily as he wore the clothes on his hard-wired body, and it had terrified her to feel that power, and to know it had been directed one hundred per cent towards her.

She shivered despite the warm torrent, remembering how vulnerable he'd made her feel with just one heated glance, one seemingly innocent brush of skin against skin. He had the gift of making a woman feel so desirable, of making her feel she was the centre of his existence and he'd used that gift mercilessly to flatter her during his pursuit, while his eyes had held a look that somehow seemed to burn its way into her soul and beyond.

And then he'd used that gift to wield her to his purpose in his bed.

She directed her face into the spray on a sigh. No, Rafe

Lombardi was like no man she'd ever met before. Little wonder he'd left a trail of broken hearts in his wake, because if a woman wasn't careful, he was everything that a woman could so easily fall in love with…

Oh, no!

She snapped off the tap and yanked the towel from the rail with a determined flick, angry with herself for letting her thoughts drift so far. Remembering how he'd made her feel, recalling the hungry look in his eye while he remained poised over her in that exquisite moment before their union, that was one thing. But building some fairy tale happy ending that could never happen…

Living in Paris must be going to her head. She'd just landed the job of her dreams. An affair was good. An affair was welcome. She wasn't looking for anything more.

Sienna wrapped herself in a towel, half aware that now the shower was turned off she could hear the sound of the news channel drifting in from the room outside. Rafe had turned it on to check the global money market report before joining her. Which he hadn't. Proof, if she'd really needed it, that she was nothing more to him than a distraction from his high-powered life.

Albeit a distraction he wanted to see again, just a few short hours away. Right now that was enough.

Her hair wrapped turban style under a towel and wearing one of the plush robes she'd found hanging behind the bath-room door, she emerged from the fog-filled en suite. There was a trolley in the room that hadn't been there before from which emanated the tantalising scent of fresh coffee and warm pastries, but Rafe was still standing near the storm-tossed bed where she'd left him, though at some stage he'd pulled on a pair of jeans that hung low on his hips, zipped but with the top button still undone. The sight was nearly enough to bring her undone, until she caught the scowl turning his face to thunder as he listened intently to the stream of frenzied Italian issuing from the television.

She moved closer, and, for the first time since they'd been together, he didn't turn towards her, didn't greet her with that soul-deep smile. After enjoying his almost instinctive reaction to her presence for the past week, she missed it more than she'd expected.

'What is it?' she asked, coming alongside, trying to follow the torrent of Italian delivered too fast for her scant knowledge of the spoken language and, at the same time, unable to resist touching one hand to the small of his back. 'What's going on?'

He silenced her with a hiss, shrugging away from the gesture, away from her, and she sensed distance opening up between them where once there had been none. She heard a name—Montvelatte—recognising it as a tiny principality strategically perched in the territorial waters between France and Italy, and saw a reporter against a shifting backdrop— what looked like a fairy-tale palace lit up against the night sky, then the line of famous casinos fringing the harbour and a picture of the former Prince Eduardo. The reporter continued talking animatedly, accompanying footage of an army of maroon-jacketed gendarmes frogmarching the young Prince and his brother into cars before being driven away from the palace. She frowned, trying to make sense of it all. Clearly something was very wrong in Montvelatte.

The reporter ended his report with a scowl and an emphatic slash of one hand accompanying the words—'"Montvelatte, *finito*!"'

The news programme crossed back to their studio before moving on to their next story. Rafe hit the remote, the screen went black and he turned his back on both the screen and her, raking his fingers through his hair.

She loosened the towel at her hair, began rubbing it in cautious circles, sensing that something major had transpired and knowing she was missing more than what had been reported in the sensational yet indecipherable television coverage.

'What's happening? It looked like the police were carting away the entire royal family.'

He spun round, his ruggedly beautiful face reduced to a mask of tightly drawn flesh over bones suddenly lying too close to the surface, his eyes both wild and filled with something that looked like grief.

'It's over,' he said, in a voice that turned her cold. Then his eyes glazed even colder. 'It's over.'

An inexplicable fear zipped down her spine. Finally he'd acknowledged her presence and yet she doubted he'd even seen her. Right now it was more as if he was looking right through her.

'What's over? What is it that's happened?'

For a minute she wasn't even sure he'd even heard her, his only movement the rapid rise and fall of his chest, but then his chin jerked up and his eyes took on a predatory gleam, finding a focus that had been lacking before.

'Justice,' he said cryptically, crossing the carpet silently in his bare feet until he stood before her, his turmoil-filled eyes holding hers hostage, his naked chest so close it took her breath away. And before she could ask him what he meant, before she could ask what any of it meant, he reached over and took the damp towel from her hands, tossing it purposefully to one side.

Sienna trembled, her pulse quickening as it always did when she had one hundred per cent of his attention, his scent and his aura wrapping around her and pulling her in.

'Tell me,' she whispered in spite of it, refusing to give herself up to his power, knowing that once he touched her, she'd be lost. 'What does it mean?'

Rafe said nothing. Instead, there was a tug at her waist followed by a loosening, and then the sides of her gown fell open. She felt the kiss of air against her skin, heard the hiss of breath through his teeth as he gazed down at the ribbon of exposed flesh, and felt that searing heat of his eyes like the brand of a torch. 'It means I want you,' he said, reaching out the fingers of one hand to scoop back the robe on one side, tracing a path down her aching breast to her nipple and circling that sensitive peak. *'Now!'*

Her body was ready, the swell of her breasts and the insistent thrumming of the pulse between her thighs telling her so. But something flashed across his eyes, and she sensed something of the torment he was feeling, and panic shimmied up her spine as she recognised the truth. He didn't see her at all, not really. She was merely a vessel, a vehicle for release from whatever demons were plaguing him, and once again, she wondered why he seemed to care so much about a tiny island principality that featured in the tabloids more for the exploits of its young Princes and their latest love interests, rather than for any financial concern Rafe would normally be interested in.

Sienna put her hands to his chest, made a move to push herself away. 'I don't know if this is such a good idea,' she warned, her head shaking even though the rest of her body betrayed her by trembling under his skilled hands, and her hands refused to lift from the wall of his chest. 'I have to get to work. I'll be late.'

'Then be late!' he growled, uncaring, before sliding a hand around her neck and pulling her to him. His lips captured hers, punishing and demanding, in a kiss in which it was impossible not to feel the turmoil that held him hostage. He tasted of coffee and need and passion—all these things she had tasted before. But now she tasted something new, something triggered by the news report that drove him, an aching fury that moved his kiss beyond mere passion to something dark and dangerous and all-consuming.

And meanwhile his mouth was everywhere—on her lips, at her throat, on her breasts, hungry as he grappled with her robe, reefing it over her shoulders, forcing it down and pulling her naked body against his. She went willingly then, melting into him because she had no real choice, her senses overloaded with the taste and scent of him, the mouth suckling and nipping at her breast, the brush of denim against her legs, the feel of his hot flesh melting her bones, the sound of his zip coming undone…

So many sensations, building one upon the other, a frenzy of feeling that threatened to consume her whole. And then he was lifting her, urging her legs around his waist, only to lower her slowly down until she felt his rock-hard length nudge at her core, and it was her turn to consume him.

He made a sound as he filled her, harsh like the cry of a wounded animal, as if it had been torn from his soul, and she clung to him, afraid for him.

Afraid for herself.

And then he was pumping into her, so fast and furious that sensation exploded inside her like a fireball. She was falling then, his arms still locked around her, barely aware of what was happening when her back met the rumpled bed and he lifted himself, easing out of her until he sat poised there, at the very brink. Through eyes still blurred with passion she looked up at him, looked into his wild eyes and saw the agony that marked his beautiful face and read the words inscribed on her soul—*it was already too late*—when with a roar he thrust into her, burying himself to the hilt again and again in a final turbulent release that sent her shuddering into the abyss once more.

* * *

It was his voice that brought her back to life, the low, urgent tones as he spoke into the phone rumbling through her like a passing thundercloud, but it was a glance at the clock that catapulted her to full consciousness and back into the bathroom to dress.

He barely noticed her go, his attention almost one hundred per cent on the words his business partner was saying. Yannis Markides, one of the few people on the planet who knew the truth of Rafc's background and the identity of his father, knew more than anyone what the television reports would mean to him.

'You have to go,' Yannis urged. 'It's your duty.'

'Now you're sounding just like Sebastiano. He's already in Paris, apparently, and on his way. He certainly didn't waste any time hunting me down.'

'Sebastiano's right to do so. Without you, Montvelatte will cease to exist. Do you want to be responsible for that?'

'I'm not the only one. There's Marietta too—'

'And the day you drop something like this on the shoulders of your little sister, is the day you lose me as a friend. Anyway, you know law dictates it must be a male heir. This is your call, Raphael, your duty.'

'Even if I go, there's no guarantee I can save it. The island is a financial basket case. You heard the reports—Carlo and Roberto and their cronies have drained the economy dry.'

There was a deep laugh at the end of the line. 'And this isn't what you and I do for a living every day? Bring the fiscally dead back to life?'

'Then *you* go, if you're so concerned. I like my life just the way it is.' It was the truth. He'd worked hard to get where he was, taking on the hardest projects out there and proving to himself time and again he was up to the task. And he'd proven something else to himself—that he didn't need to be royalty to be someone.

'But it's not up to me, Rafe. You're the son, the next in line. There is nobody else who can do what you have to do.' There was a pause. 'Besides, don't you think it's what your mother would have wanted you to do?'

Rafe should have known Yannis would hit below the belt. They'd grown up so close he was better than any brother could ever be. The downside was he also knew how to hit hard and to hit where it hurt the most. He wasn't about to admit that fact, though he couldn't deny another truth. 'I'm just glad she died before she found out his death had been organised by his own sons.'

'Not all of his sons,' Yannis corrected. 'There's still you.'

He laughed, short and hard. 'That's right. The bastard son. The son he exiled along with his bastard's mother and baby sister. Why should I go back to bail out his island nation? It's sickening what happened to him, sickening that his own sons conspired against him. But why should I be the one to pick up the pieces? I hate what happened to him, but I don't owe him a thing.'

'Why should you be the one? Because Montvelattian blood flows in your veins. This is your birthright, Rafe. Seize it. If not for your father's sake, then for your mother's.'

Rafe shook his head, trying to clear his thoughts. Yannis knew him too well, knew he felt no loyalty for a father who had never been more than a name to him, and who had discarded his own son and the woman who had borne him as easily as if he'd been brushing lint off his jacket. Even the knowledge that his death had not been an accident didn't cause Rafe any pangs of loss. It was impossible to lose something you'd never had, and Prince Eduardo had never been part of his life.

But his mother was a different matter. Louisa had loved Montvelatte and had talked endlessly of scented orange groves, of colourful vines, of herb bushes tangy with the spray of sea, and of mountainsides covered with flowers amidst the olive trees that she would never see again.

She'd never forgotten the small island nation that had been her home for twenty-one years and that had spat her out, sending her into exile for the rest of her too short existence.

Yannis was right. It had always been her dream to return. It had never happened in her lifetime, but maybe this was his chance to make it happen for her in spirit.

Merda!

Sienna emerged from the bathroom ready for work and wearing a frown. They'd made love so quickly—too quickly for either of them to have given a thought about protection. The risks of pregnancy were low, it was late in her cycle, but there were still risks and she couldn't help but regret her decision not to renew her prescription for the pill when her course had expired last month. At the time there hadn't seemed much point and finding a new doctor with everything else going on had been the last thing on her mind. She now wished she'd thought about it.

And at the risk of making her even later for work, she couldn't leave without at least broaching the subject.

'We need to talk,' she said, registering that he'd finished the call as she gathered up the last of her things and stashed them in her bag. She turned when he didn't respond. He was still sitting on the bed with his back to her, his head in his hands, a picture of such utter desolation that she would never have recognised him if she hadn't known it was him. His air of authority was gone. His power gone. Instead he wore a cloak of vulnerability so heavy that she felt the weight of it herself. 'What is it?' she asked, drawing closer but afraid to touch him, afraid she might feel the pain that was torturing him. 'What's wrong? Is this about that news report, about Montvelatte?'

For heavy seconds he didn't move, didn't speak—then finally let out his breath in a rush as he lifted his head, his fingers working hard at his temples.

'What do you know of the island?' Rafe asked, without looking around.

Sienna shrugged, thrown by the question. But at least he was talking to her and she knew that the pain would be lesser if he did. She rounded the bed and knelt alongside him on the dishevelled linen, finally game to put a hand to him, sliding her hands over his shoulders, feeling the tension tight and knotted under her fingers, trying to massage it away with the stroke of her thumbs. 'What does anyone know? Other than it's a small island in the Mediterranean, famous for both its stunning scenery and the string of casinos that have made it rich. A Mecca for tourists and gamblers alike.'

He snorted dismissively and twisted then, capturing one hand in his and pulling it to his mouth and pressing it to his lips. Hardly a kiss—his fingers were so tight around hers they hurt, his dark eyes almost black. 'And for gangsters, it turns out. Apparently they've been laundering drug money through the casinos ever since Prince Carlo took the crown five years ago.'

Behind him the clock continued to advance and she cursed inwardly. She had to get to work. It had taken some doing to land the job with Sapphire Blue Charter, only her ability to speak French and three superb references winning her the contract and making up for her being a woman, and an Australian to boot, but she was still under probation. The way she was going this morning she'd be lucky if she still had a job by the time she got to the airport. But she couldn't leave him, not like this. 'It still doesn't make sense. They've arrested the Prince and his brother in front of the entire world's media over unproven money-laundering charges? Whatever happened to being innocent until proven guilty?'

Rafe swept from the bed then, grabbing his jeans, quickly dropping those in favour of a snow-white robe that he wrapped and lashed around himself and that showed his olive skin and dark features to perfection. Through the vast expanse of window behind him it seemed the entire city of Paris was laid out like a glorious offering, the Eiffel Tower the centre-point in a brand new morning, but it was the fiery glare from his eyes that demanded her full attention.

'I didn't say they'd been arrested over the money-laundering charges.'

'Then why?'

'Because now they've been linked to the death of the former Prince.'

For a moment she was shocked into silence, her mind busy recalling the history she knew of the tiny principality. 'But Prince Eduardo drowned. He fell from his yacht.'

His hand dropped away, and his face looked even harsher then, if it were possible, his skin drawn so tight it made her jaw ache in sympathy. 'The authorities have just uncovered fresh evidence. He didn't fall.'

Shock punched into her more effectively than any fist. *'They killed their own father?'* No wonder the news reports were full of it. It was more than a scandal. It was a monarchy in crisis, a diplomatic nightmare. A nightmare that somehow held Rafe in its thrall.

'I still don't understand, though. It's horrible, but why does it matter so much to you?'

Sienna searched his eyes, dark eyes filled with grief and torment and pain that scarred their depths, and saw the shutters come down again even as he moved away from her. But the intention was clear. He'd said all that he was going to say.

A final look at the clock told her she couldn't wait any longer. 'I'm sorry, Rafe, but I really have to go.'

He didn't even turn around. 'Yes.'

She slipped on her shoes, picked up her jacket. 'I don't finish until six tonight. How about I call you once I'm home?'

This time he did look at her and she glimpsed something skate across his eyes, something warm and maybe a little sad. Then he blinked and whatever she'd seen was gone. 'No,' he clipped, 'I can't see you tonight.'

'Oh.' She swallowed, trying desperately not to show on her face how disappointed she felt. 'I've got a late shift tomorrow, but how about Wednesday, then?'

But he just gave a toss of his head and opened a closet door, pulling out a travel bag. 'No. Not then. I'll be away.'

'You're leaving?'

His eyes, when they turned on her, were cold, unfathomable. 'Like I said. It's over.'

And mere disappointment curdled into despair, leaving her feeling wrong and suddenly shaky inside her gut. Hadn't he been talking about Montvelatte when he'd said that? 'Where are you going?'

'Away.'

Crazy. She should have accepted his response for the dismissal it was intended to be—no doubt would have if she had been thinking rationally. But right now she felt crazy. He'd pursued her for a week for the sake of just one night? She'd known she would never be more than a short-term distraction for him and could live with that, but, damn it, she wasn't prepared to let it end just yet, not when such a short time ago he hadn't so much as asked her, but *told* her he would see her again.

'I don't understand.'

'I thought you were late for work!' He tossed the words roughly over his shoulder, not even bothering to look at her as he dragged things from his closet.

Breath snagged in her chest. In another life she would have already left, his dismissal of her more than plain. But not now. Not after the night they'd shared, and when he'd been the one to promise more. 'Is this something to do with that news report, because until that happened, you seemed quite happy to meet up with me again? Why is it that what happens on a tiny island in the Mediterranean is so important to you anyway?'

He stopped pulling things out of the wardrobe then and swivelled around, dumping underwear and shirts carelessly into his carry on as he fired her question right back at her. 'Why is it so important to me?'

And for just a moment, when she saw the pain etched in lines upon his face, she wished she'd never asked. 'You saw those two being carted away by the police.'

'Prince Carlo and Prince Roberto? Yes, of course. What's wrong? Do you know them?'

'You could say that.' A shadow moved across his features. 'We shared the same father.'

Then the buzzer rang and he brushed past her shell-shocked form to answer it. 'I'm sorry, but you really have to go.'

Rafe pulled the door open. 'Come in, Sebastiano,' he said, ushering in an officious-looking man in a double-breasted suit. In the same breath she was ushered out without so much as a goodbye. 'It's been a long time.'

The door closed behind her with a determined click but not before she'd heard the words the older gentleman had uttered in greeting, *'Prince Raphael, you must come quickly...'*

CHAPTER TWO

Six weeks later

THE chopper flew out of the sun, past the blade of rock that was Iseo's Pyramid and low over the line where the cliff met the azure sea. For seconds it hovered effortlessly over the helipad before touching gently down. Rafe watched the descent and landing, knowing who was on board and resenting the intrusion even before the *whump whump* of the rotors had settled into a whine of engines.

'Contessa D'Angelo and her daughter, Genevieve, have arrived, Your Highness,' his *aide-de-camp* announced, appearing from nowhere with his usual brisk efficiency.

'So I gathered,' Rafe answered drily, without putting down the Treasury papers he'd been reading or making any other move to respond. 'I think I'll take that second cup of coffee now, Sebastiano.' He noticed the telltale tic of disapproval in the older man's cheek even as he complied by pouring a stream of rich black liquid from the silver coffee jug into his cup. So be it. If Sebastiano was so concerned with finding a suitable princess for Montvelatte, he could perform the meet and greets himself. After something like half a dozen potential brides in ten days, Rafe was over it. Besides, he had more important issues on his mind, like solving the principality's immediate cash crisis. Montvelatte might need an heir to ensure the principality's future, but there would be no future for any of them if the dire financial straits his half-brothers had landed them in weren't sorted out and soon.

Sebastiano hovered impatiently while Rafe took a sip of the fragrant coffee.

'And your guests, Your Highness? Your driver is waiting.'

Rafe took his time replacing the cup on its saucer before leaning back in his chair. 'Isn't it time we gave up this wife-hunting charade, Sebastiano? I don't think I can bear to meet another pretty young thing and her ambitious stage mother.'

'Genevieve D'Angelo,' he began, sounding suitably put out on the young woman's behalf, 'can hardly be written off as some "pretty young thing". She has an impeccable background and her family have been nobles for centuries. She is eminently qualified for the role as Montvelatte's Princess.'

'And what good is it to be "eminently qualified" if I don't want her?'

'How do you know you don't want her before you've even met her?'

Rafe looked up at the older man, his eyes narrowing. Nobody else could get away with such impertinence. Nobody else would even try. But Sebastiano had been in charge of palace administration for something like forty years, and, while he'd been shunted to one side in his half-brothers' desire to rule unopposed, Rafe credited him with almost certainly being the one thing that had held the principality together during those years of recklessness and financial ineptitude. Not that that meant he had to like what his aide said. 'I haven't wanted one of them yet.'

Sebastiano gave an exasperated sigh, his attention on the re-cently arrived aircraft. 'We've been through this. Montvelatte needs an heir. How are you to achieve this without a wife? We are simply trying to expedite the process.'

'By turning this island into some kind of ghastly reality game show?'

Sebastiano gave up the fight with a small bow. 'I'll inform the Contessa and her daughter you'll meet them in the library after they've freshened up.' Without waiting for a reply he withdrew as briskly as he'd arrived. Scant seconds later Rafe noticed the golf buggy used to transport travellers between the helipad and the palace heading out along the narrow path.

Rafe sighed. He knew Sebastiano was right, that Montvelatte's future was insecure without another generation of Lombardis, and that nobody would invest the necessary funds in Montvelatte's financial reconstruction without a guarantee of the longevity of the island's status as a principality. But he still didn't like the implications.

The buggy came to a halt alongside the helicopter where his aide emerged crisp and dapper, stooping under the still-circling blades as he approached before opening the door.

Rafe turned back to his papers and the problem at hand. He had no interest in its passengers: the hopeful mother, the 'eminently qualified' daughter. He'd seen the stills, he'd seen the tapes and the two-minute interview, all of which had been provided to give him the opportunity to assess how this particular marriage prospect looked, walked and talked and how she might satisfy at least half the requirements of a future Princess of Montvelatte—that of looking the part. The other half—*doing her part*—had been apparently already assured by a barrage of eminent medical specialists.

Rafe had no sympathy for these women, these carefully selected marriage prospects, who seemed so keen for the opportunity to parade in front of him like some choice cut of meat. All so they might secure marriage to a near perfect stranger and, through it, the title of princess.

It made no sense to him. What they had subjected themselves to to prove that their families and their past were beyond reproach and that there were no health impediments to both conceiving a child and carrying it to full term, beggared belief.

On the other hand, nobody had dared question his prowess to conceive a child, for despite the scandalous circumstances of his own bastard birth thirty-three years ago, he had the right bloodlines and that, it was deemed, was sufficient.

He would have laughed, if it weren't the truth. A hitherto unknown prince had appeared on the scene in a blaze of publicity and suddenly everyone wanted a piece of the fairy tale.

Rafe glanced up, noticing Sebastiano's lips move as he handed the second of the women into the buggy, the silky outfit she was wearing shifting on the breeze, rippling like the sea.

Even from here he could see she was beautiful. Tall, willow slim and every bit as elegant as the photographs and film footage suggested.

But then they were all beautiful.

And he was completely unmoved.

He sighed. Maybe that was one good thing about this search for a princess. At least nobody would labour under the misapprehension that this was a love match. At least he would be spared that.

The woman hesitated a fraction before entering the vehicle and turned her silver-blonde head up towards the palace, scanning from behind her designer sunglasses. Was she looking for him, wondering where he was and whether the snub of not being there to greet her was deliberate? Or was she merely sizing up the real estate?

Rafe drained the last of the thick, rich coffee and collected his papers together. He would have to meet her, he supposed.

He might as well get it over with. But he would talk to Sebastiano and make him see sense. This system of princess hunting that Sebastiano and his team of courtiers had devised was no basis for a marriage. Especially not his.

Over at the helipad the buggy's cargo was safely loaded, and the buggy was pulling away when the door of the helicopter was thrown open and the pilot jumped out, running out after the vehicle with a small case in his hands.

And it hit Rafe with all the force of a body blow.

Not *his* hands.

Her hands!

He was on his feet and at the terrace balustrade in an instant, peering harder, squinting against the glare of the sun. It couldn't be…

But the pilot was definitely a woman, a tight waist and the curve of her hip accentuated by the slim-fitting overalls, and, while sunglasses hid her eyes, her pale skin and the copper-red hair framing her face were both achingly familiar. Then she turned after delivering the bag and a long braid slapped back and forth across her back as though it were a living thing.

Christo!

He pounced on the nearest phone, barking out his first ever order to the Palace Guard, 'Don't let that helicopter go!'

Sienna had to get out of here. Her knees were jelly with relief that Rafe hadn't been there to meet the helicopter, her stomach churned and if she didn't get off this island in the next thirty seconds she was going to explode. Although, the way her insides felt after that panicked dash to deliver her passenger's forgotten bag, she might just explode anyway.

Sienna sucked in a deep, and what she hoped was a calming, breath and with clammy hands pulled the door of the chopper shut, clipping on her headset. Thinking he might be there when she landed—dreading it—had put her in a cold sweat the entire flight.

And she was still sweating. It didn't help that it was so hot today, especially out here on this rocky headland, where the effect of the hot Mediterranean sun was compounded by the way it bounced off the white painted walls that coiled along the narrow road up to the castle like a ribbon. And the castle up the top—the fairy-tale castle that rose out of the rock, ancient and weather-worn and beautiful, the fairy-tale castle now presided over by Prince Raphael, last of the long and illustrious line of Lombardi.

Prince Raphael. Oh, my God, she'd slept with a prince. *Royalty.* And she'd had no idea. But nobody had back then. It had only been in the days after he'd practically tossed her out of his room that the news of the discovery of a new-found prince for Montvelatte had broken. Sensational news that had rivalled the earlier news of the downfall of the then incumbent and his brother.

And it had seemed as if every newspaper, every magazine and every television programme had been full of the news, digging into the once buried past, and uncovering the story of the young nanny who'd become the Prince's lover, only to be exiled with a young son and another baby on the way. The coronation that had followed had kept the story alive for weeks.

And his face had been everywhere she'd looked, so there was no hope of forgetting him during the day, no chance of escaping the face that haunted her in her dreams.

He was a prince!

No wonder he'd changed his mind about seeing her again. He would have known what that news report had meant—that he'd have even less reason to slum it with the likes of her.

Why would he, when he clearly had his pick of society's brightest and prettiest? There'd been a constant stream of women being brought to the island in the past few days. Nothing had been said at the base—they knew that discretion was the better part of business success—but she knew from personal experience. Prince Raphael was a man of big appetites…

Her stomach churned, the taste of bile bitter in her mouth as she completed the preflight checklist. The sooner she was away from this island and the sooner there was no risk she would run into the man who'd so unceremoniously thrown her out of his life, then the sooner this damned queasiness would settle down. Ever since she'd been told she'd been rostered on for this assignment she'd felt physically ill. Montvelatte was the last place on earth she wanted to be. Knowing she'd just delivered his latest love interest made it doubly so.

Sienna yanked herself back from that thought with a mental slap to the head.

What was she thinking? Genevieve, or whatever her name was, was welcome to him. She was out of here.

There was the roar of another engine, the blast of horns and she turned to see a jeep screeching to a halt alongside the helipad in a spray of gravel and dust, and the churning in her gut took a turn for the worst. It didn't get any better when four uniformed officers jumped out, gesturing to her to cut the rotors. This was supposed to be a simple drop-and-run. Surely there was no obscure paperwork she'd forgotten to complete?

She was making a move to open the door when it was pulled open for her from the other side. The officer saluted so properly that even over her own thumping heartbeat, Sienna imagined she could hear the snap of his heels clicking together. She'd seen that uniform before—in the footage of the former Prince and his brother being carted away—and she wasn't at all sure that was a comforting thought.

'Signorina Wainwright?'

Breath caught in Sienna's lungs and gave birth to a new strain of fear. *They knew her name?*

She shook her head, removing her headset once again. 'Y-yes,' she stammered. 'Is there a problem?'

'There is no problem, I assure you,' the officer told her in his richly accented English. 'Please, if you would just step outside the aircraft,' he added, offering her his hand to alight the helicopter. His words and actions were accompanied with a smile so seemingly genuine that for a moment she thought everything must be fine after all, that her most recent panic attack was unwarranted and that this was merely some kind of quaint formality nobody had thought to warn her about.

But once outside he made it clear that he expected her to keep moving. Towards the jeep.

Sienna stopped, the men either side of her coming to a halt also. 'What's going on?'

'It is but a short trip to the Castello,' he said, neatly side-stepping her question and throwing her thoughts into turmoil.

Her eyes swung up to the palace that sat atop the massive rock that made up this part of the island. It stared down at her with its thousand window eyes, and for the first time she didn't notice the beauty of the ancient stone architecture with its arched windows and flag-topped turrets, but the thick walls and the fortifications all around that had protected it from invaders for centuries. This time the fairy-tale palace had disappeared, and it was the fortress that she noticed, the fortress she knew instinctively would be just as hard to escape from as to break into.

The fortress that contained the man she least wanted to see in the world.

Oh, no. No way was she going there.

She swallowed back on the sick feeling in a stomach that was once again threatening to unload its pitiful contents at any time, while the hot sun wrung even more perspiration from her nervous body. Her overalls stuck to her in all the wrong places, and sweat beads slid lazily along the loose curling tendrils at her fringe and neck.

'Look, I don't really have time for this. I have to get the chopper back to base. They're expecting me.' She cast a desperate look back over her shoulder towards the helicopter, frowning when she noticed that the remaining two officers had taken up guard duty in front of the chopper, strategically placing themselves between her and the door and effectively cutting off that means of escape. Even if she could have outrun these two beside her.

'Please,' the officer urged, gesturing towards the jeep.

Finding what little shred of courage she still had left, she kicked up her chin. 'And if I insist on being allowed to leave? If I refuse to accompany you to the palace?'

He smiled again, but this time it was a little lighter on the charm, a little heavier on the menace. 'In that unfortunate case,' he said, adding a little bow, 'you would leave me with no choice. I would be forced to arrest you.'

CHAPTER THREE

SIENNA had had enough. For almost three hours she'd been stuck inside this drawing room, prowling the walls holding her prisoner like a caged lion at the zoo.

It didn't matter that the drawing room was the size of a small country and that the accoutrements, the Renaissance tapestries gracing the walls, the crystal chandeliers and fine furniture, made it much more pleasant than any zoo enclosure she'd ever seen. Nor did the constant visitors make a shred of difference, bustling in and out and offering her refreshments and any number of pastries or other tasty delights that she desired.

She wasn't about to be taken in by window dressing. The now familiar maroon-clad guards she'd spied perched at their posts outside the door every time they'd opened had made it more than clear that she was not some welcome guest, but a prisoner in a cage, albeit a very gilded one.

And while at first she'd been nervous, anxious about having to confront Rafe again and certain that he must be the one behind her detention, after waiting this long with no information she was beyond nervousness and frustration. She was furious.

Not one person she'd met here—was able to tell her exactly why she was being kept against her will or when she would be allowed to leave.

The bearer of the pastries had waved her questions aside with a sweep of a hand and had seemed insulted she hadn't been more interested in tasting the proffered wares. The tea bearer had pretended he was ignorant of both English and French and had looked benignly down his crooked nose at her when she'd attempted her rudimentary Italian.

She had a helicopter that had been due back at base hours ago and nobody had allowed her anywhere near a phone to let them know she'd been detained. A missing helicopter. A missing pilot with it. And while the fragrant sweet tea had settled her stomach, it would take something a lot stronger, if not a minor miracle, to settle her nerves. Her earlier nausea was nothing to how she felt now. She would lose her job over this for sure.

Then she heard it, the familiar whine of helicopter engines leading up to that *whump whump* of the rotors. And not just any helicopter. In fact, if she didn't know better…

She ran, her heart sinking with every step, to the large arched windows overlooking the helipad in time to see the helicopter rise up and turn to point out to sea.

Her helicopter!

'No!' she cried, slapping her open palm on the window fruitlessly, knowing there was no chance that whoever was flying the craft could see her, but continuing to slam her hand against the glass anyway as the helicopter accelerated away, already shrinking into the distance.

And mere anger turned incendiary.

There were two doors into the room—one she figured led to the kitchens from where the coffee and cakes had issued. She ran instead to the other, the large double doors she'd entered through and that she knew led to the entrance lobby, the same doors that had remained firmly closed against her until now. She pulled with all her weight against their handles, banging on the wood with her closed fists when she found them locked. 'That's my helicopter. Let me out!' When the doors stayed closed, she rattled the handles some more, her fury rising further as they refused to budge. She cursed out loud. Why the hell wouldn't they let her out?

'I know you're out there,' she yelled at the wall of solid wood, punching it some more for good measure. 'I know you can hear me. I demand to see Rafe. Right now. Where is the cowardly bastard?'

'Here in Montvelatte,' came a familiar voice behind her, a voice that sent panic sizzling down her spine like an electric shock, 'the usual form of address is Prince Raphael, or Your Highness, rather than "the cowardly bastard".'

Sienna swung around, vaguely aware of her braid slapping heavily against the timber door, all too aware of the impact of him slamming into her psyche. She'd demanded to see him and yet still she was totally unprepared for the sheer onslaught of this man on her senses.

And standing there, not two metres away from her, it was some onslaught. It was the same Rafe she remembered, but smoother, his thick wavy hair a little shorter and more tamed, his designer stubble smoothed to a mere shadow. But the sheer intensity contained in his eyes packed as much punch as they ever had. *More.* Because those eyes pinned her now, scanning her lazily from the top of her head to the toes of her boots and all points in between, until the skin under her uniform tingled, her nipples tightening to peaks under his continued scrutiny.

She swallowed, her breathing still ragged, her colour still high from her exertions on the door, if the heat she was feeling in her face was any indication, and it occurred to her in that moment the gulf between them had never been wider or more extreme. Because Rafe was now a prince and looked every part of it, so cool and urbane in his fine wool jacket, so groomed and superior, whereas she was still a nobody, and right now a dishevelled and flustered one.

But so what? She didn't give a damn about his title, not after the way she'd been treated. She was little more than a prisoner here. The last thing she would do was grovel.

'I call it like I see it,' she shot back, refusing to apologise for the outburst or the terminology she'd resorted to.

His eyes narrowed, his expression hardening. 'So I noticed. I can see your mood was not improved by the delay. I'm sorry to have kept you waiting so long. I was unavoidably detained.'

'You were detained?' She shook her head in disbelief. 'Who are you trying to kid. It was me who was detained, prevented by your goons from taking off, and threatened with arrest if I didn't go along with their plans. *I'm* the one who's been detained for hours, held here against my will, and now my helicopter's been stolen—'

'It hasn't been stolen.'

'It's gone! Someone's taken it without my permission. I call that stolen.'

'It's been sent back to base. You're not the only one who can fly a helicopter.'

'Oh? And that's supposed to make everything okay? I was due back with that helicopter. Instead I've been locked inside this prison you call a palace. Well, I've had enough. I'm leaving.'

Sienna launched herself across the room, aiming for the door he must have come through, figuring that one at least might still be unlocked, when his hand snaked out and took hold of her forearm, using her momentum to spin her back around.

'You're not going anywhere.'

The words were a whisper but deadly sure in their intent. She looked down at the hand burning a brand into her flesh, then up to his face, and almost wished she hadn't. His eyes, once filled with passion and longing and desire for her, now harsh and flat and so cold that she shivered.

'And if I don't want to stay?'

'You'll stay.'

'Why should I?'

'Because I want you to.'

The unexpected words sounded like they'd been ground through his teeth, their intensity rocking her to the soles of her feet so that she felt herself sway towards him, as if drawn by some invisible thread. Drawing her so close that his masculine scent wrapped around her and drew her even closer. She'd dreamt of such a moment, on countless sleep-elusive nights, and in pointless daydream wishes. Wished it long and hard, even after she'd seen the news reports declaring that Rafe was indeed the new Prince of Montvelatte, and realising it could never be so.

But she was here now… She searched his face, his eyes, looking for the truth, trying to discover what it meant.

And then damned herself for hoping, straightening suddenly, her back once again rigid and set. This was the man who'd thrown her out of his room and his life without so much as a goodbye once before. There was no way she'd give him the chance to do it again.

'And that matters to me because?' She wrenched her arm from his grasp. 'No, thanks. I'm leaving. And if you won't arrange my departure, I'll damn well find a way out of this hellhole myself.'

'You're not leaving.' It wasn't a question. It was a bald statement of fact and it used up the last remaining shred of patience Sienna had.

'Who the hell do you think you are to tell me what I can and cannot do? They make you a prince and suddenly you think you're the ruler of the universe? Well, let me tell you,

Rafe, or Raphael or whatever it is you like to call yourself now, you're not my prince. I didn't vote for you!'

Silence followed her words, so thick and heavy that she wished away the thump of her heart lest he hear it and read too much into it.

She was angry.

Furious.

Nothing more.

And then, totally unexpectedly, he threw back his head and laughed, really laughed, deep and loud. So deep that it was too much and cut her right where it shouldn't hurt and yet still did. So deep that she took advantage of his lack of attention and decided to make good her escape.

She didn't get far.

'Sienna,' he said, as his hands trapped her shoulders and collected her in, pulling her around until she faced him, and holding her close. So close than the room shrank until it was just his scent that surrounded her, coiling into her all over again. So close that she had to shut her eyes to block out the sight of the triangle of skin exposed by the undone-at-the-collar shirt, a patch of skin her mouth knew intimately.

'Let me go,' she protested, squirming in his arms, lashing out at her gaoler while the prick of tears was dangerously close. 'Stop laughing at me!'

'I wasn't laughing at you,' he said, with such conviction that she stopped thrashing about and dared open her eyes. And what they met was a gaze so intense and fathomless that she felt it resonate to the soles of her feet. She watched his eyes drift purposefully southwards, felt their heat on her lips before it was the touch of a finger she felt there. She gasped, her lips parting with the shock of it, and dragged in air laced with the very essence of him. 'Do you know how long it is since I've had someone really disagree with me?'

She wavered, thrown off balance by this sudden change in mood and by the electricity generated by his touch. But only for a moment. She knew what charm the man possessed—hadn't it succeeded in getting her into his bed that first fateful time, even after she'd tried everything she knew to put him off? She couldn't afford to let him through her barriers a second time.

Even so, it took everything she possessed to muster a defence. She stiffened in his arms, determined to be resolute. 'Ten minutes? Fifteen at the outside. Surprise me.'

His smile widened, as if delighted by her response, rather than irritated by it as she'd intended. 'Here I am surrounded by advisers and counsel but not one person has dared to disagree with me since that night I learned I was to become Montvelatte's ruler.' He looked down at her, smoothed a wayward tendril of hair from her brow, the touch of his fingers setting fire to nerve endings under her skin. 'Not until today when you blew back into my life like a breath of fresh air.'

His words flowed like liquid promise through her veins, spreading warmth and hope and all the things she'd missed in these past few weeks, all the things she'd known even back then she had no right to, all the things she had even less right to now. It was exactly the way he'd lured her into their previous affair, by telling her she was different, that she was special. By making her feel special.

And look how that had ended.

Bitterness spiked in her gut, lending her new strength. Sienna shook her head, shrugging off his hand and twisting out of his reach. 'I can imagine how much it must gall you being surrounded by sycophants,' she shot back. 'Now, is there a telephone or some other means of communication I can use to contact my employer and make arrangements for blowing right out of here again?'

To her surprise he let her go this time, and she edged cautiously away, forcing herself not to bolt in case those manacles he called hands locked down on her once again. She skirted the intricately carved lounge suite that held pride of place in the centre of the room in front of a majestic fireplace, all the while scanning the room's contents for a telephone she might have missed earlier, while keeping one eye on Rafe. Making sure he kept his distance. It had taken every last shred of self-control she possessed to tear herself out of his embrace. How long could she keep doing so? How many times could she be constrained by those arms before she stopped fighting altogether and gave herself up to the temptation his body offered, the temptation she had given herself up to once before?

How many times?

What a joke.

How *few* times?

But at least for now he remained where he was, seemingly content to watch her from a distance. If his stance was relaxed and casual, a smile tugging at his lips as he leant back against a polished timber table with his hands at his side on the glossy wood and his ankles crossed in front of him, there was nothing of a smile about his eyes. She shivered, reaching out to clutch the cool wood of the lounge back as she felt their purposefulness wash over her. They were the eyes of a predator, glinting and dangerous, and right now they were fixed on her, content just to watch. She turned away before he might see her fear. The sooner she was out of here and away from Rafe, the better.

Why didn't he make a move to stop her? Did he know the door she was heading for was locked and her quest to escape doomed accordingly? Her already wary footsteps slowed. Was he merely playing with her like a cat with a mouse, letting her think she would soon be free when she was trapped in here until he deigned to let her out? And would he laugh again when she turned the handle of the door to find that, too, locked?

Sienna swallowed back on a gasp that threatened to turn into a sob, tears of frustration all too close.

'It's locked, in case you were wondering,' he said behind her, reading her thoughts and her intentions with ice-cold precision.

She didn't want to believe anything he said but she believed that. Why would he allow her any chance of escape when he'd kept her locked up the entire afternoon?

So she threw him a cold look over her shoulder and changed direction, heading towards the wall of full-length windows instead of towards the door, as if that had been her goal all along. 'I don't know what you're talking about,' she lied.

She came to a halt next to the window, her arms crossed over her thumping chest, thankful that at least she'd managed to put several metres between them as she pretended to gaze out unconcernedly over a view of sea and sun and cliff-top so spectacular it should have taken her breath away.

But it was the empty helipad that filled her vision and thoughts, a sight that tore at her all over again and freshened the sting of unshed tears. How the hell was she supposed to explain what had happened when she got back?

'Why are you so desperate to leave?' Even from across the vast room, his rich voice filled the room like it was little larger than a shoebox. 'I thought we could use a little time to get reacquainted.'

She shot him a look, sending her braid flicking heavily over her shoulder. 'You really expect me to believe you mean reacquainted? Or horizontal?'

His eyebrows lifted at that one. 'I didn't realise you'd be in such a hurry, but if that's what you'd prefer…'

Her cheeks burned and she turned back towards the glass. Why the hell had she given him any idea of the direction of her thoughts? And the answer came back instantaneously, loud and clear. Because she only had to look at this man and her thoughts turned horizontal, along with her wishes and desires. 'The only hurry I'm in is the hurry to get out of here.'

'You have no desire at all to resume our relationship?'

'We never had a relationship!'

'No? What would you call it, then?'

'A fling. A one-night stand. And I would have thought that given that night is long since over, then so too is any kind of "relationship" we might have shared.'

'You think it's over?'

This time it was her turn to laugh. 'Oh, I think you made that pretty plain at the time.'

She turned, wanting to see his reaction to that but finding him suddenly closer, shocked that she'd been totally unaware that he'd silently closed half the distance between them while she'd kept her gaze fixed sightlessly at the window.

He stopped a few short paces from her, his head tilting, his gaze delving deep into her. 'You're angry with me. Because I let you down.'

'No way!' *That would imply she actually cared one way or the other.* 'I think we both got what we wanted that night. I'm over it.'

'Are you,' he said, one side of his mouth turned up as he moved still closer, 'I wonder.'

She scoffed, and continued to stare pointedly towards the window in an effort to disguise the backward movement of her feet. 'Don't be ridiculous.'

'I think you're afraid of what might happen if you do stay.'

'I'm angry, is what I am.' She lifted her chin defiantly. 'Because you think you can ride roughshod over anyone and everyone.'

'And you wish it could have turned out differently.'

Her shoulders hit something solid and she looked around to find herself wedged in the corner of the room, her frustration mounting as his words struck too close to home and his physical presence came too close for comfort. She backed up tight against the corner, thankful for the solidity of the centuries-old walls. 'Look, does this palace actually have a telephone service? I'm already late back. I really don't want to delay my departure any longer.'

'Stay,' he said, resting one hand up on the wall beside her head with his elbow bent, now so close she had to tilt her head up to meet his eyes. 'Have dinner with me tonight.'

She shook her head, wishing the action would also negate the intoxicating scent of the man that came with his proximity. 'Not a chance. I have to get back and you know it.'

'So get back later. I'm a lonely prince in a *castello*. Indulge me.'

'Indulge you?' She attempted another laugh—there was no way she was feeling sorry for him—but this one came out all brittle and false so she switched to words instead, remembering the precious cargo she'd had to transport to the island only hours earlier. 'Besides, what about your Signorina Genevieve? Won't she be expecting you to dine with her? Or are you planning on abandoning your latest plaything in order to slum it with the hired help?'

His eyes took on a feral gleam. 'My "latest plaything"? Oh, now, that is interesting.'

She regarded him suspiciously, 'What are you talking about?'

'Merely that anyone would think you were jealous. And why would you be jealous of the Signorina Genevieve unless you thought she had access to something you wanted—or perhaps, *someone?*'

'Don't flatter yourself! As far as I'm concerned, she's welcome to you.'

He sighed. 'I'm sure she would be pleased to hear you say that, but, alas, Signorina Genevieve has already departed, courtesy of the helicopter you left so carelessly unattended.' Sienna opened her mouth to protest but he cut her off with the briefest touch of his finger to her lips, a touch which caused a hitch in her breath as her senses sizzled into high alert again. 'Which means I find myself without a dinner companion tonight.' He gave a very stiff bow. 'Would you do me the honour?'

It was surreal. Whatever had transpired between them before, he was now a Mediterranean prince, bowing to a complete nobody and asking her to dine with him.

Unless he was merely desperate...

'So Lady Genevieve turned you down and you expect me to pick up the pieces?'

Rafe's hand slammed against the wall alongside her head, before he spun and strode away, his hands on his hips. And when he turned, it was a flash of fury she saw in his eyes.

'This is nothing to do with Genevieve or anyone else. This is between you and me.'

'Why?' she asked, all too aware of the breathlessness that accompanied her question. 'Why me?'

He moved closer, stopping only inches away before he raised a hand to her face and traced the curve of her jaw. 'Because the moment I saw you emerge from that helicopter, I knew I wanted you again.'

She gasped, heat rushing through her on a tide. His brazen admission shocked her to her core, but already she felt the answering call of her body to his words in the tightening fullness of her breasts and the aching need between her thighs, and she knew without a shadow of a doubt that if she didn't get out of here soon, she would once again fall victim to the sensual spell he cast around her.

'Th-that's too bad,' she stammered. 'I have to go.'

'But that's impossible,' he told her, still in that mellifluous ribbon of a voice, a ribbon that seemed to be drawing ever tighter around her. 'Because you see—' he gestured out the window to where a catamaran could be seen rounding the headland and speeding away from the island '—that's the last vessel to sail to Genoa today. And you've just missed it.'

His words blasted through the sensual fog more effectively than a dousing with a bucket of iced water. She watched the catamaran power into the distance, leaving behind twin trails of foaming water, feeling herself just as churned. 'There has to be another way off! An airport. A private charter—'

'Sadly, not today. And as you can see, we have no helicopter—'

'That's crazy. It's barely six o'clock in the afternoon. There must be something—'

'As I said, not today. Tonight there will be no moon, and Velattians are superstitious; nobody will risk travelling while the Beast of Iseo patrols.'

'What the hell are you talking about?'

'The Beast of Iseo. Surely you've heard of it.' He pointed again out the window to where the massive jagged blade of rock thrust from the sea into the sky some kilometres from the island. 'Iseo's Pyramid, the remnants of the caldera of an ancient volcano, is its home. According to the ancient legend, The Beast of Iseo emerges on the blackest of nights, foraging for wayward travellers. It's a charming legend, full of local colour, don't you think? Although it does mean you will be forced to spend the night here.'

The full impact of what he was saying hit home like a sucker punch. She was trapped here for the night. *With him.*

'I'm not staying here with you. I can't. My employer will be waiting for me. I'll lose my job…'

'Your employer has been made aware of the situation and the fact you will be staying. Besides, you have no choice; there is no way of getting you off the island, even if I could help you.'

'But it makes no sense. It's just a legend. And yet you cease all transport to and from the Island because of it?'

'You're not superstitious, Sienna? You don't believe in the Beast?'

'Oh, I believe in the Beast of Iseo. Right now I'm looking at him.'

He laughed in a way that made it plain he was enjoying his role as captor all too much, and that got so far under her skin that there was no coming out. 'You bastard. You planned all this, didn't you? You kept me here, waiting for hours, knowing I'd be trapped and that I'd have no choice but to stay on the island.'

He shrugged, looking far too smug for her liking. 'I fear you misjudge me. It was hardly my intention at all, merely an unfortunate result of Lady Genevieve's stage mother's inability to accept no for an answer. But maybe her recalcitrance was more fortunate than I gave it credit for.'

He gave another bow, this one a mere shadow of the one he'd given before. 'Now that you have no choice, you might as well accompany me to dinner.'

Sienna shook her head, knowing that way could only result in misery for her, knowing she had to be strong for her pride's, if not her sanity's, sake. 'No, thanks. Not a chance. I'll find a hotel somewhere. I'll stay overnight on the island if I have to, but I will not join you for dinner. Not after everything you've done today.'

One eyebrow raised, he turned a quizzical gaze at her. 'All I've done is to want to spend more time with you.'

'Without asking me? By risking my job? No, thanks. I don't need that kind of intervention. I'll stay at a hotel and leave tomorrow.'

'You have money for this hotel? And for the fare you will surely need? Montvelatte might only be a small island country, but we are not so naïve as to extend credit to anyone who so asks.' His eyes scanned her fitted uniform with the efficiency of an X-ray machine, making her skin prickle under the heavy-duty drill. 'Your outfit is very practical for flying, but I do not see where you might have secreted away so much as a credit card.'

She burned with humiliation, wishing away her body's inevitable reaction to his interest, remembering how once before in just one night that interest had succeeded in turning her from an under-experienced woman into a wanton.

'If you were any kind of gentleman, you'd pick up the expense of my departure, given you've disposed of my means of transport behind my back and without my permission.'

'If I were any kind of gentleman, you would not have found me half as satisfactory in bed...'

His eyes claimed victory; his mouth celebrated it in a smile.

Sienna spun away, her teeth biting into her lower lip as she battled to find a way out of this mess. Of course he wasn't going to offer her the fare out of here. And, of course, she didn't have a purse. All she had on her was her ID, a locker key and a few euros in change. But her purse and credit cards were locked away for safe keeping back at the base, the base she should have returned to hours ago.

Damn him!

'In which case,' he continued, obviously taking her silence as confirmation, 'and seeing I have caused you such distress, I feel it is my duty to offer you accommodation here, in the Palace of Montvelatte. You will find the palace very comfortable, despite its great age.'

She glared up at him, knowing she was beaten but not prepared to show it in her face.

'And I will leave the island tomorrow on the first available transport.' It wasn't a question, and right now if he argued the point there was every chance he would end up an even shorter-lived ruler of Montvelatte than his half-brother.

Once again, he made that nod of assent, almost a bow. 'If that is what you wish.'

She hesitated. Could she trust him? Dared she? But then did she have a choice? 'Then I will stay. Just for tonight. But I will dine in my room.'

His eyes glinted with something unfathomable. 'But of course,' he agreed. 'Now, let me find someone who can show you to your room. I imagine you'd appreciate the chance to freshen up.'

If she needed reminding of the state she must look, she didn't want to hear it. But she followed him across the room, already looking forward to having some breathing space to herself, a room where the air wasn't tainted by the very essence of him on every breath.

It's just one night, she told herself. *Just one night.* Tomorrow he would have to let her go. Tomorrow she would be free.

He reached the door and twisted the handle, pulling it open. 'After you.'

She froze. The door had been unlocked the whole time, the guards she'd seen earlier gone. She'd been just scant feet from the door when she'd decided she'd rather play it cool than be humiliated again. And yet she could have turned the handle and made her escape while he was still a room away. Could she have got away, past the palace guards and the staff? Was there a chance she could have made it to the port in time? She would have managed the fare somehow—offered her watch for collateral—she would have borrowed or begged some form of transport to get herself off the island.

But she hadn't even attempted to leave the room.

And somehow that was the greatest disappointment of all.

CHAPTER FOUR

THE bath was hot and deep, the foaming bath gel forming a mountain of scented bubbles that comforted her body and soothed her fragile soul. Sienna sighed as she slid down into the slippery water, letting her hair fan out around her like a mantilla and gasping as she came back up again, feeling the weight of water streaming from her hair. Heaven. For a centuries-old palace, the plumbing was definitely state of the art and a major improvement on the cantankerous contraption her landlady labelled a shower and which justified her charging fifty percent over the odds for one shoebox of an apartment in the Thirteenth *Arrondissement*.

The best part of an hour later, feeling more relaxed than she had all day, she rinsed off the last of the bubbles and wrapped herself in the large plush towels provided. Marble, gold and mirrors, she thought, taking in her surroundings. What was it about that combination that turned a mere bathroom into a destination? Yet beyond the door awaited another, even grander destination, with a massive four-poster bed hung with curtains of lace and fine silks. She couldn't wait to bury herself deep under the comforter. She hadn't wanted to be here, but now that she was, there was no way she wasn't going to enjoy this unfamiliar taste of luxury.

Her stomach rumbled and she gave silent thanks for the healthy sign. Whatever illness or nerves had plagued her earlier today, at least now she could contemplate the notion of food without feeling like she wanted to throw up.

There was a faint knock from outside and Sienna opened the bathroom door a crack to hear a woman's voice advising in rusty English that her meal was ready. 'Thank you,' she called, 'I'll be right out.'

She towel-dried her hair until it settled into shaggy ringlets around her face and then rinsed out her underwear in the sink, hanging them over the towel rail. In this warm climate they would dry in no time.

Finally she unwrapped herself from the bath sheet and slipped on the silk robe she'd found hanging behind the door. She'd loved it from the moment she'd seen it hanging there, the jade green silk shot with gold thread, the vibrant shade changing subtly as the fabric moved under the light.

It felt every bit as good as it looked, the material gliding over her shoulders like a silken kiss, teasing her nipples into awareness with every soft shift of the fabric, reminding her all too well of Rafe and his magic touch…

Rafe.

He'd told her he wanted her again.

She sucked in a much needed burst of air. In the panic of not being able to get off the island, in her anger at being manipulated, she had let those words and her body's reaction to those words slide away. But she hadn't lost them at all. Instead the words had filtered down to a place deep inside her and taken root, sprouting questions like weeds.

He didn't really want her. He couldn't, she reasoned, answering one of those questions herself. Rafe was used to taking what he wanted and she was merely convenient. Available. A man like him would have no hesitation in assuming that after the first night they'd shared, she'd be willing to fall into his bed in a heartbeat.

Ready to discard in yet another.

He was merely toying with her, continuing that cat-and-mouse game he played so well, the predator enjoying the hunt.

He'd kept her here, prevented her from leaving, merely to continue the chase, because he damn well knew the longer he did, the more likely it would be that she would once again fall into his bed.

Sienna pulled the robe tighter around her, giving the tie at her waist a savage tug. She would not think about Rafe. At least, not that way. That other night was over. It was history. Rafe was nothing to her now but a mere inconvenience, and tomorrow she would be rid of even that.

She'd begun separating her hair into sections, preparing to braid it while still damp to control its natural curl, when the scent of food, fragrant and beguiling found its way into the bathroom. Her stomach rumbled again and she paused. It had been hours since she'd had a decent meal. Her hair could wait ten minutes; it wasn't as if she had other plans for the evening.

So she abandoned the braid, working her fingers through her still damp curls with one hand as she pulled open the bathroom door with the other.

'You look good enough to eat.'

She stopped dead, a *frisson* of fear shimmying its way down her spine, a sudden rush of heat pooling in that naked place between her thighs. She abandoned her hair and clutched the robe tighter around her, crossing her arms over her chest for good measure. 'What are you doing here?'

Rafe smiled at her as he transported dishes from a trolley onto a small table set by a window overlooking cliff-top and sea. A table covered in a lace tablecloth, complete with a floral centrepiece, a candle already lit amongst the flowers even though the evening was still young outside.

A table set for two.

'The chef has prepared his signature dishes for tonight's meal. I told him I would let him know personally what you thought.'

'I said, what are you doing here?'

He looked up at her ingenuously. 'Having dinner with you.'

'Even after I told you that I wouldn't dine with you.'

'No.' This time he stopped what he was doing and stood up straight, his eyes raking over her in such a way that she wondered if he could see right through the fabric to the truth of her state of undress beneath. 'What you actually said was that you would not join me for a meal. So I decided to join you instead.'

Anger welled up inside her, any hint of the relaxation afforded by the bath diminishing by the second. 'I made it plain that I had no wish to see you again tonight.'

He shrugged, that Mediterranean shrug that told her he cared not a damn for whatever she thought. 'I did not believe that was what you meant. You should know by now that you have a very expressive body. It told me otherwise.'

Heat flooded her face and she turned away, half regretting it when the sudden play of silk over skin sent her senses shimmering further into overdrive.

'You have no right—'

'I have every right! This is my principality, my island, my kingdom. Everything and everyone on it is subject to me. And that, my dear Sienna, whether you like it or not, includes you!'

She wheeled back around, grateful for his outburst. Anger was the reaction she'd wanted. Anger she could deal with. 'So now you fancy yourself as some petty despot and you've come to take what you think is yours. Well, sorry, but you don't suck me in with all that lord of the manor garbage.

Don't expect me to fall at your feet like some loyal subject grateful to have been asked to service her lord and master.'

His eyes glittered dangerously, a muscle in his jaw popped, and for a moment she feared she'd overstepped the mark. If he wanted to take her now, by force, who would come to her rescue? She was utterly alone here, in a world that was not her own, where the laws were not the laws she understood and where he was the master, the ruler of all.

But he'd never been a prince to her, just a man, and since his oh-so-rapid excision of her from his life, not a man she respected, let alone particularly cared for. So there was no way she would stoop to playing the game by his rules.

'Oh, I never assumed it would be that simple.'

His intentions thudded into her sensibilities with all the subtlety of cannon fire. Slowly she shook her head. 'I won't sleep with you,' she said, her voice abandoning her, leaving her with nothing more than a hoarse whisper.

'That remains to be seen.'

'I mean it, Rafe. Been there. Done that.'

'If you say so. So why don't we just concentrate on what we do agree on? Are you hungry, Sienna?'

Was he talking about food? The way he looked at her, his gaze warm on her skin, his eyes electric in their dark intensity, told her otherwise.

Her stomach chose that precise moment to make itself heard. Sienna shifted her arms over her stomach, but nothing could muffle the rumble, loud and insistent.

He smiled. 'Clearly you also have a beast that requires feeding. Come. Sit.'

She was hungry, so hungry that not even Rafe's presence could make a dint in it. But there was no way she was going to be comfortable enough to eat while clad only in a thin silk robe. No way in the world.

'I... I'll just get dressed.' She turned to collect her uniform where she'd left it lying on the bed, thinking that even without the underwear still drying in her bathroom, it would put more of a barrier between them than a mere whisper of silk.

But there was no uniform. She looked around, confused, sure she'd left it on the bed before her bath. She pulled open a closet door, thinking it might have been hung up, to find the closet devoid of everything but hangers.

'Is there a problem?' he asked behind her.

'My uniform. It's gone.'

'Why should you need it?'

'I left it on the bed, and now it's gone.'

'You seem to have an unusual knack for losing things. First, your helicopter. Now your uniform.'

She wheeled around, not fooled for a moment. 'You might consider this is all some sort of game, but I don't.'

'I assure you, this is no game.' His expression sent shock waves through her system, his voice set so low and deep that the words vibrated through her, and his eyes lit with an intensity that left her breathless. 'And just for the record,' he continued, letting his lips turn up into the barest of smiles, 'your uniform is in safe hands. It has merely been taken away for laundering. You will have it back by morning. Do you have a problem with clean clothes?'

Damn the man! 'Only that you expect me to sit down and dine wearing nothing more than a silk robe. Of course there's a problem!'

His eyes flared as they cruised hungrily over her robe like a heat-seeking missile. '*Nothing* more?'

She turned away, cursing herself for her inadvertent admission, but he didn't wait for her response. 'If you feel at a disadvantage, I could similarly divest myself of a few extraneous garments.' She turned back to see him make a move to start unbuttoning his shirt and she tossed her head, determined not to let him see just how much he'd rattled her. 'Don't be ridiculous! I didn't want, and wasn't expecting, company. What I meant is I'm hardly dressed for dinner.'

'On the contrary,' his eyes raking over her with all the subtlety of a hungry jungle cat, devouring her in a single heated glance, 'you are delightfully attired. Did anyone ever tell you how much those tones complement your colouring? You have the most beautiful skin,' he said, drawing close enough to touch the back of one finger to her cheek. 'Like the finest porcelain. So pale, almost translucent.'

Her heart was beating so loud she was sure he must hear it, her nipples so rock-like under their silken covering, there was no way he couldn't see them if he lowered his eyes.

But his gaze remained fixed on her face, searching her eyes, before lingering so long on her lips that they tingled under his scrutiny, so long that she realised she'd been holding her breath the entire time. Her lips parted as she drew in air, and suddenly his scent filled her and she could taste the man on her tongue, and the hunger she had been feeling changed direction.

He could kiss her now. The thought came from somewhere from the deep, dark recesses of her mind, somewhere forbidden and unwelcome. But the path was clear. He would kiss her, and she would accept his kiss, and then she would push her hands against his chest and be the one to break it off, before things went too far, before he assumed more than he already had.

But first—*oh, God yes*—first she would have that kiss.

The air crackled around her, heavy with expectation, every breath an eternity as his lips hovered so close to hers, the tug of his fingers through her hair and the glide of his nails against her scalp an exquisite torture.

And, as she gazed up at him, something skated across his

eyes, something that told her he thought he had her right where he wanted her, something that tugged her ability to reason right back from whatever dark place she'd temporarily locked it away.

And reason told her she'd been kidding herself. Because if she kissed him now, she'd never stop. If she put her hands up to his chest it wouldn't be to push him away, but to drink in the feel of his skin over muscled chest with her fingers. And one kiss would never be enough.

'You're right.' She mouthed the words, hardly recognising her own voice as she saw the answering question in his eyes, momentarily thrown off track.

'About what?'

It was her turn to smile. 'I'm famished.' She turned her head away, forced herself to move, clumsily at first, awkward in making her body move away from where it most wanted to be, before sinking gratefully into a chair. 'What's for dinner?'

Rafe watched her go, bemused by her sudden change of mood. Seconds ago she'd been his for the taking. Seconds ago the meal had been all but forgotten and promised to be long cold before they returned to it.

She wanted him, she'd made that more than plain with her parted lips and hitched breathing. She had wanted him then and she still wanted him, if the flame-red cheeks and the way she studiously refused to meet his eyes were any indication. She was just determined not to give in to it. Just like the last time, when she'd played hard to get.

But just like last time she would capitulate. And just like last time it would be worth the wait.

It wouldn't take long. He'd give her until the end of tonight's meal. And then he'd soon change her mind about leaving any time soon. One night had not been enough; he couldn't imagine it being enough again. And, after the last few frenetic weeks, he deserved a little relaxation. What better way to get it?

Rafe sighed as he joined her at the table, pulling a chilled bottle from the antique silver ice bucket before reaching over to pour her a glass of the local wine, already looking forward to the next few nights. He needed a distraction from worries about casinos and international financing and rebuilding the world's trust in Montvelatte. He needed something to persuade Sebastiano to ease off on the wife hunt. Just for a while.

'No,' she said, holding up one hand. 'No wine, please.'

He held up the bottle so that she could see the label. 'Are you sure? It's a vintage San Margarita Superiore, the island's pride and joy.'

She was shaking her head, the internationally acclaimed wine label with its clutch of gold-medal stickers from a dozen different wine shows clearly making no impression.

He moved the bottle and poured some of the straw-coloured liquid into his own glass. 'Are you worried I might get you drunk and try to seduce you?'

For the first time since he'd sat down, her eyes flicked up to meet his. 'Not at all. I'm worried I have to fly a helicopter tomorrow morning and I'm being professional. But if my caution stops me from doing something unwise into the deal, so much the better.'

He raised his eyebrows at her words, and at the opening she'd given him. 'And would this thing you might otherwise do be so unwise?'

She flicked a napkin in her fingers, unfolding it before letting it settle on her lap. 'I think so.'

'Even though it might also be very pleasurable?'

Her chin set, she turned those deep honey-coloured eyes up to his once again, any intended coolness belied by the twin slashes of red adorning her cheeks, and he knew she was remembering, as was he, just how pleasurable that night had been.

'It would be a mistake,' she said, her tone defiant, 'and wherever possible, I try to avoid making the same mistake twice.'

The words grated on his senses, as did her ability to turn defensiveness into attack. He replaced the bottle in the ice bucket with a satisfying crunch, half tempted to tell her she wasn't going anywhere tomorrow or any time soon until he was good and finished with her.

But as he'd seen before, that would merely fuel her resistance. And he didn't want resistance. He wanted her warm and willing and begging him to fill her. And he wanted it all tonight.

Rafe forced a smile to his lips as he raised his glass to her in a toast. 'Then we must ensure you are not tempted to repeat any of the so-called mistakes of the past. Please, eat up.'

Sienna did eat up, as course after course of the most amazing food was delivered steaming-hot to her door. And she knew it must be amazing from the descriptions he gave her along the way, though she never tasted a thing, not the crayfish-filled ravioli or the lightly dusted tender calamari. Even the most succulent quail was completely wasted on her. The fine textures she could appreciate, but nothing of the taste.

Not with him sitting there, so close, so larger than life.

A man she had slept with once before.

A man who had made it plain that he wanted to sleep with her again.

And, if she were true to herself, a man who, despite everything, tempted her more than she cared to admit.

'Why did Signorina Genevieve come today?' she asked, as she contemplated the stunning dessert that had been placed before her. Fresh berries and cream lay sandwiched between wafers of meringue, creating a tower of colour and summer delights circled with a raspberry coulis and sprinkled with icing sugar, and she honestly wished she could appreciate it more, but the question had been circling through Sienna's thoughts for some time. That and the reason for the woman's sudden departure from the island so soon after arriving. The young woman had been in good spirits during their flight, and, even though she hadn't spoken a word to Sienna, it had been clear through her animated conversation with her mother how excited she had been to be travelling to Montvelatte. Sienna had figured her own reason for the visit, but given her sudden departure, now she wasn't so sure. 'Surely she would have stayed longer.'

Across the table Rafe leaned back, dragging in a breath. He crossed fingers in his lap, even though she could tell by the tightness of his shoulders that he wasn't as relaxed as he made out. 'She came for an interview, that's all.'

'She was applying for a job?'

This time he gave an ironic laugh. 'You could say that. My adviser seems to be obsessed with finding Montvelatte a princess. Which unfortunately involves finding me a wife.'

'A wife?' Sienna dragged in her own breath and fiddled with the placement of her napkin. *Rafe was getting married?*

She should have seen it coming. It wasn't a constant supply of high-class mistresses he'd had ferried to the island over the last couple of weeks—since when did they take their mothers with them?—it was potential brides.

And somehow that was no relief at all.

She did her best to inject some amusement into her voice. 'And this is how princes of Montvelatte find their wives, is it? By interview? How very romantic.'

Rafe reached for his wine glass and swirled the white wine in lazy circles, but he didn't take a sip. 'Romance doesn't enter the equation. A direct Lombardi descendant must take the throne, or the principality loses its right to exist. This is all about ensuring that doesn't happen.'

'That sounds very melodramatic.'

'Simply fact. Montvelatte's right to exist is predicated on the continuation of the line.'

'So that's where you came in.'

He leaned back in his chair. 'Even bastards have a purpose, it seems.'

His self-deprecating manner didn't fool her for a second. 'That's what was happening—that night—when the news broke on the television and they carted away your two half-brothers. You knew then, didn't you? You knew what it meant.'

'I had a gut feeling I might get a call.'

'And you just couldn't wait to take over the reins and put on that crown.'

He raised the glass to his lips and, without taking his eyes from hers, drank down the wine. 'You think I wanted this? To have my life turned into public property?'

'You seem happy enough lording it over me, holding me here against my will and forcing your way into my room when you're not welcome. Seems to me you're a natural at playing to the manor born.'

He stared at her a while, his eyelids half closed. 'If you say so.'

'And now you must have a wife. To give you an heir and to give Montvelatte the breathing space it needs.'

'That's right.'

She toyed with her dessert, making lazy figure eights through the raspberry coulis that lapped at the edges of her triumph in chocolate. 'So you're "interviewing" prospective wives. And meanwhile you're dining with a woman you once spent a night with, and who you have every intention of sleeping with again.'

It was meant to be an accusation, something that put him at a disadvantage, but the way he looked at her, the sudden widening and wanting revealed in his eyes, the planes of his face suddenly harsher in the fading light, more dangerous seemed to have the opposite effect. 'I am.'

And she felt a rush of heat infuse her skin, throbbing in places that responded eagerly to his words like an invitation. She was a fool for walking into his trap, for bringing up the one thing he'd somehow avoided talking about all night, and yet the one thing she knew he expected to happen. She looked down at her plate helplessly, at the dessert she'd barely touched, and knew there was no escape there. There were no more courses to come, the coffee already poured, the *petit fours* sitting between them accusingly. Dinner had come to an end and now he would expect her to fall into bed with him.

He needed a wife. He wanted a bed warmer. And it was clear whatever place she occupied fell into the latter category.

By rights she should hate him for it.

She *did* hate him for it.

And yet...

His gaze washed over her in a heated rush. He didn't have to utter another word; the question was there in his eyes, the hunger, the need. The promise of bliss.

Memories of the night they'd spent together surged back, rushing over her like a king tide, deep and unable to be resisted, a force of nature that could not be denied. What he'd done to her with his hands and his mouth and his perfect body. The way he'd made her feel...

The knowledge of how he could make her feel again.

Was it so wrong to feel so tempted? Was it so wrong for her body to hunger for more of what he'd given her, to experience more of that particular brand of magic?

She was leaving tomorrow.

She could have one more night. Where was the harm in that? One more night, and this time she would do the leaving. There could be no more surprises, no more disappointments. This time he wouldn't have the chance to dump her. This time she would be the one to walk away, the one in control. She could leave him to his ladies and his princesses and contessas. One of them would ultimately win him for ever, but she could have him right here, right now.

Maybe it would never be enough. But wouldn't one more night be at least something for the inconvenience he'd put her through today?

She deserved something. Surely.

He chose that exact moment to extend his hand to her. 'It's time.'

CHAPTER FIVE

'COME,' Rafe said, his voice rumbling through her in a series of tremors that threatened to unravel what was left of her defences. His long fingers wrapped around hers, circling her hand, drawing her up from her chair and against the black-clad, lethal length of him.

'Rafe,' she said, as his body received her in a swaying motion, almost as if dancing to a slow, silent waltz. 'Shh,' he whispered. 'Don't say anything.'

She couldn't say anything anyway, her reason for speaking forgotten while her senses were fully employed drinking in the feel of him moving against her, setting the silk robe to a sensual massage against her tight nipples and aching breasts.

Intoxicating.

His touch was like a drug, she decided, his hands dispensing a sensual dose everywhere they glided, everywhere they touched. And when he kissed her it was with the promise of ecstasy.

Sienna melted against him, his mouth taking possession of hers, hot and wanting and so hungry that she wanted to give him everything she had, if only he would give her more of him.

His fingers splayed wide down the curve of her spine and over her behind, holding her to him and against that rock-hard evidence of his need. She invited herself still closer, as his lips left her mouth to trail kisses down her throat. Her head fell back and he took advantage, sliding the silk of her robe apart, grazing the flesh above her breast with his teeth.

It was everything she'd dreamed of. Everything she'd missed in these last few weeks.

Make the most of it, a tiny voice in her head told her. *Because it's all you're ever going to get.*

A hand cupped her breast and she gasped, the voice in her head vanquished. 'You're more beautiful than I remembered,' Rafe murmured huskily, rolling one aching nipple between his thumb and finger before dipping his head to capture it between his lips.

Pleasure, exquisite and intense, speared deep inside, setting off a bloom of moisture between her thighs. She clung to him, knowing that otherwise her knees would give out and she would fall.

He turned his attention to her other breast, sweeping the fabric from her skin, letting her robe fall open in the process, uncaring, his hands underneath, across her naked skin. He drew back then and drank her in with his eyes, and the raw intensity she saw there terrified her.

She shivered, the tiny voice once again uppermost in her mind. What kind of man was he that he could look at her like that and then calmly turn around and marry another?

What kind of woman was she to let him?

She'd told him she wouldn't sleep with him. And yet here she was, next to naked, all but begging for him to take her. She was akin to a starving dog under the table, grateful for any scraps that might be thrown her way.

What the hell was wrong with her?

Sienna wrenched her hands from his shoulders, trusting her spine was firmer now and that her legs would hold up on their own, and pulled the sides of her robe together, lashing her arms firmly below her breasts to keep it there. She was shaking and she couldn't stop it, her body protesting at the sudden change of direction.

His head tilted to one side, his brows drawing together in a frown. 'Sienna,' he said straightening, 'are you cold?'

She shook her head, shuffling her bare feet backwards over the rich Persian carpet. 'I think you should go. This is a really bad idea.'

His eyes glinted menacingly. 'You didn't seem to think so a moment ago.'

'I told you before I wouldn't sleep with you. I'm sorry, but I haven't changed my mind.'

He took a step closer, the knot in his brows deepening. 'What kind of game are you playing? It's obvious you want this as much as I do.'

'No. I don't think so. And personally I don't think you give a damn what I want. All you care about is an easy lay.'

He growled at her coarse words. 'That's not true.'

'It is true! You decided when I landed on this island that you had an easy lay on tap. You didn't give a damn what I thought then, and you don't give a damn now. I told you I wanted off this island then and I still want off this island now. But you're still not listening. You still think you can take whatever you damn well please. Well, let me tell you, you had your chance in Paris and you made your choice crystal clear then.'

He didn't move, other than the faint tic in his jaw and the dangerous gleam in his eyes. 'Don't think you're going to gain some advantage by holding out. I'm afraid Sebastiano's short-list of potential Montvelatte princesses is already complete. There's a place for you in my bed if you want to take it, but I certainly won't beg you to change your mind.'

Cold fury at his arrogance skyrocketed her anger into overdrive. 'You think I want to marry you? Get real! I don't care that you're a prince. I wouldn't care if you were the Beast of Iseo himself. I wouldn't marry you if you were the last man left on earth. I told you I wouldn't sleep with you and I won't. Get used to it!'

His face was dark and filled with a fury that secretly terrified her. He was a prince. This was his land, his world and she was telling him how it was to be. She must be insane to think she could get away with it. But damn it, nothing gave him the excuse to act the way he did.

Nothing!

He glowered at her again, took a step closer that had her wanting to reel right away, before his tightly drawn lips finally gave way to sound. 'Have it your way.'

It was a perfect day, the rising sun already high in the sky, dazzling with the promise of heat. The infinity pool set into the gardens below sparkled and merged with the sea beyond, the perfect diamante-set blue, which in turn merged into a perfect azure sky.

A perfect day. And the perfectly wrong day for a foul mood.

Rafe sat on the terrace, holding his coffee, staring out resentfully over the beauty of the surroundings. His plans to seduce her into submission had come unstuck. So be it. If she wanted out so badly, she could have it. It was no real loss.

The chopper waited on the helipad for its pilot. He'd watched its arrival half an hour ago. He was surprised, given her vehemence of last night, that she hadn't already left.

He took a sip. *Dio!* Even the coffee tasted bitter today. He put down his cup with a clatter and stood. What was he waiting for? She was leaving. He wouldn't give her the satisfaction of seeing him watching out for her departure.

Something made him turn then, a noise, a movement, and

he saw her, standing in the doorway staring at him like a frightened animal stuck in the glare of oncoming headlights. Memories of last night's argument bubbled up like boiling mud, and his gut squeezed tight.

The only compensation was that she looked as bad as he felt. Her skin was pale. So pale against the Titian gold framing her face, even though pulled tight into that damned braid she favoured. And her eyes were smudged with dark circles that spoke of a lack of sleep that he could only hope matched his own.

What was she so scared of? Did she think he'd make another move on her? Not a chance!

'I just wanted to say goodbye,' she said, in a voice so tiny it almost got lost in the space between them.

He gave a brief nod. 'Have you eaten?'

Her face seemed to lose even more colour, if that were possible, and as he looked closer, he could see she was clutching at the door beside her for support, her grip so tight that her knuckles were white.

She shook her head, her lips pressed tightly together, her whole face looking pinched and drawn. She'd had a worst night than he had. *Good.* But as he edged nearer, he noticed for the first time that there was colour in her face after all, a strange shade of grey. 'Shouldn't you have breakfast before you go? At least some coffee?'

'I have to go,' she squeezed out between barely open lips, her eyes wider than ever as he approached. 'Thank you for your... Well, thank you.'

He nodded again, determined not to care one way or another how she felt. 'I'll have Sebastiano take you down to the helipad.'

She nodded and turned to go then, letting go of the side of the door to melt back into the house, but something about the way she moved, a slight stagger, a waver in her step, had him at her side in a heartbeat.

He reached for her arm, felt the momentary resistance in her slight frame before she sagged against him in a dead faint.

'Sebastiano,' he yelled, collecting her into his arms. 'Get the doctor!'

'She's resting now.'

Rafe stopped pretending not to be interested at the sound of the *dottore's* voice.

'Is she all right?'

'She's fine, but I've advised her to get a complete check-up when she gets home. And to think about avoiding flying while she feels like this, of course. But she'll feel better a little later on in the day. That's usually how morning sickness works.'

Clouds of black filled the space behind Rafe's eyes, an unexpected explosion of red following close behind as his heart pumped loud in his chest. 'She's pregnant, then?'

'Six to eight weeks, at a guess,' replied the doctor, oblivious to the bombshell he'd just dropped. 'So if you can do anything to reduce her stress levels, that will probably help her through this period. She does present as being very stressed.'

The doctor continued his diagnosis but Rafe heard nothing. Not while his mind processed the news, peeling back time, trying to remember. *Six to eight weeks.* Was it possible?

He'd used protection. He would never be that careless.

Except he hadn't!

He had been that careless.

The details came back in a blinding flash. He'd heard of his half-brothers' arrests and of their implication in their father's death. He'd learned that Montvelatte's existence balanced on a knife edge. And he'd been blind with anger and fury and rage that they could have been so arrogant and so self-absorbed that they had done this with pure greed in mind, and that they hadn't seen where they were heading. So blind with anger that he hadn't stopped to think, hadn't hesitated before burying himself one last time deep inside the woman who'd just happened to be there.

Had that momentary loss of control done this, resulted in a child? Was it his?

She'd almost got away. He'd been that close to letting her go, angry that she could deny him the pleasure he'd find with her, and so close to letting her walk out of his life for ever.

Would he ever have found out if she'd gone? She might never have told him.

Six weeks. Coincidence? Or fate?

Whichever, she wasn't getting away before he found out for sure.

The doctor had finished his report. 'Can I see her?'

'Certainly. Though be gentle. Right now she's a little emotionally fragile.'

Rafe blew out his breath in a rush. 'I'll just bet she is.'

Moments later he paused outside her room, his anger festering inside him, a living thing. He'd paced the terrace for endless minutes, working out the possibilities. If she'd told him last night that she was pregnant with someone else's child, if she'd thrown it in his face then and there, he would have left her alone. But she hadn't said a word. And six to eight weeks? Surely she must have known something? Was that the real reason she'd declined to have any wine?

He thought back on her determination to escape the island. She'd been desperate to get away. So desperate to escape that she'd risk flying a helicopter when she was in danger of passing out at the controls. If those facts weren't enough to spell out her guilt, he didn't know what was.

She didn't want him to know.

Which could only mean one thing.

It had to be his.

He hauled in a lungful of air, felt the oxygen fuel the fury inside him until it was in danger of combusting, until he wanted to howl at the irony.

All that time Sebastiano had been doing his utmost to find Montvelatte the perfect breeding stock.

All that time Sebastiano had spent ensuring Montvelatte would not be left without an heir.

And all that time there had been one all along.

It was a disaster. Sienna pushed herself back into pillows damp with tears, unable to assimilate the new-found knowledge, unable to come to terms with the physician's declaration.

There was nothing wrong with her, he'd calmly informed her, in the very same breath he'd dropped the bombshell that she was pregnant and suffering nothing more debilitating than morning sickness.

Nothing wrong. That was a laugh, when her entire world was shattering to pieces around her. Nothing wrong, when, in fact, nothing could be less right.

And so she'd argued and remonstrated with him. It had been too late in her cycle and she'd had a period, admittedly light, but then she'd only just come off the pill. It couldn't be possible.

And the doctor had looked benignly down at her as he'd clicked up his bag and explained that there was no mistake, that coming off the pill so recently meant her cycle could be late, and that the light period she'd assumed she'd had was most likely no more than an implantation bleed.

And then he'd asked her what she did for a living and warned her that she might have to think about not flying for a while. *Not flying?* Flying was her job. She'd just got the job of her dreams. It was her life!

And now she knew that the churning in her stomach was nothing to do with any morning sickness, but a gut-wrenching reaction to the news.

She was pregnant. With Rafe's child. That alone was bad enough. But he wasn't just a man any more.

He was a prince.

She screwed her face into the pillow and tried unsuccessfully to stem a fresh batch of tears. This couldn't be happening to her. Not with him. Not now.

He might be the father of the baby growing inside her, but he was expected to marry. Someone suitable. Someone worthy of being Montvelatte's princess.

Someone else.

Not some no-name commoner from a dysfunctional family who'd spent one night with him and ended up pregnant.

Which was fine, because she didn't damn well want any man on those terms anyway.

Sienna sniffed and sat up, grabbing a tissue to wipe away the moisture on her cheeks and blow her nose. Damn it all. Lying here crying wouldn't help; she had to pull herself together and get moving. She shoved back the covers and eased herself up to sitting on the side of the bed, swallowing air, waiting until the rocking motion inside her settled before she trusted her feet to hold her up.

Rafe wanted her gone from the island, he'd made that crystal clear, so she would oblige. And, let's face it, the last thing either he or Montvelatte needed right now was the scandal of an unplanned pregnancy with someone unsuitable. So she would get dressed and fly back to Genoa as soon as this damned nausea settled down. As soon as she'd come to terms with the shock of this latest bombshell.

Except that she was pregnant.

How was anyone supposed to terms with something like that?

There was a sharp rap on the door before it swung open, revealing the person she least wanted to see in the world. Her heart slammed into his chest as his dark eyes honed in on her, intent but frustratingly unreadable. *Please God, the doctor had not shared her news!*

She was dressed in some kind of white nightgown that fitted over her breasts and then fell softly to her ankles and he gave a silent tick of approval for whoever had released her hair from that damned braid so now it rioted around her face in a mass of colour and curl.

She looked like a virgin on her way to a sacrifice.

And then he took in her wide red-rimmed eyes, the eyes that looked up at him with something akin to terror, and revised the description. She looked like hell. *As guilty as hell.*

'What are you doing out of bed?'

'I was just getting up,' she protested, through lips inordinately pale. 'Or I was, until you once again decided to invite yourself in unannounced. So if you'll excuse me, I'd like to get dressed.'

'I thought you were sick.'

'I'm feeling much better,' she replied, adding a smile that didn't go near to erasing the caginess in those hazel eyes. 'I'm sorry. I don't know what came over me back there. I…I must have eaten something that disagreed with me.'

He almost growled. She was still trying to hide the truth. 'So now you're accusing my cook of poisoning you?'

'No! I didn't mean—' She gave up trying and shook her head. 'Look, I'm sorry to put you out, but I'll be gone soon. So if you wouldn't mind…'

She gestured towards the door but he wasn't going anywhere. He stood at the foot of the bed and leant a hand against one of the carved wooden posts. 'I don't think so. I really think leaving would be unwise right now.'

Sienna stood up in a rush and sprang away from the bed, a blur of motion as the white gown billowed around her long legs like a cloud, her bare feet pacing the carpet. He could almost see her mind ticking over as her hands busied themselves collecting her hair into a loose pony tail before letting it go to spring back wild around her face again. 'Look, Rafe,' she said, turning to him, the colour of irritation high on cheeks that otherwise looked too pale to be human, 'we've been through all this and I'm fed up with the way you think you can push me around. You agreed last night that I could leave today and, quite frankly, it won't be soon enough. As soon as I'm dressed, I'm out of here.' She was halfway to the bathroom before he caught up with her, catching her arm and swinging her around.

'Not with my baby, you're not.'

He heard her gasp. Smelt her fear. 'What are you talking about?' She was still fighting, but the guilt was there, in the defensive sheen in her eyes, in the faint tremor in her lips.

'Why didn't you tell me you were pregnant?'

Her breathing was shallow and fast, her chest rising and falling rapidly with the action. 'I don't know why you think it's any of your business, but maybe I didn't know.'

'You're lying.'

'Then maybe it's not your baby? Did you ever stop to consider that?'

He reeled back as if she'd physically lashed out, but only for a moment, before the feral gleam in his eye returned. 'You went from my bed to another's? I don't believe you.'

'You threw me out. Why should you care who I sleep with?'

'I care because I do not believe you. You were hiding it from me and you're still trying to. It's my baby, isn't it? You're having my baby!'

If he hadn't sensed her need, if he hadn't let her go, she

would never have made it to the bathroom in time. There was precious little in her stomach, nothing more than dry toast and some of the same sweet tea she'd had yesterday that had been so soothing at the time. And yet it felt like she was being torn apart from the inside with each violent heave.

And he was there, holding back her hair and steadying her shoulders as she held onto the bowl for grim death.

Oh, God, if it wasn't bad enough that Rafe should see her like this, the doctor had obviously told him why.

A total disaster had just got worse.

At last it was over; the thrashing of her stomach calmed. She heard the sound of running water, felt the cool press of a flannel against her face and she took it gratefully, pressing it to her tear-stained cheeks and wishing that there was something that could so easily soothe her soul.

The doctor had told him, and Rafe knew!

What the hell was she supposed to do now?

'Let's get you back to bed,' he said, helping her to rise on unsteady legs and steering her from the room. She went with him, the fight gone from her, her strength drained, her mind numb with it.

'I'm sorry,' she said, as he eased her down on the bed, knowing that a terrible wrong had been done, knowing she was at least partly responsible, not having a clue what to say. Having even less idea of how to fix it. 'I realize this is inconvenient. I'll go. I won't tell anyone, I promise.'

And the band that had bound his gut ever since he had heard she was pregnant grew even tighter, until even his lungs felt squeezed with the pressure. Better than any test result, it was the final confirmation he needed, banishing any lingering doubts in an instant. 'So it is mine!'

Her eyes looked up at him, pained and dull. 'Nobody will ever know. I promise.'

'*Merda!* I will know! Or are you already planning on disposing of the "inconvenience", as you so clinically put it, in order to assure that outcome?'

Her eyes sparked with indignation, their hazel lights suddenly flashing gold as if someone had thrown a switch, though her skin was still deathly pale and her voice was still rough and raw. 'As it happens I haven't had a chance to consider my options, but just what kind of person do you think I am?'

'It doesn't matter what type of person I think you are. What matters is what you plan on doing with my child.'

'And I'm supposed to believe you care? Don't bother. I promise not to go to the papers or get in the way of your precious princess hunt.'

'No.'

'What do you mean, "no"?'

'It means that's not good enough. I will not allow another generation of Lombardi bastard children to be cast aside as if they are not family. There is only one solution.'

She rolled her head from side to side against the pillow. 'You can share access, if that's what you want. I can hardly deny a child access to its father.'

'I'm glad you understand that. And there is no better way to share access…' he smiled, amazed at how neatly the whole thing fitted together—a woman he had no trouble desiring, already pregnant with his child, and an end to Sebastiano's endless round of prospective wife interviews, all rolled into one neat solution '…than to make you my wife.'

CHAPTER SIX

IF SIENNA hadn't been lying down, her knees would have given way beneath her. As it was, the breath was punched from her lungs. He couldn't be serious!

'You have to be joking. There's no reason on earth why I should marry you.'

'It is the only solution. I need a wife and an heir.'

'You need a princess, not a pilot. You need someone off that list of titled wannabes.'

'But you have something they can only promise. You have conveniently proven your ability to conceive.'

'Forget it. There's no way I'm marrying you just because I'm pregnant. No way in the world.'

'You need not be frightened of the royalty angle. You will be coached in our language and history.'

'I wouldn't say yes even if you weren't a prince! A baby is no basis for a marriage. I would never do that to a child.'

'And yet you would be happy to let that child grow up without its father. How is that fairer?'

'You can't force me to do this. Your father never married your mother simply because she was pregnant.'

'He didn't think he needed to. He already had his heir and a spare. My sister and I were surplus to requirements.'

'But your mother—'

'Had no choice! She received a substantial settlement and an annual pension on the condition she never returned to Montvelatte, and she never told anyone who her children's father was.'

Sienna threw back her chin. 'I would be more than happy to comply with the same conditions. For nothing. It wouldn't cost you a thing.'

He shook his head. 'You are kidding yourself. There is no way I would allow you to bring up our child in near poverty.'

'I have a job!'

'For how long? How can you fly in the condition you found yourself this morning? How long do you think anyone will employ a pilot who could faint at any minute? Who in their right mind would want to fly with you?'

'I have some savings. I'll take time off. Morning sickness doesn't last forever.'

'And after the baby comes, how do you expect to keep working when you have a child to care for?'

'Like plenty of other woman in my situation do. I'll cope.'

'Not with my child. Simply coping is not an option. How long do you think you'll keep the origins of your baby secret?'

'Your mother obviously managed to.'

'More than thirty years ago when there was still a measure of respect for privacy. Whereas these days, any hint of scandal, any hint of a royal baby born out of wedlock and the paparazzi will come baying at your door. How long do you think you can hide the truth?'

'I won't tell anyone if you won't!'

'And when I marry and have a wife and a family, and then the truth inevitably comes out because of something the doctor today tells his secretary or his wife, you would be happy to humiliate the woman I married with the news that I already had a child? How do you think that would look splashed across the gutter press? How do you think this child will feel when he learns that he was the rightful heir of Montvelatte and you denied him that birthright?'

'Why do you assume it will be a boy?'

'It doesn't matter. Girl or boy, you will be denying this child its place in the Montvelattian monarchy.'

'Only if it finds out. And who is going to tell?'

His arms came down on the bed either side of her, his face bare inches from her own, and it was all she could do not to cower back into the pillows at the anger and pain so starkly reflected in his features.

'I will tell. Do not think you can deny me access to my child simply because you would rather forget who his father is. I am not like my father. I will not abandon a child I sired or hide it away merely because I was not married to its mother.'

Sienna watched his eyes while he made his speech, watched the way the pain coursed so deeply through them. He'd missed out on having a father all his life. He'd been cast away, exiled with his mother, unwanted by the father who'd sired him.

And he was right. One way or another, no matter how close she played her cards to her chest, there was no way she could shut Rafe out of her child's life. But in allowing Rafe access to her child, there was no way its parentage could ever be kept secret.

So where did that leave her?

It was all too much to take in. She'd only just discovered she was pregnant, and now he was demanding that she marry him, a man she'd spent one short night with and the last twenty-four hours trying to get away from, a man who would, without a second thought, bully her into a marriage she neither wanted nor needed.

A shotgun wedding, just like her mother's. Except this

time there were no parents holding a gun to Rafe's head to persuade him to do the right thing by their daughter. This time it was Rafe holding a gun to her head.

Was it because it was the right thing to do by their child? Or was it simply because it was convenient to him?

Either way, his wanting to marry her clearly had nothing to do with her.

'You can't make me do this.' She'd wanted to sound strong and sure but her voice came out sounding more like a plea.

'It's the only thing to do. I'll inform Sebastiano and have him make the necessary arrangements.'

The necessary arrangements? Rafe had it sounding like a royal wedding was no more hassle than a trip to the local corner store.

'No! I haven't agreed to anything. You can't make me do this.'

'You have no choice.'

'I have a choice! I'm leaving and you can't stop me.' She scooted to the other side of the bed, swinging her legs over the side and pushing herself off, but he was already there, standing in front of here like a storm cloud, angry and potent and thunderous. But the hand he put to her face was gentle and warm, and she trembled into his touch. His eyes studied her face, his thumb traced the line of her lips, and her heartbeat jagged, and when his words came, it was more a promise than a threat.

'Leave and I will bring you back. Run and I will catch you. There is no escaping the truth of this, Sienna. You will marry me. You will become my wife.'

She looked up at him, afraid to blink, afraid to breathe, lest she broke this spell he'd somehow woven around her. How long he stood there stroking her face, how long she allowed him to, she didn't know. And only the sense that she was losing herself, spinning out of control into a place with no horizons, into a place she had no way of navigating her way out of, shot a burst of fear straight to her heart.

'There has to be another way,' she whispered.

His hand cupping her jaw, he dipped his face to hers and pressed the barest of kisses to her lips. 'There is no other way.'

Sebastiano wasn't so sure. He took the news of the cancellation of the remaining marriage candidates and the reason with the look of a man heading for the gallows. 'Are you sure this is wise, Prince Raphael, to marry such a woman? The role of Princess of Montvelatte is a demanding one. What background and training has this woman had in the skills necessary to undertake such a role?'

'I would imagine the same amount of training that I received in becoming Montvelatte's Prince. And yet nobody questioned my qualifications.'

'You have royal blood, Highness. There is a difference.'

'And she carries it!'

His aide gave a brief cough into his hand, too pointed to miss. 'You have something to say, Sebastiano?'

'Merely that I think it would be wise to guarantee that fact before we make any announcements.'

Rafe had no doubt. The way she'd reacted to his accusations, the way she'd apologized and promised to keep it quiet—he had no doubt at all. But Sebastiano needed facts, and it was better that they did the digging before some gossip magazine got there before them. 'Arrange for whatever tests you need—even a date will help to confirm the truth—and meanwhile find out all you can about her—her past, her boyfriends, and anyone she's seen apart from me in the last eight weeks.'

Sebastiano nodded, looking more satisfied than he had all day, and gave a little bow. 'It will be done.'

Rafe watched him take his leave and felt a pang of regret that one had to be so careful, knowing it had to be done, and knowing equally that if there was any dirt to be had on Sienna Wainwright, Sebastiano would dig it out.

He just hoped there was none.

Sienna picked up the telephone in the library and listened for a dial tone, hoping that, unlike the phone in her room, this one would not be switched through to the housekeeper. Satisfied, she nervously dialled the direct number of her boss at Sapphire Blue Charters and waited what felt like agonizing seconds for the call to be answered.

She'd been thinking about it all night. She had no way of getting to the town except by foot and she had no doubt that Rafe would find her and bring her back as promised, even if she'd had the money to buy a fare off the island. And there was no point calling the police, because the palace guard were the ones who'd threatened to arrest her if she didn't accompany them to the Castello in the first place. Asking for help from the Australian Embassy was tantamount to taking out a full page ad, and that was hardly the way she wanted to slip quietly out of Rafe's life. But Monsieur Rocher might send a helicopter, once he knew she was being held against her will.

'Oui?' The grunting voice of the owner-manager of Sapphire Blue greeted her.

She took a deep breath and crossed the fingers of her free hand. *'Monsieur Rocher, c'est moi, Sienna Wainwright. Je suis désolé—'*

'Bonjour, Sienna!'

Sienna listened in amazement as the tongue-lashing she was expecting turned into high praise as she learned she had been retained on an ongoing basis as Montvelatte's private pilot, and for three times the going rate, in response to which Monsieur Rocher had awarded her employee of the month.

'*Mais non*—'

But Monsieur Rocher was too full of praise to be interrupted. He wished her well, thanked her for her good work and bade her a hasty, '*Au revoir*', before the line went dead.

'Can I help you with something?'

Sienna turned, still reeling from the phone call, to find Sebastiano standing in the doorway, his expression looking anything but helpful. Quickly she replaced the receiver, knowing she'd been caught out. 'I...I was just calling my boss.'

'So I gathered. And did you find everything to your satisfaction.'

'I've been made employee of the month.'

He gave a slight mocking bow. 'Congratulations.'

Sienna straightened. It was clear from just his tone that Sebastiano didn't welcome her presence here, but then little wonder if she'd put paid to his plans of Rafe marrying someone from the noble classes. She could take offence that he clearly thought her unbefitting of the role of Montvelatte's Princess, or she could use it for her own purposes.

She laced her fingers together and took a step closer. 'Sebastiano, maybe you *can* help me.'

His eyes honed in on her suspiciously. 'In what way?'

'You could help get me off the island.'

This time those eyes narrowed, and he looked around before closing the door behind him. 'To what purpose?'

'So Rafe can marry someone more suitable.' She saw the glimmer in his eyes that betrayed how appealing he found her words.

'But you are carrying Prince Raphael's child, are you not?'

'It's still me he would be marrying.'

His expression remained guarded, suspicious, while his

eyes looked thoughtful. Then he shook his head. 'I'm afraid I cannot help you. But if you would like to make any more phone calls, perhaps you should know that all calls to and from the Castello are monitored for security reasons.'

Sienna shivered. So that was how he'd found her. 'Thank you, Sebastiano. So if I call my landlady to enquire after my apartment?'

'Please, feel free. But you will discover that your rent has been paid and your personal belongings sent for, to make your stay here more comfortable.'

'Thank you,' she said, *I think,* allowing herself to be led away, and feeling the noose around her neck growing tighter by the minute.

The next day under the trellised vines shading the terrace, Sienna daydreamed, thinking back to a time she could only imagine, another time when her mother had discovered she was pregnant, with a marriage to Sienna's father hastily arranged in that discovery's wake.

Had her mother felt this terror, this fear of having a new life growing inside her and all the unknowns that went with it? Had she been secretly afraid of the prospect of marrying a man who had blown into town on the tide? Or had love blinded her to those fears, so that the prospect of marrying the man she had fallen head over heels in love with, and of bearing him a child, was so utterly exciting that she'd had no doubts?

She'd been so young, barely eighteen at the time and eight years younger than Sienna was now. Surely she must have had doubts, no matter how much she'd thought she'd loved him? Surely she must have wondered if the wanderlust father of her child could ever really change?

'It's time for your ultrasound.'

Rafe's voice intruded into her thoughts, and she blinked,

the present world suddenly coming back into sharp focus as she looked up and he filled her vision, instantly kicking new life into her heart rate. How he still had that effect on her when she was basically his prisoner here, she couldn't understand and didn't want to analyse. She only knew that the sooner she could put a lid on this inner turmoil she felt whenever he so much as looked at her, the better.

To him she might only be the vessel that carried his child, and a convenient solution to a problem that threatened the Principality, but there was no way she could consider marriage to a man like Rafe—a prince—in such clinical terms. And yet if she was going to have to go through with this, she needed to be able to.

A strange fear zipped up her spine. The fact she was even considering marrying Rafe—when had that change in her thinking taken place? And more importantly, why? It was anathema to her—marrying for the sake of a child—and yet she was entertaining the idea as if it were a done deal. Last night again she'd thought about getting help. Why shouldn't she call the Embassy, and who cared if the calls were monitored? By the time they discovered who she was calling, help could be on its way, and to hell with the fall out. He had no right to keep her here against her will.

And again she'd shut herself in the library, meaning to call, fully intending to. But she'd only got as far as lifting the receiver. Only pressed it to her ear, before the fingers of her other hand had cut the connection, and she'd slammed the receiver down in frustration.

What was happening to her?

Three days she'd been on the island now. Yesterday had been filled with an endless parade of specialists, nutritionists and exercise gurus, and she'd met Carmelina, the dark-haired young beauty who was to 'manage' her new wardrobe, and lay out whatever outfits she'd need in readiness for the day's and evening's activities. When she'd protested that she'd successfully managed her wardrobe by herself for the best part of twenty years, Rafe had reminded her that soon she would be a princess, dressing for all manner of events, formal and informal, and that she could not be expected to manage a wardrobe the size of a department store.

And when a fashion consultant arrived, bringing along an entire boutique and three assistants with her and fitted Sienna out in an entire wardrobe in under two hours—and that was only the beginning, she'd assured her, planning on returning with designs made solely for her—Sienna finally believed him.

Today promised to be more of the same. Was it any wonder she felt numb from all the attention? Once yesterday's obstetrician had confirmed her pregnancy, this juggernaut that was to be a royal wedding rolled and gained momentum with every minute.

And she was still only just coming to terms with her pregnancy. Once again this morning, she'd felt nauseous, though it was more a general queasiness this time that had assailed her, a queasiness that paled in comparison to the illness of those first days here. How much had stress and high emotions played a part in that—the fear of meeting Rafe again, her fury at being held against her will and the accusation that she'd kept her pregnancy secret from him—had this all combined to magnify the worst of her pregnancy symptoms tenfold?

'Sienna?' He put out a hand to her, obviously impatient to see the proof of the child they had conceived together. 'Come.'

She regarded it suspiciously. He hadn't made a move to touch her yesterday, not after he'd discovered she was pregnant and they'd shared that one brief kiss. Out of consideration for her condition? She wondered. It wouldn't surprise her if he figured he didn't need to touch her now, his work already done.

Nevertheless she slipped her fingers into his and let him lead her inside, amazed at how comfortable his grip felt, and how much warmth could be conveyed in the touch of just one hand. It was almost enough to make her forget the litre of water she'd been asked to drink and the knowledge of where that litre of fluid now resided. Almost.

'Are you all right?' Rafe asked as they ascended the stairs slower than he obviously would have liked.

'I'm fine,' she retorted, knowing his concern had less to do with her and more to do with the welfare of his unborn child. 'Just don't stick a pin in me or I might explode.' And while his low laugh irritated her, she was still grateful for his support as she made her way up the long sweeping stairway to the first floor.

The radiographers had set up their equipment in one of the unused rooms not far from her own, turning a bedchamber fit for a queen into a suite filled with the latest in medical technology. She blinked as she took it all in. Never before had she been in the position of having a doctor, let alone specialists, come to her—to ensure privacy, Rafe had told her, and she could understand that, although part of her wondered whether he thought there was a risk she might bolt if she had the chance to visit Velatte City.

Would she bolt, she wondered as she dutifully changed out of the clothes Rafe's minions had chosen for her into the robe they'd provided? Nothing of Rafe's plans to wed her had yet been announced, nobody knew who she was, and in the cover of the harbour city, unknown and unannounced, there was always the chance she'd be able to slip the palace guard and make her way to the port and secure a ticket to somewhere.

Away from Montvelatte and Rafe, at least she would have a fighting chance of thinking straight. Already her resolve was wavering, her determination not to be steamrolled into a wedding she didn't want dangerously slipping.

Which made no sense at all. She knew marriage could falter without love to bind the couple together; her own parents' marriage had taught her that.

Although at least her mother had wanted to marry.

Sienna hadn't even been asked the question.

'Are you ready?'

Rafe's voice broke her from her reverie and she allowed herself a wistful smile. *'Are you ready?'* was about the most romantic this wedding proposal was going to get.

Moments later she was on the stretcher draped in towels with her gown raised and her naked abdomen exposed. Soothing voices explained the procedure and assured her everything would be all right before cool jelly tickled as it was spread over her belly. She felt the pressure of the sensor sliding over her skin and for the very first time considered what might happen if something was wrong.

Sienna hadn't asked for this baby, hadn't wanted it or the marriage that Rafe assumed must go hand in hand with its existence. But if something was wrong with the baby, if he wasn't getting the package deal he was expecting, there was every likelihood he wouldn't want her any more.

Just for a moment, just a fraction of a moment, she almost let herself wish for the worst.

It hit her unexpectedly then, a hitherto unknown maternal guilt that she could be so cruel to her unborn child, tumbling and crashing over her in a wave that had her clamping her eyes tightly shut as she tried to blot out the possibility that something could be wrong. Because none of this was the baby's fault. She had no right to wish away this brand new speck of life just to solve her own problems. No right at all.

And suddenly, as the scanner slid across her skin, all that mattered was that her baby was healthy. Whatever else happened to her, it didn't matter, she would somehow cope.

But please, God, let her baby be healthy!

The radiographer seemed to be taking forever, biting her lip as she stared at the screen. She said something in her native Velattian-Italian language mix that had the obstetrician nodding as he studied the emerging pictures. She turned her head to see, but the screen was angled away from her, studied intently by the radiographer by her side and by both the specialist and Rafe at the foot of the bed. She strained to get higher. 'If you could lie still,' the radiographer encouraged, putting a hand to her shoulder.

'What's wrong,' Rafe asked her, his attention distracted from the screen.

'It's taking so long.'

The woman smiled and squeezed her arm. 'Don't worry,' she said, her accented words strangely soothing. 'Sometimes it takes a little time. As soon as we have a clear picture, I'll show you your *bambino*.'

Rafe joined her at the head of the bed, pulled up a chair and took her hand between his. 'You can't see there,' she warned, knowing how much he wanted to see the evidence of this child with his own eyes.

'So we'll see our baby together.' And the way he smiled at her raised goosebumps on her skin and hope in her heart. It seemed so real, like the smile a man would give a woman when she was carrying a child conceived in love. A smile so seemingly real it made her ache for all those real things she would never have—a real marriage, a man who wanted to marry her because he loved her and not for the baby she carried, a husband of her own choosing...

Sienna turned her head away and concentrated instead on the click and whirr of the machinery and the feel of the press of the device as it traced a path across her belly, the near-excruciating pressure against her over-full bladder all but banished by the feel of Rafe's hand around hers and the lazy stroke of his thumb.

She was asked to move a little to one side, then to the other, until after some time the radiographer appeared to find what she was looking for.

'*Dottore Caporetto?*' She looked over her shoulder then to the specialist, who was suddenly studying the screen intently, a frown gathering his already bushy brows, and a chill zipped down Sienna's spine.

Something *was* wrong.

Rafe's hand tightened around hers, as if he'd picked up on the vibe in the room as well. 'What is it?' he demanded in English. Then, '*C'e' qualcosa che non va, Dottore?*'

'Something you need to see,' he said, and the consultant angled the screen so that both of them had a clear view at last, into a murky sea of light and shadow where nothing made sense.

'I don't understand,' Sienna said. She'd known her baby would be tiny at this stage but she'd expected to see something recognizable, not this unreadable blur. 'What is it?'

The specialist said something to Rafe she didn't understand but she heard Rafe's sharp intake of breath, felt his withdrawal as he pushed himself back in his chair, and she feared the worst.

The specialist's face turned into a broad smile at Rafe's reaction, before he turned his attentions to her, patting her on the ankle. '*Va tutto benissimo. Auguri signorina, lei aspetta gemelli.*'

She shook her head and looked at Rafe who suddenly looked as shell-shocked as she felt. 'I don't understand. What's wrong? What's happening?'

'Ah, excuse me, please,' the *dottore* said, looking truly contrite as he pointed to twin smudges on the screen. 'In my excitement I forgot my manners. But you have my heartiest congratulations, *signorina*. It appears you are expecting twins.'

CHAPTER SEVEN

RAFE peered at the screen and at the two dark smudges in a sea of light, smudges that proved beyond doubt he would become a father not just once but twice over in a few short months from now, a feeling of pride so huge in his chest that he wanted to howl like the Beast of Iseo itself. What fortune had brought Sienna to the island? Providence couldn't have dealt him a better hand.

'Twins?' he heard her say, her voice shaky as if she couldn't believe the news herself. 'It can't be…'

He lifted her hand then and pressed his lips against it. 'We will marry as soon as possible,' he said. 'There can be no delay.'

Rafe took her to dinner that night, insisting they celebrate the news, in a harbour-front restaurant where a private room furnished with gilt mirrors and lush curtains had been set up for them on an upstairs terrace that overlooked the lights of the harbour front and the marina. It was the first time she'd been to Velatte City, and she loved its vibrancy and colour and the handsome people, their features a blend of the best the Mediterranean could offer.

Carmelina had proven her worth as Sienna's wardrobe manager, selecting without hesitation a gown shaded from lilac through to a rich jewel-shade of amethyst that sat snug over Sienna's bustline before falling in soft, almost toga-like folds to the floor. With her hair coiled in wide ringlets and gathered up behind her head loosely for the ends to trail down, she almost felt like a Greek goddess. The way Rafe looked at her almost made her believe it.

Even so, the way he'd dressed made her wish she'd taken even more care. In a dark tuxedo and crisp white shirt he was magnificent, the Lombardi-crested cufflinks at his wrists, a burgundy tie at his throat. He looked like a man who had everything he wanted in the world, and if there was one tiny pang of regret about this whole celebration, it was that she knew that the babies she was carrying were a large part of it.

But she'd done a lot of thinking about those babies herself today, and a lot of it centered around her fears for what might happen if she did marry Rafe, and the quality of life she could offer them if she didn't.

One baby she believed she could cope with. She'd have to get a nanny, but she made decent money when she could fly. It would be hard to be a single mother, but at a stretch she would cope. Women did, all around the world, every day. Why couldn't she?

But knowing she was carrying twins had changed things, had tipped the balance. What kind of life could she offer them? What hope had she of being able to afford their care while she worked and what hope of giving them the family life they deserved? Would they grow up resenting her because she could not give them the lifestyle they would have had with their father?

But marriage without love? The one thing she feared more than anything.

How could he ask it of her?

They sat enjoying their entrées; a rare kind of peace descended on them as if Rafe too was deep in thought, while the vibrant waterfront buzzed below and the warm breeze tugged at her hair. Violin music drifted up from the main restaurant downstairs, gypsy music that was filled with life and hope and passion.

The first hint of the helicopter making its way across the harbour snared Sienna's attention like a magnet, even before the *whump* of the rotors became noticeable, and a familiar yearning surged anew. She followed its spotlight-lit path across the harbour, to where it landed atop one of the palace-like casinos lining the foreshore. She sighed as it landed. God, she missed flying, missed the feeling of soaring through the air like a bird, or skimming across the water like an insect. Missed the endless sky.

'What made you become a pilot?'

Sienna turned back to him, thinking it was odd that she was having his babies, that he fully intended to marry her, and yet they knew so very little about each other. 'The only thing I inherited from my father,' she started, 'was a love for travel. We lived on his boat my first few years, travelling the world, stopping in ports anywhere and everywhere. Until it was time for me to go to school and we dropped anchor in Gibraltar.'

'Sounds like a wonderful childhood.'

She gave a brief, harsh laugh, the sound of her father's constant taunts loud in her ears. 'I suppose it could have been.'

'It wasn't?'

'My father never wanted me. Always blamed me for ruining his life, for giving him responsibilities and putting an end to his wanderlust days. Ironic that I should inherit his love of travel, in that case, don't you think?'

Across the table, Rafe frowned, looking thoughtful. 'But boats never appealed?'

'God, no! Not after… Well, not after that. I used to lie on

the deck and watch the birds wheeling above. I used to imagine myself up there with them, it was the only way I could see to escape...' Her words trailed off. She'd said too much, revealed far too much of herself. She picked up her glass, swirling the sparkling water. 'Anyway, that's the dreary story of why I became a pilot.'

'No,' he said, squeezing her hand. 'Not dreary. Interesting. They must be proud of you.'

She looked out over the harbour and breathed in the smell of the sea and salt, finding a memory that brought a smile to her face. 'Mum was. She was ever so proud when I got my licence.' She turned and saw the question in his eyes. 'She died a few years back.'

'And your father?'

She shrugged. 'I don't know. I haven't seen him for years. He stayed in Gibraltar. We left.'

'I'm sorry,' he said.

'It's okay. Really. But can we talk about something a little more upbeat? Tell me about your sister. Where is she now?'

Rafe nodded as he sipped at his wine, and she couldn't tell if he was happy to accede to her request to change the topic, or just happy to think about his sister. 'She's fun. Where I was the serious one in the family, Marietta was always the hopeless romantic, the dreamer. She's a jewellery designer, and a seriously good one, now working in New Zealand. You'll like her, I know.'

She smiled. 'I think I will.'

A waiter came and topped up his wine, poured Sienna more lemon-flavoured mineral water and hovered just a moment too long to go unnoticed. Rafe looked up at him. 'Was there something else?'

'*Scusarmi, per favore,*' the red-faced waiter said with a nod, before rattling off a burst of language so fast and furious that Sienna had no hope of keeping up. Rafe answered, his smile genuine as he rose from his seat to shake the man's hand, only to be wrapped in an embrace that had the waiter looking mortified with embarrassment before he bowed again and again as he made his exit. *'Grazie. Grazie.'*

'What was that all about?'

Rafe gave a shrug as he sat down, as if it had been nothing. 'The waiter's father works as a teller at one of the casinos; his mother is a cleaner there. He had been frightened that they would all lose their jobs when they saw Carlo and Roberto being arrested.'

'That's not all, though,' she said, sensing more in the exchange from the odd word she'd picked up than he was letting on. 'He was thanking you for coming back, wasn't he?'

He gazed out over the harbour, rather than at her, as if he was uncomfortable with how much she had interpreted of the exchange. 'Apparently so.'

She thought about the people who'd greeted and served them tonight with smiles and warmth. She'd taken them for granted—wouldn't they meet their Prince in such a way anyway? But, looking back, there'd been a genuine warmth in their welcome, as if the people of Montvelatte had embraced their new Prince with joy. And Rafe's reaction to the waiter's comments seemed to echo those sentiments.

'You really care about these people, don't you?'

He flicked his serviette back onto his lap. 'Does that surprise you?'

She shrugged, embarrassed that she'd made so obvious her prejudgment. 'But you never had anything to do with Montvelatte before. You grew up in Paris, in exile with your mother and sister.'

'You are right, of course. All I really knew was from my mother's stories, or from the books she always encouraged us to read. But being back here in Montvelatte, living here, getting to know the people, it surprised me too how comfortable it felt. I am glad I decided to come back.' He reached across the table and wrapped one of her hands in his own, and she felt the sincerity of his words in his touch.

'Was there ever any doubt?' she asked, liking the way her hand felt in his, the way his fingers stroked the skin of her hand into sensual awareness. 'I thought you had decided that night, as soon as the reports came in, that this was your destiny.'

He shook his head. 'I wasn't planning to come at all—not at first. Not until Yannis called.' He broke off suddenly to explain. 'Yannis Markides, my business partner but more than that, my lifelong friend. It was Yannis who made me see sense. But when I did decide to come, it wasn't because I felt some inexplicable link with the island or its people.'

'Then why?'

His thumbs made lazy circles on her hand, lazy circles that sent busy signals vibrating through her veins. 'Two things. One part of me wanted to prove that a bastard son, the son his father had rejected, could make something of himself, could prove himself to be a worthy ruler.' He fixed her with eyes full of meaning. 'It seems that I, too, was blessed with a father who didn't want me.'

Sienna bristled under his gaze, not at all sure she was comfortable having something in common with him, let alone a reason to empathise with him. 'And the other?'

'Because of my mother. She loved her Mediterranean island home and hated being exiled like some criminal simply because she'd borne the Prince a bastard son and daughter. Do you understand? By coming back, I could try to make things right for her. That was my motivation. But I had no idea when I made that decision just how right it would come to feel.'

Sienna shivered, picking up on his use of past tense. His mother was dead. She recalled reading that in a magazine article after Rafe's coronation. But it hadn't occurred to her then that it was something else they shared.

She picked up her glass of water in her free hand, desperate for something to do to hide her confusion. She hated being wrong about things, hated knowing she'd made judgements based on assumptions that were misplaced. She'd assumed Rafe had embraced his new role because he'd imagined himself born to rule. Had believed it, considering the way he'd treated her. But given his story and the way the people here seemed to react to him, maybe she'd been wrong about that. Maybe he wasn't the beast she imagined him to be...

'I have something for you,' he said, interrupting her thoughts while he reached into his pocket.

She sat up straight, suddenly defensive, interlocking both hands under the table in case he was about to make some kind of engagement ring gesture. Despite their more civilized conversation tonight, and despite her shifting thoughts, she wasn't ready for anything like that yet, hoped that tonight wasn't about that. 'What is it?'

The ruby-red box looked worn, the velvet scuffed at the corners. 'It's my mother's favourite piece of jewellery. I thought you should have it.'

Sienna shook her head, while he pressed the box towards her until it would have been churlish not to raise her hands and accept it. 'But it was your mother's. Shouldn't it go to your sister?'

'Open it,' he urged. She gasped as the case snapped open, revealing the stunning jewels within, gemstones of every hue and shade, suspended at intervals from a diamond-set necklace.

'It's beautiful,' was her first reaction. 'I can't accept this,' was her second. But he was already on his feet, taking the necklace from its setting and fixing it at her throat. She put a hand to the precious piece, the jewels feeling heavy and cool against her skin, whereas the brush of his fingers felt warm at her throat, but all too light and all too brief.

He sat down again, the fire in the gems reflected in the flames in his eyes. 'They suit you.' And then, 'did I tell you how beautiful you look tonight?'

She dropped her eyes. 'Carmelina chose it.'

'It's not the dress,' he said. 'It's you. You look radiant.' He lifted his glass to her. 'Here's to you, my future bride, the mother of Montvelatte's future.'

She trembled, the responsibility of the title he'd just bestowed upon her feeling like a leaded weight. 'Look, Rafe, I haven't actually agreed to marry you yet.'

He frowned, her words clearly taking him off guard, before reaching over the table to take her hand. 'What choice do we have? Soon you will start to show. Do you want this marriage to look like some shotgun wedding?'

Like her parents' perchance? His words cut through the goodwill they'd built tonight like a scythe, sharp and deep, re-opening old wounds and laying them bare. 'If I *did* agree to marry you, why shouldn't it look that way, when that's exactly what it is?'

'I prefer to call it a marriage of convenience, for both of us.'

'And I call it like I see it. You may not be holding a shotgun to my head, but you might as well be. What choice have you given me?'

Candlelight flickered in his dark eyes. 'I'm sorry. Maybe coming out tonight was premature and you are not yet ready to see sense.'

'As you are not yet ready to see my point of view!'

He sighed and leant back in his chair, throwing his napkin down onto the table. 'And what is your point of view? That you can go on your merry way carrying two royal babies and somehow continue your life as a helicopter pilot as if nothing had happened?' He cursed under his breath and stood, signalling to the waiter for the car to be brought around.

She remained exactly where she was and jagged her chin up higher. 'I don't know any more. Two babies—I just don't know. But I do know that whatever you call it, a marriage between us will have no chance of success while we remain virtual strangers. Look at our conversation tonight, we don't know the first thing about each other.'

For a moment his jaw looked so set she thought he might just turn and leave without her, and then he breathed out on a sigh and folded himself into his chair again, nodding. '*Si*. You are right. I am rushing you. Would a month be long enough, do you think?'

He was giving her a month to decide? She rolled the proposal around in her head, looking for the catch but happy to take any concession going given the way she'd been railroaded up until now. 'That would certainly help.'

It did help. Rafe had Sebastiano rearrange his diary to free up his evenings over the course of the next week, taking her to the opera, to the opening of a play and countless magnificent dinners overlooking the lights of the city or the harbour or sometimes even both. They were photographed wherever they went, a buzz around them whenever they were spotted, and while Sienna knew there would be pictures in magazines and articles written about them, she wasn't uncomfortable with the attention. She'd made no commitment to him. She had her month and she had the time to get to know Rafe better.

At every event, Sienna was reminded of what it was that had put her under Rafe's spell from the very beginning. He could be so utterly charming, his attention focused one hundred per cent on her and her alone, to the exclusion of everything and everyone else. She'd missed that attention, especially lately. Missed the feeling that she was special for herself. And all the while he'd been the perfect gentleman, never pushing her for so much as a kiss, even though there were times she saw his need in a glance or in the tightness of his movements, like he was trying to keep it in check. She appreciated it. They'd known each other's bodies before they'd known the first thing about each other. Now they could redress the balance.

And at every outing she saw the people's reaction when they met their Prince. There was respect there, to be sure, but there was joy too as he mixed with his people, and a kind of elation lifted the crowd.

And she decided he was a good prince for Montvelatte.

They were just leaving an exhibition at an art gallery one day when it happened. A small crowd had assembled outside, cheering behind a cordon of palace guards as they made their exit. A small girl squirmed out from between a guard's legs and ran towards them carrying a hand-picked posy of flowers that she held up for Sienna to take, her dark eyes wide as if begging her to accept her gift. Sienna smiled and reached down. *'Grazie,'* she said, and the little girl beamed before throwing herself at Rafe's legs and wrapping her arms around them in a bear hug. A guard came closer, but Rafe shooed him away, instead picking up the small girl and hoisting her into his arms as he made his way to the crowd and her parents. *'Ringraziarla, la bella ragazza,'* and the child's smile widened before she threw her arms around his neck and kissed him on the cheek.

Sienna's grip had tightened around the posy, just as a band had twisted around her heart. He wasn't just a good prince. He would make a damn fine father as well.

Rafe was nothing like her own father. Though it wasn't as if he'd wanted children so much as heirs, at least he would never tell these babies that they'd ruined his life.

Was that enough?

Could she risk it?

She was almost tempted.

CHAPTER EIGHT

SIENNA sat in the library, a half-eaten sandwich and a forgotten cup of tea by her side, but it wasn't morning sickness curbing her appetite. Neither was it the Italian language study book, a handbook on royal protocol, and a short history of Montvelatte in twelve volumes that Sebastiano had so generously decided might be worth her while flicking through while Rafe was busy in Rome presenting his fiscal rescue package for Montvelatte to international financiers.

It was the parchment in her hand that had anger welling up inside her until there was space for nothing else. He'd given her a month, he'd said, to give them a chance to get to know each other, but the date on the invitation in front of her told her nothing of the sort.

She would become Rafe's bride and the new Princess of Montvelatte in less than two weeks. Rafe certainly wasn't wasting any time inducting her into the family firm or in waiting for her to make up her own mind. Neither was he wasting any time keeping her informed.

But, then, why would he? He still hadn't asked her to marry him. Simply taken it for granted that she would fall in with his plans.

And, damn it, why the hell should she? She was pregnant

with his babies, but that was where his interest in having her as his wife began and ended. She'd never been on that list of potential wives Sebastiano had been scouting, and she never would have been considered but for one unprotected moment and an unplanned pregnancy that had resulted.

And until he'd discovered her condition, he'd been prepared to let her leave the island so he could resume his search for a princess. He'd made it clear that he was willing to bed her and that was all.

She'd only been promoted to the top by default. By an accident. A mistake.

It wasn't good enough.

It wasn't *enough*.

Sienna let her hands drop into her lap and squeezed her eyes shut. What was she thinking—that this marriage might work, that if she and Rafe got to know each other properly, they might make a go of it? Because she could marry him and still end up with nothing. There were no guarantees. And babies simply weren't enough to hold a marriage together. She was living proof of that. Only love could cement a marriage together—love on both sides.

Once upon a time, in a bed in what seemed for ever ago, she thought she'd found those first magical stirrings of love. But she'd been wrong. Her sense of wonder at a wave of new-found feelings had been misplaced. Apparently it had only ever been about the sex.

And when she'd arrived on the island and was prevented from leaving, that had all been about the sex as well. Rafe had wanted to use her—and discard her—all over again.

And soon, unless she found another solution, they would be married, and still love had nothing to do with it.

Marriage. How could she do it? How could she marry a man she didn't love and who didn't love her, a man who saw her as either his personal sex toy or his personal incubator and to hell with her career, a career he was only too happy to throw on the trash heap in his pursuit of his own goals? A man who lied to her and who gave her no choice?

How could it ever work?

'Sebastiano said you wanted to see me.'

Sienna jumped, so deep in thought that she hadn't heard Rafe's approach. He obviously hadn't been back long. He was tugging at his tie, still wearing a dark suit and crisp white shirt that accentuated his olive skin. A five o'clock shadow that made designer stubble look contrived dusted his strong jawline and gave him an almost piratical appearance. How could anyone look so good no matter what they wore?

Or didn't wear, for that matter.

She dropped her eyes, trying to focus on the invitation in her hands, and why she'd been so angry, instead of the thought of the skin under that suit, skin she'd be seeing a lot more of if this damned marriage took place as planned. And that thought didn't help her burning face one bit.

Sienna stood and waved the paper in her hand, hoping he would assume that it was the reason for the heightened colour in her cheeks. 'You told me I had a month to decide what I was doing.'

'Did I?'

'You know you did. At that dinner the night of the scan. You said we had a month to get to know each other.'

'And your problem is?'

'Today I find this!' She thrust the invitation under his face so he had no choice but to take it, giving it a brief glance.

'You're not happy with the invitations?'

'I'm not happy with the date! Look at it. You said we had a month to get to know each other, a month to make up my mind before any date was set, but this says we are to be married in less than two weeks. You lied to me!'

'No! I never said you had a month to make up anything of the sort. I asked you if a month was enough to get to know each other and you said it was. Which was fortunate, as the wedding date had already been set.'

Blood pounded at her temples. 'You knew the date had been set and you didn't tell me? When you knew I thought I had a month to make up my mind?'

'And haven't we been doing that, Sienna?' he said, coming closer until there was only a hands breadth between them, and fielding her question with one of his own. 'Haven't we been getting to know each other? I thought you'd enjoyed our evenings out together?'

She could feel the heat emanating from him, but it was the scent of him that threatened to scramble her brain. A scent she hadn't realized how much she'd missed these last three days. With a strength of will fuelled by her anger, she spun away, out of range.

'That's not the point. You led me to believe that I could make up my own mind, that it would be my decision. And it will be my decision. I will not be railroaded into marrying you. I want these invitations stopped.'

'I'm afraid it's too late for that. Sebastiano informs me that they've already gone out.'

'But I haven't said I'll marry you.'

He shrugged. 'And now you don't have to.'

'How dare you!' She was sick of his arrogance. Sick of his attitude, sick of having all her reservations thrust aside as if they counted for nothing. 'And what of my life? I'm a helicopter pilot, Rafe, not a princess!'

'In less than two weeks, you will be both.'

She scoffed. 'And you would have me believe I can keep my job?'

He slammed the invitation down on the table. 'Don't be

ridiculous. I can't have my wife running joy flights around the Mediterranean. You will have work here. As Montvelatte's Princess. As mother of our children.'

'I worked hard to become a pilot! I worked damned hard to get to where I am now and not by flying joy flights. How can you expect me to throw it all away to fall in with your plans?'

Rafe sighed, pinching the bridge of his nose with his fingers. 'But don't you see, you have no alternative. Your flying career crunched to a halt the minute you became pregnant with twins.'

'And who damn well got me pregnant!'

'Guilty,' he acceded, making his way to a sideboard and pouring himself a healthy slug of Scotch that he held up in mock toast to her. 'And for my sins I will marry you. Surely you can't ask for more than that.' He threw the glass back, draining half the contents. 'Now, if that was all? I do have some work to attend to.'

He was already turning to go when she stepped forward and grabbed the sleeve of his jacket. 'Don't dismiss me like some minion with a petty grievance.'

His eyes glittered with an icy cold ferocity as his eyes scanned upwards from the hand on his forearm to her face. 'Clearly, that would be a mistake on my part. But let me make one thing patently clear. We are getting married on the date printed on that invitation, whether you like it or not.'

'And if I refuse?'

'Then I will throw you over my shoulder and carry you to the altar, if that's what it takes.'

'Why not just club me over the head and drag me there and prove to the world what a beast you really are?'

A muscle popped in his jaw, the fires in his eyes growing even colder. 'What a tempting prospect. I must keep that in mind. But rest assured, this wedding will happen. Whether or not you embrace the concept is entirely up to you.'

* * *

What was her problem? Rafe pulled off his tie and tugged at the buttons at his neck as he strode into his bookshelf-lined study. Couldn't Sienna see it was the only way? *Merda*, it solved everybody's problems in one neat package.

He threw himself into the high-back leather chair behind his desk, took one look at the untidy pile of reports and files sitting on his desk waiting for his attention and swung around to stare out the windows over the neat lines of the courtyard garden and to the azure sea beyond the cliff walls instead. He gazed out of the window, unseeing, knowing he should be tackling the paperwork. With the question of continuing the Lombardi line so neatly wrapped up, he should have been able to spend more time on the more pressing financial problems that threatened to undermine Montvelatte's economy, and helping with unravelling the intricate web of companies, dummy companies and trusts that his half-brothers had established in an attempt to ensure that the ultimate beneficiaries of the stolen casino funds would never be discovered.

They had been, but with the mess they had left behind, it would take time to get Montvelatte back on a sound financial footing.

But instead of spending time on the problem, he'd had to pander to Sienna's wishes, spending evenings with her, making her think he was going along with her wish to get to know him better. It hadn't been that onerous, surprisingly enough, the woman he'd chosen because she was pregnant with his babies, and because of how she could pleasure him in bed, turning out to be an unexpected success with the crowds.

So what was her problem? She'd enjoyed their time together, and he'd had no doubt that a month would be all it would take to convince her that marriage did not have to be the disaster she coloured it.

It had been going so well until she had spotted that invitation. How the hell had she got hold of that?

But what was worse, he'd told her that he'd carry her to the altar if she refused to marry him, and at the time he'd meant every word. Although with the cameras and the guests and the world watching, that was never on the cards. He needed her to walk down that aisle of her own free will.

Christo, but he wanted her there. Over the last few days in Rome he'd missed her more than he'd expected, and the idea of returning to her had held more and more appeal. She might not come with the pedigree that Sebastiano was so hopeful of securing for Montvelatte's Princess, but her fresh beauty could only give the monarchy a boost, and in terms of a partner, he was much happier to have someone he knew he was compatible with in bed than the pick of some highly strung finishing school graduates. *Dio,* but how he was looking forward to renewing that part of their relationship.

He swore under his breath as his thoughts turned to rock-hard reality. He had work to do, and the last thing he needed was to feel that familiar tightening in his groin.

He swivelled around in the chair and let his eyes slide over the piles of paperwork requiring his attention before this evening's dinner meeting with Montvelatte's Minister of Finance.

And then he remembered the wounded look in Sienna's hazel eyes as he'd stormed out of the room and instantly his priorities changed. For as much as she liked to call him the Beast of Iseo, he needed her to walk up that aisle willingly…

Rafe found her sitting on the side of the pool, her filmy floral skirt hiked up above her knees as she dipped her calves in the water. She looked beautiful like that, leaning back on her hands and making circles with her feet that spun with light through the water. Beautiful and yet, oh, so sad.

'Am I disturbing you?'

Sienna glanced briefly in his direction and then away. 'I thought you had work to do,' she said, but not before he'd caught the flash of surprise. Surprise and something else that had skated across the surface of her eyes too quickly to pin down, but enough to encourage him. She was angry, but there was something else there as well. That was a start.

'Work can wait. I needed some fresh air and thought, now that it's approaching evening, a walk on the cliff path would be good. Have you done that yet?'

She shook her head, sitting straight up now and sweeping her hands clean.

'Would you like to?'

She blinked once, suspiciously, and then again less so, and finally she gave the briefest of nods. 'Thank you.' She swung her legs out of the pool and reached for a towel, but he was already there with it. Their hands met as he passed it to her, and she jerked away, as quickly and gracefully as a startled gazelle.

'Come,' he said, once she'd slipped on her sandals. 'This way.'

It was still warm, but the sun was dipping lower in the sky and the scent of a thousand wild herbs and flowers played on the fresh sea air as he led her, neither of them speaking, around the Castello wall and onto the narrow path that wended its way around the headland. Low scrubby bush hugged the sides of the path, tiny pink flowers jostling with each other in the light early-evening breeze.

In the distance the shard of rock that was Iseo's Pyramid thrust savagely into the sky, with its ever-changing cloud of sea birds wheeling and circling its heights, and from this angle it looked even more dangerous, as if slicing through the water like an enormous black fin. They stopped to look at it at one point, where an enormous chair had been carved out of ancient rock.

'Tell me about the legend,' Sienna asked, standing in front of it, hugging her arms around herself as she looked across the sea to the rocky islet.

Rafe studied her face—the blandness of her expression, the tightness around her eyes. There was a vulnerability about her this evening that he hadn't seen before, almost as if she'd lost her fight and had become resigned to her fate.

He didn't like it. He liked her passive even less than he did when she argued with him. At least then she showed the passion for which he knew she was capable.

She turned her head then, her eyes questioning, and reluctantly he turned his eyes away and towards the chunk of rock she seemed to find so fascinating. 'It was the making of Montvelatte,' he told her. 'The waters are treacherous around the Pyramid; many ships have come to grief in trying to negotiate a passage between the mainland and the island. Blown off course, the pyramid was almost a magnet. Many went down. Many men died.'

'And the beast? How did that story come about?'

'There were always stories, always a suggestion that there was more to the dangers of the Pyramid than an iceberg carved from rock. And then, on a night with no moon and a savage storm, legend has it that a vessel carrying riches from the east to Genoa was blown onto the rocks and sliced in two. One man miraculously survived, only to witness the breaking apart of his vessel and the deaths of all those he'd sailed with. It was he who first saw the beast when lightning lit up the sky. The beast was standing atop the Pyramid and howling into the storm, the bloodied remains of one of his fellow sailors in its maw. That man was Iseo.'

Alongside him she shivered, and he would have reached

out an arm to bring her close, but he knew she wasn't shivering with the cold, and he sensed his arm around her shoulders would not be welcome. 'What happened to him?'

'He clung to some debris and made it here. Eventually he went mad, if he weren't already. But not before everyone had heard the story. And believed it.'

'What a horrible story.'

'Though fortunate for Montvelatte.'

She looked up at him. 'How so?'

He shrugged. 'Some enterprising pirate decided it was easier to make a living by exacting a toll from passing ships to guarantee them safe passage past the Beast, rather than bother with attacking them. It was only the ones who refused to pay that he was forced to attack.'

'Oh, my,' she said, with what sounded suspiciously like a laugh. 'Very entrepreneurial.'

And he laughed at her unexpected response, suddenly glad he'd swapped a mountain of work on his desk for a walk in the fresh air with a woman who continued to surprise him at every turn.

A woman already pregnant with his seed.

A woman who would soon be his wife.

And once again the beast inside him swelled like it had been fed. This would work, he knew in his gut that this marriage would work. *One way or another.* He just had to make her see it.

A noise interrupted them, and Rafe cursed himself for not turning off his cell phone. No doubt Sebastiano was checking up on him, his schedule thrown by Rafe's spur-of-the-moment change of plans. The caller ID confirmed his suspicions before Sebastiano's gently chiding voice reminded him of a meeting he hadn't forgotten at all. Simply wished he could.

Rafe pretended to listen while he watched Sienna turn her

focus on the ancient stone seat, running her hands over the weathered contours of the rock. He followed their progress, watching her fingers trailing across the surface, hit with the sudden memory of how those same fingers had felt dancing across his skin, her nails biting into his flesh when he'd turned his attentions to a place that had made her gasp and curl her fingers deeper.

And suddenly his body ached to feel the curl and bite of them in his flesh again.

He watched her move, absorbing the gentle sway of her hips and the sweet curve of her neck into his being as one absorbed sunshine.

How long would he have to wait? Until their marriage night? The doctor had told him there was no reason they should not resume a normal sex life, but he'd been assuming they'd had a normal sex life, when all they'd shared had been just one night. Definitely not normal. And definitely not enough.

And while he intended to remedy that the first chance he got, right now was hardly the best time.

One step at a time. He wouldn't rush her or she'd consider it just another ploy. As much as he preferred her passion to the passive sadness he'd witnessed in her most recently, the last thing he needed to give her was another reason to fight him before the wedding. That wasn't the kind of passion he wanted. Once she was legally his, there would be plenty of opportunity for passion.

But the best part of two more weeks? It would be agony.

Sebastiano's voice had long died away when she looked up and caught his gaze on her, her hands halting their exploration as her eyes widened in surprise. She swept her hands away from the rock, as if embarrassed. 'The stone is so beautiful.'

'It's called Vincenzo's throne,' he said, drawing up so close behind her that the breeze, so usually filled with the perfume of wild flowers and aromatic leaves, was laced with the warm scent of her. 'After the first Prince of Montvelatte. Nobody knows who carved the seat or when, but it was right here that Montvelatte first became a Principality.'

She flicked a nervous glance over her shoulder, as if surprised by how close he was, before spinning away and turning her attention back to the seat, running a hand along its surface. 'I was intending to read about that today,' she said. 'How did it come about?'

He allowed himself a smile as she feigned complete and total interest in the ancient relic. But he could tell by the rapid rise and fall of her chest and the slashes of colour on her cheeks that she felt it too, this hunger to renew their intimate acquaintance.

Two weeks? *Dio*, he hoped not.

'It was way back in the fourteenth century,' he began, as he watched her take her place on the wide throne, testing the seat before venturing to turn her eyes towards him again. 'A vessel carrying the royal family of Karpenthia was on its way to Genoa. At that time Karpenthia was a rich power in the north of Africa, built where the camel trade routes met the sea, while Velatte City was a seedy place of prostitutes and pirates and assorted runaways. But the King's daughter was ill with fever and close to death, so they pulled into harbour. It was a brave thing that they did, risking the lives of everyone on board, but they had no choice.'

Her eyes widened, her interest obviously piqued. 'What happened?'

'A man came forward from the crowd that came to meet the vessel. When he saw who was on board, he promised to cure the girl, and so they carried her to a hut, where his grandmother, an old crow of a woman reported to have magical healing powers, concocted a remedy made from the local herbs gathered from the side of these very cliffs.'

'The old woman saved her.'

Rafe nodded. 'The King was so grateful he drafted up a deed declaring Montvelatte a Principality in its own right, with the grandson, the man who'd promised to cure the princess, its first Prince. That man was Vincenzo Lombardi. Two years later the princess returned and became his first Princess of Montvelatte.'

'She married Vincenzo, to live amongst pirates and prostitutes?'

He shrugged as he leaned back against one arm of the stone seat. 'Legend has it that it was a great love match, and one that changed the course of Montvelatte forever. Apparently the original part of the Castello, built on the remains of ancient fortresses going back over the centuries, was his tribute to her.'

'You sound like you don't really believe it.'

'Maybe I'm a cynic, but I suspect that Vincenzo wouldn't have been backward about naming his price for saving the King's daughter.'

'But then why would the King have brought his daughter back once they'd got away? Why couldn't the story be true?'

'It's just a fairy tale. It doesn't work that way.'

'It's a legend.' She shook her head, so that her hair rippled about her head, dancing on the light. 'But why shouldn't it also be true? What better way to start a new nation?'

But that would mean loving someone could be a good thing!

He turned away, suddenly not wanting her to see his eyes. She had a way sometimes of piercing his shell and seeing inside him, of reaching into the deepest parts of him, the hidden parts of him, and of asking the questions no one else dared. Because no one else knew how he'd felt growing up and feeling his mother's pain at being an outcast, discarded like a pair of worn out shoes.

'Don't waste your time on love,' he remembered his mother softly singing as he'd lain tucked up in bed while she rocked his sister to sleep, crooning the words over and over like a lullaby. *'Don't lose your heart. Stay strong, my baby, be strong.'*

And so he'd grown up determined to be strong and to make it on his own, determined to prove to the world that a title meant nothing, that it was what one made of oneself that counted.

And given the mess his half-brothers had made of things, he had more reason to believe that than ever. He stared out to sea and to the black peak that was Iseo's Pyramid and wondered about the beast that reputedly lived there. Who needed a beast when so much darkness resided in one's own heart?

'So the pirate island becomes a Principality,' he heard her say. 'Surely the neighbouring countries objected?'

Rafe turned to see her looking up at the castle, pushing a few wayward strands of hair from her face with her hands. He bit back on a growl, forcing himself to remember his determination to wait for her. Did she have any idea how that action lifted her breasts, displaying their outline to perfection?

Sienna let her arms drop and swivelled around, and he had to prise his eyes back up to hers to meet her gaze.

'The royal families of both France and Italy held the Karpenthian King in high regard. And while neither had been interested in the island until then, content to leave it to the pirates and criminals, they imposed the condition that only a Lombardi could take the crown, that if the bloodline was broken, so too was the agreement.'

'And that's why you had to come back.'

'That's why.'

'What would have happened if you hadn't?'

'Then the pressure would have been on Marietta, as heir presumptive, to take the throne. But she's never wanted it, her links with the island even more tenuous than mine. Besides,

I couldn't put that kind of pressure on her, and I know my mother would never have forgiven me for walking away and allowing Montvelatte to lose its status as a Principality. Its land and wealth, what's left of it, for the taking.'

'By Italy?'

'Or France, depending on who makes the stronger case. Already legal teams in a dozen capital cities throughout Europe are arguing over the details, just in case.' She nodded, and he watched her stoop to pick a flower from one of the many low-growing bushes around, holding the shell-pink flower up to her nose and breathing in its fragrance. He didn't tell her that the update he'd received today had suggested that developments on the island were being keenly watched, the identity of the Prince's apparent new escort and rumours of a royal pregnancy being investigated.

Neither did he tell her of the report he'd received from the security check Sebastiano had had run on Sienna's background. And one thing shone out like a beacon. There had been no other men in her life around the time he had pursued her, or for several months before. He was the only one, confirming all he'd believed and more.

More reason then ever to get married and quickly.

They continued together, circling around the high walls of the Castello to where the hill dropped away into a steep valley behind. Terraced vineyards lined the slopes, leading down to a narrow river that curved away to the harbour where the buildings of Velatte City huddled along the shoreline. He heard her gasp as she took in the beauty before them, as mountain-bred vines gave way to the familiar white architecture of the city, which ended in a row of casinos, each more magnificent than the next, lining the white-fringed harbour far below.

'It's so beautiful from up here,' she said. 'I had no idea this path even existed.' And he felt a stab of remorse that he'd kept her largely locked away within the Castello walls, expecting her to be entertained with dusty books and language lessons when he wasn't parading her in front of the world's paparazzi, with not a hint of sharing with her the real beauty of the island that would now be her home.

And now her eyes sparkled, her smile broad as she surveyed the world over which she would soon rule by his side, and he couldn't help but take her hand in his own as she stood there, marvelling at the view. Her eyes briefly darted to his, but she didn't pull away, and he moved closer by her side, pointing out the peaks of craggy hills just visible behind the other side of the valley. 'The island extends another fifteen kilometres beyond Velatte City to the south. Predominantly small villages situated amongst vineyards and olive groves or on the coast. And, of course, like any Mediterranean island, you will find the obligatory hotel resorts, although Montvelatte's main tourism thrust has been via the casinos.'

'So beautiful,' she repeated. He watched her as her gaze scanned from one spectacular end of the valley to the other, her free hand held up to shield her eyes from the setting sun while the silken fabric of her skirt shifted and rippled around her legs in the barely there breeze.

'Without a doubt.'

And she turned towards him, her lips slightly parted, her eyes questioning.

'You could be happy,' he said, 'living here.'

And the lights in her eyes dimmed a little then. 'Rafe,' she said softly, so softly he felt his name on her breath even as he read it on her lips. Lips that beckoned him and drew him closer. Lips that made him ache with wanting her.

She shook her head, the barest, almost imperceptible movement from side to side, which he refused to accept as meaning she didn't want his kiss. Not when her eyes gave him a different message and her lips were already parted and ready for him.

And so he cupped her warm cheek with his hand, and on a tiny track, below the Castello Montvellate and above the magnificent sweep of valley below, his world shrank to just one woman, and one moment in time.

And that moment held its breath and hovered between them, shimmering with intensity as he lowered his mouth to hers. She shuddered into the kiss, and he slid his hand around the back of her neck to steady her, weaving his fingers into her hair, the taste of her flooding his senses and firing his blood.

She tasted of sunshine and vanilla, of warmth and woman, and the way her lips moved under his told him he was not the only one involved in this kiss. She was there, every part of her. She was his. He gathered her to him with his free arm, finding that sweet spot in the curve of her spine that brought her fully against his aching length.

She gasped into his mouth but she didn't fight, didn't move away. Instead she settled even closer, the subtle squirm of her hips a sweet agony that he poured into his kiss, to her lips, to her cheeks, to her eyes. And everywhere he kissed just fuelled the need that had been building ever since she'd stepped out of that helicopter, a need that refused to be compartmental-ized and set aside.

I want you, he wanted to whisper, while his teeth nuzzled at her lobe. She trembled as if he'd said the words and threw her head back, forcing her breasts harder against his chest, so that he ached to free them and reacquaint himself with their satin per-fection, longed to draw their pebbled peaks deep into his mouth.

Instead, he dragged in a lungful of air, fighting the urge to take her, right here, right now, on this lonely path high above the city, knowing it was madness when the paparazzi made an art form of lying in wait and holding out for the perfect shot, and yet still having to fight the beast for supremacy.

She'd already made him wait so long—*too long*—but soon, he told himself, encouraged by her participation, there was no doubt in his mind that very soon he would have her again.

Hesitatingly, reluctantly, he slowed the kiss, drawing back as he loosened his arms around her. She opened her eyes, and he saw her bewilderment, sensed her disappointment and very nearly changed his mind.

'We should get back,' he said, wishing she would argue, wishing she would demand that he stay and kiss her again, needing a damned good reason to let her go. 'I have a meeting I'm already late for,' he said, trying to convince himself. 'Besides which, we don't want you catching a chill.'

And before his eyes her back seemed to stiffen, her expression cooling so quickly that he ached to turn back the clock and take back his words.

'Of course,' she said, tucking the hair that had so recently coiled thick and silkily around his fingers behind her ears as she turned away. 'I'd hate to catch a chill.'

CHAPTER NINE

SHE was a fool. Forty-eight hours later, that was the only explanation Sienna could come up with as she paced to and fro under the dappled shade of the vine-covered terrace, her various text books lying open and abandoned on the table nearby.

Two nights ago she'd gone to sleep—eventually—with the memories of that cliff-path walk playing through her mind. They'd walked together along a cliff top path breathing fresh sea air scented with a myriad different wild flowers and herbs, and then he'd wrapped her hand in his as they'd gazed out over a view that was to die for. And then he'd kissed her, and the defensive walls she'd built around herself, and that he'd been unsettling ever since he'd found her poolside and asked her to walk with him, had been rocked apart.

He hadn't pushed, hadn't demanded a thing from her, and yet one simple kiss and all her defenses had been ready to crumble, like some impressionable teenager on her first date.

And for a moment there—just one tiny moment, when they'd looked out over the view and he'd asked her if she could be happy here—she'd almost imagined that he'd meant it, that he cared that she might be happy, and that he wanted her to stay. In that precious moment, and in the kiss that had followed, she'd felt the barriers she'd put up around herself tremble and shake, and her emotions tilt and slide within their unsteady walls...

And then, with one simple line, he'd firmed her emotions and her resolve. He hadn't wanted her to catch a chill. The temperature must have been in the mid-twenties Celcius with no more than a slight onshore breeze, and he had been worried about her catching a chill.

And his concern hadn't been for her benefit.

She'd ceased being someone who merited concern in her own right when she'd become his own personal incubator.

Of course he wanted her to be happy here—he needed to know the mother of his children wasn't about to take off unexpectedly, with or without them—but he'd done nothing to ensure her happiness. Merely expected it, just like he expected her to marry him.

Sienna looked wistfully over to the vacant helipad, wondering what she'd be up to and where she'd be flying now if she wasn't trapped here on this island. And then she remembered why she was trapped and that she probably wouldn't be flying anyway, and her heart sank even lower.

She turned her eyes in the direction of the books that lay open and accusing in front of her, and she questioned herself why it was that she was going along with everything as though she'd agreed to this marriage.

Maybe her work options were limited, at least while any shred of morning sickness remained, but after finding out how Rafe had betrayed her by continuing to plan a wedding she hadn't agreed to, why the hell was she still here? It wasn't as if one kiss on their walk that night was going to make Rafe forget the tiny detail she was pregnant and want to marry her for her own sake.

Fat chance.

He'd kissed her, and she'd felt—at least, she'd thought she'd felt—that there was something there, some hint of caring for her, and it had taken her unawares and she'd kissed him back.

But that faint hope had turned to nothing more than dust when he'd turned around and urged her to go back inside for the sake of her unborn babies.

Was it too much to hope that he might actually care for her for her own sake? Was that really too much to ask?

What kind of man would expect her to be able to marry someone who didn't love her?

She gazed out over the view, the blue sea and azure sky totally wasted on her. She'd promised herself it wouldn't happen. Years of watching the pain her mother felt, loving a man who'd been forced into a marriage he didn't want, years of watching her parents' marriage stagnate and fester until it had imploded in grand style, had convinced her that she could never marry a man who didn't love her.

And years of bearing the guilt that she'd been the one who'd forced her parents into a pointless marriage had made her more determined than ever that any child of hers would never be forced to bear that same burden.

'If it weren't for you, I could have made something of my life.'
'If it weren't for you, I wouldn't have a care in the world.'
'If it weren't for you...'

How many times, in how many different ways, had her father made her realize that everything wrong in his life was all down to her? All because he'd been forced into a marriage he didn't want. All because of an unplanned pregnancy.

Rafe might be a different man from her father, but his motives were hardly pure. She couldn't bear for her children to realize they hadn't been born in love, to know that their father had only wanted them for political purposes.

She couldn't bear it.

If she had to marry anyone, there was only one way it might

happen, only one way it could possibly work. If she had to marry anyone, he was damn well going to have to love her first.

Which meant that she couldn't just wait for Rafe to have the time to notice her. Whatever had motivated Rafe into taking her for a cliff-top stroll last night—probably guilt that she'd found out his duplicity—he'd not bothered to seek her company today. She knew work was his priority right now. She knew and understood that his focus was on getting Montvelatte back onto a sound financial footing, but it was also clear that if she wanted him to fall in love with her, then she was going to have to try something more than a friendly conversation.

Sienna picked up the nearest phone and dialed the number that she knew would put her instantly in contact with Sebastiano's office. The phone was answered almost immediately, the transfer to Sebastiano taking only moments longer.

'Where can I catch up with Rafe tonight?'

'Prince Raphael should not be expected back at the Castello before eleven p.m., possibly later.'

'And where can I find him before then?'

There was hesitation at the end of the line. 'Prince Raphael is currently attending a meeting of the casino finance managers at Casino de Velatte after which he's due at a recital in the casino's Crystal Ballroom.'

'Perfect,' said Sienna, already mentally trawling through the myriad evening gowns that hung in her endless closets. 'Can you take me there?'

This time the pause was longer. 'I'm not sure that's a good idea, signorina. He's not expecting you—'

'Please, Sebastiano, I know you don't think me a suitable candidate for Montvelatte's Princess, but if you won't help me get off the island, you have to help me try to make this marriage work. I wouldn't ask if it wasn't important.'

She squeezed the telephone tight in her hand, holding her breath while she waited for Sebastiano's response.

Finally his voice came. 'Can you be ready at nine?'

She breathed out on a grateful sigh. 'I'll be ready.'

Sienna was learning the benefits of having her own staff on hand. A deep oil-scented bath had been drawn for her, plump warmed towels at the ready, a professional hair stylist had miraculously tamed her mass of fiery hair into a sleek updo that shone gold under the lights, and Carmelina had selected and laid out the perfect accessories to the gown she'd decided upon.

She should have felt relaxed after such royal treatment, but inside she felt a tight bundle of nerves that coiled and fizzed and all the while tangled tighter in anticipation. She gave herself a last look in the full-length mirror and smoothed the long satin gloves up her arms, wondering how Rafe would react when he saw her. The sea-green silk gown fitted her almost as snugly as the gloves, the skilful beading around the almost modest bodice-line catching the light like a city lit up at night. Her other gowns had been elegant and perfect princess wear. But tonight she didn't want to play princess. She wanted to play seductress. He'd never seen her dressed in anything like this gown, and she could hardly wait to see his reaction. Then she spun around, glanced over her shoulder, and almost decided he never would.

The backless dress scooped low below her waistline, the beaded border hugging the dress tightly to the curves of her body and shouting *look at me* in the expensive language of designer couture.

She was no catwalk model used to strutting her stuff in make-up and high heels. She was a helicopter pilot more used to wearing overalls and a headset. Was she doing the right thing in trying to get his attention like this, or was she about to make a total fool of herself?

There was a discreet knock at the door. 'Your car is ready, *signorina*,' and the time to change her mind was past.

Carmelina nodded as she handed her the tiny purse that matched her shoes and a gossamer-thin wrap to hang from her elbows. *'Bella,'* she simply said, nodding as Sienna turned for the door.

She descended the sweeping staircase to the ground floor, unable to slow her racing heart or calm her racing mind. Because if this didn't work, if it made no impression on Rafe, and he still failed to see her as the woman she was but for the purpose he was marrying her, then what chance did she have? And what chance their marriage?

The car was waiting, as advised, in the pebbled portico, the duco of the vintage Alfa Romeo gleaming under the lighting. Sebastiano himself emerged to greet her, and for once the smile that greeted her looked more than duty-bound.

'Signorina Wainwright,' he said, with a bow, 'I would be honoured to escort you to Casino de Velatte.'

'You would?'

'It would be my pleasure.'

'Thank you. And I want you to know I'll tell Rafe this was all my idea. I would hate for him to hold you personally responsible.'

'On the contrary,' he said, with a look that was fully appreciative without losing a hint of respect, 'I bow to your wisdom. I think this is a very good idea indeed.'

Either Rafe's secretary seemed incredibly attuned to her state of nervousness, or he was simply good at relating Montvelatte small talk and delivering it in easily digestible chunks as the car wended its way down the mountainside to the city far below.

Whether it was because he thought she needed time to soak in the details, or whether it was because he knew that by saying nothing she would have more time to dwell on—and panic about—the meeting that was to come, she neither knew nor cared. She was just grateful for the company and for the quiet reassurance his presence offered.

Before long the vineyards of the slope had given way to the poplar-lined river road, studded with gated estates and grove after grove of orange trees, and then they were in the city itself, heading towards the harbour on narrow streets squeezed between two- and three-storey buildings, or beside cafés where the patrons spilled out almost to the street.

Sienna gazed out of the window, watching the city and its people, dodging through the scooter-filled traffic, which carried elegant-looking dark-haired women and men with equally dark good looks, and sometimes what looked like entire families hanging on around the driver. There was colour here, life and action, and every trip to Velatte City she found more fascinating.

And then they were on the wide Boulevard Lombardi that separated the hotels and casinos that hugged the shoreline from the marina filled with the latest and greatest in nautical accessories. And there, in the middle of the strip, she could see the dome of their destination glowing green above the surrounding buildings.

'Casino de Velatte is our oldest and most prestigious casino, often referred to as the jewel in Montvelatte's crown,' said Sebastiano from alongside. 'The recital is being held as part of the Casino's bicentennial celebrations.'

The car slowed as they approached, and land that had once been at a premium opened up before them in a series of gardens, each more beautiful than the next with their skilful plantings and water features, and cleverly designed to draw the eye up to where the gardens gave way to the towering forecourt of the grandest casino of them all.

Rafe hadn't brought her here, and she looked at the building in awe. It should be a palace, she decided, as the car pulled up at the doors, the gleaming marble-tiled entrance way glowing gold in warm splashes of light from the crystal chandelier above.

Her door was opened from the outside, and Sienna stepped out into another world, a world featuring not just the opulence of the Castello, but an extravagance she'd never experienced before. Even over the scent of the perfumed garden and the salty tang of fresh sea air, she could almost smell the money.

She didn't belong here.

In a moment of panic she turned back towards the car, but then Sebastiano was at her side, taking her arm, stilling her retreat. He exchanged a few words with the concierge and then was guiding her forwards, through the doors that would lead her to Rafe, and she was never more afraid in her life. She was no seductress. She was no princess. She was a fraud, and there was no way everybody wouldn't know it.

Inside was even more opulent, and the glances they attracted more openly curious, and if it hadn't been for the guiding hand at her elbow, she would have fled in a heartbeat. Instead she was led deeper and deeper into the building, skirting around tables surrounded by the rich and elegant, accompanied by the click and roll of the roulette ball and the hushed murmurs of encouragement to the wheel, past some of the most beautiful women she'd ever seen, wearing figure-hugging gowns, and bearing trays of champagne.

Ushered into a lift adorned in the casino's signature colours of gold, burgundy and navy blue, she let out a long breath.

'You're doing fine,' said Sebastiano, alongside her, reading her like an open book.

She looked over at him, surprised at his encouragement.

'I was wrong about you,' he admitted. 'I was afraid you

weren't what you seemed, that you were wrong for Prince Raphael.'

The lift seemed to have lost all its air. She fanned her face with her hand. 'And now?'

He smiled on a nod. 'I think you will be perfect for him, and for Montvelatte.'

She dragged in a welcome breath. 'Do you think he's going to be angry about me coming here?'

Sebastiano tilted his head a fraction, as if considering his words. Then he smiled. 'I think he's going to be delighted.'

The lift doors opened and they alighted into another opulent lobby, the chandeliers smaller but no less intricate in their workmanship or spectacular in their effect. Twin doors loomed large across the lobby, doors that opened before them, spilling out a group of men talking animatedly.

Sienna stopped as she recognized the man at the helm, and the voices similarly died away as all eyes turned towards her.

At least, she could sense their eyes upon her. Filling her focus front and central was Rafe, resplendent in a dark suit with a burgundy sash that both served to show his tall frame and his broad shoulders to perfection. Sienna felt the primitive sizzle that accompanied Rafe's every appearance, although this time it was tinged with an unfamiliar burst of fear.

So much was at stake.

So much depended on how he reacted to seeing her tonight.

Dry-mouthed she watched his eyes narrow in question, before he came closer, the dark of his eyes warm and rich and assessing every last part of her from her upturned hair to the glint of her satin sandals and every curve along the way. Lingering on those points along the way. Sienna felt her sensitized breasts swell under his scrutiny, her nipples ache as if he'd stroked them with his hot breath. 'Sebastiano,' he acknowledged, without taking his eyes from her, 'what is the meaning of this?'

Sebastiano cleared his throat and murmured his low response, so low that the pack of men behind could not overhear, so low that even Sienna had to strain to catch his response. 'Signorina Wainwright wished to accompany you to the recital.'

Rafe stared at her so hard she took a faltering step back and reached out a hand to Sebastiano for rescue, in case he might suddenly leave without her. 'I'm sorry. It was all my idea. I...I don't have to stay. I can go.'

And then she heard a sound and looked back, and when she saw where he was looking, she realized it had been Rafe who'd made that low guttural noise, Rafe who had spied the gown's clever secret as she'd turned. And the darkness of his eyes gleamed so thick with passion and need that she could feel the heat coming from him, feel it insinuate itself into her flesh and sizzle along her veins.

For the first time, Rafe nodded in Sebastiano's direction. 'Thank you, Sebastiano. You may leave now,' he said, before he slid his hand through her arm and turned to the openly curious audience behind. 'Gentlemen,' he said, with an ease at handling an unexpected situation that she envied, 'Let me introduce to you Signorina Sienna Wainwright, my companion tonight.'

The next few minutes were a blur of names and smiling faces and more hands than she could ever recall shaking in one day. Because it was the scent that coiled inside her now, that marvellous scent of clean unprocessed man. And it was the hand at the centre of her back that had her full attention, the heat generated by the fingers that were stroking her skin and stoking her own need along with it.

Someone pressed a glass of champagne into her hands and she clung to it like a storm-tossed sailor clung to anything he could grasp in the hope of staying afloat. With Rafe filling her thoughts and senses she was in danger of going under.

Finally they were led into a grand ballroom, the dimensions of which took her breath away. What looked like hundreds of people were already seated and waiting for the official party to take their seats—seats, Sienna gathered, that had had to be hastily rearranged in deference to her presence. A hush fell over the crowd as she entered on Rafe's arm and stood beside him in the royal box, a hush that immediately descended into the whispered questioning of a crowd.

Rafe leaned closer to her as the strains of the Montvelattian national anthem died down. 'Do you realise that wearing a dress like that you have well and truly set the cat amongst the pigeons?'

'Do you mind?'

And he gazed down at her with such an intense look of desire that her bones were reduced to jelly. He lifted one gloved hand and pressed the back of it to his mouth. 'What I mind most is that I have to wait until this recital ends before I can take you home and peel that damn dress right off you.'

CHAPTER TEN

SIENNA gasped, the power of his need echoing tenfold inside her, so that right then and there she felt as if he'd already peeled the dress away and that she stood naked and exposed in front of him.

He wanted her. That was good, wasn't it? That was what she had planned. He had to want her if there was any chance it could develop into anything more than a marriage of convenience.

But her plan relied on her being the one in control, the one to steer him to her purpose. Right now, though, she was being carried along on a tidal wave of his making, and that wave was towering and powerful and all-consuming.

And she wasn't sure she wanted the ride to ever end.

The recital had been interminable, the greetings they'd received on their exit taking for ever, and the purposeful silence of the car ride back to the Castello, during which she'd worried that he'd changed his mind, had been an agony.

But finally they were back within the fortified walls, where silence and discretion reigned, and Rafe took her hand and pulled her towards him. 'What did you mean by dressing like that and coming after me tonight?'

She edged backwards, fearful that he'd somehow seen her plan as the desperate attempts of a woman who wanted to be needed, but his arms held her tight and close enough for her to know his intentions hadn't changed in the least. 'Who says I wanted anything?'

His lips curved into a wolfish smile. 'You must want something, to wear a dress designed to make you look like both a virgin and a seductress.'

And she realized he knew nothing, only felt the physical need that she'd hoped he would, the need that was all she had to use to her advantage. 'Which one are you?' he asked her. 'The virgin or the seductress?'

It was easier to play the part she'd assigned herself than she'd ever imagined possible. She let her body lean into his, every curve strategically placed. 'You know I'm no virgin.'

'So what do you want?'

'It's been too long,' she told him, moving her hips just enough that she could feel his rigid length. 'I want you. I want you to make love to me.'

His eyes flared with both victory and red-hot want, and she knew she'd voiced the right words to turn his passion incendiary.

And while that was her own victory, right now the desire to make love with him was the most pressing thing in the world, and that was her obsession.

She didn't have long to wait. His mouth was on hers in an instant, his arms surrounding her, lifting her from the ground and carrying her up the stairs effortlessly, as if she were weightless. Which was exactly how she felt. Weightless. Without a care or a concern or a worry in the world except how to get this man inside her to fill this desperate aching need.

'*Christo*,' he muttered, as he surged up the stairs, 'but you are driving me insane.'

Once inside his room, he spun her against the closed door, lowering her legs to the ground, clutching the fabric of her skirt so that it bunched in his hands and left her legs near naked. He cupped her behind, his fingers squeezing into her flesh so that she gasped into his mouth. He drank it down, making her gasp once more as his fingers slid under the lace of her thong and worked still lower, while the other hand liberated a breast his hungry mouth soon captured, sucking on one sensitive nipple, tugging at the very essence of her.

Sienna clung to him, her hands tearing at his clothes, pulling his head back to her mouth, wanting to feel more, never satisfied, always wanting more of him in her mouth, on her body—inside—more that she could feel, more of what he gave her with his touch.

He parted her then with his fingers, encountered her slick need, and growled so deep in her mouth that the sound reverberated through her soul. His touch brought flesh already exquisitely tender to flashpoint, and she squirmed against his expert hand, desperation driving her as his fingers toyed with her, teased her, entered her.

She threw her head back against the door, dizzy with it all, and through the wall of his chest she could feel his heart slamming, echoing the crashing beat of her own laboured organ. And still she needed more. Needed him inside her.

As if he read her thoughts, she felt a tug and a snap, heard the hiss of a zip, and felt herself being lifted higher, the heavy door at her back, the liquid silk of her skirt rucked up high on her legs, and the taste of him in her mouth, before he set her slowly down.

Wonder consumed her just as she consumed him, letting him stretch her, fill her, her muscles working to hold him there and never let go. She could stay this way for ever, and it would still not be enough. And then he moved inside her, and the connection sizzled and burned, and before she could fight to hold him, he was gone, balancing on the brink, his breath heavy on her throat as it seemed the world hung in the balance.

And then he thrust inside her again, and this time it was better and deeper than before, the connection more powerful, the union more intense. She clung to him, his every thrust giving her more even as it expanded her need, turning it urgent and desperate and like a living thing.

She felt it rush towards her, unstoppable, inevitable, felt the same juggernaut bearing down on him, heard him meet it head on as he cried out on one final explosive thrust. Powerless to resist, she went after him, her senses exploding until nothing existed but sensation and colour and a world filled with tiny fragments of light.

He recovered first, his breathing still ragged in her ear as he lifted her into his arms again and carried her to the wide bed. He placed her down almost reverentially, kissing her on the forehead, before he turned to remove his jacket and tie and shuck off his shoes.

Sienna blinked back into consciousness and looked up at him, taking in his dark beauty and the stealthy, sexy way he moved, whether with clothes on or off, and felt the first fluttering premonition of trouble.

The sex was good—*great*—and if she'd wanted his complete attention, she had no doubt she now had it. If she was going to make an impression on him, if he was going to see her as a person, a woman with her own needs and wants, if she was going to make him *feel*, now was her chance.

And yet something was wrong.

Deep down inside her, on some fundamental level, something gnawed away at her; something wasn't right.

Rafe turned then, capturing her expression as he unbuttoned his shirt, a small crease appearing between his brows. 'Are you all right?'

'I'm fine,' she lied, her pulse skittering suddenly as her mind tried to get a handle on her unease. She pushed herself up to sitting and wrapped her arms around her knees, feeling ridiculous trying to hold a conversation lying down, while she watched his progress with the buttons down the shirt.

She hadn't meant to watch. Hadn't meant to take any notice. But the way that beautiful sweat-sheened column of olive skin grew longer, as one by one his skilful fingers brought them undone, what choice did she have?

He had beautiful fingers, long and tapered, and what he could do with them…

Oh, my, she rationalized, remembering—who wouldn't feel distinctly shaky when they'd just climaxed in spectacular fashion and a man like Rafe was only now getting around to taking his clothes off?

In preparation for a repeat performance? One could only hope.

He frowned, his face angling to look more closely at hers in the soft light. 'Did I hurt you? Are you feeling unwell? I didn't think to take it slow.'

Distracted by the sudden concern in his voice that brought with it a return of the strange gnawing feeling in her gut, her head got lost between a nod and a shake. 'No. Yes.' She closed her eyes and shook it, this time more decisively. 'Really, you didn't hurt me. I've been fine lately, so long as I avoid certain things.'

And that was the truth. The day she'd arrived at the island, and the following day when she'd tried to leave—those days had been the worst. Since then her morning sickness had been precisely that, a morning phenomenon, and if she was careful, limited to no more than a general queasiness, with no repeat of that early illness. How much of that had been down to stress and the tension of having this man back in her life?

He gave a shrug of his shoulders and peeled the shirt away, letting it drop to the floor, and in the process revealing the full glory of his muscle-sculpted chest, from the wide shoulders and the taut skin to the dusting of hair that focused to a line and drew her eyes down to where it disappeared at his belt. 'I was worried I was too eager for you. I promise this time we'll take it slower.'

She looked up. 'This time.' She repeated the words like a mantra, and he smiled.

'I told you I couldn't wait to remove that dress. I haven't changed my mind.'

Sienna swallowed as he pushed his pants down past hips lean and strong, carelessly stepping out of them. She watched, wide-eyed, as his sleek-fitting black underwear met the same fate, and she stopped breathing altogether when he moved closer. Of course once wouldn't be enough. On their one previous night together, Rafe had shown he had stamina to burn. He knelt on the side of the bed, reached out, and lifted one foot in his hands. Deftly he undid the tiny diamante-studded buckle at the side of her shoe and, holding her ankle in one hand, swept the shoe from her foot with the other, tossing it and the best part of several hundred euros carelessly to the floor behind him.

Vaguely she registered that he must have no idea how much shoes cost, or didn't care, but after a moment, she didn't care either, not when his thumbs started their dance over the ball of her foot. She groaned.

She'd read articles where people had claimed the feet could be erogenous zones, and she'd largely discounted them as fanciful and fictional, but the graze of his fingers, the brush of his skin against the silkiness of her stockings, had her trembling and rethinking her ideas. Or maybe it had nothing to do with her feet and everything to do with the way he looked at her while his fingers worked, dark eyes made darker with desire, more insistent with need.

Or maybe not, she thought, as the other shoe met a similar

fate and Rafe stroked the underside of her foot with his thumbs, causing her back to arch and a sigh of pleasure to erupt from her lips.

'Do you like that?' he said, repeating the action, and she licked her lips and nodded.

'It's…nice.'

'Only nice?' He sounded disappointed. 'Then do you like this?' His fingers trailed up her calf, disappearing beneath a sea of green silk that lapped around her legs like the incoming tide, his fingertips tracing circles higher and higher up her leg.

'It's all good,' she conceded, 'although I can't help but feel a little overdressed.'

He laughed, low in his throat, and the vibrations and the sound were almost enough to bring her undone. He reached up a hand and undid the jewelled clasp at her neck. Instinctively she reached up a hand to prevent the bodice falling down, but he stopped her arm and the fabric slid unrestrained to her waist, releasing her breasts to the air, and to his gaze.

'*Christo,*' he uttered, as he reached for them with his hands, 'but you are beautiful.' His hands cupped her breasts, his thumbs grazing her nipples before he leaned over and took one pink peak into his mouth.

Pleasure speared downwards, like arrows fired and finding their mark, to that place he'd already filled and which ached to be filled again. He worked magic on one breast, and then the other, before lifting his head and swallowing her into the perfect kiss.

She felt his hand low behind her, wondered at his expert discovery of her invisible zip, and felt the cool sweep of air as he tugged down her gown over her hips.

She made a move to remove one satin glove, and he stilled her hands, running his hand along one long satin-cased arm, running another down one silk-clad leg. 'No,' he said, 'leave these. You feel and look exquisite exactly how you are.'

She wanted to believe him, even though her make-up must be smudged beyond repair, her lips pink and swollen, and she could feel her hair coming loose, heavy coiled tendrils even now tumbling around her shoulders. But who was she to argue, when his touch made her feel the seductress she had set out to be?

'You're not angry with me,' she asked on a gasp as he pushed her back into the pillows, his tongue lapping its way first around and then into her belly button, an erotic prequel of what was to follow, 'for coming tonight?'

He lifted his head the merest fraction. 'If I had my way, you would come every night.'

She laughed a husky laugh and shuddered against the bed-clothes, her back arching as his tongue renewed its exploratory journey. 'I meant about coming to the casino. You're not angry?'

His fingers dug into her thighs; his face lay buried in her belly as he grazed her skin with his teeth. 'You have a strange concept of foreplay. What does it take, I wonder, to shut you up.' His teeth nipped at her skin, and she laughed and squirmed again, and he pushed himself higher so his mouth was once again within reach of her nipples. 'But no. Do I look angry?' He paused on the way up, laving at her skin. And he drew one perfect breast deep into his mouth, his tongue circling an even more perfect peak.

She arched into his mouth, her breath quickening. 'It's such a beautiful place.'

'Still won't shut up?' He found her other breast, lavishing the same attention for detail on that one, his hot mouth, his lips and tongue working together like an orchestra.

Teeth grazed her nipple, and she flinched, a deliciously compelling combination of pleasure and pain, a symphony of sensation. 'Sebastiano described it as the jewel in Montvelatte's crown.'

He lifted himself higher, hovering over her as he kissed her eyes, her chin and nose. His lips found hers, teased them open with his tongue and pulled her into a kiss so deep she was lost in it. Then he drew back and she opened her eyes, waiting. Perplexed.

'Sebastiano was wrong,' he said tightly, every angle and plane in his face suddenly accentuated, an exercise in barely restrained control. 'Because *you* are the jewel in Montvelatte's crown.'

And then he plunged into her in one fluid stroke that vanquished the air from her lungs and the conversation from her lips. In that hitched moment, they breathed the same air, shared the same oxygen and, as he filled her completely, shared the exact same space.

Satin-clad hands tangled in his hair, swept the powerful skinscape of his back, and held him to her. Silken-clad legs slid along his, tightening around him and urging him still deeper. And all the while his silken words tangled in her mind, part of the magic, no small part of the sensation.

It might have been a slower build up this time, less frenetic, and with more time to discover and rediscover each other's bodies, but when she came apart, it was a different kind of power that took her shuddering to completion, a different kind of wholeness that brought her back, holding him close, her limbs entwined with his.

A different feeling that left her more confused than ever.

'So that's what it takes to make you shut up.'

Minutes had passed, minutes in which the gradual calming of her breathing belied the growing turmoil of her mind.

Getting him to care for her wasn't supposed to feel like this.

She unburied her face from his shoulder, breathing in his warm male scent, relishing it, even though at the same time the amount she enjoyed it bothered her on another level. 'Apparently.'

Rafe sat up, poured a glass of water from a covered decanter on the bedside table and turned, his eyes brushing along her body as she lay, eyes that took everything in. It was ridiculous to feel shy after what they'd done and what they'd shared, but she still did, still felt exposed. And a trifle ridiculous still wearing stockings and her satin gloves. Then he handed her the glass and she scooted up in the bed, accepting it gratefully, suddenly realising her thirst exceeded her embarrassment.

'I'll speak to Sebastiano,' Rafe continued. 'Get him to free up my diary for a day or two.'

She blinked up at him, hopeful and suspicious in the same motion. 'Why?'

'I've been working too hard. And because we have a lot to catch up on.' He padded across the floor and pulled open a closet, totally at ease with his nudity. And why not, she thought, when you had a body built as if it should be immortalised in marble, every movement revealing the play of superb muscle structure beneath his skin? He was a living sculpture, perfectly proportioned in all the right places, abundantly proportioned where it mattered most. He pulled a white robe from the closet and slipped it over his shoulders, swiping another golden robe from a hanger.

He handed it to her, and for now she clutched it to her chest. 'What did you have in mind?'

'Once news gets out about the wedding, media coverage will make going anywhere a nightmare, but there's still so much you haven't seen here yet. The southern part of the island, for instance. Or we could go for a cruise around the island. Maybe take a closer look at Iseo's Pyramid if you liked?'

'That sounds good,' she heard herself say, not wanting to sound too grateful, too desperate for the opportunity.

He reached out a hand to her and she took it. 'I have to talk to Sebastiano. Why don't you start in the shower and I'll join you shortly.'

She would love a hot shower to massage her spent bones. She'd love it even more with him. She remembered another night, what seemed for ever ago, another promised shower. Maybe this time he might actually join her there. The look in his eyes told him he was definitely planning to.

Her hand in his, she stepped from the bed to the floor. 'So you won't be needing this, after all,' he said, tugging the robe from her hands so it slid to a golden pool at their feet. 'And you won't be needing these any more.' He slowly drew down first one glove and then the other until she was totally naked but for her lace-topped stockings.

His eyes gleamed with heat and fire, his breathing short and hard, and she wondered how it was possible for one man to recover so quickly, and for that man to rekindle the fire in her, so that she too was feeling that familiar ache of need.

He dropped his forehead to hers. *'Dio,'* he muttered, 'what you do to me. But I knew you would come to me.'

'You were so sure?'

'I knew. But had I remembered just how good it could be, I would have taken you that very first night.'

'You tried,' she reminded him, wondering what he'd say or do if he knew the real reason she'd decided to fall back into his bed. 'I didn't let you.'

'It was inevitable,' he said, lifting his head. 'As inevitable as the sun rising in the morning.'

She bristled, having to remind herself what she was trying to achieve and why she even cared. This marriage would happen, she could see no way out, and so she would make of it she damn well could. 'You sound very sure of yourself.'

'I am. As I am sure of you.'

Don't bet on it, she thought, as he let her go to make his call, thinking she knew less and less what it was that she wanted herself.

Don't bet on it.

CHAPTER ELEVEN

WHATEVER Sebastiano had thought of more of his plans being turned upside down, Sienna couldn't imagine, but Rafe had done it, convincing him that another day's meetings could wait. And it was paradise.

Rafe had driven them down the mountain in the sporty Alfa Romeo car, with the top down and the wheels hugging the tight curves as sure-footedly as a cat.

At the marina they'd transferred to the luxury yacht that would take them around the island. It was more like a floating palace, Sienna decided as she was given a tour. Rich mahogany timbers were set off with gold and brass fittings, mirrors and strategic lighting making the most of the space. Not that there was any shortage of that in the vast master suite.

What would it be like to make love in a floating palace, she wondered, looking forward to finding out.

And now up on deck, with Rafe by her side, the launch sliced through the azure water, the wind whipping around them, salt spray sparkling in the air. In loafers and shorts, a casual shirt unbuttoned at his neck and his hair blown freestyle by the wind, he looked magnificent, his olive skin glowing under the sun, his white-teethed smile wide. He looked more relaxed than she'd ever seen him, more together.

He felt even better, his arm looped loosely around her shoulders, his hand on her arm as he pointed out the sights of Montvelatte's coastline, naming the small villages dotted around the cliffs and coves, waving to people in passing vessels, who smiled and cheered when they recognized the royal launch and their new Prince on board.

It was paradise, but it was exhausting, so just as well it was only for a day. The night had been long and full, and the night to come promised to be all of that and more. And Sienna could hardly wait. Even now, just the heat from that looped arm was enough to set her skin to tingling, her pulse to racing. Just the faintest stroke of his fingers against her arm enough to make her nipples ache and firm.

As she'd lain in bed in the dark minutes before dawn, one hand down low on her belly while thinking about the babies growing deep inside and waiting for the first stirrings of the nausea she knew would come, she'd pondered her enthusiasm in his bed, a question that had been plaguing her all day. She'd refused to make love to him when she'd arrived, telling him there was no way she'd sleep with him, fighting off his advances like they were anathema to her. And yet, since the minute she'd invited herself back into his bed, she'd barely been out of it.

But why shouldn't she enjoy making love to him? It merely meant that she enjoyed the sex, the same as he did. It was purely physical. Purely the means to an end.

Sienna looked up at him again, at the chiselled perfection of his jaw and dark beauty of his features, and for a moment was filled with a fear so huge it threatened to consume her. He was a prince, a man whose body and looks would give the gods a run for their money, a man who could move her world with just one heated look, one sensual caress. Why should he ever love her? What could she offer him but to be a willing partner in bed and a mother for his children?

She already represented those things.

Why was she was kidding herself that he would want more? She lowered her eyes, that now familiar gnawing eating away at her gut, leaving a vacuum that she didn't understand and had no way to fill.

'Are you enjoying yourself?'

She turned her face up to his and, even with the sun on her skin, felt the warmth of the smile that greeted her permeate all the way through to her bones. 'Thank you,' she nodded, knowing that whatever happened, she would treasure it forever. 'It's wonderful.'

The boat headed out towards the pinnacle of rock known as Iseo's Pyramid, the mountainous sides reaching further and further into the sky as they approached, the seabirds forming a permanently changing cloud around the peak. Still some distance out, the skipper slowed the engines and cruised gently around the rock; yet even from this distance the rock rose sheer and majestic from the water, its black volcanic walls razor-sharp and magnificent. On one side a tiny beach clung at the base of a cleft in the rock, its white sand framed with wild olive trees and windswept bushes on one side, the jewel-blue sea on the other, and looking like the perfect picnic spot, exclusive, private and with a natural beauty that took her breath away. But there would be no picnic on the beach. 'We can't get any closer,' Rafe explained as the boat bobbed off shore.

And when she looked closer, she could see why, the shadowed outline of rocks submerged just below the surface making any passage through a nightmare, and it was easy to see why the rock had claimed so many victims in its time. For even in the bright light of day, Iseo's Pyramid loomed dark and menacing. To encounter it during a storm would be a living hell.

Sienna leaned against the side of the boat, her eyes scaling the mountain, trying to imagine what it was in the shape of the rock that Iseo had seen on that night, all those years ago.

'Where does the Beast live when it's not in residence, marauding for shipwreck survivors?'

'The Beast of Iseo? It sleeps, far below the sea, busy digesting the contents of another wayward vessel.'

'He must be hungry, then, this Beast of yours, given your embargo on sailings on nights with no moon.'

Rafe turned against the railing and looked down at her, his eyes obscured by dark glasses, yet the hint of a smile tugging at his lips. 'I never thought of that. Do you think it would be wise to make a sacrifice every now and then, in the interests of increasing the opportunities for trade between Montvelatte and our neighbouring countries?'

'Absolutely. Just make sure whoever you sacrifice is a virgin, so I have nothing to fear.'

He laughed, as he had on their cliff walk that evening, and the sound rippled through her on a wave of pleasure, and once again she asked herself why it couldn't be like this always, when one day was so special. He did enjoy being with her. He must feel something for her, to have cancelled his appointments for a day and made the time to be with her. It wasn't all about the sex, or they would never have left his suite this morning.

Shortly afterwards, the launch powered up and steered away from Iseo's Pyramid, back across the passage to Montvelatte. Out on the water the wind was rising. She heard talk from the deck of a predicted summer storm but discounted it. The sky was so blue and cloudless that it reminded her of the years she'd spent with her mother in Australia, where the land had seemed to go for ever until it met the sky. She'd loved the sense of space she'd found there, the space she'd never found growing up on a tiny in-the-middle-of-an-ocean boat or in a crowded school clinging to the side of a mountain in Gibraltar. Australia had been made of space, it seemed, and Montvelatte, an island in the Mediterranean, seemed to share the best of both her worlds—space and endless skies, hers for the taking.

A wind whipped up, tugging at her hair as the launch sliced through the water. Sienna laughed as she was caught off-balance, the hair flicking loosely around her face, her hands unsuccessfully trying to recapture the wayward locks, until Rafe captured her hands in one of his own and pulled them down low. 'Leave it,' he said, using the sway of the boat to tilt her towards him so he could kiss her brow. 'I love your hair just the way it is.'

And then he angled up her chin, and his lips met hers, her hair blowing unrestrained around them as the empty yawning hole inside her latched onto a single truth that jolted her to her core.

Please, no, she thought, feeling herself shrivel away from him in panic.

Please, not that!

But as his mouth moved over hers, the truth refused to be ignored, unfurling inside her, filling the vacuum in a revelation that could see her damned.

She loved him.

Shock wrenched her from the kiss, and when he came after her she claimed the motion of the boat was making her queasy. He had no trouble believing her, just as she had no trouble convincing him, a wave of nausea snapping closely on the heels of her discovery.

She couldn't love him.

She clung to the railing, while he insisted on fetching her some water, her world tilting and yawing in a way that had nothing to do with the motion of the boat and everything to do with a growing fear in her heart.

How could she have let it happen?

And yet, her mind recalled, one night in Paris, on a night filled with lovemaking so passionate and intense it had rocked her world, hadn't that been exactly what she'd thought? That if a woman wasn't careful, a man like Rafe was everything she could fall in love with?

But that had been before he'd shunted her out the door and out of his life without a second glance, and that was before he'd only wanted her back when he'd discovered she was pregnant to him. How could she fall in love with someone who'd treated her that way?

Too easily, it seemed. She'd allowed the same things she'd been attracted to from the very beginning to influence her now, overriding her reasons to hate him. He'd ridden rough-shod over her at every opportunity, denying her any choice, telling her that they would be married and when. And still she'd let him under her skin, wanted him by her side, in her bed. Wanted him.

And that had been the real reason why she'd wanted to flee from Montvelatte the first chance she'd had. Not just because she was angry with him for the way he'd thrust her from his room that night, but because she'd known, ever since she'd landed on the island, how he could make her feel with just one look or one touch, and so she'd had to escape, and as soon as possible.

And that had been the real reason she'd stayed. Because in spite of everything, he held the magic to make her want him.

And she did want him.

It wasn't supposed to happen this way, though. He could love her, he should love her, but she wasn't supposed to love him, not if he could never return that love.

Sienna clung to the railing, breathing in great bursts of air, as the launch lurched over first one swell, and then another, swallowing them down and wishing she could swallow down her memories. Memories of her mother, her face contorted and tear-stained, her voice cracking as she pleaded with Sienna's father to stay at home and not go to the bar that night. Begging him not to go. Telling him that she loved him.

And her father had bellowed back at her, calling her a stupid bitch, and yelling that he'd never loved her and never would and that the only reason he'd married her was because of the baby she'd been too stupid to get rid of. The hatch door had been slammed shut and he'd gone.

He hadn't come home that night. Or the next. And, worried about her mother's deepening depression, Sienna had asked her where her father was. It had been an innocent enough question. She'd known she was that baby for years, the one who had ruined her father's life. But she'd thought in her young adolescent mind that if she could find her father and tell him that she would leave, things might once again be good between her mother and her father.

She'd only wanted to help.

But her question had only brought fresh floods of tears from her mother that had answered nothing, only bringing on a sick feeling that had buried itself deep into the pit of her stomach—that it was already too late.

And that it was all her fault.

A week later Sienna had overheard the news from her friends at the English school on the side of Gibraltar's mountain, from girls who whispered in the rabbit warren of corridors in hushed tones, that her father had moved in with the woman from the bar and that he'd been boasting to everyone that he was never going back.

In the cramped society that was Gibraltar's marina, it was the best kind of scandal. Sex, infidelity and betrayal, all celebrated with a tinge of pathos for the child involved, the child who knew she was responsible for it all.

The boat lurched over the wash from a long gone passenger ferry, and a stomach that she'd been trying to keep under control lurched with it. 'Oh, God,' she cried, clamping a hand over her mouth.

Sweat broke out on her forehead; she felt sick to her core and leaned out over the railing, concentrating so hard on not letting go that only vaguely was she aware of the shouting and of the stilling of the boat. She managed a few deep gulps of air, and it was easier then to swallow back on her churning stomach, the residual wash no more than a rhythmic slap of water against the hull.

The gentle breeze cooled her sweated brow, made her aware of how hot she'd been, how close to losing everything in her stomach.

Damn it! She hated feeling this sickness, whatever the cause. Hated the feeling of vulnerability that went along with it.

She felt Rafe's hand at her back, stroking her shoulder, and almost shrugged him away until she realized that if she was feeling anything, then she was already over the worst.

'Here,' he said, and gratefully she turned and took the goblet, sipping at the cool fluid.

'I'll get them to radio the doctor,' he told her. 'He can meet us when we get back.'

She pushed the glass away. 'I don't need a doctor!'

'You're not well. You need a doctor.'

'What I need is to have my head read,' she snapped, wondering what perverse law of nature had decided that, of all the men in the world, she should be unlucky enough to fall in love with this man. 'And I'm quite sure your precious heirs will be fine, which is all you're really worried about.'

His hand fell away, the silence dragging. 'What is this?'

'Just that every time I so much as sneeze, you call in the doctors.'

'I want you to be well. Is there anything wrong with that?'

'You don't give a damn about me and don't pretend you do! Your concern for me extends no further than as an incubator for your babies. If you could get away with plugging me into a power socket for the duration, like any other incubator, you'd be satisfied.'

'You're talking rubbish.' He turned and made a signal to the skipper, who had been waiting patiently for instructions, and who now revved up the engines and cut a course back into port. 'What are you trying to turn this into—some kind of contest about what means more to me? You know how important it is for Montvelatte—for me—to have an heir.'

She swung away from him and swept a hand across her face, pushing back the loose tendrils of her hair. 'There is no contest. I'm merely acknowledging the truth of the matter. You'd never be thinking about marrying me if it weren't for two small smudges on a screen. You'd never even consider marrying me if it weren't for these two babies of yours I'm carrying.'

'And that's a problem?' He moved closer, his hands held out to her, but she jumped back out of his reach just as quickly.

'This damned marriage is all about these babies. Nothing else. If it weren't for them, you would have let me walk away weeks ago.'

His feet planted wide on the deck, he reached a hand to his head, pushing it through his hair, irritation plainly written on his features.

'We've been through this,' he said gruffly, his patience clearly wearing thin. 'We both know why we're getting married. But that doesn't mean we can't be good together. You know that.'

'Sure, we have a great time in bed. Now there's a sound basis for a marriage. Not!'

'Even forgetting the fact we'll have children between us, being compatible in bed is more than some people have.'

'And it's less than others have.'

'I'll settle for the sex.'

She scoffed. 'I'd expect you to say that. And what happens when we don't have such a great time in bed any more? When you get sick of me or I get sick of you? What happens then?'

Even behind his sunglasses, she could see his eyes narrow as they focused in on her. 'Then we get separate beds. Is that what you want to hear?' He looked away, his hand troubling his already tousled hair once more. 'What is this?' he said, turning back. 'What are you trying to prove?'

Sienna stood at the railing, looking out to sea, the wind in her hair as the boat cut through the clear blue water, and shook her head. 'I don't want it,' she said. 'I don't want a marriage based on becoming someone's brood mare.'

'A bit melodramatic, don't you think?'

'No, I don't think. You need an heir. If these…' she placed a hand low over her tummy, cradling the place her babies were growing deep below '…turn out to be girls, that doesn't help you one bit, does it? A daughter cannot become a prince. A daughter does not solve Montvelatte's problem. You need a son.'

'They will be boys; I know it.'

'How can you know it? There is no way of telling at this stage, no way of knowing. And if you're wrong, and neither of these babies is male, what will my job be?' She nodded, drawing herself up as still and tall as she could. 'I'll be expected to keep on breeding until you have an heir and a spare. But will that be enough, I wonder, given what happened to your brothers? Two sons may not be enough. So how many children must I be expected to bear? How many times will I be expected to share your bed so that you might inject me with your seed and get me pregnant? Don't even pretend you don't expect me to be some kind of brood mare for you.'

'Enough!' He drew closer. So close she could see the

corded tension in his throat, the thump of his heart beating in his temples. 'And you would have me believe that you do not enjoy sharing my bed? *Dio*, who was it who dressed herself like a temptress and paraded herself in front of Montvelatte's wealthiest like some high-society whore, trawling for sex, smelling for all the world like a bitch in heat—'

Her open palm collided against his face with a crack that slammed his head sideways and left a deep red stain upon his olive-skinned cheek.

'You bastard! I am *nobody's* whore!'

He raised a hand to his face, rubbing the place she had hit and all the while he looked down at her. 'All I am trying to do is make the best of a situation.'

'Take advantage of it, you mean!'

'Which is better than pretending it doesn't exist! Don't you think it's about time you faced the facts? You're pregnant with twins. *My* twins. What the hell else are you going to do?'

'I don't know. But maybe you might have bloody well asked me to marry you, instead of just demanding I do.'

'And would you have said yes?'

'Not a snowball's chance in hell.'

His jaw worked overtime, his eyes cold as flint. 'Then maybe it's just as well I didn't ask.'

CHAPTER TWELVE

THE engines slowed as they entered the harbour, and Rafe went and stood at the opposite side of the launch as the pilot skilfully negotiated their way into the marina and to the private landing where Sebastiano stood to attention, waiting for them to dock, the buttons on his jacket gleaming under the sun. He was looking from one to the other, a small frown creasing the skin between his wiry eyebrows.

'What is it?' Rafe asked before they'd berthed, obviously eager for a change of topic.

'The Princess Marietta has arrived. She's waiting for you at the Castello.'

'Marietta is here? Already?' He leapt onto the dock. 'I'll take the Alfa. Sebastiano, you take Signorina Wainwright and drive carefully. She's feeling a little off-colour.'

And then he was gone, and it was Sebastiano's duty to hand her from the boat. 'You're not well, Signorina Wainwright?' he inquired as intelligent eyes scanned her features, and she gained the distinct impression he missed nothing, not even the residual spark of fury that coloured her vision.

'I'm fine,' she answered, taking his hand as she stepped onto the dock. 'Rafe worries too much.'

'Prince Raphael has not seen his sister in some years. They have a lot to catch up on.'

'Lucky Marietta,' was the best response she could dredge up.

* * *

He'd tried. He'd cancelled his appointments and taken her out on a cruise around the island. He'd shown her the tiny coves and beaches that dotted the coastline, tutored her in the names of the villages and what specialities each was renowned for, whether it was to do with wine, olives, oranges or seafood.

Rafe took a hairpin bend, his tyres squealing in protest, and slammed his fist against the steering wheel. He'd done everything he could. And still she railed against him, blaming him, fighting the inevitable as if she were some innocent lamb being led to the slaughter.

Christo! What was her problem?

Last night she'd been the one to come to him, calling to every last sexual sense he had, the siren, beckoning him, wanting him to make love to her.

Hadn't he given her what she'd wanted? She'd seemed fine with their arrangement then. What the hell had changed between then and now?

The Alfa Romeo made easy work of the climb, the Castello looming larger and larger in front of him as he neared its iron gates. Maybe she was right. Maybe their marriage was a disaster waiting to happen if she could run so hot and cold in the space of twenty-four hours.

Maybe he would be better off with someone more amenable. Or maybe pregnancy was sending her hormone levels haywire. She was having twins after all. Did that mean twice the hormones?

Besides, he didn't want someone else.

Why would he when she was already pregnant with his seed?

Two babies. And she could think what she liked, but he was damned sure at least one of them would be a son and the heir that Montvelatte needed if it was to maintain its status as a Principality into the future.

It was perfect. Why couldn't she see that?

It had to be hormones.

Rafe pulled into the forecourt and was just uncurling himself from the car when he heard a sound, a familiar voice even as it turned into a squeal of pleasure. He looked up to see his little sister running down the steps towards him, and he wondered when his little sister had turned into such a stunning woman, a younger version of how he remembered his mother—blonde and beautiful and a throwback to another time, when northern Europeans had swept south into Italy. Somehow Marietta had inherited the lion's share of her genes from their mother. As for him, he'd inherited her height, but the rest of his genes he could attribute squarely to his typically Mediterranean father.

He was glad she'd won their mother's blonde good looks and that they sat with such apparent ease on her. Maybe he hadn't taken any notice back then, or maybe it had just been too long a time since he'd seen her. How many years was it since they'd seen each other? Whatever, it was way too long.

'Raphael!' she squealed, launching herself at him, and the years faded away, and it was his little Marietta back in his arms. His same little princess. Although now with a discernible hint of a New Zealand accent. 'I'm so sorry I missed your coronation.'

He grimaced. 'Don't be. It was a dry and dusty affair. You didn't miss anything. But you're here early. I wasn't expecting you until just before the wedding.'

'I finished a design project early. Thought I'd take off before they lumbered me with another. I hope you don't mind. It's just so good to see you at last.' She kissed both his cheeks and then stood back down, a grin tugging at her lips as she gave him a look of mock seriousness. 'Or should I call you "Prince Raphael" now?'

He squeezed her to him again and spun her around, returning the kiss with one of his own. 'Only if you let me call you princess.'

'But you always did,' she said on a laugh as she settled back to ground level, taking his arm as they headed into the Castello. 'But who would have imagined one day I would actually be a princess for real—and that this—' she swept her arm around in a wide arc '—would all be yours.'

'It's not mine. Technically, I'm just looking after it.' She turned and switched on that same electrifying smile that had got his mother noticed by a prince who'd lost his wife, only to be thrust into oblivion when he had tired of her, and something tugged at him from way deep inside.

This hadn't been a happy place for his mother, bearing babies who were destined never to rule, in love with a man who had only sought her comfort on the rebound.

'You always were a stickler for doing it by the book,' she said with another laugh, dragging him away from the pit where lay his memories of the time. 'Can't you sit back and enjoy it, just a little? I've been having a ball looking around this old place. I only know it from photographs.'

He led her into the library, the aroma of fresh coffee and warm rolls reminding him that he'd had a full appetite-building day on the water, a day that had ended less than spectacularly, which meant the comfort factor of the food wasn't lost on him either. He sat down and poured coffee for them both, adding a liberal dash of cream to his own.

Marietta took the cup he proffered, slipped off her shoes, and curled them beneath her, holding her cup with both hands as she blew across its surface. 'Plus I think I have incorporated into my memories all those things I heard you and Mama talking about—when you did talk about Montvelatte.' She took a sip of her coffee, and when she spoke again her voice was subdued. 'I can't believe what happened to our father. He never cared for us, never gave us a thought, but I thought he loved his sons. How they could do such a thing to their own father—' She looked up at him. 'Have you seen them at all, Carlo and Roberto?'

Rafe leant back in his chair and stretched his legs out long in front of him. 'I visited them once in the prison.'

'And?'

He remembered the day, before his coronation, when he'd gone to see them. He wasn't even entirely sure why he'd wanted to go, just that if they could talk, maybe he could make some sense of what had happened, but all he'd got was their hatred, their sneers and looks of derision, reminding him how he had felt long ago, as if he was still the bastard son who counted for nothing. He shook his head. 'Nothing's changed.'

She blinked and took a deep breath, then turned her eyes up at him over the cup and smiled apologetically. 'What am I talking about? You're getting married, big brother. How amazing is that?'

'Why should it be amazing? I'm thirty-three years old. High time I settled down, wouldn't you say?'

She laughed and put her cup down. 'Except you were the one who was never going to settle down.'

He looked away. Wondered why he hadn't yet heard any sound of Sebastiano returning with Sienna.

'Where is she?'

'What?'

'Your fiancée. Where is she? When do I get the chance to meet her?'

'Oh.' He shook his head. 'Soon. I'd like you to be one of her bridesmaids. It's probably just as well you're here early.'

'That's what I figured,' she said, sipping at her tea innocently. 'Anyone else I know in the wedding party?'

'Probably only Yannis. I've asked him to be my best man, of course.'

The cup stilled at her lips, and something briefly clouded her eyes, something he didn't quite understand, before she looked up at him and threw him one of those dazzling smiles that lit up the room. 'Of course. Who else? Anyway, what's she like, this bride of yours. Tell me about her. This is so amazing, big brother, I've never know you to stick with a woman for more than a month in your life. She must be something to have got you to commit.'

'She is,' he said with surprise, his voice choking, his ears straining for any sound. 'You'll meet her soon.'

'Is she pretty?'

He jerked his head around, his fingers tangling together, his feet itchy, unable to keep still. Was she pretty? In his mind's eye he saw her hair, coiling around her face, refusing to be restrained, and shining copper against the most perfect translucent skin. *Dio*, she wasn't just pretty, she was breathtaking, a breath of fresh air on a stifling summer's day, a slice of paradise in every smile. 'She'll make a great first lady for Montvelatte,' he said, realising how lame the words sounded the minute they'd left his mouth.

Marietta considered him carefully, her long-lashed eyes as calculating as any computer. 'But you love her, right?'

Sienna had made a hash of the afternoon. Blown any sense of camaraderie she and Rafe had been building up because she'd had an epiphany. An epiphany she wanted to run kicking and screaming from. A thunderclap that, at first, had seen continuing her endeavours to make him love her all but pointless.

She'd wanted to wallow in the depths then. She deserved to wallow. To consider herself lost, like some storm-tossed traveller at sea, miles from home, without a sign of land, and bereft of loved ones. Iseo's Pyramid had never looked so appealing.

But there was no escape, and nothing would change the truth. She loved Rafe Lombardi. *Prince Raphael Lombardi.* She wasn't supposed to love him, but she did.

And she could deny it all she wanted. She could rail against the injustice of it. She could drive herself and everyone around her crazy by fighting it and fighting them, but then what good would that do?

Or she could keep going with her plan. Just because her father had never loved her mother, didn't mean that Rafe could never love her. She was sure he felt something for her. There was a spark—something—that was worth pursuing, no matter how much he tried to compartmentalize her usefulness in his life between recreation and procreation.

It was no consolation that her mother had probably felt just as sure that she would be able to make Sienna's father love her. It was no help at all.

But if she was to win through this, then she had to look to the positives. Rafe could love her, she was sure.

She had to be sure.

Sebastiano seemed to respect her need for quiet and drove at a gentle pace up the mountain to the Castello, the shadow thrown by the building casting the road into a half-light that seemed strangely to fit her mood.

Half-light. Where she felt now, knowing she loved Rafe. Knowing he didn't love her.

Half-light. A possible future of unreciprocated one-way affection if she didn't try.

Did she want to live life that way? Hell, no.

Rafe's car was still in the driveway when they pulled up, but something else captured her attention. The JetRanger sitting pretty in the centre of the helipad below, the familiar navy-and-white colours of her former employer proudly displayed. Just the sight of it was enough to rip open the scar of losing her recent life.

Sebastiano opened the door for her, caught the direction of her lingering gaze, and sought to explain. 'Princess Marietta arrived in it two hours ago. I believe the pilot is waiting to collect a delivery before taking off.'

She turned to him. 'Who's the pilot? Do you know?' She hadn't been with the company that long, but just the thought of connecting with someone from her former life—anyone— lifted her spirits immeasurably.

Sebastiano gave a nod. 'I will find out for you. But if you would like to step inside, I dare say Princess Marietta would like to meet you.'

Sienna hesitated a fraction longer, her gaze on the chopper, her fingers itching to hold a joystick again. She'd missed flying, missed being part of the endless sky. A gust of wind came from nowhere, and her eyes scanned further afield, to where the sky was deepening and even the water below was chopping up, looking more threatening. Maybe they were right. A summer storm. That would be something to see.

Then, with one last look at the helicopter, Sienna followed Sebastiano inside.

She heard voices coming from the library, Rafe's rumbling deep tones and a woman's voice, her laughter light and infectious, and, without having even met the woman, Sienna liked her already. It would be nice to have another woman around, nice to have someone to talk to, and she was about to enter the room when she heard it.

'But you love her, right?'

Sienna stopped short of the doorway, holding her breath, her senses on red alert. There was only one person they could be talking about.

The silence stretched on for ever as Sienna waited, her ears straining to hear his response over the pounding of her heart.

'Did you know she was pregnant?'

She looked to the ceiling, her fingers clenching and un-clenching as Rafe deftly sidestepped the issue. From inside the room, she heard the sounds of Marietta's delight, her squeal when she heard the news about the twins, while outside the room Sienna closed her eyes and breathed deep. She knew she couldn't keep standing here eavesdropping forever. She would have to enter the room, meet Rafe's sister, and pretend everything was all right. When nothing was right and every-thing was all wrong.

Desperately wrong, when a perfect day could turn upside down. Where a fragile peace was going to be the best they could ever hope for.

She couldn't meet Marietta now, couldn't pretend that ev-erything was all right and that she was the blushing bride. Brides were supposed to look radiant, and right now she didn't have a sailor's chance against Iseo's Pyramid of pulling that off. As quietly as she had come, she turned and headed for the stairs.

'So, big brother,' his sister said, 'anyone would think you were avoiding the question. You do love her, then?'

His sister hadn't changed a bit. He'd thought he'd thrown her off topic with the news of the twins, but she could always be like a dog with a bone when it suited her. He got up and walked to the windows, noticed the darkening sky and the brooding light, but it was on noticing the car parked next to his that he frowned. *Where was she?* He turned back to his sister. 'You always were a hopeless romantic, Marietta.'

'And you were always a hard-nosed cynic.'

'With good reason!'

She got up and joined him at the window, her hand on his arm. 'Raphael, what happened to Mama, it doesn't have to be like that.'

'It won't be. I've made sure of it. Sienna will make the perfect wife.' *Once she could get her hormones under control.*

'Without love?'

'We get on fine.' *Although, given today's events, it could be better.*

'So,' she continued, and he sighed, knowing the interrogation was far from over, wishing Sienna would arrive so that he might be spared, and his sister would turn her powers of inquisition in her direction. 'You're marrying this woman, who's carrying your twin babies and who is expected to become part of some royal fishbowl, but you don't love her?'

'It's easier that way,' he said, turning his attention once more out the window, Iseo's Pyramid growing more evil-looking in the darkening sky, the usual cloud of seabirds absent, as if they'd all already hunkered down for the storm.

'So what's in it for her?'

'She gets to be a princess. Isn't that every little girl's dream? It used to be yours.'

Marietta conceded his point with a nod. 'Although my father was a prince, so it's slightly different. But is Sienna happy with that?'

'She will be.'

'And she doesn't love you?'

'Of course not!' And after the things he'd said to her today, he'd be surprised if she was even talking to him. He flinched when he remembered. He shouldn't have likened her to a high-class whore. She hadn't deserved that.

'Just as well.'

'What do you mean?'

'Only this, big brother. Our mother adored our father and

all for nothing because he was incapable of returning that love. She died lonely and bitter because of it. So if you care at all for this woman, don't let that happen to her.'

He had to prise his teeth apart in order to speak. 'It won't.'

Rafe found her in her room, collecting up her damp towels, freshly showered and smelling like a new morning after a night of rain showers. And even in the jeans and singlet top she'd changed into, her hair pulled into a loose ponytail behind her head, she looked so beautiful that the desire to possess her swelled up large in his chest.

'Marietta was hoping to meet you.'

Her eyes were cool, noncommittal, and he figured she was still angry with him from their argument on the boat. 'I'm sorry. I needed to freshen up. Is she staying?'

He nodded, watching her carefully, searching for any sign that Marietta could be right, and that Sienna might somehow have fallen in love with him. 'She's joining us for dinner.'

'Fine.' She made a move towards the bathroom with the wet towels.

'Sienna…'

'What?'

'Somebody else will get those.'

'They're only towels. It's no trouble to hang them up.'

He followed her into the bathroom. 'Look, I shouldn't have said what I did, on the boat.'

She looped one towel over the rail, not even looking at him. 'Which bit, exactly?'

He reached a hand behind his neck and massaged muscles tight and stiff. 'When I likened you to some high-society whore. I shouldn't have said that.'

She sniffed, sliding the other towel over the rail to join the first, fussing with the edges so they exactly aligned. 'I don't know, I actually thought referring to me as "some bitch in heat" was equally as offensive.' Satisfied with the place-ment of the towels, she turned and pushed past him, back into the bedroom, sitting down on the bed, slipping sandals on her feet.

'I was angry.'

'I'll say, not that I think that excuses you. Seems to me that it's okay for you to demand sex and to tell me that you want me, but that the moment I do, I'm some kind of whore.' She stood up. 'How does that double standard work, exactly?'

'I'm sorry. I was out of line.'

'Yes, you were. Now, if you'll excuse me?'

'Where are you going?'

'Just for a walk.' She felt no compunction to tell him where and what for, no need to tell him that the pilot of the helicop-ter was a former colleague and that she was looking forward to talking to someone she'd known longer than ten minutes. Sebastiano had promised her he'd be able to give her a few minutes before the chopper had to take off, before the curfew came into effect. 'To clear my head.'

'The wind's getting up. Don't take the cliff walk.'

This time she managed to dredge up a smile. 'No. I wouldn't dream of it.'

'And, Sienna.'

She turned just inside the door. 'Yes?'

'Marietta was worried about you.' He noticed the slight frown that puckered her brow. 'I thought I should say something.'

Her frown deepened. 'About what?'

'About how things are between us. About how they have to be.'

He had her full interest now, every cell in her body sitting up and taking notice. She shut the door and turned towards him, crossing her arms in front of her. 'So tell me.'

'This won't be a normal marriage.'

She gave a brief laugh. 'You think I haven't picked up on that? But why should Marietta be worried about me. We've never even met.'

'Because of what happened to my mother. A long time ago.' He dragged in a breath and threw his eyes to the ceiling, looking as if he'd rather be anywhere but here, and meanwhile she waited, caught between wanting to flee and to protect her emotions from yet another roller coaster ride, and wanting to stay and hear what he had to say. To get to the bottom of his fears and hang-ups, to have him open up to her about his family and what made him the person he was—surely he wouldn't do this unless she meant something to him? She didn't want to raise her hopes, only to have them cut down again. But neither could she live without hope. Had Marietta made him see something he hadn't seen himself?

'My father's first wife died suddenly,' he began, 'and he was left to raise two young sons.'

'Carlo and Roberto,' she said quietly, filling in the blanks, and he nodded.

'He was devastated for a time, thrown completely by her loss and by the unexpected responsibility of deciding what happened to the next generation. My mother was enlisted to help the nanny, and she was very beautiful. When you meet Marietta you will see what I mean; she is very much like her mother, who was not only beautiful, but a rare blonde in an island filled with dark-haired people. She stood out and she was noticed. My father was still grieving his lost wife, but he was smitten with my mother's beauty and seduced her, wanting no more than relief from the anguish of losing his wife. Meanwhile she was young and overcome by his apparent affection, and she had fallen in love with him.

'When she became pregnant, he moved her out of the palace, but still he went to her. And still my mother took him in. I think she believed that one day he would marry her and make her his princess.

'But she fell pregnant again. Meanwhile my father found another mistress, younger and with more time on her hands, and my mother was distraught. He sent her away, offering her a settlement if only she never returned. So she left.'

The seconds ticked away, an antique mantel clock that she never noticed except for the deepest, darkest nights, sounding like a drumbeat in the ensuing silence, with only the wind whistling outside for company.

'Why are you telling me this?'

'So that you know the risks.'

'Risks?' She battled to make sense of it all. 'I still don't understand. What's your mother got to do with me?'

His eyes were so dark and deep, she felt in that moment she could fall into them and never find her way out. 'She fell in love with a man who was incapable of loving her. I'm warning you not to do the same thing.'

CHAPTER THIRTEEN

THE wind suddenly howled outside the windows, a loose shutter somewhere banging. But inside the room, Sienna's blood had turned to ice, her heart stilled with the cold.

'You're warning me off.'

Rafe nodded.

'Telling me not to fall in love with you?'

'Telling you how it has to be.'

'Because you don't love me.'

'Because I can't love you. I can't love anyone.'

She shook her head, the injustice of it all threatening to swamp her, the sheer unfairness too much to comprehend. 'But you don't know that.'

'I know what I saw what my mother go through. I know I will never put myself in such a position.'

'And you're trying to tell me that this is the only way this marriage can work, by you not loving me and me not loving you.'

He held up his hands. 'We can still have a good marriage.'

She took a step back towards the door, the pleas of her mother running through her head, begging her father not to leave them. The sound of her father yelling back, telling her that he'd never wanted her, that he'd never loved her. The sound of the hatch slamming down, as he'd left them for ever.

That was not going to be her future. But it would be if she married Rafe. She could fight and fight and do everything she could to try to make him love her, but his mind was made up. She'd already lost him.

'No.'

His eyes narrowed, his stance more alert. 'What do you mean, *no*?' And just like his stance, the tone of his voice had also changed, shifting from conciliatory to wary in a moment when he realized he didn't have the upper hand any more.

'I'm not prepared to marry you on those terms. I could never marry someone who didn't love me—who was incapable of loving me. Don't you see? My mother was just the same as yours. She loved my father with all her heart, and he turned that power back on her and crushed her with it. And nothing, not even the child that had forced them into marriage, was enough to keep them together.

'I made a promise to myself years ago that I would never marry a man for the sake of an unplanned pregnancy, especially without that man's love.' She looked at him, her eyes scanning his features, wanting to imprint his face on her memory so that she might remember every last perfect detail of him in case it was the last time she saw him this close, beginning to believe it might very well be. 'And I was starting to think it might work. I thought there was a chance—that we could make it work. But, no. I can see that's not possible.' She glanced at her watch, cursing to herself when she saw the time. So much for catching up with an old colleague. The chopper was probably already gone, just one more disappointment in what had turned out to be a gut-slammer of a day. But that didn't matter right now. She just wanted to get away, find some space, sort out a head too full of cries of injustice and a heart too shredded with pain.

She reached for the door, pulling it open. 'I guess the only bright spot is that it's lucky we had this conversation now, before we went through that farce of a marriage.'

The door slammed shut, Rafe's hand and his weight behind it. 'What the hell are you saying?'

She stared up at him, surprised he'd moved so fast. Unsurprised at his anger. He'd still expect her to marry him come hell or high water. What did it take to make him realize nothing could make her settle for a loveless marriage? 'What do you expect? You don't leave me with much choice. I can't marry you, Rafe, babies or no. I can't stay here with a man who can't love. I won't be my mother all over again.'

'Who's asking you to? You said yourself that your mother loved your father. It doesn't have to be that way for us. That's what I'm trying to prevent.'

She laughed then, a release so unexpected that it left her almost dizzy in its wake, dizzy and so close to tears she could feel the moisture seeping through. 'But that's the problem, Rafe, it's already too late. Because I...I love you.'

Stunned didn't come close to expressing the way Rafe felt. She couldn't be serious. She couldn't be.

Dio! He wheeled around, both hands clutching at his temples, tangling into his hair, searching for answers he couldn't find. It was the last thing he wanted to happen. It was the worst thing that could have happened.

'I don't believe you.'

I don't want to believe you.

'You think right now I care what you believe?'

'Yet you say you love me.'

'Do you think I want to? Do you think I went looking for love with a man who practically dragged me kicking and screaming into a marriage I didn't and still don't want? What kind of masochist do you think I am?'

He couldn't answer. He didn't know. All he knew was that

something was wrong, his convenient marriage slipping beyond reach, sliding towards a disaster he'd never seen coming.

A disaster he'd been trying to avoid ever since he'd been a child.

'Don't waste your time on love.

Don't lose your heart.'

He couldn't love and, damn it all, she wasn't supposed to love him.

He looked up at her, at her face of porcelain-like skin, at her hair kissed gold by the sun, her eyes wide with questions he knew he'd never be the one to answer. And inexplicably he ached with that knowledge, the gears in his chest crunching and grinding together.

And he didn't have the faintest idea of how to stop them.

'You must go,' he said, his voice a coarse whisper, while in his mind the tear-streaked face of his mother played, kissing him goodnight the nights she'd managed to stay up longer than he did, the scent of perfume more and more giving way to the fumes of alcoholic despair. He didn't want that fate for Sienna, but neither could he bear to witness it here, where he couldn't give her what she needed. 'Get out now, before it's too late!'

She hovered uncertainly, her eyes shining, or was that merely his?

'Rafe,' she said, putting out a hand to him. 'It doesn't have to be like this. Can't we talk about it? There must be a way, has to be a way.'

'There is no way!'

'But your babies. One day we will share children, maybe even the heirs Montvelatte needs. You're not thinking straight.'

'Send me the first-born son!' he yelled, the pulse in his head pounding like drums. 'You can keep the other.'

She reeled back as if he'd physically thrust her aside. 'Rafe. I'm sorry.'

'No, you're not! You've been trying to figure out a way to get out of this marriage from day one. And now you've finally hit on the perfect plan. You knew I could never do to a woman what my father had done to my mother. I'd told you what he'd done! What better way to secure your release.'

'Rafe, it's not like that. Listen to me. I love you.'

'And for the last time, I don't want your love! Get out. Go! I never want to see you again.'

Blinded by tears she could no longer control, Sienna somehow stumbled out of the room, blundering past curious staff, who called out to her in concerned voices, past the palace guard that had held her hostage that first day and now stood by to let her flee.

Outside the wind tugged at her hair, the sky an ominous shade of grey, but she took no notice, running full pelt for the one person she knew might help her. The one place where escape lay waiting.

It was still there, the small pick-up truck just driving off. Any minute the JetRanger and her lifeline to the outside world would be gone. She screamed out, but her words were carried away on the wind, and the pilot climbed into the cabin and pulled his door shut.

She had time. She knew the time he would take to get the bird off the ground, to turn on the master electrical switch and avionics, to check fuel levels and turn the fuel valve master on.

She was halfway down the road as the navigation lights turned on. Right on cue.

She pushed herself harder as the rotors began to turn, ducking down low as she made for the pilot's door, her fist slamming on the window.

The pilot, Randall, looked around, first in shock, a smile of recognition tinged with concern spreading his lips wide a moment later before he opened the door. 'Hey, there,' he said in his lazy American drawl. 'I thought you weren't coming. What's up?'

She gulped down air into burning lungs and did her best to smile while she swiped away at her damp cheeks. 'No time for small talk. Just get me out of here.'

'I love it when a lady tells me exactly what to do.' He grinned and waited until she was in the seat alongside him, her seatbelt buckled, before he raised the helicopter from the ground. 'You almost missed me,' he said, shouting to make himself heard. 'Any later and we would have been stuck here for the night. Damn curfew.'

She nodded, still trying to regain her breath. She knew all about the damn curfew.

'We missed you at the office,' Randall said, as the bird moved under his expert hands. 'Been taking a vacation?'

'You could say that.'

He flicked a glance into the back. 'You didn't bring any luggage.'

'Sudden change of plans.'

'Only there was this rumour going 'round, y'know, that you were maybe stuck on Montvelatte for good.'

'Big storm coming,' she said, pointing out the windscreen, and the pilot beside her laughed. 'I get the picture. And, yeah, it might get a bit bumpy, so hang on.'

The bumps didn't worry her, at least not the bumps in the air. It was the bumps that life dealt out that were infinitely worse. She turned around, trying to gauge their distance from the island, wondering when she'd ever be far enough. Escape had been ridiculously easy in the end. But, then, Rafe had practically thrown her out.

Sienna sat back down in her seat, letting out a long breath. To their left the looming peak that was Iseo's Pyramid claimed sovereignty over the surrounding waters, a dark prince in a darker sea, and she shivered as she let her gaze drift over its frightening dimensions, its sheer size just as overwhelming from above as below. She wasn't afraid. She'd left the real Beast of Iseo behind on Montvelatte, but still the dark brooding shape held the power to fascinate, the power to disturb.

She sensed it rather than heard it, something no passenger would notice but an experienced pilot would. She looked across at the pilot and then down at the gauges at the exact same time he did. 'What is it?'

'I don't know.' His eyes scanned the controls, nothing evident, and then it happened again, a tiny blip, a momentary loss of power, and this time Randall's hands were hard at work. 'Damn,' he yelled. 'Whatever it is, we'll have to turn around back to Montvelatte.' And her spirits plummeted. To be foiled when she was so close to escape! How could she return to that island? How could she ever risk facing him again, the man who had banished her because she had been foolish enough to love him? But right now there was no other choice.

Then a bolt of lightning rent the sky in two, the world around her appearing in black and white, like some crazy negative, and she would have sworn the bolt hit the very rock itself. Birds erupted from the peak like magma from a volcano, a cloud of huge seabirds, panicked from sleep and lumbering through the air in every direction. Normally they would have been fine where they were, far enough from the rock and the wheeling cloud of birds that they would be in no danger, but these birds were stunned, beyond instinct other than to escape.

'Watch out,' she cried, as Randall continued to do battle with the handicapped craft. But it was already too late. There was a bang as something hit the rotors and the aircraft shuddered and yawed to one side, the smell of smoke filling the cockpit. And now she was helping him with the controls, battling to put the chopper into autorotation and regain control, but it was no use.

'We're going down,' he called, 'we won't make it to the island.' But she was already at the radio, barking out a Mayday call.

'Head for the rock,' she said, and the pilot tossed her a look that said she was as mad as Iseo himself. 'There's a small beach,' she shouted, clutching at the controls, 'around the side.' And the only place they had a chance of making an emergency landing.

For a few hairy seconds she almost thought they would make it, the two of them almost enough to get the helicopter under control. Until the second bird hit. It penetrated the cockpit like a missile, a sickening crunch that sprayed blood and gore everywhere as it slammed into the pilot.

'Randall!' she screamed, as he slumped over his controls, feathers stuck to blood she had no way of knowing belonged to him or the bird.

She battled to push him back into his seat while trying to manage the controls for both of them, the rock looming ever larger, the wind wilder where the rock ended and the sea began.

And then there it was, the tiny patch of sand, barely visible in the growing darkness but there, calling out to her like an invitation, a siren's call.

'Let's hope not,' she muttered through grim lips as she battled the wind and rock and a failing aircraft.

Rafe was still fuming, stalking around Sienna's room, waiting for her return, when Sebastiano found him. 'Prince Raphael,' he said with a small bow.

'Not now,' he said gruffly, turning away, not interested in the minutiae of the affairs of state when something of momentous proportions had just taken place. Something he was still battling to get a handle on.

Sienna had said she loved him. Why? How could it have happened when their mothers' stories were so similar? How could she embrace love after what her mother had gone through?

But she *hadn't* embraced it.

He thought about her arguments, her protests. She hadn't wanted to love him. Something he could identify with.

And yet she did love him. There was something totally unidentifiable about that. Though, at the same time, something unexpectedly and oddly satisfying.

'I think you will want to hear this.'

'Didn't you hear me? I said, not now!' He was still trying to make sense of it, trying to work out why his gut felt so twisted and torn and just plain wrong when he'd done what he'd thought was right and got rid of any chance of someone loving him.

Except knowing he'd achieved that didn't make him feel any better. It made him feel a damn sight worse. And he was damned sure his father had never felt this bad when he'd exiled his mother, or he would have changed his mind in a heartbeat and kept her for his own.

And the gears crunched some more before settling into a new configuration, something that worked on a different level.

And he remembered another time, another evening, when he'd walked that cliff-top walk with her, and he'd felt the swelling inside that had told him that this marriage would work, and at last he realized what that feeling had truly been. Not a beast inside him, needing to be fed, but a heart so crusted in tragedy and pain that it had taken a woman like Sienna to shed light and crack it free.

He hadn't had to make her see this marriage would work. She'd shown him the light, she'd made it possible.

He couldn't send her away, because he needed her here now, with him every day of his life. And without fully understanding why, something told him that he had missed an opportunity back there in her room to tell her what he really thought, feelings he was still trying to come to terms with, feelings that would not be suppressed, no matter how much he denied them.

'But it concerns Signorina Wainwright.'

The wind gusted around the castle then, pummelling the walls and rattling windows until they shook, and a niggling seed of premonition buried itself inside him and took root.

'What is it?'

'She was seen leaving in the helicopter. The one that brought Princess Marietta.'

He looked to the windows, where the tops of trees could be seen dancing wildly in the wind, leaves flying past, the rumble of thunder like an omen.

'She's out in this? Why the hell didn't anyone stop her?'

Sebastiano crossed his hands in front of him and dipped his head. 'That's not all. There's been a Mayday call reported from the helicopter. Some kind of electrical fault, coupled with a birdstrike.'

Rafe didn't hear the words. He felt them like boulders raining down, their pain etching his soul. 'How far did they get from the island?'

'The *Guardia Costiera* has been alerted, although in these conditions…'

'How far did they get?'

Sebastiano hesitated, clearly uncomfortable with imparting his next piece of information.

'Iseo's Pyramid.'

Rafe's blood ran cold. He'd sent her away. He'd told her to go. He might as well have sent her to the very Beast himself. *Christo*, why had it taken so long for him to realize what should have been so obvious all along? That he wanted this woman because he loved her, in spite of every warning he'd had, he loved her.

And he wanted her back.

Ice filling his veins, he somehow made it to the rain-lashed terrace, his eyes searching out the familiar black outline of rock against the clouds and the storm tossed sea. But there was no missing it. Not today, even on the darkest night, no missing that other cloud that rose unnaturally from the other side of the island.

A single plume of smoke.

CHAPTER FOURTEEN

IT HAD taken every shred of every ounce of pulling rank that Rafe could find, every firm promise that the Beast of Iseo was a myth and that the weather was their worst enemy, but finally he'd convinced the *Guardia Costiera* that he was going with them. Rain lashed his face, his hair was probably wetter than the sea right now, but he felt nothing. Nothing but this great yawning pit that had opened up inside him.

He'd sent her away. Damn well told her to get out, and she'd done exactly what he'd wanted.

What he'd thought he'd wanted.

He must have been insane! Cursed with some kind of madness, because right now the thing he wanted most in the world, the thing he wanted more than anything, was the one thing he'd told her he didn't want.

Her love.

Because that would mean she was alive.

How could he have let her go?

How could he have sent her into the darkness, crying and distressed? And the yawning hole in his gut snapped shut, catching him in the inescapable truth.

He was his father all over again.

Casting aside her love. Telling her it was unwanted. And

in trying to protect himself he'd damaged himself even more. By lashing out at the one person who could show him otherwise. Who could show him how to love.

Rafe looked from the boat, his eyes always on the slick black rock, searching out any detail, anything out of place. The plume of smoke was long gone, but if there had been smoke, then the helicopter must be there, somewhere. For now that was all he would focus on. And if the helicopter was there, then so too was Sienna.

He would find her. And then he would tell her what had been so glaringly obvious the moment he'd known she'd gone, that he wanted to change places with her and smash himself into the rock in her place.

He was such a fool.

The cruiser rounded the rock, the beams from its powerful lights doing the best job they could to cut through the rain and illuminate the shore, every eye on board not concentrating on keeping the boat from the rocks, but searching for any scrap of evidence of the helicopter's position.

And then there was a glint of white where there should be none, and a cry went up to launch a dinghy. Rafe pushed his way to the front. 'I'm going,' he said.

Strange that she should feel cold. The thought came from nowhere, a kind of hazy realization that it was summer, that she shouldn't feel cold. It was wrong.

Sienna tried to move, but something was pinning her in her seat, something that kept groaning and waking her up, when all she wanted to do was sleep. It groaned again, the sound vaguely human.

Randall.

He lay slumped against her, sharing the scent of his fresh kill, and she remembered where she was, a helicopter down

on Iseo's Pyramid, and laughter bubbled out of some un-
tapped place.

She'd landed a helicopter on Iseo's damned Pyramid with
the ugliest landing in history. But they were alive! At least for
now, until that damned Beast found them.

She reached a hand for the radio, but her wrist screamed
out in pain and she pulled it back, sinking back once more into
grateful oblivion.

Inch by inch, with one coastguard hanging over the edge to
check for rocks that might slice the dinghy's shell to shreds,
the boat had made it to the tiny sandy beach. To Rafe it had been
an eternity. An eternity of waiting. An eternity of wondering.

And now that they were finally here, was it already too late?

His feet were amongst the first to splash into the water's edge,
the waves still surging in, sucking at his calves with ferocity.
But then he was running. Splashing through the shallows and
running for the unnatural egg-shaped object, its blades angled
askew, the lighting from torches showing how they'd decimated
the shrubs and bushes as the chopper had come down.

He reached the passenger door a scant second before the
man behind him. He pulled at the latch, heaved it with all his
might when it wouldn't come, and wrenched it open.

And there she sat. Sleeping.

Pray God, she was sleeping!

'Sienna!'

Her eyelids flickered open with the play of torchlight on
her face, and he breathed out a breath he hadn't realized he'd
been holding. She looked up at him, confused. 'I knew the
Beast would come,' she mumbled, before slipping back into
unconsciousness.

A doctor pushed his way in front of him, and he gave him
room, while another worked on the pilot alongside. Rafe stood

back then, the angry sea sucking around his ankles, the shadow of the rock looming high above.

Oh, yes, if there was a Beast of Iseo, he was worthy of the title.

It was unsafe for everyone to move them from the Rock in the night, but they'd established there were no spinal injuries and they'd splinted Sienna's wrist, and now she lay on a stretcher in a tent, Rafe by her side, stroking her hair.

Deep in the night, the wind dropping as the storm dissipated, she woke up to the touch of him, and she stirred.

'You're here,' she murmured.

'Where else would I be?'

'But those rocks… You're crazy. You came through those rocks?'

'I came to find you. Do you think rocks were going to stop me?'

'I don't know. But I never expected anyone to come so late on such a night. I guess I should thank you for that. I suppose you told them that the future heirs of Montvelatte were at stake.'

He lifted up her good hand and pressed his lips to it. 'No. I told them that the jewel in Montvelatte's crown was at stake, and if they didn't find you, I would personally feed them to the Beast of Iseo, one by one.'

'You told them that?'

'My exact words.'

'But why?'

'Because I realized after you'd left that there are more important things than avoiding love. And then I heard you were missing, and that your helicopter had gone down, and I was afraid I'd never get the chance to tell you.'

'Tell me what?'

'That I love you, Sienna.' He smiled down at her and felt

his heart expand tenfold with the joy he saw reciprocated, even in a face shadowed in the low lamplight. 'And I am sorry for all the pain I caused you, all the assumptions I made, all the decisions I made without even considering you.'

'You're sorry for all of them?'

'I know,' he admitted, 'there were plenty of them. I'm sorry it took me so long to realize. Sorry I made you feel like you were trapped. Looking back, it should have been obvious to me. Even back after that one night in Paris, I was annoyed that events in Montvelatte had intervened, that I would not see you again.'

'You were? I thought it was these babies of ours you were after—your potential heirs.'

He smiled and nodded. 'They were an excuse, and a good one. But even back then I knew I wanted more of what you had to offer. I'm so sorry it's taken me so long to wake up, so sorry you had to go through all this.'

'It wasn't so bad. I kind of enjoyed being behind the joystick again.'

'I heard. The pilot said you'd saved his life. And I got to thinking, Montvelatte needs a helicopter pilot.'

'You don't even have a helicopter.'

'No, but if my refinancing plan works, we could have. And I'll need someone to fill the position. If you're not too busy to fly me around, that is.'

She smiled. 'I think I accept.'

'That's good. And I have one other favour, that I really have no right to ask.'

'What is it?'

'I'd like to celebrate my love for you by asking you to share my life for ever. Will you marry me, Sienna, and become my wife?'

She blinked up at him. 'You're actually asking me?'

'I'm asking you. Pleading with you if it comes to that. And if you don't want to get married, I'll even settle for that, so long as you promise to live in sin with me forever.'

'But then your children will be bastards, forever.'

'I don't care,' he said. 'It never did me any harm. So long as I can have you.'

And then he kissed her, and she knew forever would never be long enough.

EPILOGUE

S<small>UNLIGHT</small> poured through ancient stained glass windows, showering the congregation in puddles of fractured light. Organ music filled the cathedral, and the scent of fresh orange blossom filled the air as the tiny page boy and girl marched their slow march down the aisle.

Sienna waited at the head of the aisle, watching the procession, wondering how it would look if instead of waiting serenely until last, she skipped past her attendants and claimed her husband.

Not the way royals were supposed to behave in front of their own, but then she was only new at the job, and she still had a lot to learn.

Her soon to be sister-in-law, Marietta, gave her a final smile and squeeze of the hand, before she too set off down towards the altar. Where Prince Raphael of Montvelatte, her Rafe, stood waiting for her, tall, dark and utterly devastating.

She felt a flutter deep down inside her, touched one satin-gloved hand to her stomach, and knew with a woman's instinct that it was more than mere butterflies. She smiled. The day could not become more wonderful.

Or so she thought. Until minutes later, when she joined Rafe at the altar and changed her mind. There, with the eyes of the world watching, together they exchanged their vows, and she could not believe that anything would ever come close to that feeling.

'I love you,' he murmured, as he drew her to him for the bridal kiss that would seal their agreement and their future together. And, as he drew her deeper into the kiss, to the delight of the entire congregation, she knew it to be true, and that the Beast of Iseo had finally been tamed.

Cavelli's Lost Heir

LYNN RAYE HARRIS

Lynn Raye Harris read her first Mills & Boon® romance when her grandmother carted home a box from a yard sale. She didn't know she wanted to be a writer then, but she definitely knew she wanted to marry a sheikh or a prince, and live the glamorous life she read about in the pages. Instead, she married a military man and moved around the world. These days she makes her home in North Alabama, with her handsome husband and two crazy cats. Writing for Mills & Boon is a dream come true. You can visit her at www. lynnrayeharris.com.

To Mom and Pop, who took me to live in
fascinating places, bought me lots of books,
and didn't blink when I locked myself in
my room for hours on end to read.

CHAPTER ONE

CROWN PRINCE NICO CAVELLI, of the Kingdom of Montebianco, sat at a fourteenth-century antique desk and reviewed a stack of paperwork his assistant had brought him an hour ago. A glance at his watch told him there were several hours yet before he had to dress and attend the State dinner given in honor of his engagement to a neighboring princess.

Nico had a sudden urge to loosen his collar—except it was already loose. Why did the thought of marriage to Princess Antonella make him feel as if a noose were tightening around his neck?

So much had changed in his life recently. A little over two months ago he was the younger son, the dissolute playboy prince. The prince with a new mistress every few weeks, and with nothing more pressing to do than to decide which party to attend each night. It wasn't the whole truth of his existence, though it was the one the media enjoyed writing stories about. He'd been content to let them, to feed their need for scandalous behavior. Anything to keep their attention away from his emotionally fragile brother.

Nico pinched the bridge of his nose.

Gaetano had been the oldest. The delicate one. The legitimate one.

The brother that Nico had spent his childhood protecting

when he hadn't been fighting for his own honor as the product of a royal indiscretion. Ultimately, he couldn't protect Gaetano from the ramifications of his choices, or from the fateful decision to aim his Ferarri at a cliff and jam the pedal to the floor.

Per Dio, he missed Gaetano so much. And he was angry with him. Angry that he'd chosen such finality, that he hadn't fought harder against his personal demons, that he hadn't trusted Nico with his secret years ago. Nico would have moved mountains for Gaetano if he'd known.

"Basta!" Nico muttered, focusing again on the paperwork. Nothing would bring Gaetano back, and nothing would change Nico's destiny now. He was the remaining prince, and though he was illegitimate, the Montebiancan constitution allowed him to inherit. In this day and age, with modern medicine being what it was, there was no doubt of his parentage—if, indeed, there could be any doubt in the first place; Cavelli men always looked as if they'd been cast from the same mold.

Only Queen Tiziana disapproved of Nico's new status— but then she'd disapproved of him his whole life. Nothing he ever did had been good enough for her. He'd tried to please her when he'd been a child, but he'd always been shut out. He understood now, as a grown man, why she'd disliked him. His presence reminded her that her husband had been unfaithful.

When he'd moved into the palace after his mother's death, the queen had seen him as a threat, especially because he was stronger and bigger than Gaetano, though he was the younger of the two. That he was now Crown Prince only drove the pain deeper. He was a constant reminder of what she'd lost. It didn't matter that he'd also loved Gaetano, that he would give anything for his brother to still be alive.

Since he couldn't bring Gaetano back, he would do his utmost to fulfill his duty as Crown Prince to the best of his ability. It was the only way to honor his brother's memory.

A knock on the door brought his head up. "Enter."

"The Prefect of Police has sent a messenger, Your Highness," his assistant said.

"I will see him," Nico replied.

A moment later, a uniformed man appeared and bowed deeply. "Your Serene Highness, the Prefect sends his greetings."

Nico tamped down his impatience as the man recited the ritual greetings and wishes for his health and happiness. "What is the message?" he asked, somewhat irritably, once the formalities had been observed.

Though it was indeed the Crown Prince's duty to oversee the police force, it was more a symbolic role than anything else. That the Prefect was actually communicating with him about something filled him with an uncharacteristic sense of foreboding.

Ridiculous. It was merely the awareness of his loss of freedom that pinched at the back of his mind and made him feel uneasy.

The man reached into his inner pocket and pulled out an envelope. "The Prefect has tasked me with informing you that we have recovered some of the ancient statues taken from the museum. And to give you this, Your Highness."

Nico held out his hand. The man stood to attention while Nico ripped into the envelope.

He expected the sheet of paper inside, but it was the photograph of a woman and child that caught Nico's attention first. Their faces filled the frame as if someone had stood very close to snap the picture. He recognized the woman almost instantly—the wheat-blond hair, the green eyes and the smattering of freckles across her nose—and felt a momentary pang of regret their liaison had not lasted longer. His gaze skimmed to the child.

Sudden fury corroded his insides. *It was not possible.* He

had never been that careless. He would never do to a child what had been done to him. He would never father a baby and walk away. It had to be a trick, a stunt to embarrass him on the eve of his engagement, a ploy to get money. There was no way this child was his.

His mind reeled. He'd spent only a short time with her, had made love to her only once—much to his regret. Wouldn't he have remembered if something had gone wrong? Of course he would—but the child had the distinct look of a Cavelli. Nico couldn't tear his gaze away from eyes that were a mirror to his own as he unfolded the paper. Finally, he succeeded in wrenching his attention to the Prefect's scrawled words.

Nico dropped the paper and shoved back from the desk. "You will take me to the prison. Now."

Lily Morgan was desperate. She was only supposed to be in Montebianco for two days. She'd been here for three. Her heart beat so loud and hard in her ears that she'd half expected to have a heart attack hours ago. She had to get home, had to get back to her baby. But the authorities showed no signs of letting her leave, and her pleas to speak with the American Consulate were ignored. She hadn't seen a soul in over four hours now. She knew because she still had her watch, though they'd taken her cell phone and laptop away when they'd brought her down here.

"Hey!" she yelled. *"Hey! Is anyone there?"*

No one answered. There was nothing but the echo of her voice against the ancient stone interior of the old fortress.

Lily sank onto the lumpy mattress in the dank cell and scraped her hand beneath her nose. She would not cry. Not again. She had to be strong for her boy. Would he miss her by now? She'd never left him before. She would not have done so now had her boss not given her little choice.

"Julie's sick," he'd said about the paper's only travel writer just a few days ago. "We need you to go to Montebianco and research that piece she was working on for the anniversary edition."

Lily had blinked, dumbfounded. "But I've never written a travel article!" In fact, she'd never written anything more exciting than an obituary in the three months she'd been at the paper. She wasn't even a journalist, though she'd hoped to become one someday. She'd been hired to work in the advertising department, but since the paper was small, she often did double duty when there was a shortage.

The only reason the *Port Pierre Register* had a travel writer was because Julie was not only the publisher's niece, but her parents also owned the town's single travel agency. If she was writing about Montebianco, there was probably a special package deal coming up.

But the mere thought of traveling to Montebianco had turned Lily's legs to jelly. How could she enter the Mediterranean kingdom knowing that Nico Cavelli lived there?

Her boss was oblivious. "You don't need to write it, sweetheart. Julie's done most of the work already. Just go take some pictures, write down how it feels to be there, that kind of thing. Experience the country for two days, then come back and work with her on the write-up."

When she demurred, he refused to take no for an answer. "Times are getting tough, Lily. If I can't count on you to do the job when I need you, I may have to find someone who's more willing. This is your chance to prove yourself."

Lily couldn't afford to lose her position at the paper. Jobs weren't exactly thick on the ground in Port Pierre; without this one, she couldn't pay her rent or keep up with her medical insurance premiums. She could search for other employment, but there was no guarantee she'd find anything quickly. Once she'd gotten pregnant, she'd had to drop out of college. She'd spent the last couple of years bouncing from one low-paying position to another, doing anything to take care of her baby.

The job at the paper was a major break and a huge step up for her. She might even be able to return to school part-time and finish her studies someday.

She simply could not endanger Danny's future by refusing. She'd gone without many things as a child when her mother had been out of work or, worse, had dropped everything to run off with her womanizing father again. Lily would not do that to her own baby. She'd learned the hard way never to rely on anyone but herself.

She had no choice but to accept the assignment, though she'd comforted herself with the knowledge that her chances of actually crossing paths with a prince were pretty slim. She would leave Danny with her best friend, spend two days touring Castello del Bianco, and then she would be on a plane home. Simple, right?

But she'd never bargained on winding up in a prison cell. Would someone call the authorities when she didn't return? Had they already done so? It was her only hope—that someone would report her missing and the American Consulate would insist upon an accounting of her movements within the kingdom.

A distant clanging brought Lily to her feet. Her heart thumped harder if it were possible. Was someone coming to see her, to let her go? Or was it simply a new prisoner being brought into the depths of this musty old fortress?

Lily gripped the bars and peered down the darkened hall. Footsteps echoed in the ancient corridor. A voice spoke until another silenced it with a sharp command. She swallowed, waiting. A lifetime later, a man came into view, his form too dark beneath the shadows to distinguish features. He stopped just short of the pale light knifing down from a slit in the fortress wall several feet above his head. He didn't speak.

Lily's heart dropped to her toes as a fresh wave of tears

threatened. Oh God, he couldn't be here. *He simply couldn't.* Fate could not be so cruel.

She couldn't say a word as the prince—for so she had to think of him—moved into the light. And—oh my—he was every bit as handsome as the pictures in the magazines made him out to be. As her memory insisted he was. His black hair was shorter than she remembered, as if he'd cropped it closer in an effort to look more serious. He wore dark trousers and a casual silk shirt unbuttoned over a fitted T-shirt. Ice-blue eyes stared back at her from a face so fine it appeared as if an artist had molded it.

My God, had she really thought he was just a graduate student at Tulane when she'd met him at Mardi Gras? Could she have been any more naive? There was no way this man could ever be mistaken for anything other than what he was: a wealthy, privileged person who moved in circles so far above her that she got altitude sickness just thinking about it.

"Leave us," he said to the man at his side.

"But Your Highness, I do not think—"

"Vattene via!"

"Si, Mio Principe," the man answered in the Italian dialect commonly spoken in Montebianco. He gave a short bow and scurried up the passageway. Lily held her breath.

"You are accused of trying to smuggle Montebiancan antiquities out of the country," he said coolly, once the echoes from the man's footsteps faded away.

Lily blinked. "I'm sorry?" Of all the things she'd expected him to say, this had not been even a remote possibility.

"Two figurines, *signorina*. A wolf and a lady. They were found in your luggage."

"Souvenirs," she sputtered in disbelief. "I bought them from a street vendor."

"They are priceless treasures of my country's heritage, stolen from the state museum three months ago."

Lily's knees went weak. *Oh, God.* "I know nothing about that! I just want to go home."

Her pulse hammered in her ears. It was all so strange. Both the accusation and the fact he didn't appear to recognize her. But of course he wouldn't! Had she really expected it? She gave her head a tiny shake. No, she hadn't, but after all she'd been through the last two years, it hurt nonetheless. How could he not look at her and know? How could he not be aware of her the way she was of him?

Prince Nico drew closer. His hands were thrust in his pockets as he gazed down at her, his cool eyes giving nothing away. No hint of recognition, no sliver of kindness, nothing. Just supreme arrogance and a sense of entitlement so complete it astonished her. Had she really spent hours talking with this man? About *what?*

Without meaning to, she remembered lying beneath him, feeling his body moving inside hers. It had all been so new to her, and yet he'd been tender and reassuring. He'd made her feel special, cherished.

Now, the memory seemed like a distant illusion, made all the more so by his lack of awareness of it.

She dropped her gaze, unable to maintain the contact. His eyes were unusual in their coloring, pale and striking, but that wasn't the precise reason she couldn't look at him.

No, she couldn't look because it made her heartsick for her child. She hadn't realized it until she was face-to-face with the prince again, but Danny was the exact image of his father.

"I am afraid that is impossible."

Her head snapped up, her eyes beginning to tear again. *No.* She had to be strong. "I—I have to get home. I have responsibilities. People need me."

Prince Nico's gaze sharpened. "What people, *signorina?*"

Lily's stomach hollowed with fear. She couldn't tell him about Danny, not now. Not like this. "My family needs me. My mother depends on me." She hadn't seen her mother in over a year, but he didn't know that.

He studied her, his quick gaze sweeping over her with interest. And something more. Her nerve endings prickled.

"No husband, Lily?"

His use of her name was like the subtle caress of his fingers against her skin: shocking, unexpected and delicious. At first she thought he must recognize her, must remember her name after all—though he'd called her *Liliana* in their time together. But nothing in his demeanor indicated he had. *He'd gotten it from the police. Of course.*

She felt like a fool for thinking otherwise. But why was he here? Did a prince really come to the prison when someone was accused of theft? She felt as though she was missing a piece of the puzzle, as though there was something she should know, but she couldn't quite grasp what it was.

"No, no husband," she said. She couldn't mention Danny, she simply couldn't. Fear for her baby threatened to overwhelm her. If Nico knew he had a son, would he take her baby away from her? He certainly had the power and the money to do so.

She pressed closer to the bars, beseeching him, pouring every ounce of feeling she had into her words. "*Please,* Ni— Your Highness," she corrected, thinking better of calling him by name. "*Please* help me."

She thought he looked puzzled, but it was gone so fast she couldn't be sure.

"How is it you expect me to help you?"

Lily swallowed the hard knot in her throat. Could she confess just a little bit? Would she endanger her baby by doing so? Or was she endangering him by not speaking? What if she never got out of here? Would Carla raise Danny as her own? "W-we met once. In New Orleans two years ago. You were kind to me then."

If she expected awareness to cross his features, she was disappointed. He remained distant, detached.

"I am always kind to women." His voice was as smooth and rich as chocolate. And as cool as an Alpine lake.

Heat rushed to Lily's face. How could she stand here and have this conversation with him, with the man who'd fathered her child and didn't even know it? She'd been right about him, right not to persist in her efforts to track him down once she'd learned he was so much more than an ordinary man named Nico Cavelli.

She still remembered the shock of finding out who he really was, the endless parade of photos and sensational tabloid articles once she'd discovered his identity. Prince Nico of Montebianco was nothing more than a playboy, a jet-setter on a global scale who'd once gone slumming in New Orleans. He did not remember her, did not care about her, and certainly wouldn't care about Danny.

Just as her father hadn't cared about her or her mother. Of all the men in this world, how had she chosen *this* one to initiate her into the ways of intimacy between a man and a woman? It was mind-boggling how ignorant she'd been, how duped she'd been by his charm and sincerity. He hadn't exactly lied about who he was, but he hadn't told the truth, either. She'd known his name and where he was from, but she hadn't known he was a prince until later.

Once he'd gotten what he wanted from her, he'd abandoned her to her fate. She'd stood in the rain for over two hours that last night, waiting for him. He'd promised he would be there, but he never showed.

God, he made her sick.

Before she could gather her thoughts to speak, to think of another method of approach, he whipped something from his shirt pocket and thrust it toward her. Gone was the cool facade. In its place was a wrath so deep it would have frightened her had there been no bars between them.

"What is the meaning of this? Who is this child?"

Lily's heart squeezed. She shoved her hand between the bars, tried to reach the picture of her and Danny, but the prince snatched it away. A sob tore from her throat before she could stop it. They'd gone through her things, dismantled her suitcases as if she was a common thief and passed her possessions around for comment. Worst of all—*he knew her secret!*

"Who is he?" the prince demanded again.

"That's my baby! Give me that," she cried, clawing between the bars. "It's mine!"

He looked furious. And a little bit stunned, if that were possible. But he recovered quickly. "I don't know what you think will happen now that I've seen this, but it will not work, *signorina*. This is a cheap attempt to blackmail me, and I will not bow to it." His voice dripped menace.

Lily stopped struggling and stared at him, her head buzzing with emotion. "Blackmail you? Why would I do that? I want *nothing* from you!"

Her mind raced. Nico didn't know anything for certain. He was only concerned about himself and his money. If she hadn't been locked up, it might have been a relief in an odd way to have her opinion of him confirmed. She had to make sure he understood that she expected nothing from him. If he didn't feel threatened, he might help her to leave this place.

Lily closed her eyes, struggled for calm. "All I want is to go home."

Why had she ever been worried he would take her baby away? He was not the kind of man who would care about his child. He kept many mistresses, and had fathered several children already. She usually avoided the gossip magazines, but the occasional blaring headline about Nico still had the power to attract her attention. She knew, for instance, that he was about to marry.

A pang of feeling sliced into her and she pushed it down deep without examining it. How must his wife-to-be feel about his philandering ways, about the many children with no real father? She had certainly made the right decision not to get in touch with him two years ago. Danny deserved so much better than a father like him, a father who would never be bothered to spend any time getting to know his child. She didn't want her baby to grow up the way she did, with a wastrel father who only came into her life whenever it suited him—and left it again without concern for the emotional wreckage strewn in his wake.

"What are you doing in Montebianco?" he demanded, his tone distrustful and suspicious. "Why did you come here, if not to try and blackmail me?"

"I was doing research," she said, her temper flaring. "For a newspaper article. And why would I want to blackmail you?"

"Do not play games with me, *signorina*." He tucked the photo back into his pocket. He looked murderous, as if he could order the guard to forget she was down here and throw away the key. A sliver of fear knifed into her; he probably *could* do such a thing.

"I hope you are comfortable, Lily Morgan, because you are going to spend as much time in this cell as it takes for me to learn the truth."

"I told you my boss sent me. I didn't come for any other reason!"

"You do not wish to tell me this child in the photo is mine? You did not come all this way to do just that? To demand money?"

Lily wrapped her arms around her body, surprised she was trembling, and looked away. "No. I want to go home and forget I ever met you."

Nico moved so fast she jerked back a step, forgetting the bars between them. His hands were the ones gripping the metal this time, his pale gaze lasering into her. "I don't know what you're playing at, Miss Morgan, but I assure you I will get to the truth."

When he shoved away and strode up the passage, she didn't make a sound. It wouldn't have mattered anyway. Prince Nico had no heart.

Nico strode into his apartments in the palace and summoned his assistant. Once he gave the order to find out everything about Miss Margaret Lily Morgan—oh yes, that had been a surprise, finding out she used her middle name instead of her first; and yet it explained why he'd never found a trace of her when he'd inquired two years ago—he went onto the terrace and gazed out at the city below.

The encounter had affected him more than he cared to admit. Lily Morgan was not at all what he expected. She was not the soft, almost shy girl he remembered, his Liliana who was as pure and fine as the flower she was named after. The night in prison should have frightened her, made her cooperative. Yet this Lily was fierce, determined.

But determined to do what?

He did not know, but he would not leave her there for another night—was, in fact, somewhat appalled she'd been held there without his knowledge in the first place. Nico's mouth twisted in distaste. It made sense that the old fortress was still used as a prison, but the conditions could be improved. Yet another thing he would change now that he was Crown Prince.

He slipped the photo from his pocket, held it between two fingers without looking at it. The photograph had been altered, he was sure of it. Any talented photographer with the right computer equipment could make a photo say anything he or she wanted it to say. How well Nico knew this. Today was not the first time he'd been presented with such a lie. The media tried all the time to place him somewhere he'd not been, or with someone he'd not been with. The photographs were doctored, easily disproved, though it was irritating and inconvenient to do so.

And yet it was the life he'd chosen, when he'd chosen to be the foil for Gaetano. Nico shoved a hand through his hair. He could handle it. He'd always been able to handle it. He would do so now, and he would send Miss Lily Morgan back to America where she belonged.

Madonna diavola, this was also not the first time he'd been presented with a paternity claim—though he'd never been presented with it in quite this way. Lily hadn't mentioned the child at all until he'd shown her the picture. And then she'd been desperate to get the photo from him, had never actually come out and said the child was his. But it *must* be her intention. What else?

He lifted the photo, studied it—and felt that jolt of awareness and recognition he'd never experienced before. Unlike the children that two of his former lovers had tried to assert were his—each incident had been disproved and the claims retracted, though Nico still gave money for the children's care since it was not their faults they'd been born without fathers— this boy had the look of a Cavelli. It was more than the eyes— something in the dark curls, the smooth olive skin, the shape of jaw and nose, the firm set—even in a toddler—of the lips. The likeness was remarkable, yet surely it was a trick.

He'd been captivated by her, he remembered it well, but not so captivated he'd forgotten to take precautions when he'd made love to her. He never forgot to take precautions. It was as necessary to his existence as sleeping or eating. He'd grown up the product of an indiscretion, and he would not ever cause a child to suffer the way he had. When he had children, they would be legitimate, wanted, and loved.

But what if those precautions had somehow failed? Was it possible? Could he be this boy's father? And, if he was, how could she have kept him from his son for all this time?

But no, it was not possible. He would have remembered if something happened to the condom; nothing had. The child could not be his, no matter how strong the likeness. It was a photographic trick.

Satisfied, he dropped the photo into a potted plant. He would not be played for a fool by this woman. Soon, he would know the truth. And tonight he would formalize his engagement to Princess Antonella, would move forward with the effort to unite Montebianco and Monteverde by honoring the commitment his family had made to the Romanellis when Gaetano was still alive. Antonella Romanelli was a beautiful woman; surely he would be well pleased with her as his wife.

Nico turned from the view and strode toward the terrace doors. He only took a few steps before faltering. With a muttered curse, he retrieved the picture and tucked it against his heart.

CHAPTER TWO

LILY BOLTED UPRIGHT on the musty cot, panic gripping her. Where was she? Why was she so cold?

A moment later, she remembered. The thin blanket she'd huddled under just wasn't enough protection. She scrubbed both her hands through her hair and got to her feet, hugging herself against the chill settling into the damp fortress walls as night crept over the city. How had she managed to fall asleep after her encounter with Nico?

Her eyes were gritty and tired, and her head throbbed. She'd cried so hard she'd given herself a migraine, though it was thankfully nothing more than a dull pain now. The sleep had helped at least.

The sudden clanging of the metal door in the passageway startled a little cry from her. Her heart pounded as she backed toward the opposite wall of the cell. A naked bulb overhead gave off only meager light and she squinted into the darkness outside the bars. A big shape shuffled into view and thrust a key into the lock. The door swung open just as she made out the uniform of a Montebiancan police officer.

"Come with me, *signorina*," the man said in thick English.

"Where are you taking me?" Fear, sharp and cold, slashed into her. Did the prince plan to have her thrown off a cliff somewhere?

Stop being silly.

"Come," he said, motioning. She hesitated only a moment longer, deciding she might have a better chance once she was out of this cell. She could give him the slip if the opportunity presented itself, or perhaps she could scream for help. It wasn't much of a plan, but it was better than sitting here another night.

The policeman ushered her up into the bright light of the rooms above the ancient cells. Before she could grow accustomed to the light, she was outside in the cool night air. A Mercedes limo idled near the exit and a man in a dark chauffeur's uniform snapped the car door open.

Lily faltered. The policeman held out his hand, motioning at the car. "Please," he said.

She hesitated, glancing at the street beyond the black iron gates. There was no escape that way, so she climbed into the car, her mind racing with possibilities. The door slammed behind her and a moment later the car whisked into traffic. Her questions about where they were going didn't penetrate the glass between her and the driver, so she settled into the plush leather of the interior and watched the city lights slide by as she planned her escape.

Lily gripped the door handle in a damp palm, her heart racing. When the car came to a halt at a light, she pulled, intending to slip out and disappear into the night before the driver could blink—but the door was locked. She jerked it again and again, but it refused to open. The driver didn't even glance at her. The car started moving, climbing steadily uphill, and Lily bit her lip, tears of frustration choking her.

Soon, they passed beneath an archway and into a courtyard. The car came to a halt. Lily pulled in a deep breath as her door swung open. Whatever was about to happen, she would *not* be a blubbering wreck. She was stronger than her fear, stronger than Nico Cavelli could ever imagine. She'd had to be.

A man in a colorful palace uniform beckoned her. Only then did it dawn on her that they'd arrived at the Cavelli Palace. The Moorish fortress sat at the highest point of the city, its white walls gleaming in both sun and moonlight. It commanded sweeping views of the sea and sparkled like a diamond in the center of a pendant. She'd gazed at it for two days, wondering if Nico was here, what he was doing, if he ever thought of her.

She'd certainly gotten her answer, hadn't she?

She was hurried through a door and down a series of corridors, finally arriving at closed gilt double doors. The palace guard rapped and spoke in Italian. A moment later, a voice answered and the doors swung open.

Blood rushed to Lily's head as she crossed the threshold. The room was a confection of ornate Moorish arches, mosaics, antiques, priceless artwork and tapestries. The gilt alone could pay for Danny's college tuition wherever he chose to go. A massive crystal chandelier threw glittering light into every corner. Her senses were overwhelmed as she tried to take it all in.

The doors clicked shut behind her and she whirled, her gaze colliding with that of the man walking in from an adjoining room.

If he wanted to intimidate her, he was doing a fine job. He was tall and broad, his body encased in a glittering uniform that surprised her with its ornate formality. A red sash crossed from his right shoulder to his waist. The uniform was dark, black or navy, and studded with gold. Medals draped across his chest in a colorful row of ribbons and polished silver discs and stars. A saber, dripping with tassels, was strapped to his side.

He lifted his hands and peeled off first one white glove and then the other while she gaped. He tossed them onto a chair with the hat she hadn't noticed before.

Desperately, Lily tried to conjure the image of the somewhat shaggy-haired student she'd thought him to be in New Orleans. He'd smiled a lot then. Laughed. How could this person be the same? Did he have a twin, perhaps? A twin who'd given her a false name?

For once, she wished she'd read more about him. Her knowledge was limited to gossip magazines and celebrity Web sites. She'd steadfastly refused to find out anything more once she'd discovered just how colossal a mistake in judgment she'd made. What good would it have done to pore over his biography when she was never going to see him again? Lily Morgan dating a prince—yeah, that was freaking hilarious.

"This is what is going to happen," he said coolly. "You are going to answer me truthfully and completely, and then you will call your friend Carla—"

"I want to call her now," Lily said firmly, only mildly surprised he knew her best friend's name. He'd been busy the last few hours, that's for sure. "She must be frantic with worry, and I want to know my son is well."

Nico held up a hand. "All in good time, *signorina*. First, you answer my question, and then you call."

Lily was tired and achy from too little sleep and the cold prison cell, and her head still throbbed dully. Her temper was on its last thread, and she no longer cared if she was talking to a prince or not. He put his pants on the same way as everyone else—not to mention he'd once deigned to sleep with her—so that gave her as good a reason as any to speak to him as an equal. "I'm calling her now, or I'm not answering."

Nico's eyes gleamed with suppressed annoyance. "You do not wish to test me, *signorina*. Your position is precarious enough, do you not think?"

Lily's chin nudged up a notch. "What do you plan to do, throw me back in that dungeon?"

"Perhaps. Trafficking in stolen antiquities is a significant crime in Montebianco. We take our heritage very seriously here."

Lily's right temple pounded. "I didn't steal anything. If you check with the street vendor, you'll know it's the truth."

"We are having some difficulty locating him. Not to mention that street vendors do not typically sell priceless artworks as if they are cheap trinkets."

"You're lying." The man had a stall in the market, for goodness' sake. How hard was it to find him again?

"I assure you I am not. He seems to have disappeared. If ever he was there in the first place."

Lily's bravado leached away under the weight of his arrogant surety. She was too tired to fight him, and too worried about her son to care about matching wits with this cold-blooded man any longer. She just wanted it over with. "Fine—what do you want to know?"

"I want you to tell me if this child is mine."

Lily's lungs refused to work properly. Liquid fear softened her spine, her knees, but somehow she remained upright. "What kind of question is that?" she asked on little more than a whisper.

His eyes flashed fire. "It is the kind of question you will answer truthfully if you wish to remain free."

She nearly choked. "You call this free?"

"Lily," he said, a hint of exasperation in his voice. And something else. Pain? Weariness?

She swallowed, dropped her gaze to study the tiles at her feet. Her heart pounded so hard she felt dizzy. It was the moment of truth, the one she'd never thought would come. Would he somehow care for her and Danny? Would he help them, be a father to her boy?

Of course he wouldn't. He was marrying a princess, God help the poor woman, and he wasn't about to change his ways just because he had yet another illegitimate child in this world. He might give her money to take care of Danny, but Lily knew that everything came with a price. She'd basically taken care of herself since she was fifteen years old, and she would continue to take care of herself and Danny on the strength of her will and determination. She would not accept handouts from Nico.

A finger under her chin tipped her head up. She hadn't realized he'd moved so close. The touch stung, brought memories to the surface she'd rather forget. His eyes were mesmerizing, as pale and blue as a winter lake. She'd wanted to drown in them once. Wanted to drown in him.

Part of her still did.

"Why does it matter?" she said, fighting a wave of panic.

His gaze never wavered, piercing her to the core. The contrast of his soft words was jarring to her senses. "Is this boy mine?"

In a split second, a million possible outcomes crossed her mind. And yet there was only one answer she could give, no matter how it tortured her to do so. "Yes," she whispered.

She was utterly still as his hand dropped. A moment later, while time stood still, he twirled a lock of her hair around his finger. "I remember this hair," he said softly. "It is still like the finest silk in my hands."

He'd moved closer than she'd realized, his body mere fractions away. The hilt of his sword grazed her beneath the ribs. "You remember?" she said, then cursed herself for sounding so desperate for an affirmative answer.

His gaze dropped to her mouth, lingered long enough that warmth blossomed between her thighs. Had she ever been kissed so thoroughly as when he'd kissed her? She stared at his lips, remembering the first brush of them. Remembering how his tongue dipped in to stroke her own, the way she'd sighed and opened to him, the utter rush of desire that flooded her as the kiss deepened into something that left them both gasping for breath and sanity when it was through.

He smelled so good, like citrus and spice and warm Mediterranean nights. She wanted to lean into him, wanted to kiss him again, wanted to know if what she'd felt with him had been real or a fluke.

"I remember you," he said. For an insane moment she thought he might really kiss her. With a soft curse, he moved away, unstrapping the sword as he walked. It clattered to the floor beside the chair with the rest of his gear before he spun and fixed her with a glare.

"I remember that we met in Jackson Square when a pick-pocket tried to steal your purse. I remember meeting you for three nights in a row in front of the cathedral. But most of all, I remember the last night. Mardi Gras. You were still a virgin."

Lily didn't care if she had permission or not. She moved to a plush couch and sank down on it, aware that she hadn't showered since yesterday and that she probably smelled as musty as the dungeon. But her legs wouldn't hold her up any longer.

"But when you came to the prison…" Her voice trailed off as she thought about how cold and cruel he would have to be to put her through that ordeal earlier. This was not a man to lose her head over, not a fairy-tale prince on a white stallion. This was a petty, privileged man who didn't care about anything but his own pleasure.

"This is what you will do now," he continued. "You will call your friend Carla and have her bring the boy to the airport. She will turn him over to a woman in my employ. Her name is Gisela—"

"No!" Lily shot to her feet. "I'm not telling Carla to give my son to a stranger—"

"*Our* son, is he not, Lily?"

Her heart battered her ribs. She would not lose her baby to this man! "Surely you can't be prepared to take my word on it," she flung at him with far more bravado than she felt. "Let me go home and you'll never hear another thing from me, I swear."

"That I cannot do, *signorina*." Irritation crossed his features as he stalked toward her again. "And I already know the truth. Our son was born nearly seventeen months ago, on November the twenty-fifth, in a small hospital in Port Pierre, Louisiana. You were in labor for twenty-two hours, and the only person at your bedside was Carla Breaux."

Lily sank onto the couch again as her legs gave way. *He knew the truth.* "Why did you ask me if he was yours if you know so much?"

"Because I wanted to hear you say it."

Lily felt as if she were collapsing in on herself. Her body folded over, slowly, until her head was nearly between her knees. Fury and fear mingled in her gut, bubbled into a great howl of rage that erupted from her throat, astonishing her.

Astonishing Nico, if the alarm on his face was any indication.

"You are *not* taking my baby away from me," she vowed. "I'll go back to that cell and stay there, but I will *not* tell Carla to hand over Danny to you."

He went to the bar set against one wall and poured a measure of caramel-colored liquid into a glass. Then he returned and held the cut crystal out to her. "Drink this."

"No."

"You are overwrought. This will help."

She gripped the glass in both hands, more to make him go away than anything. When he stood so close, her head felt fuzzy. Thankfully, he retreated a few steps. He picked up a phone, issued what she assumed were a set of orders since whoever was on the other end never had time to speak before he hung up again.

"You will call your friend Carla and tell her to bring Daniele to the airport tomorrow morning."

"I won't," she said quietly, resenting the way he so easily Italianized her son's name.

"Indeed you will," Nico replied. "You can make this easy, or you can make it hard. Should you not cooperate, you might never see Daniele again. Because you will not leave Montebianco. He could grow up motherless, and alone."

Numbness crept over her. "You would do that to your own son? You would deny him his mother?"

She didn't miss the nearly imperceptible clenching of his jaw. "I will do what it takes to make you see reason, *cara*. If you cooperate, this will not have to happen, *si?*"

"How can you be so cruel?"

He shrugged an elegant shoulder, and Lily saw red. The spoiled bastard! The glass tumbled to the floor and shattered against the tile as she lunged for him. Nico was faster, however. He swept her high into his arms and carried her across the room as she kicked and struggled.

"*Dio,* woman, you are wearing sandals. Do you want to slice your feet to ribbons?"

Lily didn't care. She simply didn't care about anything any longer. This man, this cold evil man, was trying to take away the one person in the world who meant the most to her. It was her greatest fear come to life. She would not allow it.

She twisted in his iron grip, throwing him off balance so that he stumbled. Lily pressed her advantage and they fell to the thick Oriental carpet together, Nico taking the brunt of the impact. A moment later, he flipped her and she found herself on her back, Nico's hard form pressing into her, breast to belly to hip.

"Stop fighting me, *cara,*" he said harshly. "It changes nothing."

Lily wiggled beneath him, tried to shake him off. His solid form didn't budge. The point of a star-shaped medal dug into her ribs. "Why are you doing this to me?" she cried. "You have dozens of children with your mistresses, so why do you care about mine?"

Rage, disbelief, frustration—they chased across his face in equal measure. "I have one child, Liliana. Only one. And you have kept him from me."

"I don't believe you," she gasped out.

Nico shifted and the medal's point thankfully stopped pricking her. He gripped her arms, forced them above her head. He seemed to hover on the edge of control. "Have you never thought that gossip magazines might lie?"

"They can't all be lies." There had to be a grain of truth, right? Perhaps they exaggerated, but there must be something to it. Not one of the reporters she knew at the *Register* would dare write something so patently false.

Nico's laugh was short and bitter. "You have obviously never been the victim of these carrion. They feed on outrage and misdirection. There's hardly a single thing they print about me that is true."

"Now I know you're lying. I've seen photos of you with lots of women—"

"I have had many mistresses," he said, cutting her off. "This is to be expected—"

"Why? Because you're some kind of God's gift—"

"*Basta!* You seek to exasperate me, *signorina,* and you succeed. Nevertheless, I have *one* child."

Lily's chest heaved in frustration as she stared up at him. But her eyes closed as the truth of his words sank in. Gossip magazines thrived on scandal. She knew that. But she didn't want to believe he spoke the truth. Because if he did, so much she'd thought about him would be wrong. The blood drained from her head as the implications sank in.

"But if Danny really is the only one, that would mean—"

She couldn't finish the sentence, uncertain what to say next. Was Danny in line for a throne? *Impossible.*

Nico said it for her. "Yes, *cara,* our child is my heir and second in line to the throne of Montebianco."

Her insides were jelly. "How is that possible?" she managed. "We aren't even married."

"It just is," he said, his accent thickening suddenly as she moved.

Lily took advantage of his distraction to try and buck him off. She arched her back and flexed her body upward, shoving into the cradle of his hips. His arousal sent a jolt of sensation sizzling through her.

In spite of her anger and frustration, the feeling was delicious. Dangerous.

Nico's breath caught as she shoved against him. The sound was slight, but she heard it nonetheless.

And just like that she was on fire, absolutely aflame with longing. How could it be possible? How could she feel sexual desire for him when he wanted to ruin her life? He'd given her the most precious thing in her world, and now he wanted to take it away. And her body didn't seem to care. She redoubled her efforts to throw him off.

"Maledizione," he ground out between clenched teeth. "Stop moving—or would you like to take this into the bedroom and do it properly?"

Lily's palms pushed against the crisp material of his uniform. A desperate, greedy part of her did indeed want to *do it properly.* But her common sense, her anger, her sheer dislike of the man won out. "Get off me."

"As you wish," he said, then bounded up and left her to climb to her feet alone.

Lily hugged herself, her body still tingling with the shock

of desire. How could she want him? She closed her eyes, squeezed her arms tight around her middle. My God, she really was her mother's daughter.

She could not afford the distraction of such thoughts. She had to focus. "What now?"

He whirled on her, his uniform as crisp and perfect as if he hadn't just been rolling on the floor with her. His royal bearing was absolute. She wondered that she'd never noticed it in the three days she'd spent with him in New Orleans.

"You will call your friend and instruct her to turn over the child."

Lily shook her head. "Why? So you can marry your princess and raise my child with her? Not just no, but hell no."

Nico's brows drew together. "We will need to work on that mouth of yours. It's unfit for a royal."

Lily snorted. "But not unfit enough for you two years ago when you seduced me, huh? Go to hell, Nico," she said, stressing his name without the title.

"You most definitely require etiquette lessons, *cara mia.*" His gaze raked her from head to toe. "And a suitable wardrobe."

Lily stiffened. Her clothes might not be the height of fashion, but they were usually clean and neat. Unlike now, when she'd spent the last twenty-four hours in a prison cell and just wrestled on the floor with a prince.

Nico retrieved a cell phone from a table. "You and your son will never want for anything again. You will no longer have to work. I will take care of you both."

Lily stared at the gleaming phone held so casually in his hand, his words more seductive than she cared to admit. Never to have to struggle again? Never have to worry about keeping her apartment or her health insurance? Money and freedom from the fear of not having enough to take care of her baby?

But no. What was he offering her—the chance to be a kept woman while he married his princess and had babies with her?

She'd work herself half to death before she accepted such treatment. She'd taken care of Danny this long; she could continue to do so just fine on her own.

"I can take care of my son without you," she said.

His expression grew so chilly she had to suppress a shiver. "Apparently I have not expressed myself in a manner you understand. There is no choice, Liliana. You and the boy belong to me."

Lily snorted. "Even you can't own people, Nico."

He merely smiled at her. A frisson of warning raced down her spine and pooled in her belly. A moment later, he lifted the phone to his ear and began speaking in Italian. This time, it was a conversation, not simply a set of orders. When he finished, he laid the phone on a nearby table.

"What did you do?"

His self-satisfied smile did nothing to ease her tension. "Five million dollars is a lot of money, no? Do you think your friend will turn this down for you?"

Black spots swam before her eyes, but Lily refused to buckle. "My God…"

"*Si,* it is not likely, is it?" He moved closer, shadowing her like the predator he was, impossibly male and utterly beautiful in spite of the hatred she felt for him in that moment. "She will not turn it down, Liliana. Shall I tell you why?"

When she didn't reply, he continued, "Carla has a boyfriend with a little problem. He likes the game tables in New Orleans a bit too much, yes? He has taken much from her in the last three years. Her savings are gone, her house leveraged in excess of its current value. This money represents a new life, *cara mia.* She will not say no."

Lily blinked up at him. She knew she was defeated. Carla hadn't told her the extent of Alan's problems, but Lily had known that it worried her. Carla was almost as bad as her own mother when it came to her slavish devotion to a man who cared more for himself than for her.

His fingers stroked down her cheek, impossibly tender when compared with his actions. She shuddered in spite of her vow not to react. "What do you plan to do with my baby?"

His eyes hardened, his hand dropping away. "*Our* baby, Liliana."

Lily faced him squarely, ready to do battle, heartsick and heartbroken all at once. "You can't buy me off, too, Nico. I will never leave Danny with you willingly."

"Clearly not," he said, his voice deepening with anger. "But you will not need to do so."

Lily gaped at him. "My God, you *are* unbelievable—how do you think your wife-to-be is going to feel about me and Danny, huh?"

"Why don't you ask her yourself?"

"What? Are you insane?"

Nico grabbed her by the arm and propelled her toward the opposite wall, her puny resistance not slowing him in the least. He approached a door, and for one crazy minute she thought it was a bedroom and there was a woman inside. He would throw open the door and there she would be, the Princess Antonella Romanelli of Monteverde, a black-haired gray-eyed beauty, sprawled across silk sheets and pouting prettily because her lover was taking too long to get the *baby mama* under control.

Abruptly, they slammed to a halt, Nico pivoting behind her, the full length of his body pressing into her. She tried to jerk away, but he gripped her chin—more gently than she expected—and forced her head forward.

Lily gasped. "Is this a joke?"

She stared at her reflection—their reflection—in the mirror. The darkness of his fingers against her skin, her hair wild and tumbling around her shoulders in a silky mess. Her pink cotton shirt was stained over her left shoulder, and her eyes, though tired, gleamed with fury. Nico, in contrast, was cool and unruffled. If not for his quickened heartbeat against her, she'd almost think him bored.

But no, there it was, that flash of something in his eyes, in the set of his jaw, that spoke volumes without a sound being uttered.

"No joke, Liliana. I have broken a long-sought-after treaty between my country and Monteverde, not to mention embarrassed my father and our allies, so that I can do what should have been done the instant you conceived my child."

"I—I don't understand," she whispered, searching his face in the mirror, her heart slamming into her ribs.

"Of course you do," he replied, dipping his head until his lips almost grazed the shell of her ear. Almost, but not quite.

"You, Miss Lily Morgan, are about to become the Crown Princess, my consort, and the mother of my children."

CHAPTER THREE

SHE LOOKED UTTERLY STUNNED. Not that he blamed her; he was still somewhat stunned himself. He had a son with this woman, a fact that had the power to punch him in the solar plexus and leave him gasping for breath every time he thought of it.

A son she'd kept secret from him. The electric current zapping through him as he pressed against her was most certainly rage, nothing more.

"You can't be serious," she finally squeaked out. Her green eyes were huge as she blinked at him in disbelief. The platinum color of her hair made her almost ethereal. Surely, this is what had attracted him to her in the first place. That and the fact she'd been blissfully unaware of his identity. The experience was so novel that he'd quite possibly been more attracted to her than he would have otherwise been. She'd treated him like an ordinary person and he'd found it refreshing.

"I am indeed serious, Liliana." He'd gotten his answer in the moments before he'd left his quarters to attend the State dinner. His investigators worked remarkably fast, and what they'd turned up was evidence he could not ignore. She'd given birth almost nine months to the day from the night he'd made love to her. She could have found another lover right away, true, but the child's resemblance to him was too strong to discount. He would of course take the official step of verifying the child's parentage, but it was merely a formality at this point.

When he considered how he'd missed the first seventeen months of his boy's life, how this woman had kept his son from him, he wanted to shake her and demand to know how she could do such a thing. He let her go before the urge overwhelmed him and took a step away.

He would marry her because his personal code of honor would permit nothing less. It was his duty. But he didn't have to like it. Or her.

She spun around to face him. "B-but I'm not a princess, I don't know how to be a prin—"

"You will learn," he said harshly. She wasn't the ideal bride for him, but she could be trained. She was attractive enough, and she'd already proven she had the moxie required to stand up beneath the pressure. When she was coiffed and dressed appropriately, she would no longer appear so common. She was not as beautiful as Antonella, but she was quite lovely in a natural way. Antonella didn't affect him one way or the other. He could take or leave the Monteverdian princess.

But Lily—

Nico crossed to the bar and poured another cognac. This time he downed the liquid himself, welcomed the burn of fine Montebiancan brandy. *Per Dio,* it'd been a hell of a night thus far. And he wasn't finished fighting with himself.

Part of him, a mad and primal part of him, was so completely aware of the woman across the room that he wanted to haul her to his bed and strip her slowly before burying himself inside her for the rest of the night.

Madness. Sheer madness. The urge filled him with both hunger and rage, and he worked to force it down deep and put a lid on it.

In the two months since Gaetano had died, he'd mostly ignored the sensual side of his nature as he'd worked to further

Montebiancan interests and be the kind of heir to the throne that his people deserved. He was sorely regretting the lack at the moment. It made Lily Morgan seem far more irresistible to him than she should be.

"Surely we can work this out another way," she said, her voice small and hesitant. "You can have visitation and—"

"Visitation," he exclaimed, slicing her words off before she could finish. He shrugged out of the sash and tossed it aside, then worked the buttons of his uniform jacket with one hand, throwing it open with an angry gesturc to lct the air from the terrace door he'd left ajar cool his body. This night had thrown him so far out of balance that he half wondered if he would ever recover his equilibrium. "You are quite lucky this is no longer the Middle Ages, Liliana. As it is, you are getting far more from me than you deserve."

If he thought she would be chastened by his words, he was in for a surprise. She lit up like a firecracker. *Dio,* she was lovely. And she'd just cost him five million dollars, a trade treaty with a neighboring kingdom, and every last shred of credibility he'd built since becoming the Crown Prince. Being illegitimate, and having the playboy reputation he'd had before his brother's death, he'd had to work doubly hard to prove himself.

Now, all his effort lay in tatters around him. The thought fuclcd the angcr roiling in his gut.

"More than I deserve?" she said, her voice not small any longer but large and strong. "How dare you! I've been on my own for these two years, enduring what you could not begin to imagine in your ivory tower, taking care of a baby and—"

"Silence!" There was no way on this earth he would listen to her berate him for what had been essentially her decision to keep him in the dark about their child. She would pay for what she'd done. He was far too angry, far too close to losing the last shred of his control. "If you are aware of what is good for you, *cara,* you will not speak of this any further tonight."

She opened her mouth, and he slapped the crystal on the table and moved toward her. When she scurried backward, her eyes widening, he checked his progress. He was on the edge of emotions he'd never felt before, torn between wanting to protect and destroy, and it made him reckless.

He snatched up the phone and pressed the button that would summon his housekeeper. When he put it down, Lily was chewing her lip, arms folded beneath her breasts as if to protect herself. Or to keep warm. The night was probably cooler than she was accustomed to in her native Louisiana. A tremor passed over her, confirming his observation. Beneath her shirt, her nipples peaked, small and tight, and goose bumps rose on her skin.

Nico swallowed, remembering how perfect her breasts had been when he'd first bared them to his sight. How responsive she'd been as she'd moaned and clutched his shoulders when he kissed the tight little points.

Dio, *this was insane.*

Nico shook the memories away and peeled off his jacket. "You are cold," he said as he closed the distance between them. "Take this, *cara.*"

He placed the jacket on her shoulders and she clutched the material around her, thanking him softly. He turned his back on her and moved away.

He heard the intake of her breath, braced himself for what she might say next—but there was only silence.

Finally, she spoke. "Nico, I'm sorry that—"

The door opened and the housekeeper entered, interrupting whatever she'd been about to say. Nico didn't look at her again.

"Please show our guest to her room," he told the woman awaiting his instructions. "And send someone to clean up the broken glass."

Signora Mazetti gave a short bow and waited for Lily to

join her. Out of the corner of his eye, he saw Lily remove the jacket and place it carefully over the back of the settee closest to her. Then she followed the housekeeper without complaint.

Lily awoke to the sound of china and silverware delicately clinking together. She sat up, yawning, and blinked as she tried to take in her surroundings. Brocade curtains hung from a canopy and were drawn back to let light filter into the giant bed. For a moment, she thought she'd been upgraded to the best suite the hotel had—but then she remembered.

She was in the palace, in Prince Nico's apartment. If you could call a wing of a royal palace an apartment. And she was as much a prisoner here as she'd been in the dungeon cell of the old fortress.

A woman in uniform stood off to one side, fussing with a tray. She turned and dropped a curtsy before coming forward and settling the tray laden with bone china and thick silverware across Lily's lap.

"His Highness says you are to eat and dress, *signorina*. He wishes you to join him in precisely one hour."

The woman curtsied again and slipped out the door, closing it behind her. Lily started to set the tray aside, but the scents of coffee and food wafted up to her, reminding her how hungry she was. She'd been unable to eat during the twenty-four hours she'd spent in prison. Last night, all she'd wanted was to shower and sleep—but now her stomach rumbled insistently.

She thought about tossing on her clothes and trying to find a phone—maybe she could call Carla and explain she was being held against her will. Or maybe she could call her boss and tell him she'd been kidnapped. She'd call the consulate herself except she couldn't waste precious time looking for the phone number. *Someone* would help her, she was positive.

Her suitcase had arrived, but her laptop, cell phone and passport had not been returned, naturally. Nico had cut off not only her contact with the outside world, but also any chance of escape. But Lily Morgan did not give up so easily, damn him.

Her stomach growled so hard it hurt, and she had to acknowledge that if she didn't eat something now she wouldn't get very far. Lily wolfed down the fresh bread and thinly sliced meats and cheeses along with a soft-boiled egg and two cups of strong coffee with cream.

Half an hour later, after she'd showered again and dressed in jeans and a T-shirt, she tried the door. It was unlocked and she slipped into the corridor, looking right and left. Which direction had she come from last night? She couldn't remember, so she started down the hall and tried doors. When she emerged into the living room where Nico had coldly informed her she would be his wife, she stumbled to a halt, a shocked "Oh" escaping her. With bright sunlight spearing through the windows and through the terrace doors, the room glittered with gold and colored glass mosaic.

She dragged her gaze from the opulence of the room and searched for a phone, finally finding it on an inlaid cherry-wood table beside one of the velvet couches. Lily snatched it from the cradle, not sure who she should call first.

"You have to go through the palace operator, I'm afraid."

Lily jumped and slammed the phone back down. Nico stood across from her, a newspaper in one hand, a cup in the other. He was so tall and elegant. She didn't usually think of men as elegant, but Nico was. Elegant, gorgeous and so masculine he shot her pulse through the stratosphere just looking at him.

He wore a dark gray suit that was clearly worth more money than she'd ever made in six months of work. The fabric looked beyond expensive, perfectly tailored. He also wore a crisp white shirt with no tie, and black loafers. A ruby signet ring glittered on his right hand.

"I want my phone back."

"You will have a new phone, Lily. And many other things besides." His gaze raked her from head to toe and she bit the inside of her lip. No doubt he saw a poor ragamuffin, a woman unfit to be a princess, and was disappointed. Well, by God, she *was* unfit to be a princess. Nor did she want to be one. She would never, ever fit in here. It was preposterous.

Lily thrust her chin in the air. "I've reconsidered your offer," she said. "You can visit Danny whenever you like, and I will bring him to Montebianco often, but it's impossible for me to marry you. We'll just have to manage another way."

"Manage?" He set the cup and paper down and came over to where she stood, looming above her. He seemed surprised—or maybe he was amused—but quickly masked it with his trademark arrogance. "You have misunderstood once again, Liliana. There was no offer. There is simply what will be."

"You can't possibly want to marry me," she said softly, staring up at him with her heart thudding into her throat. Did he have to be so darn breathtaking?

"What I want is of no consequence."

"It's not what *I* want."

"Perhaps you should have thought of that two years ago."

Lily blew out a breath. "I don't think either of us was thinking much that night, were we?"

A muscle in Nico's jaw ticked as he watched her. "Clearly not. But what about after, Lily? What about when you learned you were pregnant?"

She studied her clasped hands, suddenly unable to look at him. "I didn't know who you really were."

"But you found out. Why did you not contact me then?" His voice was controlled, as if he were struggling with his temper.

Lily put distance between them, instinctively wrapping her arms around herself. How could she tell him she'd been afraid? Afraid he would take her baby away and paradoxically afraid he'd be the kind of father she'd had growing up? Instead, she focused on the one truth that was easily explainable. "Assuming I could have figured out how to get past the layers between you and the public, would you have believed me?"

"Eventually."

Lily bit back a bitter laugh. "Oh yes, how lovely *that* would have been."

Nico sliced a hand through the air, as if cutting through their conversation. "None of this is important now. What is important is that you *still* had no plan to inform me. Had you not found yourself detained here, I would never know of our son's existence, would I?"

"No," Lily said quietly, forcing herself to meet his gaze.

Nico's eyes hardened. "Trust me, *cara*, if there were another way, I would send you far from Montebianco and never see your deceitful face again. As it is, I think we shall have to make do with the situation, *si?*"

"I'm deceitful?" she said, her voice rising. "*Me?* What about you? Not only did you fail to tell me you were really a prince, but you also seem to have forgotten you were supposed to meet me in front of the cathedral—"

"I was called back to Montebianco unexpectedly," he cut in, his voice rising to match hers. "I sent someone to inform you."

"I didn't get the message."

His expression didn't change. "You have only yourself to blame. When my man was unable to find you, I sent out inquiries. Had I known your real name was Margaret, I might have been able to contact you."

Lily bit down on her bottom lip, surprised at how quickly she found herself on the verge of angry tears. She would *not* allow this man to affect her so strongly. Not now. It was too late to discuss what-ifs.

"I've always gone by my middle name. Why would I have told you my legal name as if you were a prospective employer or something? It simply didn't occur to me."

She shook her head. Wasn't it just the story of her life to have something so vital hinge on something as simple as a legal name? "I don't want to be unhappy. I don't think you want to be unhappy, either. And if you force me to marry you, we will both be miserable. You have to see this is true, right?"

"It is too late for that," he said harshly.

Lily tried to sound reasonable. "Why? You could still marry your princess and have children with her. And how can Danny be in line for the throne anyway? Don't princes have to be born legitimate?"

Nico's face was a stone mask. "In Montebianco, royal is royal."

"I don't want this for my child," Lily insisted. "I want him to grow up normal." The wealth frightened her. And not only Nico's wealth, but the atmosphere he lived in. How could Danny be anything but spoiled rotten if he grew up here? How could he become a decent young man, and not a womanizing lothario like the prince standing before her? It terrified her, the thought her boy would be lost to her once he arrived. And that he would become the kind of man she despised most.

Oh God, how could she be tied to a playboy prince for life? Because no matter that she was the only woman he'd ever gotten pregnant—and it must be true considering the lengths he was going to in order to keep her here—he was still the worst sort of Casanova. Would she become just like her mother, desperate for one man's affections and willing to put up with whatever he dished out just to be with him?

Worse, would Nico be a fair-weather father?

"He is *our* child, Lily. You have already tried to deprive him of his birthright with your selfishness."

She blinked. Selfish? Was she? Was it possible?

"That's not true," she said. She sounded defensive to her own ears. And perhaps a bit guilty. In protecting her baby, had she really been trying to keep him all to herself? Had she really been afraid Nico would take him away? Or had her motives been purely because she'd believed he was not the kind of man who could be a good father?

"You will do so no longer," Nico continued. "Daniele is my son and I *will* be his father in truth from this moment forward. If you expect to remain in his life, then you will stand before the authorities and agree to be my wife. That is your choice, Lily."

"That's not a choice," she said, her throat aching with the effort to speak normally. "It's a command."

Nico's gaze was unreadable. "Then perhaps we finally understand one another."

When Nico had said she needed a suitable wardrobe, Lily hadn't realized he'd meant to fly her to Paris to visit couture shops that very afternoon. While they were winging their way to France, he'd finally let her call her boss and explain that she wouldn't be back at work tomorrow as planned.

Hell, she wouldn't be back at all it appeared, though she didn't say that. Darrell was curious, but Lily had no words to explain what had happened. She assured him she was safe, said she would e-mail him her impressions of Montebianco along with the photos she'd taken, and ended the call.

Then she looked over at Nico. He was typing something

on his laptop. "I need to use a computer," she said firmly. "I have a job to finish."

"All in good time, Lily." He didn't look up.

She tried to keep her cool as she explained. "The paper paid my way here and they expect me to finish the job. I can't leave them high and dry."

This time, he did look at her. "Of course. But it can wait until we return to Montebianco, yes?"

"I'd prefer to work on it now."

He closed the lid of his laptop. "Did you not keep notes on your computer?"

"Of course I did. But the police confiscated it."

"It was turned over to me. You may have it back when we are in Montebianco. And then you may access your notes. Does this work for you?"

A current of frustration zapped through her. "Does it *work* for me? What you really mean is that I don't have a choice. Why not say so?"

He smiled, though it held no humor. "Your *choice, cara,* is to wait until we return to Montebianco or to use this laptop." He looked at his watch, glanced out the window. "However, you will need to work fast, as we will be landing very shortly."

Lily crossed her arms and looked away. She knew she'd been snappish, but she couldn't apologize. Not after all he'd put her through the last few hours. When she didn't say anything, he stowed the laptop; twenty minutes later, they were on the ground and exiting the plane.

Once they entered Paris, her black mood lifted a little. Seeing the Eiffel Tower as they drove through the streets was exciting. She wanted to see everything, to spend hours exploring the sights she'd only read about, but Nico informed her they did not have time for touring.

Instead, she was ushered in and out of Prada, Versace, Louboutin, Dior and Hermès—and those were only the names she remembered. She'd never seen such an array of expensive clothes and handbags in her life. Nor had she ever thought she'd own a single piece of clothing from any of them, never mind an entire wardrobe. It was overwhelming to see the bags and boxes piling up.

"Nico, this is ridiculous," she finally said as they drove to the next shop on his list. "No one needs this much stuff."

"*Principessas* do." He looked up from his paper, half-bored, and gazed at her coolly.

"*No* one does," she shot back. Why did he make her feel as if she was six years old?

He dropped the paper onto the leather seat of the Rolls-Royce with a sigh. "Principessa Liliana Cavelli must be as chic and polished as it is possible for any woman to be. She will be the envy of some, the bane of others, and always—" he held up a finger when she would have spoken "—always she must be elegant and beautiful and a proper representative for Montebianco. She will dine with kings and queens, ambassadors, heads of state, and yes, perhaps even her own American president."

Lily felt her eyes widen.

"She is the wife of the next king, and the mother to the king after him. She must look the part and she must never, ever bring shame to the Cavelli name—or to her son—by refusing to do so. It is about more than her own desires, after all. It is about duty and honor, and centuries' old tradition."

"But it seems so extravagant," she said defensively.

"It may appear so now, but you will witness the truth for yourself soon enough. And you would not thank me if I allowed you to be unprepared for the role."

Lily turned away. Damn him for making her feel petty— and over what? Hundreds of thousands of dollars in clothing, shoes, handbags, luggage, belts, scarves, coats and lacy underwear. How did he manage it?

She thought of Danny, of his adorable baby smile and the way his eyes lit up when she came home at the end of each day, and her heart filled with love. Because of this crazy turn of events, her baby would never go hungry, would never do without medicine or a roof over his head or the warmest clothes in winter. He was her entire world; for him, she would wear sackcloth and ashes—or Prada and Gucci.

She despised the idea of accepting so much from Nico— and yet she realized she had no choice. Lily vowed she would teach Danny that money did not make the man. He would not grow up as spoiled and selfish as his father. Somehow, she would make sure he understood.

They didn't speak again and he went back to reading his paper. Soon, she found herself seated in a posh salon with a team of women hovering over her and one of Nico's hulking security guards standing by in the corner—yet another reminder her life had changed drastically. Was she really at risk in a salon? Quite possibly, she supposed. What kind of life would this be, always looking over her shoulder and wondering if danger lurked close by?

A question to which there could be no answer.

Nico stated that he had business elsewhere and would return for her in a couple of hours.

In the salon, at least, she absolutely refused to allow anything to be done that she did not feel comfortable with. Clothes were one thing; they were impermanent, changeable. But her hair and makeup were another thing all together. Hair grew back, but she wasn't accepting a cut that wasn't *her*. Fortunately, the women were under no orders to transform her into something of Nico's design.

Once her hair had been washed and trimmed, it was wrapped in some sort of healing hair mask—or perhaps that was *masque* since she was in France—while two women gave her a pedicure and manicure. A trip to the nail salon had been a little indulgence of hers before she'd had Danny. Since he'd been born, she'd not been able to spare any money, and she'd forgotten how much she missed it.

When the women were finished and she sat with her hands under a portable dryer, her attention was caught by a woman entering the salon. She had an entourage, and she was easily the most elegant, coolly beautiful woman that Lily had ever seen. She carried a tiny Pomeranian dog in one arm. Sable hair hung halfway down her back, rippling like silk when she turned. Beneath her jacket, she wore a thin sweater that rested midthigh with skinny black jeans and vibrant red stilettos. Huge sunglasses looked chic on her, though they would certainly make Lily look like a bug.

That was the kind of woman Nico needed. The kind he wanted her to be. The thought was a little depressing.

The women in the salon flocked to the newcomer, made her comfortable, brought her a café and spoke to her in hushed whispers. A moment later, she was on her feet, striding purposefully toward Lily's chair.

She whipped off the dark glasses, her reddened eyes spearing Lily with a glare. "You are Liliana Morgan?"

"Uh, yes," Lily replied, too shocked to correct her name. And too horrified. She'd only seen a couple of pictures, but she recognized the woman standing over her so angrily.

"I," she said imperiously, "am Princess Antonella Romanelli. I believe you have stolen my fiancé."

Lily swallowed. Oh. Dear. God.

"I'm sorry," she said. "Truly I am." Did she explain everything to this woman? Keep her mouth shut and hope she would go away? What did one do when confronted by an angry princess?

Antonella propped a bejeweled hand on one lean hip. "Of all the places, yes? Here I am, running from Montebianco to soothe my wounded pride, and you appear. Could the world be any crueler?"

Surprisingly, her eyes filled with tears; Lily found herself reaching for the princess's arm almost without thought. But what could she say that would help?

Antonella shifted out of reach before Lily touched her. "I have a habit of chasing away prospective grooms."

She grabbed a tissue from a box on the table and dabbed at her nose. Her gaze moved over Lily, not rudely, but assessing. "How has he chosen you? What have you done to him? *Dio,* I do not see it," she said. "Surely a child is not enough to make a difference."

"I'm sorry for your pain, Your Highness," Lily said, smarting from the remark and feeling her temper rising in spite of the princess's obvious distress, "but not everyone is as privileged or as beautiful as you. And my son is none of your concern."

Antonella laughed, a sweet sound that had no humor in it. "Oh my dear girl, forgive me for insulting you, but you cannot know what you've cost me. You cannot know."

Before Lily could reply, the princess was striding across the room, snapping her fingers and speaking in rapid Italian. She took her dog from an assistant as her entourage regrouped and scrambled to follow her out the door.

Lily numbly watched her progress, a horrifying realization striking her—Princess Antonella was in love with Nico. Did that mean that Nico was in love with her, too?

By the time Lily was finished in the salon, she barely recognized herself. Once the treatment had been washed from her hair, it had been blown out into a sleek mass of shiny, silky platinum before being pulled back into an elegant ponytail. Though Lily was no stranger to cosmetics, with a baby to look after she didn't usually have the time or the money for more than a tube of lip gloss and mascara. Now, she'd been shown how to apply a hint of blush and eyeshadow to accent her natural features. Her lips were a pale pink, and her lashes were long and lush.

She'd been shown to a dressing room where a selection of clothing from today's excursion waited for her. She changed into the slim pencil skirt and white top with tiny pearl buttons down the front. A wide black belt, silk trench coat and sky-high patent pumps finished the ensemble. She rolled up her jeans and sweatshirt and shoved them into the oversize Fendi bag that sat on the cream damask chaise, then studied herself in the mirror.

Did she look like a princess? Maybe. She certainly looked more elegant than she ever had in her life.

But she still felt like Lily Morgan from the wrong side of town, the girl with a chain-smoking, hard-drinking mother and an absentee father. She thought of Princess Antonella, of her beauty and sadness, and felt like the worst kind of human being. She'd come between two people who were right for each other—worse, she was almost glad for it. When she thought of Nico holding his princess, kissing her...

Well, she just couldn't think of it, that's all.

Lily left the salon with the guard at her elbow, guiding her toward the idling Rolls under the awning a few feet away. They were almost to the car when a bright light flashed in her face. And then another and another.

The guard shielded her with his body, moving her forward the entire time as voices called to her in French and flashbulbs lit up the surrounding area like lightning. A second later, the car door opened and she was thrust inside. Her pulse was unsteady as she craned her neck to watch the scene disappear behind her.

"Put this on," a smooth voice said.

Lily spun around, her heart in her throat, to face Nico. She hadn't even known he was in the car. His gaze flicked over her. Was that approval she saw? Oddly enough, she wanted his approval. The thought was not a welcome one, and she dropped her head to look at her clasped hands, her heart refusing to beat normally.

"Lily," he said, and she realized he held out a box. After a moment's hesitation, she accepted it. She didn't bother to ask what it was; she simply opened the lid—and felt the blood draining from her head as she contemplated the sparkling ring.

"It's very big," she said. "A very pretty sapphire."

Nico grasped the box and tugged the ring free. "It is a diamond." He took her hand and slipped it onto her finger before she could protest. The ring was too big and twisted beneath the weight of the diamond. Nico frowned. "We will have it sized in Montebianco."

"I can't wear this," she said, horrified at the size and weight of the hunk of metal and rocks on her hand. A blue diamond? So blue it looked like a sapphire? How much did something like that cost? She didn't even want to think about it.

"This is your engagement ring. You will wear it."

Hurt and confusion cascaded through her as she searched his face. Was he thinking of Antonella? But his expression was emotionless.

Her gaze dropped to her hand and the strange weight on her finger. She'd envisioned shopping for rings someday with a man she loved, going from store to store and trying them on, searching for the perfect one. It would be a joyful thing they shared, not a chore or a duty. Or a command.

This ring was nothing like what she'd imagined her engagement ring would one day be.

"I don't like it," she said, then regretted it the instant their eyes met. His expression was bored, irritated. He did not care. If he'd told her it was a family heirloom, and he was expected to give it to his bride, at least she would have known this meant something to him. But no, he'd walked into a jeweler's—or sent someone, more like—and told them to bring him a rare, expensive ring. This was about status, not tradition, not their child, and certainly not about love.

What would he have chosen for Antonella?

No. She couldn't go there, she simply couldn't. Lily closed her eyes, breathed deeply.

"It's too late," he said. "No doubt someone has already rung the press to inform them I bought this ring. It cannot be taken back."

Lily stared at the diamond, its glittering mass like a huge neon sign of ownership. Everything between them would be very public, she realized. Every look, every gesture, every word. Everything he did was for the cameras. In the space of a day, her life had turned into a reality show. The paparazzi were already swarming, if the incident a few moments ago was any indication. Would she ever know a moment's happiness, aside from the time she spent with Danny?

"How did New Orleans happen?" she said softly, realizing how uncharacteristic it must have been for him. He moved in his own circles, not in hers. It was an anomaly that they'd even met.

Nico studied her. She thought she saw a glimmer of admiration in his eyes. But it was gone quickly and she decided she'd imagined it.

"My life was different then."

"So why me?" She wanted to know, especially now that she knew firsthand the world he came from. Had seen the kind of women he was linked with in the pages of magazines the world over. Women unlike her. Glamorous women, gorgeous women.

Women like Princess Antonella.

"Because you did not know my identity. I found it novel."

The truth was raw, like an open cut, and he'd just poured salt onto it. Of course she hadn't known him. She was from a small town in Louisiana, not a glamorous metropolis. Oh what a cliché she'd been. The country mouse in the big bad city. Everything about New Orleans was grand, and different than she was accustomed to. Clearly, it had affected her judgment. She'd allowed herself to be swept away by his attention and charm, and by the wild abandon of Mardi Gras.

"If not for Danny, I could wish we'd never met," she replied.

He shoved a hand through his hair, the gesture full of frustration and regret. "*Si,* I wish this, too. But it is too late now. You are the mother of my child. Nothing can change that."

No, nothing could. How he must hate her for forever dividing him from the woman he had chosen to marry. He'd as good as told her that he regretted everything about his brief relationship with her. He was marrying her for Danny, nothing more.

Lily turned her head, the landscape blurring as the Rolls glided toward the airport. This was not at all the way she'd imagined her life would turn out.

But for her son, she would endure. He deserved a father, and Nico seemed determined to be one. It was more than her own father had ever done for her. Jack Morgan had never fought to be in her life. He'd seen her more as an inconvenience when he'd been there. If she were truthful with herself, she'd often believed that each time he left, it was because of her. Because she'd been bad or unlovable.

She dashed her tears away before Nico noticed. She was a woman now; she knew it was never the child's fault when a parent left, and yet the memory still had the power to sadden her and make her feel inadequate. She would not ever allow Danny to suffer the same way she had.

The car snaked through heavy airport traffic, finally turning and making its way over the tarmac toward the Boeing 737 that sat with engines idling. The red carpet leading up to the stairs still had the power to surprise her. It was so opulent, so unlike her ordinary world. If not for the red path leading to the stairs pushed against the plane, she might think it simply another passenger jet. There were no markings to indicate who the owner was—deliberately, Nico had informed her—because it provided a certain anonymity.

They exited the Rolls and hurried up the carpet as a group of reporters clamored from behind a line a couple hundred feet away. Nico sent her before him, catching her around the waist when she stumbled on the stairs and righting her.

"Careful, *cara,*" he said in her ear as her heart thudded from his nearness and the sizzling touch of his fingers through her clothes. She made it the rest of the way without incident, greeting the flight attendant at the door with a quick smile.

Two men sat at one of the polished mahogany tables, rising when she and Nico entered the plush black and gold interior. They both bowed, and one motioned to a folder on the table.

"The documents are ready, Your Highness," he said. "We can perform the ceremony as soon as you wish."

Lily whirled to Nico. "Ceremony?"

Nico took her hand in his, squeezed, his eyes flashing a warning. "Why wait, *cara mia?*"

"Wait?" she repeated, her brain having trouble catching up to what, in her heart, she knew he was telling her.

"We are ready," he told the men, anchoring her to his side with an arm wrapped around her. He looked straight into her eyes as he said the next part, "You may marry us now."

CHAPTER FOUR

NICO WATCHED a range of emotions cross Lily's face. Shock, anger, fear—and resignation, *grazie a Dio*. She would not fight him this time.

"Why does it have to be now, like this?" she asked.

He touched her cheek, wasn't surprised when she flinched, and dropped his hand away. He'd expected her to be transformed this afternoon, but not like this. She was more beautiful than he'd thought possible. He still couldn't quite put his finger on it. Was it the smooth silkiness of her hair? The creamy velvet of her skin? Her wide, green eyes?

He didn't know, but he was having trouble remembering that he was supposed to be angry with her. He couldn't forget what she'd done to him, but now was not the time to dwell on it or to allow it to color his actions. There was plenty of time yet to deal with her treachery. And he would most certainly do so.

"A variety of reasons, Liliana," he said. "You must trust me."

She blinked. "Trust you? How do you expect me to do that?"

He grasped her arm, gently, and tugged her away from the magistrate and his assistant. Nico turned her so her view of the two men was blocked. He put his hands on her shoulders, slid them up to her face, cupped her cheeks and stroked her skin. Her breath caught, sending a warm current of need through him. *Dio,* if nothing else, he would enjoy taking her to his bed.

He might be marrying her out of honor and duty, but there were parts of it he could enjoy. *Would* enjoy.

"We must do this for Daniele," he said softly, knowing those words above all others would soothe her. He could tell her they *had* to marry now, in France, before returning to Montebianco, but he didn't think it would persuade her.

He could also tell her that his father was furious, that Antonella's father and brother were demanding retribution, and that unless they married right now, she would very probably be arrested on her return to Montebianco and thrown back into the fortress on charges of receiving stolen property and trafficking in antiquities.

He had no idea whether it was true or not—he was beginning to suspect it wasn't, though it was still quite odd that priceless art would find its way to a street vendor to be sold for a pittance. And yet nothing in her background indicated she knew the first thing about antiquities. But until they located the vendor, or caught the mastermind behind the theft, Lily was vulnerable to charges.

That was why it was now or never. If she went to prison, he would have Daniele—but his son would not have a mother. He would not marry Princess Antonella and raise his child with her; he had enough experience as the illegitimate child to know how his son would be treated by a woman who hadn't given birth to him. He would not take the chance that another woman would view his child as a threat, as Queen Tiziana had always viewed him.

Lily was the boy's mother. No matter how Nico felt about her, his son deserved a mother who cherished him.

"I want to see my son first," she said. "I want to know he's safe and well."

"He will be arriving in Montebianco very soon, *cara mia.* The plane carrying him left American airspace over five hours ago. There is no reason to wait."

She looked both elated and crushed at this news—glad she would be reunited with her baby and sad that her friend had betrayed her. Poor Lily, she'd had no idea that everyone had a price, that those closest to you could always be bought.

"It is time, Liliana."

She still looked hesitant, looked as if she would argue, so he dipped his head and touched his lips to hers—light, brief, the barest caress. And was shocked that he wanted her instantly, wanted to carry her to the back of the plane and the private bedroom there, wanted to make her his before another hour passed.

He would not, of course. When she didn't resist, he ran his tongue over the seam of her lips, testing. She opened to him, and he invaded, tangling his tongue with hers. Their strokes were light at first, teasing. And then, lightning quick, more desperate. He wasn't sure who was driving the kiss any longer, but he dug down deep and found his control, pulled back.

She looked dazed. Nico kissed her again, pressing his advantage as she leaned into him and clutched his lapels, moaning so softly that only he could hear.

When he lifted his head this time, they were both breathing a little harder. "Marry me now."

"Yes," she whispered.

Nico pulled her back to the two men before the effect of his kisses wore off and she dug in her heels again. He held her hand firmly in his, tried not to dwell on how small and cold it was. She'd not been cold when he'd known her in New Orleans. She'd been warm and innocent and vibrant. To see that gone from her now was oddly disquieting.

The magistrate said a few words, they answered ques-

tions when prompted, then signed a couple of documents—
and it was done.

"You will file these immediately, *si?*" Nico said as Lily
drifted away from his side and plopped into a seat as if she
were on autopilot.

The magistrate handed the folder to his assistant. "Of
course, Your Highness. Congratulations."

"*Grazie.*"

The plane was airborne within minutes after the two men
left the jet. Lily hadn't moved from the black leather club
chair. She absently held the stem of a champagne glass a
flight attendant had handed her. She hadn't touched the
alcohol. Nico waved off the attendant when she came to offer
a refill. Lily turned, her expression troubled.

"How did you manage to do that? Aren't there laws that
must be followed when marrying? Didn't we need blood tests
or documents or something? We're not even French."

"Neither were they," he said. At her quizzical look, he continued. "They were from the Montebiancan embassy, *cara.*
This plane, while I am on it, is Montebiancan soil. Legally,
we were married in Montebianco, but a copy of our license
will be filed in France."

She shook her head. "I don't understand."

Nico sighed. "The marriage is recognized in France
because of a reciprocity agreement we have with them. Even
the king cannot dissolve our marriage now."

He watched as understanding clicked. She was very fast,
his wife.

"Your father disapproves, doesn't he? And you believe he
would have refused his permission?"

"Something like that, *si.* It no longer matters now. You,
Principessa Liliana, are my wife."

He thought she would say more, but she simply lifted the
glass in a mock toast. "For better or for worse." Then she

plunked it down untouched and stood, lines of strain brack-eting her mouth. "I'm tired. Is there somewhere on this flying palace where I can lie down?"

"But of course," he murmured. "An attendant will show you."

Far better to send someone else with her. His blood still hummed from the kisses they'd shared. If he took her to the bedroom, it would not be to rest.

Lily was numb. She'd gone to Paris for the first time in her life, but instead of it being a wonderful memory shared with someone she loved, it was a duty she'd been expected to fulfill. She'd been married in the most romantic city on earth—yet her wedding could hardly be called romantic. She stared at the rock on her hand as they rode in silence from the airport to the Palazzo Cavelli. She, Lily Morgan from Port Pierre, Louisiana, was now a princess. She should be happy, shouldn't she?

Principessa Liliana. Princess Lily. Neither of them sounded right to her ears.

She glanced at Nico from beneath her lashes. He was so handsome, so remote, and yet he could be tender. Like when he'd kissed her. Dear God, he'd taken her breath away. She hadn't known who she was or where she was or what she was doing as his mouth slanted over hers. She'd only known hunger and a feeling of rightness that was shocking in its utter conviction. She'd been dazed and ready to do his bidding—which was certainly what he'd intended.

"Marry me now."

"Yes."

But how could he kiss her like that when only a day ago he'd been set to marry Princess Antonella and share his life with her?

Lily didn't understand, and it frustrated her. She had very little experience with men. And all of it was with this particu-larly exasperating specimen beside her. She had to protect herself, protect her child. She was smart enough to realize that if she didn't watch out, Nico would thoroughly confuse her. And that was dangerous for Danny most of all. He was her first priority and she must keep a clear head for him.

When they finally reached the palace, the light was waning. The chauffeur opened the door and Nico exited, turning around to hold his hand out for her.

She reminded herself he was acting a role, just as he was when he'd caught her on the stairs to the plane. It was a public facade, a show for any observers. He appeared solicitous, loving—like when he'd kissed her in front of the magistrate and his assistant. He was a very practiced seducer of women, this playboy prince.

She put her hand in his, trying to ignore the sizzle of awareness that blasted through her. As she emerged onto the cobblestone path, her attention snapped to a helicopter buzzing low overhead.

"It is the media," he said as they started to walk, her hand still caught in his. "I had hoped to keep them away for a day or two longer, but it seems as if the story has broken."

"But you said someone would call them when you bought the ring. Why is it a surprise?"

Nico's expression was stormy. "It is not the ring alone that will have brought them. Someone informed them about our trip today."

She thought of Antonella, wondered if it could have been her. But she was reluctant to say the name to Nico, unwilling to see even a hint of regret or longing in his face. Right now, she felt brittle enough that it wouldn't take much to shatter her steely facade.

"What do we do now?" The helicopter whirred closer as it made another pass.

He slipped his arm around her and guided her toward the doors that were being held open by two palace guards who snapped a salute as they approached. "We carry on as planned."

They passed between the doors and into the ornate gallery that was the main entrance. Nico stepped away from her, his arm dropping. She tried not to be disappointed, was in fact angry with herself for even considering it.

"What *is* the plan?" Lily said, her body still humming in response.

"We are married, Liliana. We will pretend to be deliriously happy with this state of affairs, *si?* You will be obedient and, while we are in public at least, you will play the role of happy wife."

Lily nearly swallowed her tongue. He'd taken everything from her in the space of hours and he wanted her to be happy? She still hadn't come to grips with the fact she would no longer be able to pursue a career, let alone that she'd suddenly become a housewife for all intents and purposes. "Excuse me? I am to be *obedient* and *happy?* What is your role in this farce?"

He looked every bit the arrogant prince in that moment. "I have had much practice at living in the public eye. I do not need instruction. You, however, do."

"So I'm to do as you say, is that it?"

"*Si,* this would be best."

"Did you not consider that I might have had a life planned before you interfered?"

He didn't look in the least sympathetic. "And how could this *life* compare with what you have gained by marrying me? You will never have to work again, Lily. Many women would kill to be in your situation."

Lily's laugh was bitter. "Oh yes, clearly they are banging down the doors. And I'd trade with any one of them in a heartbeat."

His teeth ground together before he whirled from her and strode in the direction of his apartments. She was so busy trying to keep up that she couldn't say anything else as she hurried after him, cursing the platform stilettos pinching her feet. He entered his private wing, then crashed to a stop.

Lily slammed into his broad back, cussing. "What the—?"

A child's giggle registered in her brain.

"Danny!" she cried, darting around Nico's immobile form and sweeping her little boy into her arms. "Oh my baby, my little sweetie, Mommy missed you *so* much."

She hugged him close, burying her nose in his fresh powdery scent. Until this moment, she'd feared she might never see him again. He started to squirm and she lifted her head, smiling at him so broadly her cheeks hurt. He reared his dark head back, his pale blue eyes so much like his father's as they opened wide to look at her. His little lip trembled.

"It's Mommy," Lily said, "Mommy's here. Oh how I missed you, my darling!"

Danny burst into tears.

Lily closed her eyes in relief when Danny finally drifted off to sleep. It'd scared her when he started crying, but she quickly realized she must look different to him. Plus he'd just had a long trip with a strange lady. Not that this Gisela woman seemed to have any trouble relating to him—in fact, she'd come forward quickly when Danny started to cry, and the little boy reached for her. But the last thing Lily needed was to surrender her child to a stranger and watch *her* soothe him. Not after everything else that had happened that day.

She'd ripped her hair from its confinement and mussed it up, smiling and talking to him the whole time. He'd calmed when she looked more normal to him, though he was still a bit fussy, and she'd carried him to her bedroom to lay him down for a nap. It was only midday back home, and he was accustomed to that schedule. It would take time to adjust. No one tried to stop her, and indeed she forgot all about Nico and

Gisela as she walked to the room she'd stayed in last night with Danny in her arms.

Lily's heart was near to bursting with love, but her fingers shook as she smoothed a lock of dark hair from her sleeping baby's face. She'd missed him, and she was frightened for him. For them both. Their lives would never be the same. But for now she was just relieved to see him.

She looked up as the door swung open. Nico stood there, his face clouded with a riot of emotions she didn't pretend to understand. He'd removed the jacket he'd been wearing. The contrast of the white shirt with his olive skin was stark, delicious in a way she didn't want to contemplate but couldn't stop herself from doing. Her husband was a stranger to her, and yet he was connected to her in the most intimate way possible. This child she loved so much was half his.

Half. Lily licked her lips nervously. It seemed incredible they'd come together long enough to make a baby; the man in the entry was so foreign, so unlike anyone she'd ever known. How had they gotten past those differences? How would they ever get past them again?

Nico came over to the bed, gazed down at the child sleeping amidst the pillows Lily had piled around him. Her heart pounded in her temples, her throat. They were so much alike. So very much.

"It is amazing," he said softly, a touch uncertainly. "I had thought perhaps—"

He shook his head, and Lily bit her lip. She wanted to ask what he'd thought, but wasn't brave enough to do so.

Nico reached out, and Lily instinctively grabbed his arm. "No," she said. "You'll wake him."

His tortured gaze met hers. It surprised her to see him look so vulnerable, so unsure. He was Nico Cavelli, the Crown Prince of Montebianco—and yet at the moment he looked like a man lost and alone. It made her heart ache. He dropped his hand to his side, and she felt that aching guilt all over again. Was it truly so wrong to let him touch his son? Or was she being overprotective? She didn't know, and yet instinct made her want to enclose her baby in her arms and never let anyone touch him for fear they would take him away from her.

"I have always been so careful," Nico said, still watching his child. "This was not supposed to happen."

"No," Lily whispered. "But I'm not sorry it did."

Nico's sharp gaze turned on her. "Indeed not. You have gained a kingdom out of the bargain, and more wealth than you could have dreamed possible."

Lily gritted her teeth in an effort not to scream at him. "I was talking about our son. I could care less about the rest of it."

He snorted in disbelief. "Yes, very easy for you to say when there is no question you've benefited enormously from giving birth to my heir."

Anger and hurt warred in her breast. And the desire to lash out. "I do hope you've made sure he's yours before you committed your esteemed royal self to us for life."

He looked at his son. "There is no denying this child belongs to me. But even so, I am certain of it."

A prickling sensation danced on hot feet over her skin. "How? How are you certain, Nico?"

His gaze was haughty. "No matter how strong the resemblance or how convincing the evidence, did you think I would not order a paternity test? He is mine."

Lily grabbed his arm. The muscle beneath her fingers was warm and unyielding. "You stuck a needle in my baby without telling me? How dare you!" She wasn't surprised he'd done it, now that she thought about it, nor was she surprised he could get the results lightning fast. But still, she was furious about the pain it would have caused Danny to have blood drawn. If her baby hadn't been wearing long sleeves, she'd have noticed the mark.

"Do not be a hypocrite, *cara*. He's been vaccinated, which certainly involves needles the last time I checked. It was a necessary precaution."

Lily glared at him. Her voice shook as she spoke. "Don't you *ever* do anything to my child again without permission."

"You mean *our* child, Lily." Danger saturated his words, warning her to beware. He shrugged out of her grip, turned away to look at Danny sleeping. "This is my son. He will be king someday."

And then he began speaking in Italian, shutting her out completely. Lily didn't say anything as he spoke quietly, though she trembled from the force of the emotions whipping through her. Danny was no longer solely hers, no longer her little boy to raise and love. He was a prince, a future king, an exalted being she couldn't understand from her perspective as a small-town American girl. Would he despise her someday?

She couldn't bear to think it, and she sucked in a sharp breath as Nico reached out and touched Danny's cheek. This time, she didn't try to stop him.

A moment later, he turned to her, his gaze icy. "We dine in an hour. Be ready."

Lily crossed her arms beneath her breasts. Why did she feel as if events were escaping her before she could truly understand them?

"I think I should stay with Danny. He's had a long day. He needs me."

"Gisela is qualified to look after him, I assure you. She is a very fine nanny."

"I don't want a nanny," Lily protested. "There's no need."

He shook his head, clearly pitying her. The thought made her angry. And bewildered. Why did she feel so out of sorts around him? Why did she let him intimidate her? She'd spent three evenings with him two years ago, and she'd never once felt less than his equal. Now? Oh God, now she felt as though she would never measure up, as though everything he said or did was a criticism. She was out of her depth, and she resented it. Resented him.

"You have much to learn, Lily. Princesses have many duties. A nanny is required if you are to perform them all."

Lily took a deep breath. "He needs a mother, not a nanny."

"Dinner is in an hour," Nico said. "We are dining with the king and queen. Refusal is not an option."

Lily couldn't find her voice as he walked away. At the door, he turned back. "Wear something formal. Gisela will come to look after our son."

Dinner was held in the king and queen's private apartments in a different wing of the palace. If Nico's quarters were grand, these were opulent. Lily tried not to stare wide-eyed at the priceless paintings, the frescoes and bas-reliefs, the gilding and the footmen, who looked as if they'd been plucked from another era complete with powdered wigs and silk knee pants.

Earlier, she'd thought Nico believed her incompetent because he'd sent not one, but two women to help her dress. Thank God he'd done so. She had to acknowledge that she'd have never managed alone. She was gowned in a dress as fine as anything a movie star had ever worn to a Hollywood awards ceremony, her hair was pinned into a smooth chignon, and she sported an absolute fortune in jewels. Nico had placed the diamond choker around her neck himself, and she'd put on the earrings and bracelet with shaking hands while he thankfully refrained from commenting.

And yet, in the hour since they'd been here, the queen refused to look at her and the king frowned a lot. Worse, they spoke in Italian. Or perhaps that was ideal since she didn't have to formulate responses to any questions or think up appropriate conversation.

She had no idea what they spoke about, and yet she could

see the tension lining Nico's face. Especially when Queen Tiziana said anything. His fist clenched on the table each time. She wasn't even certain he was aware of it. What must it have been like growing up with these two for parents? The thought made her shiver involuntarily.

What had she gotten herself into?

She vowed that Danny would never spend a single moment in their company without her being present. She wasn't certain if they were truly cold, or if it was simply some sort of royal reserve. Perhaps they were perfectly nice people once you got to know them—but she thoroughly doubted it. And until she knew for certain she would protect her son fiercely.

When Nico stood and informed her it was time to leave, she put her hand in his without argument and allowed him to lead her from the table. The king said something, but Nico ignored him. The king spoke again, more sharply, and Nico ground to a halt.

Slowly, he turned, spoke a few words and bowed. The king's face softened, though the queen's did not.

"Good night, my son," he said. "And goodnight, Liliana. Thank you for joining us."

Lily blinked and dropped into her best grade-school curtsy. It seemed the appropriate thing to do. "Thank you for inviting me, Your Majesty."

By the time they entered Nico's quarters, Lily had managed to work herself into a temper. Why had he forced her to endure that? It was *humiliating*. Even when she'd been working the ten to two a.m. shift at Lucky's gas station for minimum wage, she'd never been so mortified. It was as if she'd been invisible.

"What happened tonight?" she asked, an edge to her voice as she dropped her wrap on a velvet couch.

Nico's gaze was shuttered as he contemplated her. "You dined with their royal majesties, the King and Queen of Montebianco. Charming, are they not?"

She didn't think he required an answer. Indeed, he went and poured a measure of brandy into a glass, held it up in silent question. Lily shook her head. He stoppered the crystal decanter and moved to a window, his back to her, one hand in his pocket as he sipped the drink.

Oddly, she felt sorry for him. And worried for her own child. "It must have been quite different growing up in a palace," she said. "I never realized *how* different."

She turned her head to look at her surroundings, seeing them for the first time in a different light. How would a toddler ever play in a room like this? It was filled to the brim with things that could break or be stained in the blink of an eye. And with things that could injure—sharp corners, glass, small objects that could be swallowed.

In short, it was a nightmare.

"True," he said. "But I haven't always lived here. I spent the first six years of my life with my mother."

Lily blinked. "Your mother? But, I thought the queen—"

Nico laughed, but the sound was more a snort of derision. "Queen Tiziana is not my mother, *cara*. My mother died many years ago."

Lily twisted the rock on her hand, suddenly uncomfortable. Moments like this, she regretted never learning more about the man who'd fathered her child. "I'm sorry, I didn't mean—"

"It matters not," he replied. "Life is uncertain, *si?* We cannot look back with regret. It changes nothing."

She felt her anger dissipating, her curiosity about her husband growing. Clearly his life had not been one of unbroken perfection. "Where did you live before coming here? Was it very far?"

He took a seat opposite her, the brandy cradled in his palm. "Not far enough."

Lily didn't quite know what to say to that. She didn't think he meant to share so much—but perhaps he did. Did it change her opinion of him, knowing he'd lost his mother at an early age and been taken in by that icy couple sitting in their miserable grandeur on the opposite end of the palace?

She didn't want to soften toward him, didn't want to have a reason to look at him differently. He'd forced her to marry him, had bribed Carla to turn over Danny, had uprooted her life and changed it so thoroughly she could never go back. And he'd done it all without any care for her wishes.

She despised him and his autocratic ways. And yet—

"My mother had an apartment in Castello del Bianco, and a luxury villa a few miles south on the coast. It was not a bad life." He shrugged, leaned forward. "I'm sorry you had to sit through dinner with them, Liliana. My father is truly not so bad, but when the queen is near, he is more reserved. He is angry with me, but he can do nothing to change it now. He will get over it."

"I—thank you." Good grief, she certainly hadn't expected that!

He stood and set the drink on a side table. "Come, let me remove that necklace for you."

Lily's hand fluttered to her throat. Oh yes, the necklace. The one with the tricky clasp that she'd never manage on her own. He'd changed gears so quickly it threw her, but she went to him, turned and waited, her pulse thrumming so fast that he must surely see it beating in her throat.

His hands, large and smooth, settled on her bare shoulders, sent a chill skimming down the indent of her spine. Lily didn't speak, in fact didn't realize she'd been holding her breath until his fingers slid toward the nape of her neck and it rattled out of her in a shaky sigh.

"So," he said, his fingertips slipping beneath the diamond choker, stroking her skin with little motions that made her crazy, made a feeling she didn't want to examine shoot straight to the liquid center of her, "it is our wedding night, *cara*. What would you have us do first?"

"D-do?"

"*Si*, there are many things we could do." His lips touched her nape, lifted after the barest shivering caress. "Or perhaps we should go straight to bed."

CHAPTER FIVE

HE NEEDED A WOMAN. It'd been too long since he'd lost himself in the pleasures of a female body. Tonight, more than any other, he could use the oblivion a few hours of bed play would bring. He was on edge, perilously so. When he'd walked into this apartment earlier and seen his baby playing on the floor with the nanny, he'd felt as if he'd landed on a different planet. He, Nico Cavelli, had a son. *A son.*

It terrified him in the oddest way. He still didn't understand it. But for the first time since Gaetano had died, Nico wanted to walk away from his duty and his country and return to the carefree life he'd had as one of the most eligible bachelors in the world.

A life he understood. Being illegitimate, he'd never had to live his life a certain way. He hadn't been expected to marry or produce heirs. He'd lived to excess, always pulling the attention away from Gaetano. Tiziana resented him for it, but Gaetano had been grateful. His brother wasn't cut out for the spotlight, had dreaded his upcoming wedding to a woman not of his choosing.

Pain blanketed Nico. The night before his brother drove off the cliff, Nico had told him to be a man. To marry and do his duty and, for once, stop worrying about the public scrutiny.

Nico regretted that he'd not been more sympathetic, that he

hadn't listened to what Gaetano was trying to tell him. Because he knew, didn't he, what had really sent Gaetano over the edge?

No.

Nico dragged his attention back to the woman standing in front of him, her creamy skin glowing in the refracted light from the chandelier as she bent her head to allow him access to the necklace. He needed to focus on her, to shove away the pain. She'd carried his child in her body, had given birth to a son who would carry on the Cavelli name. The knowledge made him possessive.

And more. The blood of his ancestors pounded through him, urged him to storm her defenses, to conquer and pillage, to make her his and plant his seed inside her again. She was his wife now. It was right that they make a brother or a sister to join Daniele. His boy would never be lonely, not as he'd been.

Until he was brought to the palace and had Gaetano to love, he'd had no one. Before her death, his mother had used him as a pawn in her game with the queen. And though Queen Tiziana tried to separate Nico and his brother, Gaetano's love for him was mutual. They were practically inseparable until they were grown and life separated them naturally. And more than life, since Gaetano had chosen to take the final step.

Was it his fault?

"Basta," Nico muttered, turning Lily in his arms, wrapping her in his embrace and lowering his head to capture her lips almost savagely. He *would* have a few hours peace, *per Dio.*

He took her by surprise—and yet on a deep, instinctual level she'd known what was coming. Lily's head dropped back, her mouth opening beneath the onslaught of his before she could think twice about it. This kiss was like the one on the plane, but notched up by several hundred degrees.

This was what she remembered from two years ago, this all-encompassing inferno. A part of her knew she had to resist him—and yet she didn't want to. She wanted to lose herself in the heat of him, wanted to feel again all those things she'd felt before. She hadn't been with a man since that first time, hadn't *wanted* to be with anyone.

In spite of her anger at the circumstances that had bound them together as man and wife, she sensed something deeper than just a physical need in him, something that cried out for contact and closeness. After what he'd revealed to her about his childhood, she was confused by the conflicting feelings crashing through her. Had he done it on purpose to elicit her sympathy?

She didn't know, and she was on the verge of not caring why. He held her tight, his tongue stroking against hers, his mouth both gentle and fierce at once. He tasted like brandy, sweet and edgy and sharp.

Lily trembled involuntarily as he pressed her close, as the hard contours of his body fitted to the soft curves of hers. She had no doubt where he was taking them. There was something altogether bewildering about kissing this man she shared a child with. He was a prince and she was just a girl from the wrong side of town, but right now those distinctions didn't seem to matter.

She wanted him, and she wanted to push him away.

His hands slid over her back, the curve of her hips, and then he found the hidden zipper at the side of her dress. Lily dragged in a rough breath. Should she let this happen? Could she stop him?

Did she want to?

"Lily," he said against her cheek, his hot mouth skimming along her jaw, her neck. And then his lips were on hers again and she knew she was losing the battle with herself.

When her arms went around his neck, Nico knew he'd won. He would get her beneath him, get her out of his head and into his bed and place her where she belonged in his life. This crazy sense of being on a runaway train would subside and he could carry on the way he always had. Once he compartmentalized her, he would have peace again.

And yet something wasn't right. The thought niggled at him, poked at the rawness in his soul until he had to force himself to examine what was wrong. And when he did, he knew it would be a mistake to take her like this.

His history with the Palazzo Cavelli was so twisted and painful that simply being inside it affected him in ways he couldn't quite predict. After that farce of a dinner with his father and the queen, he was especially vulnerable to his bitterness. If he took his new wife now, it would be in anger.

Anger at his father, at Gaetano, at the queen—and, perhaps most of all, at Lily for deceiving him.

It was no way to begin.

He tugged her zipper back into place as he extracted himself from the kiss. She looked up at him in confusion, her pink lips lush and wet, a line forming between her brows. He put his hands around hers where they were still clasped about his neck, separated them gently and lifted them away.

"You should go to bed now, *cara.*"

When he let her go, she hugged herself, a gesture he'd noted she often did when unsettled. She looked vulnerable, confused.

He pushed his fingers through his hair, turned away from her. Away from temptation. God knew he was unsettled, too. His body throbbed with thwarted need. A long, cold shower was definitely in the cards for him tonight.

"I—"

When she didn't finish speaking, he turned to look at her. *"Si?"*

She fingered the diamond collar. "I still need your help to remove this."

"But of course," he replied, making quick work of the clasp and moving away from her as the necklace dropped.

She caught it before it fell to the floor. "Where would you like me to put these jewels?"

"Put them? They are yours, Lily. Take them to your room; stuff them under your mattress or leave them lying on the dresser. It matters not to me."

She clutched the sparkling ornament to her breast, her chest rising and falling a little faster with each breath. "I hope you aren't congratulating yourself for what just happened," she said, the color high in her cheeks.

He stifled a bitter laugh. "Hardly, *cara.*"

"Because you won't catch me unaware again. Next time, I'll be ready."

Nico ignored the painful throb of his groin, the reminder he'd been so close to paradise and pushed it away. One thing he had to give her—even when she was uncertain or afraid, she barreled forward as if she knew exactly what she was doing.

"I do hope so, *bellissima.* It makes the game more fun."

Lily punched her pillow and flopped onto her side. She'd gone to bed more than two hours ago, once she'd finished her report for the *Register* and e-mailed it off, and she had yet to fall asleep. She wasn't certain what had been more humiliating—the dinner where she was ignored, or afterward when she'd practically ripped her clothes off and screamed "Take me" only to have Nico pull back inexplicably.

Inexplicably, hell. She knew why. He'd kissed her because he'd felt sorry for her after the way the king and queen treated her—or maybe it was because with her back to him, he'd been thinking of Antonella, thinking how he should be undressing *her,* kissing *her,* stripping *her* slowly and making love to his exotic princess instead of his ordinary wife.

Lily bit back a groan. Oh God, she'd really debased herself, hadn't she? She thought of the way she'd clung to him, the way she would have done anything he asked in that moment—

and felt shame suffuse her body like the glow of a hot coal. Twice today she'd been ready to do whatever he wanted simply because he'd kissed her.

She *was* pathetic. But no man had ever kissed her the way Nico did. Maybe she should have tried harder to find a boyfriend in the last year or so, find out if another man could affect her the way he did. But she'd always been so busy raising Danny and trying to make ends meet. She'd had no time for men.

And she was sorely regretting it at the moment. Maybe if her mother had tried harder to find another man, she wouldn't have been so vulnerable every time Lily's father rolled back into town and decided he wanted a place to stay. And a woman to take advantage of.

Lily turned onto her back, heard the contented gurgle of her baby in the crib nearby, and felt her exhaustion and anger melt into relief, even if only for a moment. Danny was her reason for being, her *only* reason for being. She would not lose her head over a man, and certainly not a man who didn't care for her as she deserved. Nico was smooth, treacherous. He was a playboy prince, accustomed to women falling into his bed at the mere suggestion they should do so.

He was toying with her, punishing her perhaps. She would not allow him to humiliate her again.

The next morning didn't start off so well. Lily awakened in her room alone, then panicked as she ran through the apartment trying to find where her baby had gone. In the moment she woke up, she hadn't thought of the nanny; she only knew her baby was missing. Had he crawled out of the crib somehow? He was a little dynamo, had been known to escape his crib at home a time or two as he got bigger.

She'd been ready to tear the palace apart when Nico found her in the living area calling Danny's name and on the verge of tears.

"He is not here, *cara*."

Lily's breath froze. "Where is he? What have you done with him?"

Nico's expression grew frosty. "I've not kidnapped him, Liliana. He is fine."

For once, Lily felt chastened. But only slightly. "I want to see him."

"You cannot." He checked his watch, then speared her with the full force of his stare. "We are retiring to my private *palazzo* for a few days. I have sent Gisela ahead with Daniele. They will meet us there. You must get dressed."

Though Lily was furious with him for making a decision about Danny without consulting her, it did no good to rail at him. He merely shrugged it off and told her to hurry.

Now, she sat beside him in his silver Maserati and watched the miles fly by as they snaked toward their new abode. Montebianco was far more beautiful than she'd realized. At one point, they drove through a lush, almost tropical forest before emerging onto the coastal road. Around every corner, cliffs jutted out to sea, their white faces stark and beautiful. Below, the turquoise water lapped their bases.

In fact, the farther Nico drove, the less traffic they encountered and the fewer homes, except for those perched on the cliffs overlooking the Med. It was all so exotic, so exciting. She, Lily Morgan—no, Lily *Cavelli*—was zipping along the Mediterranean coast with a prince. Who would have ever thought it?

The sun was strong and bright, and Lily was thankful she'd gotten new sunglasses that wrapped around the corners of her eyes to minimize the light. She'd been uncertain how to dress, but she'd finally chosen espresso capri pants with a cream top and a pair of low-heeled sandals. Her French-manicured toes looked very elegant, she thought. Nico hadn't commented on her attire, so she supposed what she'd chosen was appropriate.

"How far is it?" she finally asked after they'd been on the road for nearly an hour.

Nico glanced at her. "So you do remember how to talk."

Lily shifted in her seat to look at him. "I was waiting until I could speak without the urge to shout at you."

His mouth lifted in a grin that sent her heart skittering. "It took a long while, yes?"

"I'm sure the urge will return quite soon," she replied. "This conversation may be brief."

He laughed, a warm rich sound that she'd not heard since they'd sat together at a restaurant in the French Quarter two years ago. She'd forgotten how much she enjoyed the sound. She'd been captivated with him then, and his easy laugh had certainly been part of the charm.

"We are nearly there," he said. "You've wasted the entire trip pouting."

"I was not pouting."

"Indeed you were. I am quite accustomed to women's moods, *cara*. I recognize pouting when I see it."

Lily chewed her lip. Mention of his experience with women did nothing to enhance *her* mood. She chose to ignore it and move on. "What will we do in this new place that we could not have done in Castello del Bianco?"

Nico's hands flexed on the wheel. "We will have some peace from the curiosity seekers, for one. And far fewer people to deal with. No king and queen nearby. We can play on the beach, take walks, swim. It is like your American vacations, yes?"

Vacations weren't something she'd ever had time for, but she understood what he meant. She latched onto something he'd said. "What do you mean by curiosity seekers?"

He seemed to consider for a moment. "You cannot imagine our hasty marriage has not garnered attention."

"No, of course not."

He glanced at her again. "You are new to this, Lily, but you must realize that the media will go to extraordinary lengths to pry into our lives, to find stories to tell, and some of those stories may embarrass or anger us. It is something you learn to live with."

"Don't you fight when the stories are wrong?" The *Port Pierre Register* was small, and yet they always printed corrections when someone disputed an article.

He shrugged. "It is almost never worth the effort."

"No one bothered you in New Orleans. I would have certainly remembered if you'd gotten media attention."

"*Si,* this is true. But I was in the city anonymously, and my brother was still the Crown Prince. The American media are not so interested in European royalty, yes?"

Lily tucked a lock of hair behind her ear as she watched him. "You have a brother?"

His jaw tightened as he concentrated on the road. For a moment, she thought he might not answer. "*Had* a brother, *cara mia.* He is dead."

"Oh." Impulsively, she reached out and touched his arm. "I'm sorry."

"*Grazie.* He died two months ago and I miss him every day."

Lily swallowed a lump in her throat as she turned away. She'd been so focused on Nico as a tyrant and a playboy that she hadn't imagined him to have a softer side, a side that felt deep emotion and experienced pain. Of course she knew he must, but she'd not expected he would let her see into his life like this. Not so soon anyway.

Just then, they rounded the final turn and a sprawling complex appeared before them. It was sleek, modern, not at all what she'd expected. "I thought you said we were going to a palace!"

"It is a palace—but it is *my* palace. I had it built a few years ago, and I consider it home." He pressed a button in the car and the black iron gates swung open to admit them. Moments later, he pulled into a sleek garage beneath the house and shut off the engine.

Inside, the house was nothing like the ornate confection of his apartments in the Palazzo Cavelli. The furniture was sleek, modern. Soft leather couches, hardwood floors, plush Oriental rugs, and modern art. It was very masculine—and yet, it was beautiful in its restraint.

Nico looked at her. "We will probably spend a lot of time here, *cara*. If you wish to change something, this is possible."

She shook her head slowly. "No, I'm not sure I would change a thing. I like it."

"Nevertheless, if you should change your mind." He tossed his keys onto a table behind the sofa. "Now, if you wish to see Daniele's room, follow me."

The house was large, but not as big as the palace, so when they came to her baby's room she wasn't quite prepared for the sight that greeted her. Toys filled every corner of the room, giant stuffed giraffes, pandas, a bear—Lily's hand went to her mouth as she took it all in. The furniture was grand—a plush couch, an entertainment center with a flat-screen television, a chair—but there was no crib, no dressers. Perhaps there hadn't been time. He'd only learned he had a son two days ago.

Nico grinned at her. "It is a suite, Lily. Here." He took her hand, led her through the room, into a palatial bathroom, and out the other side to another grand room—only this one had a crib, dressers, a changing table and a wall of bookshelves filled with children's books. Gisela sat in a rocker, but she popped up and curtsied when they walked in. For the first time, Lily realized how young the girl was. She was barely twenty, Lily would bet. Far too young to know about babies. She made a mental note to speak with Nico further about this nanny idea.

"Mamamamamamamama!" Danny cried, wobbling toward her as fast as he could on his little legs.

Lily's heart filled. She dropped to her knees and held her arms wide as her baby ran headlong into them.

"Mama," he said contentedly as she stood and hugged him tight.

"Who's my little Dannykins? Who's mama's baby? Is this mama's baby?"

Danny giggled in delight as she pulled his shirt up and blew a raspberry on his belly. She laughed, then glanced at Nico. His expression was not at all what she expected. A mixture of pain and anger played across his handsome face. She turned away, cradled Danny against her as her heart picked up speed.

"Mama," Danny said again, then began babbling something unintelligible. He stretched his arms out, trying to get down, and she set him on the floor again. He promptly toddled back to the little truck he'd been playing with on the soft carpet.

Nico watched Danny play, his nostrils flaring, his jaw tightening. He flexed his fingers at his side, though she didn't think he was aware of it. It was as if he wanted to move, wanted to touch Danny—but couldn't bring himself to do it.

And it hit her that he must feel like a stranger in this little triangle. He was the one left out, the one looking in.

"He's learning new words all the time," Lily said softly, her mind reeling with conflicting thoughts. Danny was his son, and they were strangers. Could she bring herself to help him? She frowned, torn between the desire to keep Danny to herself, to protect him, and the knowledge that she was being selfish, that Nico was Danny's father and her son deserved the best father possible. If Nico remained the outsider, how would that benefit Danny?

Lily swallowed her trepidation. "If you went and played with him," she said, "it would help him get to know you."

Beside her, Nico stiffened. His face, when she dared to look, was a blank mask. But his eyes—

Oh God, if his eyes were flames, she would surely be burned to a crisp in them right this second.

"It will take time," she offered, trying to make him understand. "But you have to—"

Nico turned and left the room.

CHAPTER SIX

LILY WENT AFTER HIM, but Nico knew the house much better than she did and he was gone before she could catch him. She stood in the empty living room, uncertain whether to keep looking for him or to return to Danny.

Why had Nico left so abruptly? She'd been trying to help him, trying to make him understand it would take time to get to know his son. The pain on his face had twisted her heart, pricked her with guilt. It was her fault he was a stranger to Danny. In that moment, she hadn't liked herself very much and she'd wanted to make it right.

Unable to find him, she eventually went back to Danny's room, sent Gisela away and played with her baby until he crashed. As she tucked him into his crib, a fat tear dropped onto the back of her hand. She scrubbed it away, then dashed her hands beneath her eyes to get rid of the rest of them.

What was her problem? She'd tried to help, but Nico refused her advice.

She needed to move around, needed to burn off some of her restless energy. She found Gisela on the couch in the other room and asked her to please keep an eye on Danny while he slept. Then she wandered the big house, poking into rooms and stepping onto myriad terraces that all had fabulous views of the sea. She hoped she might find Nico, might explain to him that he needed to spend time with Danny, that it would all be well if he would do so. But he wasn't in the house.

She found the clothes he'd bought for her in a closet the size of her apartment back home. Another closet, as masculine as hers was feminine, adjoined it, and she knew she'd probably stumbled into the master suite. Beyond the closets, a bathroom the size of a small city had floor-to-ceiling windows that looked out at the ocean, and a giant spa tub sunk into the floor in front of them.

Unbelievably, there was a butler's pantry attached, complete with a refrigerator and wine rack. Perfect, she supposed, for entertaining guests in the tub. Female guests, no doubt.

Princess Antonella?

Lily shoved the thought aside with a mental growl. She hesitated at the bedroom door, then slid it open on silent rollers and stepped inside. It was a large room with a king-size bed that dominated one wall. Again, floor-to-ceiling windows looked out on a view as spectacular as any she'd ever seen. She crossed to the terrace doors, but stopped when her attention was caught by a trio of framed photos on a table beside a club chair.

In the first, two boys, close in age, stood with their arms around each other, smiling. The next was of a young man, caught in a moment of exuberance, laughing at the camera— Nico's brother, she guessed. The third was a formal portrait of Nico as a child; it must have been shortly after he'd come to the palace. He looked so solemn. Unhappy. He wore a uniform much like the one he'd had on the other night, though without the medals, sword or sash.

Lily picked up the photo, studied it. The resemblance to Danny, even now, was remarkable. She wondered why the picture was important to Nico, why he displayed it when the boy in the frame looked so unhappy. Didn't most people surround themselves with photos that evoked pleasant feelings?

"It reminds me of who I am."

Lily whirled, clutching the frame to her chest. "Oh God, you scared me."

Clad in head-to-toe black, he looked as dark and devilish as any demon. It took her a moment to realize he was dressed in motorcycle leathers. For some reason, her heart rate jumped.

He rode a motorcycle? He raced the hairpin curves they'd driven on the way out here? Challenged the sheer drops that plunged to the sea? How could he be so irresponsible? What would they do if something happened to him?

He came to stand beside her, the scents of warm leather, wind and, yes, even oil permeating her senses. Her nipples tingled in response, shocking her. Her boyfriend in Louisiana, before she'd ever met Nico, had worked on a farm. He'd often smelled of grease and outdoors, and she'd never once found that sexy.

But Nico, a gorgeous, wealthy prince—

The contrast aroused her for some reason. Pathetic.

His shoulder bumped against her as he pointed at the picture of the two boys. "Gaetano is on the left."

"He's not as tall as you," she said stupidly, only half paying attention. Threads of fire spread through her at his nearness, currents of sweet need thickening her veins. What was wrong with her? Why could she not control this feeling when he was around?

"*Si,* and he was older by three years. Very interesting, yes?" He didn't wait for an answer. "The other is a few years later. Gaetano was laughing at something, I don't remember what. We went to Australia that summer, and I'd never seen him freer. It was quite extraordinary, but then you would have had to know my brother to understand."

"Maybe he didn't like being the Crown Prince," she ventured. Who would, as unhappy a place as the Palazzo Cavelli seemed to be?

Nico nodded slowly, surprising her. "Yes, I believe it was that. And more. He never told me exactly."

Lily thought of her mother, how she'd never understood the choices the older woman made. The way she lived her life for one man in particular, then fell apart during the periods he was gone. Maybe it wasn't the same thing, but at least Lily understood what it was to love someone and not understand them or be able to penetrate the armor they cloaked themselves with.

"What happened to him?" she asked softly.

Nico took the frame she still held, gazed at the child in the photo. "It was suicide, *cara.*"

Shock and sorrow crashed into her. She'd known a girl in high school who took her own life. The blow was too much for her parents to weather; they'd divorced not quite a year later, and the mother left town. The girl's brother had withdrawn, too, finally quitting school and spending time in jail. All their lives had been irrevocably changed by that one act.

How had Nico's brother's death affected him? The king and queen?

"I'm very sorry," she said. "No one should lose a family member like that."

It seemed such an inadequate thing to say, but it was all she could do. He kept his gaze focused on the photo. "No, no one should," he said.

She wanted to ask him more about his brother, but she was afraid to do so. She was, in fact, amazed he was even talking to her after the way he'd looked at her earlier. She wanted to reach out and hug him, but instead she changed the subject.

"How old were you in that picture?"

"Six. My mother had died three days before."

He couldn't miss her indrawn breath. There'd been so

much pain in his life. It broke her heart to think of it, to think she'd contributed even a fraction to his sorrow.

Leather creaked as he shifted toward her. "It was not so bad after a while. I adapted."

She felt her eyes filling. "But you were a boy. You should have had more time."

"Life does not always cooperate, *si?* I lost my mother, but I gained a brother."

A brother he'd lost, as well. "No one should only get one or the other."

"No, this is true."

"Was it very bad? Being raised in the palace, I mean?"

"I have nothing else to compare it to."

She couldn't imagine the queen being very kind to a motherless boy, especially one whose presence reminded her that her husband had gone outside their marriage vows. "You must have missed her. Your mother."

"I hardly remember her now, *cara.* She was always busy— and then one day she was gone."

Lily swallowed the hard lump in her throat. *No child should be that lonely.* She stood beside him, unmoving, feeling his presence so strongly that his every breath felt as if it were her own. She could not have moved away if her life depended on it.

But he could. He set the photo down and stepped away. In the next instant, the oily *zrrittt* of a zipper filled the silence before his jacket landed on a chair. He stood before her in a tight white T-shirt that clung to sweat-dampened muscles. His hair, she realized, was also damp and hugged his head in a mess of runaway tendrils that she ached to touch.

The leather pants were tight, well-worn in patches from gripping his legs around the motorcycle. He also wore heavy black boots with buckles that cinched over the pants, and she found her breath catching in her chest.

It wasn't fair. He threw her off balance looking like that, like every girl's bad boy dream. She could see him roaring up to a smoky nightclub, riding off into the night with a woman wrapped around him—a woman who knew a night of sinful pleasure awaited her.

Lily wanted to be that woman. She wanted to peel the shirt from his chest and lick her way down—

Oh God.

"Need something, Lily?" he asked softly.

Her pulse quickened. "No, I—" She pulled in a deep breath. "Of course not. Why do you ask?"

"Perhaps I can give you what you need," he said. "You have only to ask."

"I'm—" *Breathe, Lily.* "No, it's nothing. I was just thinking about something. I'm sorry, what were you saying?"

"It is not important," he said, watching her. "I'd much rather talk about what *you* were thinking."

"I—I better go see if Danny's awake," she replied, shivers chasing over her body. How did he do this to her? How could he look at her with such hatred earlier and then flirt with her now?

Because he was an expert, that's why, a Don Juan who'd seduced hundreds of women. She could not forget who she was dealing with. He didn't care about her. He was merely reacting to the vibes she was giving off.

Stop it now, before you do something stupid.

Nico closed the distance between them. "What's the matter, Liliana? Afraid to admit what we both know?"

She tilted her head back, meeting those piercing eyes, the depths that were awash in humor and something more. Desire?

"I'm not afraid of you," she said.

His smile was instant. Devilish.

Delicious.

"Did I say you were?" He reached out, twirled a lock of

her hair around a tanned finger. It was only hair, yet she trembled as if he were stroking her skin. "It's inevitable, Lily. We *will* end up in bed together. Quite probably sooner than you think. There is no need to fight it."

She had to struggle to speak normally. "I'm not fighting anything. You're delusional."

"Am I?" His fingers slipped to her collarbone, stroked their way up her neck to her jaw. He grinned when he passed over the thrumming beat of her pulse. "Perhaps we should test this theory...."

Lily marshaled what shreds of willpower she had left and jerked away from him. "There's nothing to test, Nico."

He didn't try to touch her again, but his mouth was still crooked in that knowing grin. His voice was a sensual purr. "Run, Lily. Run far and fast before you find yourself sprawled naked on my bed. Because if we begin this, I will not stop until it's finished."

Her entire body shook with fear. No, not fear. *Desire. Need. Want.*

In another minute, she'd be the one shoving him backward onto the bed, the one tearing at his shirt and slipping her hands into his pants—

Lily ran, his mocking laughter following her down the hall.

Nico slid beneath the shower spray, the cool water a welcome relief from the heat of his wild ride along the coast. No, it was more than that. He needed the cold water to calm his raging desire for his wife. *His wife.*

Only a day later and he still felt a mixture of amazement and bewilderment that he had a wife, much less one that twisted him up inside unlike anything he'd ever experienced. It was simply her proximity, the fact she was desirable and that he hadn't had a woman recently—not to mention the way she'd looked at him a few minutes ago.

As if she'd spent a week in the desert and he was the first glass of water she'd seen in all that time.

He'd been more than willing to quench her thirst. He still had a hard-on, damn her. He let his soapy hand slide over it, groaned. He could relieve himself, certainly, but it wasn't the same. He twisted the shower dial to cold and resisted the urge to shout as the needles of icy water pierced his skin.

He closed his eyes, leaned his forehead against the tile and willed his raging libido to subside. For now anyway.

How could he want her like this when he'd watched her with his son earlier and had it driven home how much he'd missed in his boy's life thus far? Danny—for so she always called him—said *mama*. He walked. He knew who his mother was and ignored the man standing beside her.

Ignored his *father*.

She'd urged Nico to go play with the boy, but he'd felt like his heart was on the outside, like if he did so she would see how uncertain he was, how much it hurt to be a stranger to his child. He didn't know anything about children, not really. He'd spent minutes with them, not hours. He, who was in supreme control in every other instance of his life, had no idea what to do with his son—and it bothered him.

Instead of going to his son, he'd fled. *Dio,* like the worst kind of coward. But he'd felt too much in that moment and he hadn't quite known how to handle it. A long ride on his Ducati with the wind slipping past and the purr of the motor beneath him was exactly what he'd needed to clear his mind.

When he thought back to that moment when his baby ran to Lily, every feeling he'd ever had of not belonging, of being the outcast, crashed through him once more. Remembering those feelings helped him not want Lily so much.

But he still wanted her. And he knew what he needed to do. He would not creep around his own house, avoiding his wife and remaining a stranger to his son. No, he would learn how to be a father to his boy—and he would bed his wife.

Very soon, she would beg for his touch. She'd nearly done so just now. If there was one thing on this earth he knew how to do—and do well—it was seduce a woman. Though he could command her to share his bed, the idea was nearly laughable. Prince Nico Cavelli did not ever need to order women to get naked for him.

He would not start now, and certainly not with the woman he'd married.

Lily was feeling quite cranky when she woke and dressed the next morning. She'd spent the night in a state of flux—one minute she was cold, the next hot and throwing off the covers. Unfortunately, all the times she woke up in a sweat coincided with short, intense dreams about a certain prince in motor-cycle leathers.

She hadn't dreamed of sex in a long time, but she'd more than made up for it in the span of one night. She'd had shadowy impressions of skin against skin, of his lips against hers, of his hot velvet length sliding inside her, filling her so deliciously that she thought she might die from the pleasure of it.

She could almost believe those things had really happened if she hadn't awakened alone each time, panting and aching with desire. No matter how delectable her dreams, she had to resist the temptation to give herself to him. Because down that path lay ruin and pain. She wasn't naive enough to think she could manage a lifetime with him without being intimate—they were married and he would want more children, as did she—but there had to be a point at which she could isolate that most vulnerable part of herself and keep it locked away.

It would simply take time to find it, but she would do so. For her sake, and for Danny's. Until then, she would have to be careful.

When she emerged from her dressing room, she first went to Danny's room. He wasn't there, so she continued toward the kitchen. This time, she wasn't panicking that Danny'd been spirited away.

Lily heard voices and smelled food as she approached the kitchen, but the sight that greeted her when she stepped inside the large, sunny space was not one she could have ever expected. Nico stood at the stove, a pan in one hand, a spatula in the other. He smiled when he saw her, and her heart tripped.

"Ah, so you have decided to grace us with your presence after all."

"It's only eight-thirty."

"Yes, but we have been up since six."

She looked beyond him to where Danny played in a corner with a set of building blocks. When he saw her, he launched to his feet and toddled toward her, babbling happily. She caught him in her arms and covered his face in kisses while he laughed.

When she looked at Nico, he'd turned his attention back to the pan. "What are you making?"

He glanced up. "Eggs. For you."

Lily's eyebrows climbed toward her hairline. "For me?" she practically squeaked.

"*Si*." He grinned at her. "Do not look so frightened, *cara mia*. I am capable of cooking quite a few things, eggs being one of them."

"Why would a prince need to cook?" She'd imagined him with a personal chef and a staff of waiters, had seen it in action in the palace in fact. But she'd never imagined him cooking. And never for her. That was certainly not something that happened in any of the fairy tales she'd ever read. What an unexpected man her prince was turning out to be.

"Princes need to know many things," he said, moving the spatula around the pan. "Besides, the queen considered it edifying to have me learn tasks she thought menial."

Lily frowned. "Did your brother learn them, too?"

"He did, but only because he defied her to be with me." He shrugged. "Let us not talk of this anymore, hmm?"

Danny started to struggle and she set him down. He immediately went back to his toys. "You watched Danny all morning?"

She sensed the sudden tension in the set of Nico's shoulders, and it troubled her. Why was he afraid to spend time with his son? Did he think she would disapprove? It bothered her to realize that only twenty-four hours ago, she would have. And, while a part of her was still jealous at the idea of Danny needing anyone but her, she wanted what was best for her child.

A father—a happy, involved father—was best for them all.

"Gisela fed and dressed him, and we have been playing for the past hour while she uses the gym."

"Gym?"

Nico grinned at her again. "You are full of questions this morning, *Mi Principessa*. Food will cure that, perhaps. But yes, there is a gym in the house. Very good for keeping one's figure."

She imagined him pumping iron and thought her heart would stop, especially when her brain insisted on clothing him in leather pants and a damp T-shirt. He indicated a bar stool at the large center island. Then he set a plate in front of her, and she dug in with her fork while he poured coffee.

"Wow, it's good," she said, and he laughed.

"You did not believe I could do it, did you?"

Lily couldn't hide a smile. "No, I really didn't. Who would risk telling a prince his eggs taste like burned cardboard? I thought perhaps no one ever told you the truth before."

She stabbed her fork in again, took another bite of the perfectly scrambled eggs. They were creamy, silky and tasted like butter. How much time had he spent in a kitchen anyway? Lily decided she disliked the queen even more. "It really is delicious."

"I would have done this for you two years ago," he said,

jolting her with the memory of that morning, "but we had no kitchen in our room."

She took a hasty sip of coffee, hoped she could blame the rush of heat to her face on the hot liquid. This was too intimate, sitting here with him as if they were a happy couple, and she felt too exposed. She didn't want to talk with him about that night, not now. Perhaps if she moved on to the most obvious contradiction, he would leave it alone. "It must have been quite an experience for you, spending the night in a cheap hotel like that one."

His eyes gleamed wickedly. "I don't remember the room, *cara*. It had a bed. The rest is unimportant."

"You left before I woke." She knew her voice held a note of accusation, but she couldn't seem to prevent it. She'd been disappointed that morning to find him gone—but he'd left her a scribbled message, and she knew it was only a matter of hours before they would meet again.

Except he'd never shown up. And she'd cried for two days when she realized how foolish she'd been. She'd given herself to a man who'd used her for his pleasure and abandoned her.

How familiar was that?

He placed a hand on hers where it rested on the marble counter. "I did not want to go, but duty called, as I have said before. Unfortunately, it also called me back to Montebianco when I found out the true extent of the problem."

"What happened?"

She *wanted* to understand. The feelings she'd experienced had been so new, so amazing and tender, and she'd wanted to keep them for far longer than she'd been allowed. That had been her first real heartbreak. Because a part of her had fallen hard for the man she'd chosen to give herself to, and the truth of how wrong she'd been about him had been devastating.

His thumb traced a path on the back of her hand, sending

spirals of sensation rolling through her in waves. "It was the first time my brother attempted suicide, Liliana."

His sadness lanced into her. She'd been so focused on herself and her feelings about that night that she hadn't considered something terrible might have happened. And now she felt that aching guilt again. It was almost as if the universe had conspired to keep them apart.

Silly. Even he had been there that night, it wouldn't have lasted between them. He was a prince, for pity's sake. She was no one.

"I'm really sorry, Nico. I can't imagine how hard it must have been for you and your family to go through that with a person you loved."

He caught her chin in his fingers, forced her to look him in the eye. "And it must have been difficult for you when I did not return, yes? I would have been there had it been possible."

Perhaps he would have. But she refused to dwell on it. That naive girl was gone, buried under the weight of harsh reality and motherhood. She pulled free of his grip. "We can't change the past."

"Yes, but—" He looked down, his brows drawing together. "*Si,* little one?"

Lily dropped her fork and pushed herself up in her seat, leaning as far as she could over the island. Danny stood beside Nico, clutching his pant leg with one hand. The other arm was stretched up, his little hand opening and closing. A sharp pain pierced Lily's heart—but was it joy or fear?

"He wants you to pick him up," she said softly, biting her lip hard to keep her silly tears from spilling.

Nico looked at her for a split second, a mixture of terror and confusion on his handsome face. She could have laughed if her heart weren't breaking. "It's okay, Nico. Pick him up. He'll want down again in a minute."

Miraculously, he bent over and scooped Danny into his

arms. And then he looked at her as if he feared he'd need more instruction. Danny, for his part, looked thrilled at the new heights he'd reached. Nico was indeed tall, and Danny seemed to delight in it.

Finally, he put his arms around Nico's neck and burbled a string of unintelligible words.

"What did he say?"

Lily shrugged and tried not to laugh. "I wish I knew."

"I thought women were supposed to understand baby talk."

"I know when he wants something, but sometimes it's not so clear. He likes the sound of his voice, I think."

Danny touched Nico's nose, then touched his own. *"Naso,"* Nico said. "Nose."

Danny laughed. The sound coaxed an answering smile from Nico while Lily could only stare at them both in wonder. Two dark heads so close together, smooth olive skin—Nico's was darker, of course—and eyes that could be a mirror to the other when they both turned to look at her.

Nico frowned. "Why do you cry, Liliana?"

"What? Oh." She swiped the tears away guiltily. "It's nothing."

"Ma-ma."

Lily smiled. "Yes, baby boy?"

He stretched his little arms toward her. She looked at Nico hesitantly, but he was already leaning forward, letting Danny reach for her. A second later, she had her baby in her arms. She tickled him, blew raspberries on his belly while he laughed uproariously, then kissed his little face until he protested. Another minute and he was down, his attention caught by the blocks once more.

"He is amazing," Nico said with that sort of singular pride that all parents had in their babies.

Lily felt a bubble of joy lifting toward the surface of her

soul. "Oh yes," she said solemnly, "the most amazing baby in the world."

Nico looked at her, his mouth crooking into a grin. A second later, they were both laughing.

The next few days were some of the most idyllic of his life. Nico spent time with Lily and their son without any expectations. He continued his slow seduction of Lily's mind and body, not rushing the process in the least. He was in fact enjoying it. He touched her as much as possible, brushing up against her as he passed, reaching across her to pick something up, his arm skimming her breast if he could manage it.

It was driving him crazy, touching her without *touching* her. He wanted to strip her, explore her with his hands and mouth, wanted to do all the things he'd realized were impossible due to her inexperience the first time. He wanted to spend days learning her body, wanted to know what drove her crazy and what made her come unglued in his arms.

He was driving himself crazy, but more importantly he was driving *her* crazy. When they made love for the second time, it would be well worth the wait.

He was also, gradually, becoming more comfortable with his son. He no longer felt stirrings of panic when Danny wanted to be picked up, no longer worried he would drop him or hold him wrong. In fact, it was almost ridiculously easy to make the child happy. Why had he not realized this before? Tickle him, make faces, talk silly—and the little guy was fascinated. So, Nico realized, was Lily.

Still, he didn't play with their son because it made her happy. He played with him because it made Danny happy. And Nico.

For the first time since Gaetano had died, he felt content. He took his little family to the beach, took them for drives and hunted down obscure restaurants where the owners were discreet and they could enjoy themselves like anyone else. He'd had the reporters who'd camped at the gates to the palazzo run off, and he'd been pleased they hadn't returned. Only one helicopter had invaded his privacy, but a single phone call and it was gone, as well.

After yet another day at the beach with Lily and Danny, Nico strode into his office to find a letter from his father waiting. Nico ripped into the envelope—the man was too old-fashioned to use e-mail—and scanned its contents.

As expected, King Paolo of Monteverde remained an unhappy man. Paolo was widely reputed to be violent, though Nico didn't think the king would go so far as to initiate hostilities between the countries simply because his daughter had been jilted.

He dropped into a chair, unmindful of the sand clinging to his body, and propped his forehead on his hands. The truth was that Montebianco could suffer if the trade issues didn't get worked out. His country depended on olive oil, textiles and raw ore from Monteverde. They could procure the items elsewhere, certainly, but at what cost? How many jobs would be lost? How many households would suffer a reduction in their income?

Nico had counted on Monteverde's dependence on Montebiancan wines, leather goods and produce to even the balance and make King Paolo see reason.

But the king was more stubborn than he'd anticipated. *Madonna diavola.*

As much as he wanted to stay out here with his head buried in the sand, it was time to return to the Palazzo Cavelli. Montebianco's people needed to know their prince was concerned about their welfare, that his pleasure took a backseat to their future. He could not let them down.

The day before Gaetano had died, he'd said, "*You* should

have been Crown Prince, Nico. You're stronger, more capable. Montebianco needs a man like you."

Nico had told him not to be so ridiculous, told him he was a fine prince and would be a good king. Gaetano had only smiled.

But later that day, they'd argued.

"I don't want to get married, Nico," Gaetano had said for what seemed the hundredth time.

Nico, tired and frustrated with his brother's reluctance to do his duty when he'd always been so privileged, had lashed out. "Sometimes you have to do what you do not want, Gaetano. It's your duty as Crown Prince, as our future king."

Gaetano had looked at him with such sadness. "But I *can't* be a husband to her."

"Dio," Nico had said, pushing shaky fingers through his hair. "All you need to do is get her pregnant, ensure the succession."

"You don't understand, Nico. I can't. She's, she's—"

Nico had feared what was coming, had said firmly and without sympathy, "You can. You *must.*"

Gaetano had looked away, swallowed. To this day, Nico regretted not letting his brother say what had been on his mind. *I can't because she's a woman, Nico.*

Why had he been afraid to hear it? Why, when he'd always known? Why hadn't he simply hugged his brother and told him he loved him, no matter what?

He'd never gotten the chance to say those words. Early the next morning, Gaetano drove off the cliff.

Nico would give anything—*anything*—to bring him back again. Since he couldn't, he would do the only thing he knew how. He would honor Gaetano's memory by being the kind of Crown Prince his brother believed he would be.

He would do his duty, no matter the personal cost.

CHAPTER SEVEN

LILY'S HEART CLIMBED into her throat and took up residence there. "You want to do what?"

Nico came into the room, swinging a helmet from one hand. "Come with me, Liliana. It will be fun."

His expression didn't exactly look fun loving. No, if anything she'd say those were lines of strain around his eyes. "I—I've never ridden a motorcycle. I don't know how."

"You have only to hold on to me." He caught her around the waist with one broad hand, pulled her toward his leather-clad body. "You can do that, *si?*"

If she fainted from the light-headedness he induced in her with his mere presence, would she get out of the ride? It was a thought. But there was something in his eyes, something that told her she didn't want him to go alone.

"I'm not sure it's safe."

Nothing about Nico was safe. Over the last few days, he'd managed to somehow make her like him the way she had in New Orleans. In spite of the way they'd begun this time, her heart was bound tighter each time she saw him with Danny. Whether he tried to teach their baby Italian, talked nonsense to him or made him giggle, Lily felt herself melting a little more with every moment they spent together.

Having a baby changed people. Had it changed Nico? Was

he enjoying fatherhood? Was Danny as important to him as he was to her? The evidence said yes, but she'd learned not to trust herself so easily. Her father had often made her mother happy for varying lengths of time before he broke her heart yet again. It was a lesson Lily needed to remember.

Especially now, when he looked like sin wrapped up and tied with a bow.

"We will go slowly, I promise."

She motioned at his delicious fantasy of a body. Oh that formfitting leather! She hadn't been able to get it out of her mind since the first time he'd worn it. "I don't have the appropriate attire."

"Jeans, boots and a jacket will do for where we are going."

She blinked. "Where would that be?"

His smile was genuine, and it sent her pulse into overdrive. "It's a surprise."

Fifteen minutes later, Lily found herself climbing onto the back of a wicked-looking motorcycle and cinching a helmet into place. She wrapped her arms around him while the engine hummed and the smell of leather, rubber and motor oil filled her nostrils. The bike was sleek—red and silver—and purred like a kitten. Until he revved it.

Lily clutched him tighter as they roared up the drive. The gates opened and he shot between them. A news van sat around the corner from the entrance, and it launched forward as they passed.

"*Maledizone,*" Nico said, the sound coming clearly through the helmet mike. There were a few more words in Italian—which she decided were not in the least polite—and then he said, "Hold on, *cara.*"

"Nico, please," she said, her heart thrumming as she thought of her sweet baby back at the house, of the last few days of bliss—oh God, *why* had she agreed to this? "I don't like going so fast!"

"Trust me," he replied. "A few moments, we will lose them. I will not hurt you, Lily."

She didn't reply, simply tightened her arms around him and laid her head against his back. The motorcycle was designed in such a way that she sat higher than he did, and when he leaned over the bars, she had to lie against him or let go. She chose to flatten herself against him.

The bike roared at incredible speeds down the coastal road. "We are approaching a turn. Lean the way I do, *si?*"

As if she could do anything different. He braked only a hair, then arrowed into the corner, dipping deep to the left, laying the bike nearly flat—and then they were out the other side as if they'd been fired from a gun. Her breath stuck in her chest.

She dared to turn her head as much as possible against the wind and blurring landscape. Behind them, the van was nowhere to be seen.

"I think you lost them!"

"I can hear you, there is no need to shout."

"Sorry."

"Another few minutes, and we'll get off the road."

Lily held tight to his torso, finally breathing again when the motorcycle slowed. He made a turn onto a path that led downhill. It was a dirt trail, wide, and lined with brush. They rode on it for several minutes before he turned again and they emerged onto a remote beach.

He took the motorcycle down to the water's edge and drove along the packed sand there. They went slow enough that Lily was able to sit up and gaze out at the cresting waves. A dark band of clouds had moved in, blocking the sun. The day had gone from bright to gray in the space of a few minutes.

"Will it rain?" she asked.

Nico looked up. "Possibly."

He didn't seem too concerned, so she didn't say anything else about it. A few minutes later, he slowed even more, then came to a stop beside a huge ragged limestone rock that sat like an island in a sea of sand.

"Take my hand and climb down," he said. "Be sure to watch out for the pipes. They are very hot."

Lily did as he instructed, removing the helmet while Nico swung a leg over and stood on the sand beside her. He unsnapped his helmet and tugged it off. "That was fun, yes?"

"Um, not all of it," Lily said. "It was a little fast."

"Sometimes fast is best," Nico said, his mouth lifting in that wicked grin that always sent her heart into overdrive. He appeared more at ease now than he had when they'd started. She wasn't sure what had changed for him, but she was glad for it.

He set his helmet on the seat, placed hers there, as well, then took her hand and led her toward an outcropping of rocks a few feet away.

"Where are we going?" she asked again.

"We're almost there."

She had no idea what he wanted to show her. Another rock? More sand? She'd thought he'd already taken her to some of the more beautiful spots on this coast. They rounded the cliff face and Lily jolted to a stop.

Nico turned back to look at her. He seemed oddly solemn. "It is extraordinary, isn't it?"

Lily could only nod. The cliff face bowed inward at this point, creating a half-round bowl that held the skeleton of a wooden ship. The vessel lay on its side, the wood darkened through years of enduring the elements. The remnants of a tattered flag flapped in the strong breeze coming from the direction of the ocean.

"Is it a pirate ship?" she asked, and then felt silly for doing so. She'd been watching too many Hollywood blockbusters.

"No. In fact, it's not all that old. It is a replica of the days when Montebianco's wealth came from command of the shipping lanes. But it sank in strong seas during a regatta many years ago and washed up here."

"Why wasn't it moved to a museum?"

He shrugged. "Not enough interest, I suppose." He walked toward the ship, and she followed, her imagination spinning out a tale. Though he wore leather, she could easily picture him in breeches, standing on the deck and commanding his men to sail into battle. And though the ship was a replica, it made her think of the history of this country and the long line of kings her husband must descend from.

The long line of kings her son descended from.

And suddenly she felt so out of her depth that it frightened her. What was she doing here? Why had a prince—a future king—married *her?* What happened when he realized she was completely unsuitable?

He would take Danny from her and send her back to America, that's what.

No.

He would not do such a thing. He couldn't. He'd lost his own mother, hadn't he? That had to count for something.

He bent over and grabbed a rock, then hopped up onto one of the thick logs at the base of the ship and hurled it. Lily stopped and watched him, her memories of the last few days tumbling together with her fears. He seemed preoccupied as he put his hands on either side of a gap in the hull and peered inside. Eventually, he pushed away and turned back to her.

His expression changed in a heartbeat.

"Cavolo!" He jumped down and ran toward her. "We must get under cover," he said, grabbing her arm and spinning her back the way they'd come. That's when she saw what had alarmed him.

Black clouds hung lower in the sky than before, and the wind picked up speed, whipping her hair across her eyes. She could taste the salt on her tongue from the cool air, and she scraped her hair away so she could see. A funnel cloud danced along the water, moving toward the beach.

"Is that a tornado?" Good God, they had tornadoes here? She'd thought those were a nightmare she'd left behind in Louisiana.

His voice was grim. "It is a water spout. Probably won't come ashore, but the rain will be quite hard for a while." They reached the motorcycle and he tossed a helmet to her. "Don't put it on," he said when she started to do just that. "We don't have time to get away."

"What are we going to do, stand here beside this rock and hope for the best?"

"There is a cave nearby. We'll wait inside for the worst to pass." His smile belied the seriousness of the situation. "Don't worry, *cara,* the sun will be shining again in half an hour."

He wheeled the bike toward the cliff, skirted along for a few feet, then slipped between an opening in the white rock. Lily followed, not sure what she'd find inside. A tiny, dank space where she couldn't see two feet in front of her face? The idea did not make her happy.

But no, the cave opened into a large area with a roof that soared thirty feet or more. Light filtered in from gaps in the rock much higher up the face. The walls glittered with what looked like tiny crystals.

"It was a sea cave once," Nico said, parking the motorcycle and turning to face her. "Millennia ago."

Fine, powdery sand covered the floor, punctuated here and there by rocks. He went over to a ledge of smooth rock against one wall and sat down. "I used to come here with my brother," he said, as if in answer to her unspoken question about how he knew where to find it. "It was very far from the family palazzo, and forbidden—but we did so anyway."

Lily imagined the two boys in the picture, laughing and running and knowing they were doing something wrong but unwilling to stop. "Did you come often?"

He leaned back against the rock, hands clasped casually on

his knees. "Not often, no. It was very far, and difficult to get to. We found the ship one summer, and we tried to come as often as possible. As you can imagine, a wreck would have much fascination for young boys."

Outside, the rain began to beat against the rock. The wind whipped inside the cave, stirring up the sand. The storm had moved very fast. She imagined them caught in it, shuddered. Thankfully he'd known where to take them or they would be huddling in the wind and rain right this moment.

"Come," Nico said, holding out an arm. She went and sat beside him, reveled in the warmth of his body as he tucked her in against him. Maybe she should have said no, but she didn't want to. Not this time.

Nico's chin rested on her head, and she found herself burrowing closer, her arm going around his waist. It seemed natural, inevitable. If only they could stay like this forever.

"Gaetano died here," he said softly, and she jerked back, her eyes searching his face. The pain in his eyes was raw—and yet controlled.

"Nico, I—"

"Shh," he said, pressing a finger to her lips. A thrill of sensation shot through her. "It's okay, *cara mia*. He made his choice."

"What happened?" she said when he took his finger away.

"He drove his car off a cliff nearby."

Lily shuddered. How awful for them all. "Why did you want to bring me here if it makes you sad?"

He tilted her chin up, his eyes capturing hers for long moments. But then they closed, and he leaned back, away from her. "I sometimes think he's waiting here. I know he is not, but it gives me comfort to think so."

Lily couldn't help herself—she cupped his smooth jaw in her palm, spread her fingers along the fine, strong bones of his face. He felt closer to his brother in this place, and he'd brought her with him. It touched her more than she could say.

"I don't think that's wrong," she said softly. "It happened so recently, you're still growing accustomed to it."

He pressed his hand over one of hers, then dipped down and touched her lips with his own. Gently, lightly—so lightly that she was the one to lean forward, the one to demand more.

But he did not give it to her. "There is something about you, Liliana," he said, his breath hot against her skin. "I don't know what it is."

"Perhaps you just don't know me very well," she replied, her heart thrumming as their breaths mingled. It was so intimate, so thrilling. She *wanted* him to kiss her again, as he had the night of their wedding. He hadn't attempted it in days now, and she was a little too uncertain of herself to kiss him first. "I'm a mystery."

He leaned away from her, and she bit back a protest. Not at all the effect she'd been aiming for. She wanted to howl in frustration.

"Then tell me something."

She gaped at him, a hot achy feeling settling in the pit of her stomach. "Isn't it usually the woman who wants to talk first?"

Nico threw back his head and laughed. Lily tried not to join him, but she couldn't help herself. It felt good. A week ago, she'd have never thought she could share a light moment with him— and yet, in the space of the last few days, she'd seen a side to him she'd only hoped existed.

Was that the real Nico? Or was she dreaming of something that wasn't truly there?

"Indulge me, Liliana. Tell me something about yourself."

"I don't know what to say," she replied, her eyes downcast as she felt suddenly shy. What could she tell him that wasn't mortifying? He was a prince, completely unaccustomed to the sort of life she would have led in Louisiana.

"Surely there is something."

"I'm an only child."

"I know that." When she looked up, he was smiling gently. "I know the facts, *cara*. I don't know how you feel about them."

All the facts? That was a rather frightening prospect. Lily twisted her fingers into the fabric of her jacket. How could she reveal her deepest longings and hurts to him? "I've never had the luxury of dwelling too much on the past."

"Were you lonely without siblings?"

"Sometimes. But I had friends. I had Carla," she said, frowning.

"Do not blame her, Lily," he said, going to the heart of what she was thinking. "Very few people can resist the lure of such money, especially when they do not have it."

"I don't *blame* her," Lily said. "How could she say no? You wouldn't have let her anyway." She couldn't blame Carla, though it still hurt. Would she have done the same thing if their positions were reversed? She liked to think she wouldn't, but how could anyone know what they would do until faced with the choice?

"No," he said very solemnly. "I would not."

"And has the price been worth it?" A coil of heat threaded through her veins. He'd bought her and her son as though they were chattel, had put her friend in an impossible position. It still had the power to anger her when she considered it. Their lives were forever altered now.

"I believe so, yes," he replied. He caught her hand and brought it to his mouth, sucked the tip of her finger. "I'm not sorry, Lily, because our son is worth any price to me."

Am I?

Lily shivered, but she could not ask the question. "He is the best thing that ever happened to me."

"And the most frightening, no?"

"It wasn't easy, if that's what you're asking. But I wouldn't trade it."

"I know you would not." He dropped her hand, shifted

away from her on the stone ledge. "You had no right to keep him from me for so long."

Lily swallowed the lump in her throat. She'd thought she was doing the right thing for her baby, but now she realized she'd hurt the man who'd fathered him with her silence. They still had a long way to go, but he seemed to genuinely adore his son. "No, I should have contacted you."

His gaze was sharp. "Do you mean this?"

"Yes." She glanced away. "I—I was afraid you might take him away from me."

His eyes burned into her. "We still have much to learn about each other, it seems."

Feeling somewhat awkward in the silence that followed, Lily leaned back to look up at the soaring ceiling; outside, the rain pounded down. "We get storms like this back home, but they can be much worse. I was terrified of thunder when I was little."

"But not now?"

Lily shook her head. "No. I had to stop being afraid. I was often alone in the house, and I'd have gone crazy otherwise."

It was hard staying frightened when you had to learn to take care of yourself because your mother was off in some bar or another. Storms ceased to be significant.

"But you were afraid for a while, yes?"

Lily sucked in a breath. "I learned to deal with it. It was that or go around jumping at every little sound and hiding under the covers whenever it rained."

"That seems reasonable," he said gently. "Though it couldn't have been easy."

Lily shrugged. "Nobody ever said life was easy."

Nico's gaze was thoughtful. "I'm learning what it is about you, I think," he said, his voice barely reaching her as the rain picked up outside. "You are strong, Liliana. Brave. I find this very compelling."

"I—"

He swooped in and cut her off with a kiss, his mouth claiming hers hotly. It was shocking, but Lily had no wish to argue about it: she opened to him. Their tongues met, sucking and stroking—pulling her deeper under the tidal wave of desire cresting inside her body.

This. This was what she wanted, this spark, this beautiful passion. All of it, hers.

"*Dio,* I want you," he said against her mouth.

"Yes."

The knowledge sent a thrill through her. He wanted *her.* Not Antonella, but her.

Strangely, she wasn't scared. She'd had sex with him once—had only had sex *once* in her life. And, oh God, she was burning up with the desire to do it again. It'd been pretty good that first time, though mysterious and somewhat frightening, too. But now?

Oh, now…

She knew what to do, knew what to expect. Lily ached with the need for release, felt as if she would die if she didn't reach that culmination. To hell with her fears. Right now, she wanted her prince.

She put her arms around his neck, pressed in closer. He was warm and big, his body sizzling against hers. One of his hands worked the buttons on her shirt, spreading it open as he moved downward. The air wasn't all that cool, but against her heated skin, it felt like an arctic breeze. Lily shivered, not from the chill, but from anticipation.

When Nico had her shirt open, he spread the material wide, his lips blazing a trail down her neck, over her collarbone—

Lily gasped as his mouth grazed the soft mound of her breast. "It's a front clasp," she managed, and Nico chuckled before releasing the bra and freeing her breasts from the lacy cups. He shaped them, pressed them together, and she leaned back on her hands, thrusting her chest up, toward his seeking mouth.

She wanted him inside her. Her body ached with it. More than anything, she wanted to feel the heat of him, the hard length of him, his naked skin against hers as they moved together. There had been pain the last time, just a little, but she knew there would be none now—in spite of the fact she hadn't had sex again since that first time, she was more than ready for him.

When his lips closed over one tight peak, she thought she would come simply from the exquisite sensation.

"Oh, Nico," she gasped.

He growled low in his throat, a sound of possession and male satisfaction. The vibrations shuddered through her, gathered in the center of her feminine core and threatened to shatter her senses. How could she be on the edge so quickly?

He laved each nipple with his tongue, dragged his teeth across the aching points with just enough pressure to make her back arch toward him.

She couldn't allow it, couldn't be the only one about to explode with the feelings and sensations of all he was doing. Lily reached for the snap to his pants, smiling to herself as his breath rattled in on a sharp hiss.

The sound emboldened her, and she tugged his zipper down enough to get her hand inside. He was hard, his penis thick and hot beneath her hand. He growled at her again as she wrapped her fingers around him.

"Lily, *Dio*."

And then he dragged her into his lap, kissed her hard. She stroked him, tentatively at first, then more boldly as he shuddered beneath her touch.

Finally, he tore his mouth away. Swore. "Stop, Liliana."

"But you like it," she said, shocked at how sensual her voice sounded.

He grasped her wrist, pulled her hand away from his pants. "It is not a question of like, but a question of control. Keep doing that, and we'll be finished before we begin. I want you too much for play."

"Then we need to begin."

He closed his eyes, swallowed hard. "*Madonna diavola,* had I known you would be so eager, I would have taken you to bed and skipped this ride."

Heat crept up Lily's neck to her cheeks. "Had you kissed me first, maybe we'd still be there instead of here."

Nico kissed her knuckles, laughing brokenly, while she tugged her shirt back into place with her free hand, suddenly self-conscious and confused at his hesitation.

"No," he said, catching her fingers and opening her shirt again.

"Nico, for heaven's sake, what's the point if all you're going to do is talk?"

"Your eagerness is most gratifying, *cara mia.* A man likes to know he is wanted."

As if he'd ever had a problem with *that.* "So does a woman," she shot back.

"Oh, I want you," he said as he stood and started shrugging out of his jacket. The dark T-shirt he wore molded to his muscular torso, and Lily dragged in a deep, sustaining breath that smelled of salt and sea, hoping it would steady her erratic heartbeat. The man ought to come with a warning label that proclaimed one word loud and clear: *Danger!*

"Then what do you plan to do about it?"

His lip curled in a wicked smile. "As many things as I can get away with."

CHAPTER EIGHT

SHE INTRIGUED HIM as no woman had ever done. Nico allowed himself a small frown as he slipped out of his leather jacket. No, that wasn't quite right. He was certain he'd been fascinated with other women before Lily. *Hadn't he?*

But it'd been a long time since he'd wanted one so badly he was ready to spill himself like an eager teenager. Even now, looking at her, he had to keep a tight rein on his need. She sat on the ledge, her hair mussed, her lips swollen from his kisses. Her shirt and jacket gapped open, exposing her soft breasts, the high-tipped points of her nipples and petal pink of her areolas. Quite simply, he wanted to devour her.

He was torn between taking her here in this place and waiting until he had a soft bed to lay her down in. But his baser nature didn't want to wait. And apparently, neither did hers.

"Come here," he said, tugging her up and against him. He tossed his jacket on the smooth ledge where she'd been sitting, then dropped his mouth to her exposed collarbone, followed the line of one shoulder as he pushed her shirt down her arms. He wondered if she would protest, but she went for his waistband again. He hissed when she closed her fist around him. She'd certainly learned a thing or two in the last couple of years.

The thought of another man making love to her, while his son lay in a crib in another room, repulsed him. *Infuriated him.* She should have been his. All this time, she should have been *his.*

He wrapped a hand in her glorious hair and tugged her head back, exposing her neck to his questing mouth. A moment later, he let her go and unfastened her pants. He couldn't wait another second to see her, to touch her womanly softness.

"Nico—" She gasped as he shoved the material down, dropping to his knees in front of her. She was trapped by her pants and boots, but hc was free to do whatever he liked. A state of affairs he intended to take full advantage of. His cock strained against the confining leather, the ache driving him almost to distraction. He wanted to thrust into her, *now.*

But he would deny himself until he'd given her this.

Her buttocks were round and smooth in his hands as he pressed a kiss to her belly. He intended to go slowly, to drive her as insane as she was making him, but the satiny feel of her, her womanly scent, the heat and lushness—he couldn't wait.

Nico licked a path down her abdomen, sliding into her femininity, finding the little point of her pleasure. He spread her with his fingers, ran the flat of his tongue over her clitoris, varying the pressure.

Her fingers wound in his hair as she threw her head back, little panting sounds of delight bursting from her. She was eager, wet, her body humming with the tension he wound tighter and tighter. He knew not to let her go over yet, backed away each time he sensed she was close. He wanted to drag it out, wanted to give her so much pleasure she would never desire another lover.

He slipped a finger inside her tight passage—and her knees buckled as she cried out. Her body clutched at him greedily as she shuddered and shuddered.

Dio, she'd reached her peak.

Just like that.

The wonder of it staggered him. He held her up when she

would have dropped, stood and lifted her onto the ledge when the tremors subsided. She was so wild and beautiful in her abandon, leaning back on her arms, her breasts thrust into the air. Another moment and he would free himself, would thrust into her and—

Her eyes were closed, tears slipping down her cheeks. He stilled in the act of unsnapping the leathers. He ached to touch her again, to take her over the edge and show her how beautiful it could be between them. But for the first time ever, he stared at a woman and found himself uncertain.

Had he hurt her? But no, she'd gotten pleasure; he knew she had. Maybe he'd gone too fast, driven her relentlessly to the point of surrender and now she regretted it.

Or was it something deeper? Had he pushed her too far when he'd asked her to tell him about herself? Had he forced her to reveal too much of her soul?

Yes, he knew many things about her—but he felt as if he knew nothing. Facts on an investigator's report weren't the same as whispered confidences.

And then it hit him. The idea was so ridiculous he almost rejected it out of hand. But, *per Dio,* he wanted her to love him. His entire body stilled as he absorbed the idea, examined it from all angles. He *wanted* her to love him. He wanted *one* person in this world to look at him with the kind of loving adoration his brother had. It was the only feeling of belonging he'd ever had, and he missed it. Perhaps that's why he'd brought her here today: it was an effort to merge the two very different halves of his life.

Was he that transparent, that desperate?

Nico drew in a breath, closed his eyes. He needed time to think. The rain had stopped, and the sharp smell of the sea filled his nostrils. He would take her home, give her time to recover, give them both time to regroup. He couldn't push her now, not like this. She deserved better.

"Liliana," he said, reaching for her shirt and jacket and laying them across her. His penis throbbed in protest at what he was about to do. "Put these on and we will go."

Her eyes glistened as she sat up. "W-why? You haven't—"

"Shh." He dropped beside her, her taste still on his lips, his body screaming for release. "The storm is over, we need to go before we are missed."

A tear spilled over her cheek and he caught it before she could scrub it away. "I don't understand," she whispered.

"It is best this way, *cara.*" The hurt shining in her eyes bewildered him. Wasn't he doing the right thing? He shoved away from her and refastened his pants. Behind him, he could hear her dressing.

A moment later, she was passing him, grabbing her helmet off the motorcycle and waiting for him to push it out to the beach. He picked up his jacket and crossed to the bike.

"Why do you always back away?" she demanded. The other side of passion was anger—and she looked like a pint-sized Amazon, eyes flashing, cheeks flushed, hands on hips.

Always? He'd stopped himself twice, both times against his will. And he was damn sure paying for it the way his body ached. "Now is not the right time," he told her. "It's not you."

She dragged in a laugh that ended brokenly. "'It's not you, it's me.' I've heard that before, Nico. Usually it happens when some high school boy wants to break up with you because he's heard that the girl down the road is an easy lay."

Nico kicked the stand from the Ducati and blinked at her. She was angry with him when he was being considerate of her? When he wasn't falling on her like an animal? Frustration crashed into him. "What the hell is an 'easy lay'?"

Her chin quivered. "A moment ago, I'd have said me."

It took him a second to process the English idiom, but then he understood. "Lily—"

"Don't say anything to me right now, Nico. It won't help."

He considered it as he watched her fight with herself, realized she was right. They'd already come too far down this path to turn back. There was too much hurt and anger to make it right at the moment. He wheeled the bike from the cave, Lily on his heels.

They rode back to the house in silence, humiliation a drumbeat in her veins. Nico had proven his mastery over her, had made her desperate for him, and then walked away as if she were as easy to dismiss as an annoying fly. He gave her an orgasm, certainly, but how embarrassing was it to fall apart like that under his expert attention and then have him zip his pants and tell her they had to go, as if he'd done something as mundane as tuned up the motorcycle?

And why, *why* had she said that to him about high school boyfriends? God, how pitiful and revealing was that? Before she'd gone to New Orleans and met Nico, her longtime boyfriend—the one she thought she might marry someday—had broken up with her because she wouldn't sleep with him. She'd believed that if she gave away her virginity, she'd somehow become like her mother. So she'd guarded it fiercely—until Jason broke up with her and she'd met Nico a few short months later.

When they arrived back at the house, Lily went immediately to the shower and tried to scrub the feel of his lips and tongue from her body.

It didn't work. Nothing worked. She only wanted more.

Heaven help her.

She couldn't figure him out. One minute he was hot and vibrant and on the edge of control; the next he was cool and collected and so in control she wanted to scream. It wasn't fair, not when she couldn't seem to find her balance around him no matter how hard she tried. Just when she thought she had it figured out, he did something to shake her up.

And whoa, he'd certainly shaken her up in that cave. She couldn't erase the image of him kneeling before her, his mouth on her body, waves of sheer bliss thundering through her like the surf outside.

But what happened next wasn't at all what she'd anticipated. She'd expected him to join her on the ledge, to slide into her and ease the incredible ache she'd still felt.

Except he'd lied—or he enjoyed manipulating her. She wasn't sure which. But the truth was that he didn't want her as much as he'd claimed he did. He wanted Antonella, perhaps—or one of his sleek mistresses. He did not want a low-born American girl who was more mutt than pedigree. In fact, she wouldn't be surprised if he'd left the palazzo again and went to one of his many female admirers for comfort.

Though wouldn't a womanizer take what was offered to him? Why would he go that far and no further? God, she didn't know! She didn't understand him at all.

Much later, when she couldn't sleep, Lily decided to go to Danny's room and check on him. Gisela was close by, of course, but Lily just wanted to sit in the dark and listen to her baby breathe. If she were with her baby, she'd find her center of balance again.

She'd wanted to keep Danny in the room with her, as she'd done since he'd been born, but she had to admit it was time he had his own room. Though it was hard to let go even that much, she didn't want him growing up frightened to be alone in the night.

Lily slipped into her robe and made her way down the hall. She padded into the outer suite on silent feet, then crept into Danny's room—

And drew up short. An ocher night-light burned against one wall, casting a soft glow on the room—illuminating the man who lay on the chaise with his son on his chest. Against her will, Lily's heart knotted.

Man and boy slept soundly. Even in sleep, Nico had a protective arm over Danny, anchoring him in place. The sight brought her both joy and pain—joy that they had each other, and pain that her baby now had someone else besides her.

She hesitated on the edge of the threshold, uncertain whether to go or stay—would Nico's hold on Danny eventually relax? Would her baby fall to the floor? Or did her husband have the situation well in hand?

Lily bit her lip, warring with herself so intently that she didn't notice Nico's eyes flutter open. When she looked at his handsome face again, he was staring back at her. Her heart turned over in her chest. He was a beautiful sight, masculine and strong—and yet tender enough to hold a sleeping baby.

Wasn't that what every woman wanted?

Carefully, he shifted Danny and sat up. She rushed forward to help him, but he shook his head and she crashed to a halt, her fingers twitching with the urge to assist. He managed to rise and lay Danny back into the crib. Her little boy curled into a ball, his arms wrapped around the blue plush dinosaur he'd fallen in love with. His old teddy bear sat in one corner of the bed if he needed it.

Lily joined Nico beside the crib, reassuring herself that Danny was indeed asleep. Then, the two of them left the room. When they'd gone a short distance, Lily asked, "Was he awake when you went in?"

"I heard him crying." Nico ran a hand through his hair. "It took a long time for him to sleep."

Lily's heart was in her throat. "Danny was crying? Why didn't you call me? Where was Gisela?"

"Gisela is feeling unwell, *cara*. I told her to go back to bed."

"You should have called me."

"Why? What could you have done differently?"

Nothing probably. Lily bit her lip. "I'm his mother," she said defensively.

"I am aware of this."

Oh God. When he used humor on her, she wanted to melt into a sticky puddle. She crossed her arms, trying to shore up her defenses. She absolutely would *not* think of how amazing his mouth felt on the most sensitive part of her.

"Perhaps I should go back, stay with him—"

"No."

Lily gaped at him. "What do you mean no? You can't order me around like I'm the hired help. I'm his *mother*, and if I want to spend the night watching over my son, I will."

He took a step closer, his large form crowding her in the darkened hall. She refused to step backward, though her pulse kicked up. He smelled like citrus and spice, with the faintest hint of an ocean-scented breeze. To her dismay, she wanted to lick him like a lollipop.

"There is no need, Lily. He's asleep. It's simply an excuse to get away from me."

"That's not true." Except it was.

"You still want me and you don't like it."

She lifted her chin. "You really are full of yourself, aren't you?"

"I know when a woman is—how do you say—*turned on*. You, Liliana, are very much so."

"You're kidding yourself if you think so," she said coolly. "You had your chance, Nico. You turned it down."

He tilted his head, let his gaze slide down her body and back up again. The perusal was slow, thorough, and her blood pressure spiked at the heated look in his eyes. But she'd experienced that look before, hadn't she? And it hadn't mattered one damn bit.

She stared back at him with all the iciness she could muster.

His smile was wolfish. "Very good, *cara*. You will make a fine princess yet."

"Don't mock me, Nico."

"I would not dream of it, *Mi Principessa*."

For a moment she thought—or was it hoped…feared?— he was about to kiss her anyway.

His expression changed, seemed troubled for a moment. But then it passed. "I forgot to mention we are returning to Castello del Bianco in the morning. You must be ready by eight."

Just like that, he'd changed direction again. Fury burned through her. "I'm not doing this," she vowed fiercely. "I'm not living the rest of my life taking orders and jumping to your tune. Is this how you would have treated Antonella? How you would have treated *anyone* but me?"

"Keep your voice down before you wake Daniele."

How dare he insinuate she didn't care about her baby's welfare! Lily shoved him as hard as she could. Which didn't amount to much since he only moved back a single step. The next second he'd wrapped his hands around her wrists. Then he pushed her against the wall, trapping her arms above her head.

His head dipped toward her. Lily turned away, pressed her cheek to the wall. Rejected him the way he'd rejected her earlier.

He nibbled her earlobe. Lily's eyes closed as a current of need rocketed through her, settled in her core. She bit back the moan that tried to escape, but not before he heard a fraction of it she was sure.

"*Dio,* you are fiery. And I've been too careful with you," he said. "I erred on the side of caution when I should have done no such thing." He transferred her wrists to one hand, then used the other to slide beneath her robe and cup her breast. "Perhaps I should take you to bed and keep you beneath me for the rest of the night."

"You talk a fine game," she managed, her heart drumming as her nipple rose to his touch, "but we both know you won't do it. You don't seem to have any staying power."

She'd thought he would be angry at her insult, but a laugh rumbled in his chest. "Now that," he said, "is where you are wrong."

"Then why do you keep stopping before you begin? Maybe you have a *premature* issue or something and you don't want me to know you can't keep it up long enough to—"

His bark of laughter startled her. The next instant, she was in his arms and he was striding down the hall. He kicked his way into the nearest room. She realized it was his as he set her down and ripped his dark T-shirt over his head.

As he advanced on her, naked chest gleaming in the soft lamplight, she scrambled backward, torn between resisting and helping. A dark line of hair arrowed down toward faded jeans, which rested just below his hip bones and showcased the hard muscles of his abdomen. He was a spoiled prince, and yet he looked like a demigod, all bronze and delicious with a sculpted body, tousled hair and bedroom eyes.

Sexy.

That was the word that popped into her head as he reached for her. So incredibly sexy.

"You're not going to force me," she declared. "You wouldn't do such a thing—"

"I might," he said, unknotting the belt of her robe, "but I doubt it's necessary."

"No matter what you think, you aren't irresistible, Nico."

The robe fell from her shoulders; he grabbed the hem of her favorite sleep shirt after taking a second to grin at the cartoon cat on the front. His expression grew serious. Hot. "I might have believed you had I not tasted your desire earlier. Are you wet for me now, too, Lily?"

Before she could formulate an answer, the shirt disappeared and he was pushing her backward onto the buttery-soft leather couch in the sitting area. He followed her down, his naked chest against her skin, the rigid bulge in his jeans riding against her silk panties.

And she realized she hadn't yet tried to resist. Lily closed her eyes, swallowed hard against her doubts and insecurities. "Stop, I don't want this."

She didn't sound very convincing.

"You are a poor liar, Liliana." His head dropped, and then his teeth were scraping her jaw, his big hands spanning her hips, lifting her against his erection.

Lily bit back a moan. What was wrong with her? How could she let him do this to her? She'd trusted him earlier, trusted that he wanted her the way she wanted him, and he'd made a fool of her.

He would do so again if she let him. He took pleasure in tormenting her like this.

"No," she gasped as his mouth closed around one aroused nipple. His fingers slipped beneath her panties, found the sensitive heart of her desire.

"You *are* hot for me, Lily."

She gasped as he stroked her. "Nico, no."

He stilled, lifted his head, his eyes searching hers. "Tell me to stop, right now, and I will do so. But if you don't say the word, Lily—" he softly squeezed her clitoris, eliciting the most delicious sensation "—if you don't tell me to leave this instant, there will be no turning back, *capisci?* You *will* be mine."

Her lungs stopped working as she gazed up into his handsome face. He was heart-stoppingly beautiful, and he was about to make love to her. Or was he?

"I want you to stop," she blurted. Because if she didn't say it, if she didn't make him cease this sweet torture, he would humiliate her once more.

Nico looked at her in disbelief. And then he swore violently. But his hand slid up, out of her panties—

Until she caught his wrist. She wasn't even aware she'd done so until he looked at where she'd grabbed him.

"What's it going to be, *Principessa?*"

Oh God, he'd given her the choice. He'd lobbed the ball

into her court and she was messing it up badly. Her heart pounded, her vision tunneling in on the man above her. She could see nothing but him, nothing but his piercing eyes and sculpted features. But she couldn't let him go.

"Tell me you want me," he commanded.

"I—I can't."

He reversed the progress of his hand, slipped between her folds again. Her eyes closed as he found her.

"So wet, Lily. So ready for me. Why would you want to deny us this?"

"You denied us first—"

"I thought you needed more time, that I'd pushed you too fast. Clearly, I was wrong."

One finger entered her, then another. Slowly at first, then faster, he mimicked the motion of what he would do with his body.

"Nico—"

He made a sound low in his throat. "Do you like this?"

"Yesss."

"Do you want more?"

"I—yes."

"Good, because I am through waiting, *tesoro mio.*"

She moaned in protest when he lifted away from her, but he unsnapped his jeans, shoving them down just enough to free himself. Lily could only stare as his penis sprang free. He was more than ready for her. And, oh my God, she was a lucky, lucky woman.

Nico lowered himself onto her again, hooking his fingers into her wispy panties and shoving them aside. She'd forgotten all about them while she'd devoured his body with her eyes.

Suddenly, she knew this was it. He was done with preliminaries, done with the give-and-take dance that had gotten them to this point. There was no turning back now. Fear gripped her—and anticipation.

He lifted her hips with one broad hand beneath her bottom and drove into her.

Lily cried out from the shock of it. This was what she'd wanted from him earlier, this incredible pressure and tension, the sweet aching beauty of male possession. But not just any male—*this* male, this gorgeous, amazing man.

"Lily, *sei dolce come il miele,*" he groaned.

She had no idea what he'd said, but it sounded beautiful.

"You feel so good." His eyes were closed, his head tilted back. "I want to stay like this…."

Lily wrapped her legs around him, lifted herself until she could catch him around the neck and pull him down to her. She had to taste him. "Kiss me," she begged. "Please kiss me, Nico."

His mouth fused to hers, hot and wet, his tongue plunging into the moist recesses of her mouth to tangle with her own. He moved his hips, sliding away from her while she tried to hold him tight.

And then he plunged forward again and her scalp tingled. *Everything* tingled. Every last nerve ending, every last cell. Her entire body was alive with the sensations of what he did to her.

What they did to each other. Because Lily was not passive, not this time. She might not have had sex again until this moment, but she'd had a baby and she was no longer naive. Her pleasure was as much her responsibility as it was his.

She ran her hands down his sides, cupped his buttocks as she lifted her hips to him. Her body was ready for him, and yet she knew she would be somewhat tender when it was over. And she didn't care. She pushed up into each long stroke, meeting him at the top, the pressure more exquisite each time.

"Lily," he groaned. "What you do to me, ah *Dio…*"

"Don't stop, Nico. Please don't…" She squeezed her eyes shut. "I can't…can't last…it's been so long…."

He growled something in Italian, something hot and

dark—and then he let go of his control. Soon they were both beyond restraint, slamming into each other urgently.

As the tempo increased, he buried his face against her neck, his breathing as ragged as her own. She could feel it coming, hovering on the edge of her senses, the culmination of an orgasm that was so much more complete than the one she'd had earlier. That had been blissful, shocking—but this, oh, *this*.

Her breath caught as the first tendrils of it uncoiled inside her. Nico seemed to sense it and angled her pelvis higher so the pressure changed as he stroked into her.

And Lily exploded into a million bright lights. A moment later, Nico followed, his hips grinding into her as he came, a broken groan spilling from his lips. A groan that sounded like her name.

But she couldn't be sure because she was still trying to gather the pieces of herself back together.

Long minutes later, he pushed away from her. She mourned the loss of him, but welcomed the cool air where it flowed over her sweat-dampened body. She lay with her eyes closed, one hand flung over her face, trying to process everything that had just happened.

In two years, she'd not felt even the slightest stirring of desire for any man. Nico was the one who'd filled her dreams, who'd starred in her fantasies, the one who'd fathered her precious child. But Danny was the product, not the reason, of what she'd felt for him that night two years ago.

Was it love? Fear wrapped around her like ice. She could *not* be in love with him. It was far too soon, and she didn't know him well enough. But her heart didn't seem to care.

"*Dio,* Lily, you feel amazing." He lowered himself and ran his tongue across her belly, spread his fingers over her abdomen. "These marks—are they from the pregnancy?"

She tilted her head up. He traced a fine, silvery stretch mark. It was so fine she was surprised he'd noticed. But then, it wasn't as if she'd been naked for anyone since having Danny. How would she know what a man might notice?

"Yes."

He bent to trace it with his tongue. "I'm sorry I did not get to see you carrying my child."

The comment made tears press against the back of her eyes. Until his fingers fanned over her possessively, stroking her sensitized skin. His dark head moved up her torso, and then his mouth fastened on a distended nipple. Lily clutched him to her, the sweet tension in her body nearly unbearable.

She hadn't recovered from the last orgasm and already she wanted him again. He made her feel special, cherished. Hot and achy.

He suckled her other nipple, advanced and covered her mouth, his tongue dipping inside to tease and torment.

"We should move to the bed," he murmured between long, deep kisses. By the time they made it, she'd lost her panties and he'd lost his jeans—and then he was inside her again....

And Lily knew she was the one who was lost.

CHAPTER NINE

NICO COULDN'T breathe properly. Every lungful of air was filled with the sweet scent of the woman beside him—she smelled like flowers and spring rain with a hint of cinnamon; she smelled like the Lily he remembered. He gently traced the line of the sheet where it lay above the swell of her breasts. He ached with the need to lose himself in her once more, but he knew he should not demand it of her. Not again tonight.

She lay with her head to one side, her eyes closed, her chest rising and falling evenly. They'd both fallen asleep after the second time, but now he was awake—wide-awake—and wondering what he should do.

If she'd been one of his mistresses, he'd have dressed and left her apartment. Not that he never spent the night with a woman—he often did—but just as often he felt the need to return to his own home and enjoy his solitude. Tonight he wanted no such thing.

"Nico," she breathed.

"Yes, *tesoro mio?*"

"I should check on Danny again—"

"I went a little while ago. He is sound asleep. As you should be." He threaded his fingers between hers, kissed her knuckles.

"You're not."

"I do not need much sleep."

"Maybe our son gets it from you then," she said, yawning. She turned into him and he wrapped his arms around her, pressed her naked body against him. Why had he waited so long to take her to his bed? He dipped his head, touched his lips to her shoulder.

It was far more pleasant this way. He flexed his hips against her and her breath caught.

"*Oh...*"

"Good *oh* or bad *oh?*"

"Definitely good. But Nico," she said, a note of worry creeping into her voice.

"Yes?"

"I'm not sure I can do this again tonight. It's, um, it's been a while."

He tried not to react, but he felt his body stiffen as he wondered exactly when the last time for her was. And who it was with. "I understand, *cara.*"

"Do you?" she said, her hand resting on his cheek. "Because that felt a lot like you didn't."

He turned into her palm, kissed it. "Has it been very long since the last time?"

She laughed. "Yeah, two years."

He stilled. Blinked. She could not be telling him what he thought she was telling him. "I don't think I heard you correctly."

She kissed his chin. "You did. You're the only man I've ever been with."

A fierce feeling of satisfaction permeated his entire being. She was his, had only ever been his. "How is this possible?" he asked. "*Sei bellisima,* Liliana. Any man would kill to have you."

"I never found another one I wanted," she said very softly.

"You do me much honor," he replied, uncertain what else he could say to express how grateful he was for the gift of her innocence and trust two years ago, and for her confession now. It was primitive of him, but he liked knowing she'd only been his.

She laughed. "Oh, Nico, you make it sound like we're living in the Middle Ages or something. For a man who knows how to do the things you do with your tongue, you sound awfully formal and prudish just now."

"Do I?" He grinned at her. "Perhaps I should remind you how wicked I can be, yes? I'm sure I can think of a few things that won't abuse your tenderness."

"I'm counting on it," she said breathlessly as he rolled her to her back and began another thorough exploration of her delightful body.

Lily had no idea what time she awoke, but when she did she found that Nico had made her breakfast again—only this time he served it in bed. When she finished eating, he ran her a bath in the gorgeous sunken tub, shedding his wet clothes to join her after she playfully splashed him.

She climbed on his lap, facing him, her legs wrapped around him and their bodies touching in that most intimate of places. He was engorged, ready for her, yet he made no move to enter her in spite of the way she rubbed against him.

Instead, he held her gently, grabbed a sponge and squeezed it over her breasts. Her nipples were tight little points that seemed to tighten even more when the air drifted over her wet body.

"*Dio santo,* you are beautiful," he said.

She wasn't, but she loved to hear him say it. Loved him, in fact. How had she committed such a colossal mistake? She had no idea, but she didn't care. She was in love with the man she was bound to for life. How bad could it be? He could learn to love her eventually, she was sure of it.

He was *not* like her father. Nico had honor and dignity. He loved their son, he cherished her body, and he felt deeply about many things. He was a man capable of love; he would not abandon her to raise their son alone, would not leave her for long stretches of time and then return and ask to be forgiven only to repeat the entire cycle in a few months or years.

Would he?

No, of course not.

"You're beautiful, too," she said, reaching beneath the water to wrap her hand around him.

His breath caught. "You are insatiable, *cara*. I quite like it," he finished, dropping the sponge and fusing his mouth to hers. While he kissed her, she managed to wriggle herself up high enough that the tip of him nudged her entrance. She caught his moan in her mouth, then gave it back to him when he thrust the rest of the way inside her.

"I am yours, Liliana," he said brokenly. "Do with me what you will."

Hers.

She'd never felt more powerful in her life as she began to move her hips. His head tilted back on the edge of the tub, his eyes drifted closed, and joy suffused her. She rode him slowly at first, drawing out the torment for them both. But then she needed more, so much more. Water sloshed over the rim of the tub to soak the tile, but he didn't seem to care.

And, oh God, neither did she.

"Nico," she gasped as her body began to shudder. *No, not yet.*

She changed the angle, slowed her thrusts. But he caught her hips tight, held her in such a way that she took him deeper with each thrust.

His eyes opened, burning into her. Burning *for* her.

"Take me, Lily. Take all of me," he growled.

This man, this gorgeous beautiful prince, was in ecstasy because of *her,* because of what she did to him. It amazed her, and humbled her. And sent her tumbling over the edge far too quickly when she wanted to drag it out forever.

"Nico," she cried as she shattered. "Nico, oh, I…" *I love you.*

Her heart was full with all she felt and could not say. It was too new, too raw, and she wasn't yet sure how to deal with it. He held her rigid when she would have folded against him and drove into her again and again, drawing out the pleasure for them both. When she came a second time, he was with her, his groan mingling with her sharp cry.

"I'm sorry, Lily. Don't cry," he said long moments later when her heart rate had almost returned to normal. He held her gently, fingers dancing up and down her spine. "It is my fault. I should not have made love to you again so soon. You make me lose control when I should know better."

She reached up to touch her cheeks, realized they were moist with tears. "Oh. No, I'm fine, really. It's just so... overwhelming."

"*Si,* it is that," he said, tucking a lock of her damp hair behind her ear. "There have been many changes for you."

That wasn't what she meant, but how could she tell him?

"And for you." She cupped his face in her hands. "I'm sorry, Nico. I should have contacted you when I found out I was pregnant. I made a mistake."

His gaze was troubled, but then it seemed to pass. "We will have to make another baby, yes? A little brother or sister for Daniele."

Lily's heart ached with love and a feeling of rightness. "He would like that. *I* would like that," she finished somewhat shyly considering what had just happened between them.

Nico's grin was genuine. "It is my solemn mission, *cara.* I shall rise to the occasion—just as soon as I recover from this one."

They returned to the city that afternoon, the journey seeming to weigh on Nico with every mile. The closer they got, the less he spoke, the less he smiled, the less he seemed the same man to her. Lily concentrated on the white buildings and red roofs in the distance, feeling as if Castello del Bianco were a tangible force drawing the life from her husband. And she didn't know how to fix it.

By the time they reached the Palazzo Cavelli, he'd returned to the coolly arrogant prince she'd thought was gone forever. It confused and irritated her. What had happened to the effortlessly sensual man she'd had a bath with this morning? The man who'd shared his body and his soul with her, cooked her breakfast and slept with a toddler on his chest?

This man, this prince, was not the sort of person who would do any of those things.

Had she judged him wrongly once more? Had she made him into what she wanted him to be when in fact he only did what was expedient to his wishes?

He didn't stick around for long once they were inside their apartment. He said he had to meet with the king, then left without so much as a smile or a kind word. Lily stared at the closed door for long minutes after he'd gone. Fear, anger and hurt mixed in her stomach, pounded through her with the refrain that she wasn't really a princess, that she'd given her heart to a man who didn't love her in return, and that she'd lost any chance she'd ever had at happiness when she'd married him. He'd taken her career, such as it was, her baby and her heart.

After Lily checked on Danny, she retreated to the room she now shared with Nico. The opulence of the palace no longer staggered her, but still her breath caught at the magnificent antique bed, the gilded walls and plush furniture, the marble and crystal and priceless paintings. It was like living in a museum. She, who'd only been to a single art museum in her life, now lived in the middle of one.

It only added to her Alice-in-Wonderland confusion.

A knock on the door sounded and she turned toward it, almost grateful for the interruption.

"Yes?" she said, and then wondered if there was something else she was supposed to say. What did princesses say? *You may enter?*

A young woman in the palace staff uniform entered, her eyes downcast. "*Scusi, Principessa.* For you," she finished, holding out a box.

"*Grazie,*" Lily replied. The girl shot her a wary smile, then backed out of the room and closed the door.

Lily went over to a table and pulled the lid off the box. She lifted out a stack of newspapers and magazines, confused as to why they'd been sent to her.

Until she realized that it was *her* picture in a grainy news photo. The paper was in Italian, so she shuffled through until she found something she understood:

Crown Prince Marries Daughter of Alcoholic Stripper, Endangers Relations with Neighbor

By the time Nico made it back to his quarters, he was mentally exhausted. He'd spent the last several hours wrangling with King Paolo and his father over the state of the treaty between their nations.

Paolo had at first demanded he divorce Lily, repudiate his son and marry Antonella. The man was insane and Nico didn't mind saying so. His father, however, urged a different course. Paolo was posturing for the best deal he could and using whatever ammunition he had in his arsenal to get it. The public humiliation of his daughter was fairly substantial in his mind, though it would never have escalated to this point had he not bandied it in the press. Nico felt sorry for Antonella, but only because her father was a self-important fool. She was a beautiful woman and would command many offers for her hand once her father let this go.

Now, Paolo wanted to hold further talks about the treaty in Monteverde. Nico didn't want to go, but his father urged him to do so. As Crown Prince, it was his duty. As architect of the current impasse, it was his responsibility. He could hardly refuse the invitation. To be seen in Monteverde, with his wife, would go a long way toward normalizing relations. It would show that Montebianco needed Monteverde's good-will, and it would give Paolo a chance to appear both important and magnanimous.

The residence was quiet when he entered. He wasn't as late as he'd thought he might be, though perhaps Lily had gone to bed. Nico headed for the bedroom, anticipation pumping through his veins. Would his wife be naked in their bed, waiting for him? Would she be dressed in something slinky and enticing? Or would she be wearing that silly shirt with the cat on it?

It didn't matter which garment she wore—or didn't wear—because his reaction was the same with each image in his head. He wanted her, plain and simple.

But when he opened the door, the sight he found was not what he'd hoped for.

Papers littered the floor. Lily sat in the center of them, reading. She looked up at him, her eyes red. "Hullo, Nico. Have a good day at the office?"

He crossed over and snatched a paper off the floor. Fury settled into his bones like a permanent chill when he realized what these were. He would make whoever did this pay. An upended box lay under the table, and he knew that someone had saved everything until they'd returned.

Queen Tiziana, no doubt. It was just like her to be so heartless. The more innocent the victim, the crueler she could be. Her treatment of him had changed in proportion to his size and age, but when he'd first arrived, he'd been fresh meat. Just as Lily was. If the queen outlived his father, she would be lucky if Nico didn't banish her from the kingdom entirely.

He'd known there would be articles, but he'd avoided the papers during their honeymoon. He regretted it now. He was so accustomed to shrugging off what they said that he hadn't stopped to think he might need to prepare his wife better.

Obviously, he'd been wrong.

"They know *everything*," Lily said numbly. "My mother, my father—the town I grew up in, the fact our family took public assistance, that my mother once stripped for a living. They called me a gold digger, said I tricked you, that Danny isn't yours—"

"I know Danny is mine."

She waved the paper she was holding. "Yes, well maybe you'd like to tell them that? Issue a statement perhaps?"

"It does no good to answer these swine," he bit out.

She climbed to her feet, faced him squarely. Fury, he was surprised to see, was the dominant emotion. "I don't know how to do this, Nico. I'm not a princess. I'm not meant for this. I won't let them hurt Danny—"

"No one will hurt Danny," he vowed.

"Then you will make them retract these lies?"

"Montebianco is a free society, Lily. I can't make them do anything. Nor can I make the European gossip rags do what I wish, either. The best course is to ignore them."

She looked stunned. "Ignore them? You would ignore people calling your son a bastard and your wife a whore?"

Nico stiffened. "*I'm* a bastard, *cara*. And I assure you it makes no difference. The furor will die down soon enough. You are the Crown Princess now, you must learn to handle these things."

"I didn't realize that part of the *job* was learning to ignore lies and put up with insults."

"You worked for a newspaper," he said harshly. "How can this surprise you?"

"I worked with reporters who had integrity, Nico. No one would dare to print a lie that was easily disproved. It isn't professional."

Nico raked a hand through his hair. "Yes, well tabloids

don't have the same standards. They thrive on lies, the more outrageous the better."

She gaped at him. "How can you be so dismissive? It's embarrassing to me, but it makes *you* look incompetent."

"You are missing the point, Lily. It doesn't matter. It will go away tomorrow, or the next day. As soon as there's nothing left to feed on, they will move on to another target." He reached for her. "Come, let's go to bed and forget this. It will look better in the morning."

She jerked away. "I can't believe you would allow an insult to our son to go unchallenged. Of course I don't expect you to defend me, but—"

"There's nothing to defend," he roared. "*Cavolo,* I don't have time for this! We are flying to Monteverde tomorrow. I need you to be prepared."

She wrapped her arms around herself, looked away. Her chin quivered and guilt speared him. Perhaps he should be more patient, should help her through this with more compassion. He'd had a bad afternoon, but that was no excuse. "Lily—"

"Monteverde?" she cut in. "Isn't that where Princess Antonella lives?"

"*Sì.*"

Her laugh was unexpected. "Fabulous, just fabulous. What if I refuse?"

Cold anger flooded him. "You cannot refuse. It's your duty."

"No, it's *your* duty."

Nico stiffened. "You are my wife, Liliana. We *will* be in Monteverde tomorrow night, and *you* will appear to be happy about it."

"Of course, Your Supreme Majesty," she bit out. "Is there anything else you wish to command, oh Lord of Everything?"

"Lily," he said, unable to keep the sudden weariness from his voice.

She sucked in a breath, her chin quivering faster now. He knew it wasn't from weakness, but from anger that she cried. "I didn't ask for *any* of this, Nico. I'm here because you forced me to be here. You've tried to turn me into something I'm not. If you don't like how I do the job of being your wife, then you have only yourself to blame for making a poor choice."

Nico gritted his teeth. "I did not force you to give me your virginity two years ago, nor did I rip the condom so you would get pregnant. It happened, Lily. Now we deal with it."

She made a sweeping motion with her hand. "So this is how we deal with it? Ignore the lies and hope they'll go away? Have you stopped to think what might happen when they actually manage to track my mother down in whatever third-rate honky-tonk dive she's holding up a bar stool in and ask her how it feels to have a daughter marry a prince?"

"They won't find her."

She went very still. "What do you mean they won't find her?"

"Because I found her first. She's in a treatment facility."

She looked as if he just said he'd sold her mother into slavery. But of course he'd had her family investigated. And what he'd learned about her mother necessitated action. The woman had been drunk in a Baton Rouge nightclub when his people found her. And, contrary to Lily's belief, she was most certainly still stripping for a living. Once she'd sobered, she couldn't even remember her grandson's name. Had, in fact, insisted she wasn't old enough to be a grandmother.

"You sent my mother to rehab? Without telling me?" He watched as a range of emotions crossed her face. Her voice sounded hollow when she spoke. "I haven't talked with her since shortly after Danny was born. How did you find her? Why?"

"I have many resources. And I had to do something for precisely the reason you've stated."

"I wanted to help her, but she never would listen and I

didn't have the money...." He had no idea what she might do next, but she suddenly gave up the fight and crumpled into a nearby chair. "You've thought of everything, haven't you? I should have known you would."

"I have no choice, Lily. I must do what's best for Montebianco at all times."

"Maybe you should have thought of that before you married me."

"There was no choice in that, either. I married you because we have a child together."

She laughed, but the sound was broken. Then she swiped her fingers beneath her eyes. "Not the best criteria, was it? But duty called, I suppose."

He resented the way she made it sound as if he'd committed a crime. He'd done what was right. And he'd done it at a personal cost that was still being tallied. "Yes."

"I wish you'd considered how it would affect me and Danny before you imposed your royal will."

His brows drew together. What could he have done differently? He'd given them wealth and privilege and a life far removed from what it would have been. "Your lives are immeasurably better now that we are married."

She speared him with a watery gaze. "Oh yes, very much so. I've never been happier."

In spite of her sarcasm, he wanted to go to her, wanted to sweep her up and take her to bed and make this whole thing go away. Because she had been happy just a few hours ago—he'd have staked everything he had on it.

But she wouldn't welcome him with open arms, not like this morning. It bothered him more than he cared to admit.

He went and picked up the phone, gave orders for someone to come clean up the mess.

"Go to bed, Lily," he said over his shoulder. "Tomorrow will be a long day."

She didn't answer for a long minute. When she did, her voice was so soft he had to strain to hear. But he didn't miss a word.

"I liked the man I knew in New Orleans, the one I spent the last few days with. Where is he? Because I don't like the Crown Prince very much at all."

Nico swallowed a hard knot in his throat. Was he so different when he was here in the palace? He knew he felt more constrained, but he'd not thought he completely submerged his personality beneath the pomp and circumstance of his duty. Perhaps he did. Perhaps she was far more perceptive than he.

"I am the same man," he said without turning around.

"I wish that were true. But I don't believe it is."

A few moments later, he heard papers shifting and crinkling as she stood and walked across the floor. A door closed. For the longest time, he heard nothing else. And then the snick of the lock fell into place.

The next day was a whirlwind of activity. Lily welcomed the distraction. She was caught in a flurry of fittings and beauty appointments to prepare for the gathering at the Romanellis' residence in Monteverde later that night. Unlike the trip to Paris, these women came to the palace to attend her. Gisela brought Danny in from time to time, and he amused the ladies to no end with his baby chatter and adorable antics. Lily was gratified by the comments that he looked exactly like his father.

Of course he did. Anyone with eyes could see he was his father's child, and yet she was still angry with Nico for refusing to correct the tabloids. When she'd worked at the *Register,* people sent in corrections to stories all the time. And the paper printed them.

She'd thought she wanted to be a journalist someday, but now she knew that was impossible. And she'd realized, after last night, that she really didn't have the necessary bulldog attitude it required. Some of what the papers said was true—her mother's alcohol addiction, the fact she'd once been a stripper—but Lily would never be able to write something so cruel and see it published if it meant someone would be hurt by it.

She'd been lulled by her short time at the *Register* into thinking that all papers and all stories were like the ones in her hometown. Naive of her, she knew. Especially now. She was news, and whatever a reporter could dig up about her was fair game. No wonder Nico was so jaded about fighting back.

But when he had right on his side, she refused to understand how he couldn't fight the battles that mattered. She didn't so much care about herself, though it hurt that Nico wouldn't defend her, but Danny, her sweet baby—he did not deserve the aspersions on his parenthood.

It had infuriated her to read them. This morning, she'd asked for the papers to be delivered to her. She'd thought Nico might have issued orders to the contrary, but within moments a maid brought all the English language papers she could find. The articles had thinned somewhat, though there was a picture of her and Nico on the motorcycle. And a grainier one of them and Danny on the beach.

She scanned the articles, then bunched the papers up and stuffed them in the trash. Privacy was no longer a guarantee. It would take getting used to, but she would survive it, same as she'd survived everything else in her life. It would take more than a few negative stories to defeat her.

By the time evening fell, Lily hadn't seen Nico all day. When she'd gone to bed last night, she'd locked the door. She'd been angry, and maybe she'd behaved childishly, but she hadn't expected him to avoid her completely. She'd spent a very lonely night awake on cool sheets, aching for the man she loved and dying inside because he wasn't the person she'd begun to think he was.

He'd married her for Danny. She wasn't stupid; she'd known it was the truth. And yet, to hear him say it so baldly, so blandly—it squeezed her heart into a tiny ball. She'd done everything wrong. She'd meant to insulate her heart from him, meant to learn how to live with him without falling for him—but she'd failed.

And now she was paying for it. Was this what her mother had felt all those years? This aching emptiness that could only be filled by one man? Maybe so, but she would not be the woman her mother had been. Danny was her priority. Nico did not care about her, so she would not expend her energy agonizing over him.

She would do her *duty,* but that was all. She would go to Monteverde and smile as though she was the happiest princess in the world.

After she was dressed, she awaited Nico in the living area. She'd been gowned in the most exquisite silver dress that hugged her curves from breast to ankle. The dress had a small train, and she'd been fitted with a sash like the one he'd worn the first night she came to the palace. Long white gloves went up to her elbows, and a diamond tiara perched on her head. She'd stared at herself in the mirror for long minutes, unable to believe the sight of all those diamonds winking like a neon sign.

When she was eight, she'd had a cheap plastic tiara with paste jewels that her mother had gotten from a thrift store. She'd shut the door to her room and pretend to be a princess, waltzing with her prince at a grand ball. Every night, until the tiara disappeared in one of their moves. She'd cried for a week. That her life should now imitate her childhood dreams was too surreal.

But in her dreams, the prince loved her. Too bad reality was so different.

When Nico entered the room, her heart leaped at the sight of him. He was resplendent in the ceremonial uniform of the Montebiancan navy. Though he had the sash and medals, this time the sword was missing. He drew up short when he saw her.

"Sei belissima, Principessa," he said.

Lily clasped her trembling hands together. She'd had protocol lessons today, but she had to admit she was nervous about this evening. "Thank you. I think."

He smiled as if nothing bad had happened between them. "It means you are beautiful."

She dropped her gaze to the floor, swallowed. She couldn't look at him and pretend nothing was wrong.

"You are prepared for this?" he asked.

Lily lifted her head. "Yes. I will do my duty, Nico."

She didn't have to wonder if he heard the bitter twist she put on the word. Something sparked in his eyes—but was it guilt or resentment?

Or neither?

He held out his arm for her in silence. She took it and they headed for their waiting helicopter. She was beginning to understand that she really didn't know him at all, no matter what they might have shared.

He'd married her for Danny's sake. But if duty demanded it, would he divorce her just as quickly?

CHAPTER TEN

THERE WERE THREE KINGDOMS, Lily learned on the flight to Monteverde's capital, that had once been a single country. But more than a thousand years ago, three feuding brothers divided the country between them when their father died. Montebianco, Monteverde and Monterosso were now ruled by the descendents of those brothers—though the connection was so far in the past they were no longer related except in the most distant way.

Montebianco and Monterosso had good diplomatic ties, and had done for over one hundred years now. But Monteverde was the odd kingdom out, the one ruled by a tyrant who controlled his people's access to news, the Internet and travel. They were an insular people, but they had many things to offer if free trade could be established. The Monterossan king refused to negotiate with King Paolo, but Montebianco was the peacemaker of the three. Good relations, Nico explained, would benefit everyone.

Lily had never ridden in a helicopter, but she had a feeling this one did not quite count. The interior was plush, like Nico's jet, lined with cushioned seats and polished wood. "Marrying me ruined everything, didn't it?" she asked when he'd finished his discourse on regional politics.

His expression didn't change. "It did not please Paolo, no."

She wondered if he regretted his hasty decision to marry her, but she could not bring herself to ask it right now. She'd been angry last night, and she'd as good as said that her life would have been better if he hadn't forced her into marriage.

And yet she wasn't certain it was the truth. Yes, she'd have her independence—but she wouldn't have the freedom to be the kind of mother she'd been lately, the sort of mother who had the luxury to spend as much time with her baby as she wanted. She'd still be working long hours to provide a good home for them both and wondering when life would ever get easier. Her baby would be spending most of his time in day care instead of with her. Though Nico had taken much from her, he'd also given her a precious gift. If he said that he regretted it, she wasn't sure how she would handle it.

Instead, she turned to the window and watched the darkness slide by until the lights of a city appeared on the horizon. Once they arrived at the seaside fortress belonging to Monteverde's king, their six-man security team, clad in black suits and probably packing enough artillery to take over a small country, preceded Nico and Lily out of the helicopter and took up stations to await their descent. Nico went first, then held out his hand and helped Lily to the landing pad.

A man in a white dinner jacket and bow tie came forward and bowed deeply. "Serene Highnesses, welcome."

Lily bit the inside of her lip and followed Nico's lead. She had to relax, had to get through this night and the inevitable meeting with Princess Antonella so that she could return to the palace and hug her baby close again.

Would she lock the bedroom door tonight? Or should she encourage Nico to join her? She was still angry with him, but perhaps they could move forward if they reconnected on the intimate level they'd shared at his house on the beach.

"Relax, Lily," Nico said quietly, looping her arm inside his and placing his hand over hers. "You are the Crown Princess of Montebianco. You outrank everyone here with the exception of the king. Remember this when you feel overwhelmed."

"I just want it over with," she said through the smile she'd pasted on her face as they passed between two rows of onlookers on the portico.

"It will be so soon enough," he said as they entered the interior.

Not soon enough for her liking.

They stopped in front of a large set of double doors, and the man who'd escorted them spoke to Nico in Italian. When he was finished, Nico bent to whisper in her ear.

"They will announce us, and we will enter onto the ceremonial staircase. We stand while the photographers take our picture, and then we descend. The king is not yet in attendance, but will appear after we've arrived."

"So we don't upstage him?"

"Precisely, *cara*."

Somehow, she got through the grand entrance, the photos, and then down the stairs—without stumbling on her high heels—to a large ballroom that had fewer people than she'd expected. It wasn't empty, but it wasn't packed, either.

Nico handed her a champagne flute. She took it, but did not drink. If anything, she needed a clear head tonight. They did not have long to wait before King Paolo arrived. He was a large, florid man, dressed in a uniform that was dripping with jewels and medals. At his side was a woman who made Lily's heart stutter in her chest.

Princess Antonella was the most graceful, elegant creature she'd ever seen. Her long, thick hair was swept into a pile on her head; her tiara made Lily's look puny, and she wore a deep ruby gown that set off her hair and skin to perfection. She walked with a lush, sensual roll of her hips that was most surely designed to rivet the attention of any male within sight. Lily wanted desperately to look at Nico, to see if there was regret or lust on his face, but to turn away would be an insult to the king.

And perhaps it was a blessing she couldn't look at Nico. Was she truly prepared to handle what she saw there?

Instead, she focused on the couple coming down the stairs. Antonella's beautiful face was set in a cool, detached mask while the king looked gruff and arrogant. From the corner of her eye, Lily saw Nico bend at the waist. At the last second, she remembered to drop into a curtsy.

"Welcome to Monteverde, Your Highness," King Paolo said to Nico, ignoring her altogether.

"We are delighted to be here, Your Majesty," Nico replied smoothly, though she knew it was anything but the truth. "My wife and I thank you for your hospitality."

"Come then, let me introduce you to some of my government ministers," the king said to Nico. "Antonella, entertain the prince's companion."

Lily watched them go, her heart pounding so hard she thought everyone could surely see it, and then turned to the woman who would have been Nico's wife had it not been for her. She expected to see hatred, but Antonella's expression remained cool and controlled. "*Principessa,* do join me."

She led the way to a small sitting area off one end of the ballroom. A few other women occupied the space, but found a reason to leap up and fade into the background as soon as Lily and Antonella appeared.

Lily sank onto a chair facing her beautiful rival. "I'm sorry you have to do this."

How hard it must be for Antonella to have to entertain her in public, knowing everyone was watching her be nice to the woman who'd ruined her happiness.

Antonella raised her champagne glass. "It is my duty," she replied before taking a delicate sip.

That word again. Lily was beginning to hate the sound of

it. She turned her head sideways, studying the other woman. Something about her makeup…

"Are you okay?"

Antonella shifted in her seat, rotating the right side of her face away from scrutiny. "Yes. It is nothing," she said, her fingers straying up to her cheek. "I was clumsy and ran into a door."

It was possible, Lily supposed, but she didn't quite buy it. Still, the bruise under Antonella's eye was none of Lily's business. It was well hidden under her makeup, though upon closer inspection the purpling skin was obvious when compared with the left side of her face.

Who would hit her? Her father? The idea horrified Lily, but then she'd disliked the man on sight—and Nico's description of him hadn't exactly been warm.

But Antonella seemed uncomfortable, so Lily didn't mention it again. The minutes ticked by as Antonella made small talk, and Lily soon relaxed. She found she couldn't help but like the princess even if the other woman was so well schooled in proper behavior that her questions were merely polite and not truly because she was interested.

"Your son, he is talking now?"

Lily laughed. "He talks quite a lot, yes."

"I think I would like a baby someday," she said almost wistfully.

Lily bit her lip and leaned forward. She hesitated to speak, but decided she had to do it. For her own peace of mind, if nothing else. "I'm sorry if I've caused you pain. But I'm not sorry Nico chose to be a father to his son."

Antonella's exotic eyes widened. "You love him?"

She'd gone this far; there was nothing for it except to be honest. The feeling was still so raw and new, but she wanted to share it with someone. Was it wrong to do so with this woman who had loved him, too? Or was it right to let Antonella know where she stood? "Yes, I do."

"Then I am very glad for you. To be in love, it is extraordinary. I wish to feel this for a man someday." Antonella's smile was startling—and genuine.

Lily blinked. "You aren't in love with Nico?"

"Oh good heavens, no," she laughed.

Lily felt as if a weight had been lifted from her soul. Antonella did not love Nico!

"You seem quite pleased," the princess said, smiling once more.

"I have to admit I am. I was afraid I'd ruined all your dreams." But what about Nico? Had he been in love with Antonella? She didn't think so—but she wasn't certain. It seemed unlikely. Or did it?

Antonella shook her head. "I was engaged to Gaetano first. Poor man. He chose his path, and that is all any of us can hope to do—though not so tragically, one would hope. When Gaetano died, my father negotiated to wed me to Nico instead."

Lily remembered her conversation with Antonella in Paris. She'd said she had a habit of chasing away grooms. Now it made sense.

"You *will* find someone," Lily said. "It'll happen when you least expect it, I imagine."

Antonella frowned. "I am not so sure. Love is perhaps not for me." Her gray eyes were piercing suddenly. "Be careful, Lily. Prince Nico, he is handsome and pleasing, but he knows these things about himself. He knows how to make women love him. He also knows how to break hearts."

Lily realized she was clutching her hands in her lap. "I—yes, I know."

Antonella reached across and squeezed her hand. "I do not wish to upset you. You are a nice girl, but Nico is a jaded man. I would not say this if I didn't know the truth. He had an affair with one of my school friends a few years ago. She'd been expecting marriage, I think. But Nico found a new woman to amuse himself with and moved on. This is often the way with such men."

"Such men?" Lily repeated, feeling the twist of the vise around her heart with every word.

"He is a prince, gifted with a handsome face and raised on entitlement. Trust me, I have a brother. I understand this quite well. But do not fret yourself, Lily! Nico may very well be tamed by marriage, and I will have upset you for nothing."

"No, you're right. I'd be naive to think otherwise." Lily sipped her champagne because she needed something to do. The liquid was no longer cold, and the bubbles nearly made her sneeze.

Perhaps she'd need to take champagne-drinking lessons before the next official soiree, she thought sourly. The idea would have made her laugh had her conversation with Antonella not tweaked that insecure part of her that was simply waiting for Nico to live up to his playboy reputation.

And what did she expect anyway? It'd been a little under two weeks since he'd married her, only a couple of days since they'd started having sex. Did she really think he could feel the same for her as she did for him? That his fascination with her body was anything more than the excitement of being with a new lover?

Until last night, he'd said all the right things, complimented her and seemed to enjoy their lovemaking. But was that enough to build a real relationship on? Without Danny, the entire scenario would be moot. He would not have lifted a single custom-shod foot to tromp down to her cell in the police station if she hadn't been carrying a picture of her baby. It was enough to make her breath catch painfully.

Antonella's gaze went beyond Lily's shoulder, her expression morphing from confusion to horror. Lily pivoted in her chair to see what was going on. A group of men in uniform, carrying automatic rifles, stomped toward them. Antonella bolted to her feet. Lily joined her more out of instinct than anything, surprised when the other woman gripped her hand and moved her body in front of Lily as if to shield her.

"What do you want?" Antonella demanded when the men fanned out, taking up position around them.

"*Scusi, Principessa Antonella,*" a tall, lean man who seemed to be the group leader said. "But we are under orders to take this woman into custody."

"This *woman,*" Antonella pronounced, "is the Crown Princess of Montebianco. Surely you are mistaken."

"No, *Mi Principessa,* I am not."

Nico sat in the king's private study, listening to the man expound on his theory of a united Monteverde and Montebianco forcing Monterosso to bow to their collective wills. It was entertaining, if pointless. The man had despotic tendencies and ambitions that were no good for his country, especially if he truly attempted to put any of his plans into action.

Nico had been introduced to several government ministers, who were only yes-men to Paolo, and then shown to the king's study where Paolo insisted he share a vintage bottle of Montebiancan brandy and talk.

Or, as it turned out, listen.

Nico was more than ready to leave. He glanced at his watch. Another minute, and he was making his excuses, retrieving his wife and flying home. He'd already been here two hours and Paolo had yet to commit to any of his proposals for getting the treaty back on track.

Maybe Nico's heart wasn't in it. He'd been out of sorts since his argument with Lily last night. He'd wanted to go to her, wanted to bust down the door and make love to her until she screamed his name, but he hadn't been able to make himself act. She'd said he'd made her life worse by forcing her into marriage. And he'd wanted to rail at her that in contrast he'd made *his* life worse. He was the one justifying his actions to his father, to this irritating man pontificating about alliances and the future, and to himself as he began to wonder whether he'd done the right thing or not.

He'd never wanted a child of his to endure a life like the one he'd had, but had marriage been the necessary vehicle to take care of Danny? Could he not have found another way to provide for them?

Basta, no. He'd done the right thing, the *only* thing he could do. Lily would learn how to be a princess, and Danny would grow up as a prince and the heir to the throne. What was done was done.

A man came in to hand Paolo a paper, leaning over to whisper something in his ear as he did so. Paolo's face split into a grin.

"Prince Nico," Paolo said when the man had gone again. "It seems as if we have caught a thief."

"A thief? How extraordinary."

Paolo's mouth twitched. "Indeed, she is quite extraordinary."

Nico's skin prickled in warning.

"I am so sorry to inform you, Your Highness, but it seems as if the woman who accompanied you tonight is part of an international gang of antiquities thieves."

Nico shot out of the chair just as the door burst open to admit several armed men. He stood there in impotent rage, fists clenched at his side, heart racing, and glared at the man who watched him with an amused look on his face.

"If you've hurt her—"

How could he have brought her here tonight? How could he have put her in danger? He should have refused, no matter what his father or Paolo demanded. Ice dripped into his veins. He needed to deal with this man coldly, on his level. He could not afford the distraction of *any* emotion right now.

"This is what you will do," Paolo said coolly, all pretence

gone. "You will divorce this woman and marry my daughter, as you should have done in the first place."

"You dare to imprison my wife? To threaten me? You're risking war, Paolo."

"You would take your country to war over a woman? Like Menelaus, yes? You know what happened to Menelaus—the beautiful Helen ran off with Paris willingly, and the Greeks spent ten years trying to get her back. Was it worth it?"

"It's not about the woman," he bit out. "It's about sovereignty. You insult my nation with this act of aggression against her Crown Prince."

Paolo's face turned an alarming shade of purple as he banged a fist on his desk. His crystal tumbler rattled violently, brandy sloshing over the side to splash the wood.

"You *will* marry my daughter. I insist on it. I have worked too hard to be thwarted by one such as you." Spittle formed at the corners of his mouth. "If you don't do as I say, I will have you both killed."

Nico was tempted to laugh—until he realized Paolo meant the threat. The man's eyes gleamed with barely contained madness. He'd thought Paolo was simply stubborn before, but it was much more than that. The King of Monteverde was unbalanced. There'd been rumors to that effect for a few years now, but there were always rumors coming out of royal palaces. He knew that firsthand, which was why he'd given them little credence.

Nico sized up the man before him. He could resist, but what was the point? If he agreed to do what Paolo wanted, then he had a chance to save Lily. Because he would not allow her to remain here as Paolo's prisoner—even if he had to die to free her. He'd put her in danger, he would get her out again.

"Very well, Your Majesty. But I want to see Lily first. And I want your assurance she will be well treated."

* * *

That this cell was far more luxurious than the one in which she'd been imprisoned in Montebianco was not a comfort. Bars were bars, and guards were guards.

Lily wrapped her arms around herself and stood in the middle of the sumptuously appointed room, an actual palace room with a cell door welded to the frame. Very odd, but then she'd learned that nothing was as she expected it to be since she'd left Port Pierre. Part of her could hardly believe she was here. Another part wanted to howl.

The lean man with the blade-thin nose had told her she was under arrest for her ties to an international ring of thieves who dealt in artifacts. The idea was preposterous, and yet here she was.

She rubbed her gloved hands over her bare shoulders. The chill ricocheting over her skin was the result of bone-deep fear, not from a lack of warmth in her prison. No, the room was everything a guest could want—were she a guest.

Lily sniffed back angry tears. This was all a mistake. She had faith that Nico would fix it. He would not allow his wife to be imprisoned by a neighboring monarch.

Antonella, bless her, had resisted mightily—but orders were orders and the guards were determined to carry them out. Lily finally agreed to go, certain it was a mistake and that it would all be sorted out.

When Nico finally appeared, relief threatened to buckle her knees. Lily flung herself at the bars, reaching for him. "Nico, what's going on? Get me out of here!"

She had only a glimpse of the fury on his face before he turned away from her as King Paolo came into view. Nico was coldly, brutally angry. If she were Paolo, she'd shrink in terror.

Yet the king merely looked smug. "You have seen her," he said in English, no doubt for her benefit. "Now you will return home and divorce her."

"Your word she will not be harmed, Paolo, or the deal is off."

The deal? "Nico? What's going on?"

He ignored her. A chill snaked down her spine, even colder than the chill she'd felt when she'd been brought to this room. Why was he so calm, so dispassionate? Didn't he care that she was in a cell? Or was he truly making deals with this awful man?

The possibility of it staggered her. And the truth. Montebianco came first. He'd told her that more than once. If he had to sacrifice her for his country, he would do so.

Oh God—

"She will not be harmed," Paolo said. Then he chortled gleefully. "Oh this is fun! I may have forgotten to mention, by the way, that I will soon have your son in my custody. Just in case you have any ideas of reneging on our agreement."

Lily's heart stopped. It. Just. Stopped.

How could she worry about herself when her baby was in danger? She wanted to choke the life from this man. From *both* of them. Fury, dark and cold, ate her from the inside out.

"If you hurt my child," she swore savagely, "I'll kill you myself."

Paolo spun toward her, laughing. "Oh ho, a threat to the monarch's life. This as well as her involvement with that despicable gang of thieves."

"You lying bastard," Lily hissed.

"Lily," Nico said sharply. "Enough."

"No," she shouted, gripping the bars in her fists. "How dare you stand there so passively when this—this *man* threatens our baby?" Her gaze swung to Paolo. "Tell me *right now* what you've done with my child!"

Paolo's glee was unholy. "Your nanny is a sweet creature, is she not? And yet she has a price. Everyone does—is that not right, Your Highness?" he asked Nico.

A muscle in Nico's jaw ticked, but he didn't reply. How could he stand there so mutely? She wanted to shake him, scream at him, *make* him act! He wouldn't correct the media, and now he wouldn't stop this evil king? What kind of man was he?

"Yes," Paolo said again, "everyone has a price. Mine is that you marry my daughter and make her your queen."

Lily felt as if someone had yanked the floor out from under her. She gripped the bars in an effort to hold herself up. Nico would not agree to this. *He would not, would not—*

"I have said I will do so," Nico replied. "But I want my son back immediately. Without him, there is no deal."

CHAPTER ELEVEN

SOMETIME DURING THE NIGHT, a team of black-clad men with face masks, night-vision goggles, headphones, and weapons burst through the outer doors to her prison and incapacitated the two guards. A voice ordered her to stand back, and then a flash of light split the gloom. Before she could process the popping sound, her cell door swung open and one of the men swept her into his arms.

Lily had no idea who they were or where they were taking her, but she prayed to God it was somewhere safe and that she would be reunited with her baby. She clung to her rescuer's neck, tired and aching and so, so ready for this nightmare to be over.

The men rushed up to the landing pad where a black helicopter descended onto the tarmac, blades whopping and doors wide-open. They piled in as shouts went up from below. Moments later, the craft levitated to the metallic burst of gunfire.

This helicopter was much louder than the executive version she'd flown in earlier, a stripped-down military monster that made conversation impossible. Lily tried to get away from the man still holding her, but his grip didn't loosen. As her struggle intensified, he reached up with one hand, stripped off the mask and headset and let them fall.

Lily's shock lasted only a second. Then she slapped him.

* * *

The city looked the same as it had yesterday, and yet nothing was the same. Lily refused to speak to him. Not that Nico blamed her. He sat at his desk staring into nothingness. He couldn't concentrate on the papers his assistant had given him earlier. The events of the night before had been outrageous, brutal and shocking. He'd wanted to strangle Paolo with his bare hands, yet to do so would have been a death sentence for them both.

Instead, he'd wasted no time once he'd left Monteverde in ordering Lily's rescue.

He shoved away from the desk and made his way to the nursery. He knew she would be there. She hadn't left their son's side since he'd brought her home. He hadn't wanted to leave, either, but his presence seemed to upset her. For the time being, he'd respected that. But no more.

Sunlight speared into the nursery. Danny was in his crib, napping. The sight of his son curled up with the blue dinosaur sent a wave of emotion through him. If not for the nanny's decision to do the right thing, he might have lost his wife and child both. A wave of despair tumbled through him at the thought.

A movement caught his eye and he turned his attention to the window. Lily lay on the window seat, head turned to look outside, a book dangling from one hand.

"Liliana," he said, surprised at how rough his voice sounded. At the mix of feelings tumbling through him. He shut them down without mercy, as he'd learned to do long ago. He already felt so out of sorts that he couldn't process them right now.

She turned bloodshot eyes on him. "Go away."

"No."

She didn't respond, simply stared out the window. He went to her side, took the book away and sat facing her, trapping her between him and the casing.

"Please don't touch me," she said, her voice cracking with the effort to control it.

"I apologize for what happened. I should have refused to take you to Monteverde. I did not trust Paolo, but I didn't know he was crazy enough to carry out such a scheme. He did not harm you, did he?"

She shook her head.

"Lily—*Dio,* I'm sorry you had to think I would go along with his plan, but it was the only way—"

"How did he get to Gisela?"

Nico shoved his fingers through his hair. "She has a brother, *tesoro mio.* He has been in much trouble in the past, and he'd once more fallen in with a gang. He disappeared a few days ago, no doubt on Paolo's orders. Gisela was offered money and the return of her brother should she hand Danny over when ordered. Instead, she chose to go to the authorities when the command came."

Wisely, since Paolo would have killed them both once he had Danny. Fortunately, Nico's men had located her brother; he was now free and would receive the rehabilitation he needed.

Her lip quivered. "I *am* grateful for that, but—oh God— he's just a baby. I wanted him to have a normal life, and now this. Will he always be at such risk?" Her head dropped to her knees as she brought them up in front of her, shielding her face from his view. "Of course he will, and it terrifies me. How do you live like this? Wait, don't tell me—*duty.*"

"Nothing like this has ever happened before—"

She speared him with a glare. "But that doesn't mean it won't again! I thought the media was bad, but what if something happened to one of us? Or both of us? What would Danny do then? And if you tell me the king and queen would take care of him, I'll scream. Those two shouldn't be allowed to take care of a goldfish, much less a child—"

"Nothing will happen, Lily," he said firmly, though he

couldn't disagree with her assessment of the royal couple's child-rearing skills. "We have taken the men who were behind the thefts into custody, and many of the artifacts have been recovered. It was a Monteverdian gang that Paolo sanctioned in order to finance his greed. Some of the art had been lost along the way, which is how those statues ended up amongst the ones the vendor had. It's over now."

"Maybe this time—but what about the next?"

"There will be no next. Paolo was a desperate man, *cara*. He steered Monteverde into bankruptcy over the years of his rule. The union with Montebianco was necessary for him to infuse his failing government with cash, but it was his last resort. His son has challenged his rule and it looks like he will be removed from power. Then the healing will begin."

"Things like this don't happen where I come from. Life is *normal*." She gave a half-hysterical laugh, sucked it in sharply. "My God, until last night, I had no idea you were actually in the military, that you would risk yourself in a rescue operation—"

"Did you think the uniform was simply for show?" he said gently. He wasn't an active member of the Montebiancan navy any longer, but he'd been trained extensively during his time in the service. He'd been advised against the mission because he was the Crown Prince, not because he wasn't prepared. Nothing, however, could have kept him from going.

"I don't know what I thought. But I do know I hate it here," she said softly, her eyes filling with tears again. "I've been nothing but miserable since the moment I set foot in this country—no, since the moment I met you two years ago." She pressed the heels of her hands to her eyes. "God, what an idiot I was to get involved with you."

"Then why did you do so? You should have given yourself to someone more worthy, then married him and bought your house and picket fence, as you Americans say."

Her comment stung, though he knew she wasn't wrong. Far better for her if he'd simply prevented the pickpocket from taking her purse and said goodbye. Instead, he'd been intrigued by her sweet innocence.

She shook her head. "I wish I had. I wish Danny was someone else's child."

If she'd pierced his heart with a hot knife, she couldn't have caused him more pain. But he knew something else now, something he should have recognized long ago.

"Lily, look at me. Please." He waited until she did so. The move was reluctant, but it was enough. "I should have told you who I was that night. I would say that I shouldn't have made love to you, but the truth is I don't regret that. If I'd realized in time, then yes, I should have stopped. But when I knew you were innocent, that I was your first, I should have been truthful with you."

He lifted his hand to touch her, thought better of it. "The first time is special, for a woman most of all I think. It is your right to know who you give yourself to."

Her shoulders slumped. "So many *shoulds,* Nico. Will we ever get it right?"

"Does anyone?"

"When there's love, then yes, I think so. But you don't love me. And I don't love you." She wouldn't look at him when she said it. Her words hurt him more than he'd have thought possible. She didn't love him. What did he feel?

His life was happier with her in it. But was that love? He didn't know, and couldn't focus on figuring it out when he was still smarting from the knowledge she didn't love him.

"I am fond of you, Lily. You have courage and integrity. You are the mother of my son, the mother of my future sons. We will have a good life together."

"But you *will* tire of me eventually. And then you'll go back to your mistresses and party-boy ways."

"I want no one but you," he protested, stung.

"Now. It will change, Nico. You're that kind of man."

He didn't know what to say, how to reach her. He just wanted to hold her, but he knew she would not let him right now. "Let us not talk about this yet. When the time comes, we will discuss—"

"When the time comes?" she hissed. She shoved herself up. The book fell to the floor with her sudden movement, but she ignored it. She popped her fists onto her hips and glared at him. "I thought you were out of your mind last night when you came bursting in with a group of commandos, but this absolutely takes the cake—"

Danny's cry interrupted her speech. She hurried to the crib, swung Danny into her arms and turned back to fix him with a hard look. "Go away, Nico. I don't want to talk to you right now."

Danny began to wail as she rocked him too hard. He saw the worry and self-loathing on her face, but then she seemed to take a deep breath—and calm washed over her. Danny's wailing turned softer as she crooned rhythmically.

Nico watched her soothe their son, something in him growing tight and heavy. She shot him another glare, then turned her back on him, shutting him out. Danny looked over her shoulder, but even he turned away without acknowledging his father.

Long after Nico was gone, Lily still wanted to walk out onto the terrace and scream at the top of her lungs. Maybe she would feel better. Most likely, however, she would make her throat hurt even worse than it already did. She'd yelled herself hoarse when Nico left her in the prison cell last night, then she'd cried when she thought she was doomed to stay there. She'd truly believed Nico had sacrificed her for his country's sake.

But, damn it, she was finished with crying. She had no one but herself to blame for the way she felt about him. She'd known what he was before she'd fallen in love with him. Why he'd risked himself in the rescue operation was beyond her. She did not fool herself he did it because of her.

She watched Danny play with a red fire truck and felt an urge to pick him up and hold him tight. She'd already done that so many times today that he was getting quite fussy whenever she gave in to the urge.

But she'd almost lost him, and it made her feel panicky and on edge. Still, she sat on her hands and watched him play, unable to leave him for more than a few moments at a time. Nico had already sent a new nanny—an older woman with a kindly smile—but Lily was reluctant to retreat for some much-needed rest.

Nothing about her life had been even remotely normal since the moment she'd arrived. She wasn't kidding Nico about that, though she'd perhaps been a bit harsh when she said that she wished Danny were someone else's child. She'd been upset, confused. She just wanted a normal life for her and her child. Why was that so much to ask?

"Oh God," she said, pressing her hands to her eyes again. She had to stop this weepiness. It was ridiculous.

He wasn't a bad man; he was a good man, a man with a strong belief in doing what was right. He'd married her so Danny would have a father, no other reason, and she had to admit it was noble—even if she didn't agree with his method or the fact she'd had no say in it once he decided. After his own childhood as the unwanted son under Queen Tiziana's thumb, she could understand why he did not scatter illegitimate children in the wake of his liaisons.

When he'd learned of Danny, he'd been truly shocked. Since then, he'd done the best he knew how to take care of them both. He was not at all the irresponsible womanizer he'd been made out to be in the media.

She was angry with him, angry with herself, but she'd been wrong to lash out at him the way she had.

And yet, in spite of the way she felt about him, she knew for an absolute fact that she could not live the kind of uncertain life he wanted to restrict her to. She couldn't share his bed, couldn't love him and bear his children, all the while knowing he didn't feel the same. That's why shc'd licd and said she didn't love him. How could she give him that kind of power over her?

And how, if she did, would she be any different than her mother had been? She'd grown up watching her mother reorder her life—*ruin* her life—simply to accommodate a man she couldn't seem to stop loving no matter how he treated her.

Lily would not compromise herself that way. Not ever. And she intended to tell Nico that just as soon as she apologized for saying she'd been miserable since she'd met him.

"Signora Cosimo, can you watch Danny?" she said as she went into the adjoining room.

"*Si, Mi Principessa,*" the woman replied, curtsying deeply.

He'd made a mess of everything.

Basta! Nico threw down his pen and put his head in his hands. Why, in trying to do what was right, did he keep getting everything wrong?

He'd made a mistake in bringing Lily here. She was beautiful and vibrant, and she loved their son to distraction. And he'd nearly lost them both because *he* had put them in danger. By forcing her to be his wife, by claiming his son, he'd put their lives on the line. They weren't accustomed to this life. Danny was young and would learn, but was it fair to force Lily to be something she did not want to be?

He loved his child. And, though his feelings were in a

tangle he was having trouble sorting out accurately, he knew he felt something for Lily. It wasn't the same as what he felt for Danny, which was why he couldn't quite figure it out. But he cared for her, cared what happened to her—cared very much about her happiness.

She didn't love him. She'd told him so only hours ago. It still hurt.

What kind of a selfish bastard was he to ask her to give up her life for him? Weren't there other solutions? He had money, power and the ability to travel when and where he liked. If he let her go, could they work it out somehow?

He didn't want to let her go. An ugly, selfish part of him raged at the thought of not having her in his life. At the thought of some other man making her his wife. But after everything that had happened, he owed it to her to give *her* the choice. She deserved far better than he'd done by her thus far. She deserved happiness.

If it was the last thing he did, he would give it to her. No matter how much it hurt.

Reluctantly, and with a sharp pain piercing his chest, Nico picked up the phone.

"Liliana."

Lily turned her head, stomping down on the current of pain and joy she felt each time he entered the room.

She'd looked for him everywhere earlier, but his assistant informed her he'd gone out. Exhausted, she'd finally given in to the urge to nap. Once she awoke, she'd showered and changed, then she sat on the terrace and watched the white lights of a cruise ship in the distance. It wasn't dark yet, but the sun had set and ribbons of crimson and purple still stretched across the horizon.

"I've been waiting for you," she said. "Anselmo said you were gone on business earlier."

"*Si,* there has been much to attend to." He moved with the shuffling gait of someone who was physically exhausted. He dropped a folder on the table before falling into a chair across from her. Before she could say anything, he pushed the folder toward her.

Her mouth felt suddenly dry. "What's that?"

"The answer, I hope."

"Answer to what?"

He rubbed his forehead absently, fixed her with a look. "Sign those papers, *cara,* and our marriage is no more. I am setting you free."

Lily had to work very hard to sound normal. "Is this a joke?"

"Not at all." He flipped the folder open, took a pen from inside and clicked it. Laid it with the top facing her. "Sign, Lily, and you may go."

Anger, fear, despair—she felt them all. "You aren't taking my son away from me. I told you before that I wouldn't leave him."

"Of course not. He will remain with you."

Lily gaped at him. Was he in his right mind? After everything they'd been through, everything he'd done to bind her to him and get Danny? "You aren't making sense, Nico."

"No? It is simple enough, *tesoro mio.* We will share our son, as many divorced couples do. He is still my heir, and he will need to spend more time in Montebianco as he grows up. But you will have a house here and will be with him."

Goose bumps prickled her skin. She was so cold all of a sudden. "You're divorcing me, but you want me to remain in Montebianco?"

"I am settling one hundred million of your American dollars on you, *cara,* and more in the future should you need it. You may buy a house on every continent should you wish. But I require you to spend time in Montebianco with our son so that he may learn his heritage and his position. Should he choose not to follow me when he is old enough to do so, that is his right."

Lily stared at the pen in front of her through a blur. He was offering her everything she could have hoped for. Danny would be safe and well. He would only have a part-time father—but that was better than no father. Or, at least it was when that father was Nico. He would not neglect his son, not ever. They could work it out, and her baby would never be in danger again.

Signing was the right thing to do. Earlier, she'd wanted to tell him she would not be a passive participant any longer. They could be married—because she truly hadn't thought he would divorce her—but she would not share his bed and wonder when he would cast her aside. She felt too much when they were together, and she wouldn't torture herself like that.

She deserved a man who loved her the way she did him. She wanted that man to be Nico, but clearly he never would be.

"If you are pregnant, *cara*—"

"I'm not," she said fiercely, not caring when a tear spilled free and dropped onto the paper. She'd gotten that news when she'd woken from her nap. There would be no baby.

"Ah."

She stared at him for a long minute, waiting for what she did not know. Did she expect him to confess his love? To tell her it was an elaborate ruse for some reason she couldn't fathom?

She picked up the pen, hesitated. Would he stop her? But he didn't move.

Lily had to lean closer to see the line. Another tear spilled, landed with a fat plop on his signature. Quickly, she scratched the pen across the line below his, then dropped it and shoved away from the table.

CHAPTER TWELVE

NICO DIDN'T TRULY FEEL the effects of what he'd done until many hours later, when he wandered into the nursery and found it empty. He'd been operating on autopilot, and now…

Now his son was no longer there, no longer ready to smile and babble at him and ask to be picked up. Nico liked holding his boy. The little guy put his arms around his neck and held on tight while Nico carried him around and talked to him in that silly voice parents often used with children. He'd never quite understood the urge to do so until he had his own child.

And then he hadn't cared how ridiculous he might sound, or who might overhear him.

He stood at the crib's edge and gripped the railing tight, staring into the emptiness with an unseeing gaze. Danny was gone, and the knowledge ripped him in two.

How had he managed to let them go? Why had he done it?

Part of him, the part he'd shoved down deep, howled in rage and grief.

He'd done the right thing; he'd given Lily her freedom because she had a right to find happiness with someone she could love. She deserved to be safe and well, to not live in fear. He could give her that much. If it hurt him to do so, he would get over it. She came first.

He could feel the weight of the blue diamond ring he'd given her in his trouser pocket. She'd left it on his pillow before she'd gone, and he'd carried it around for hours now, the solidity of it searing him like a brand. Reminding him of what he'd lost.

A hot, possessive emotion washed over him. He wanted her.

But it wasn't just a sexual need.

She came first. The feeling buffeting him was so strong, so overwhelming, that he wondered how he'd not been bowled over by it sooner.

He'd been happy with Lily and Danny. Lily was the only woman who'd ever seemed to care more about the man than the prince. Hadn't she told him she didn't like the prince? That the man was the one she preferred?

She'd given herself to him when she had no idea who he was, other than plain Nico Cavelli. She hadn't known about the money or the privilege, hadn't known he was from an ancient and royal family. She'd thought he was a foreign student visiting New Orleans for Mardi Gras.

Dio, she *loved* him. Nico couldn't breathe as he gripped the railing. Anguish ripped through him. She'd never said the words, but he knew she did. How had he been so blind? She'd lied to him and he'd believed her.

Madonna diavola, what a fool he was!

She'd told him she didn't love him because she hadn't believed him capable of loving her. Why had he not seen this? Why had he not told her the truth?

Because he *did* love her. She meant everything to him. When Paolo took her, he'd thought he would go mad with the urge to kill the man. Her safety had been his paramount concern. Not his own, not his country's—hers. Hers and Danny's. He would have died for them both if it had been necessary, and to hell with duty.

He was in love with the woman he'd married, the woman

who'd borne his child all alone—and he'd let her go. He'd sent her away because he'd believed she wanted her freedom, that she would be happier without him.

Dio, Dio, Dio.

Nico rubbed his chest, but the raw, empty hole did not go away. He'd let her go because he'd wanted to right the wrong he'd done her when he forced her to marry him.

But, once again, he'd gotten it wrong.

He spun away from the empty crib and strode through the apartment to his office. It was very early in the morning, and he hadn't slept at all, but he had much to do.

This time, he would get it right.

In the end, it was extraordinarily easy to leave her life in Montebianco and return to Port Pierre. She'd kept hoping— through the numbing ordeal of being ferried to the airport, boarding the royal jet and getting settled for the flight—that Nico would suddenly appear and tell her he'd been wrong, that he wanted them both to stay.

But the jet took off and there was no turning back. She'd chosen Port Pierre because it was familiar, but she had no idea where she would truly end up. Perhaps she'd move to Paris, learn French and find a handsome Frenchman to settle down with. The thought was so strange that it seemed like a film she might view rather than an idea about her life. She was wealthy beyond her dreams, yet she felt poorer than ever and sad.

When they landed in New Orleans, Lily took a room in a nice hotel in the French Quarter. She needed to prepare for her return to Port Pierre. She hadn't quite considered the logistics of it when she'd told Nico that's where she wanted to go. He'd ordered the jet made ready without question, and she'd felt that she had to carry through with it or look like a fool.

But if she were truly to return, she would need a place to stay that was big enough to accommodate the full-time nanny and the security team Nico sent with her. She'd thought the bodyguards would return to Montebianco when they delivered her to her destination, but no, they were as permanent as a presidential Secret Service detail. Danny was a prince, and the heir to the Montebiancan throne. He required security. She hadn't escaped the danger after all, no matter how far she'd run.

Lily spent four days in the city, putting off the trip to Port Pierre each morning as she contemplated her next move. She went to see her mother in the treatment facility. Nico had spared no expense in getting the best help possible. Donna Morgan looked better than Lily had ever seen her. Her skin wasn't so sallow, and she was actually filling out a bit. And she asked about her grandson, which shocked Lily and made her cry. When Lily left, Donna asked her to send pictures and to stay in touch. It was more interest in her life than her mother had shown in years and it touched her deeply.

On the sixth day, Lily hired a car and made the hour trek to her hometown. Port Pierre was exactly as she'd left it—and yet everything had changed. She knew she couldn't work at the paper anymore, not when she *was* the news. Everyone stared at her as she made the rounds of the shops and businesses she'd once frequented.

She even went to visit Carla, but it was awkward. Her friend had bought the historic home in Port Pierre's center that she'd always wanted and was fixing it up with the money Nico had paid her. Carla apologized over and over, though Lily told her she understood. But she left the encounter feeling more alone than she ever had. Something had changed between them in the short time Lily was gone, and she knew their relationship would never be the same. They would remain friends, but they would never have that easy camaraderie they'd once had. Their paths had diverged forever.

Lily returned to New Orleans more confused and upset than ever. It really was true that you could never go home again. She was untethered, blowing in the wind like a dried husk, uncertain where she would land or if she would survive the trip. Violent storms were an unfortunate part of life in Louisiana, but you could rebuild after a storm. How did you fix the damage left in your soul when it was a man who'd caused the devastation?

But of course she would survive, she thought angrily. It would just take time.

As if on cue, an afternoon thunderstorm blew into the city, lashing furiously at the windows and cracking booms that frightened Danny and made Signora Cosimo's eyes widen in alarm each time. When it was over, and everyone was soothed, Lily decided to walk the rain-washed streets alone. She needed to release some of her energy, needed to make a decision about what to do next, and she was determined to accomplish it this afternoon.

New Orleans was still a vibrant city, full of equal parts danger and exhilaration. She avoided the decadence of Bourbon Street, instead choosing the more elegant Royal Street a block over. To think she could now walk into any of the fancy shops and buy anything she wanted was still beyond her grasp. She was so accustomed to living frugally, with the exception of her two weeks as the Crown Princess of Montebianco.

Eventually, she had to pass St. Louis Cathedral. She hesitated only a moment before looping around to the front of the building on Chartres Street. The white facade of the church practically glowed in the pale light that remained after the storm had passed. Lily crossed the street to Jackson Square, then turned and looked up at the three spires of the church.

She sighed, then decided to start toward the hotel again. A man ambled toward her through the square and she stopped, struck by how he reminded her of Nico at this distance. He even wore a hooded running jacket, the same as Nico had that first time she'd met him. At the man's back was the Mississippi River, turning golden as a ray of setting sunshine spilled over its surface. A barge glided by in the distance and she focused on it wistfully.

But when her gaze returned to the man, her heart quickened. It could not be...

It took a very long moment for her to realize that her heart had recognized what her eyes still did not want to admit.

"Liliana," he said, drawing up in front of her. His hands were in his jeans pockets, but he took them out and pushed back the hood.

"What are you doing here?" she asked, dumbstruck. It was too much, the sight of him. All her memories of meeting him here two years ago crashed down on her. And everything since. She felt as though she needed to sit, so she retreated to a park bench a few feet away and thunked down on it.

Nico followed, though he stood over her and didn't join her on the bench. He looked...sheepish. And as if he hadn't slept in days. Lines of strain bracketed his mouth, and dark circles lay heavy under his eyes.

His beautiful eyes.

"I want you to marry me," he said.

If he'd announced he was joining the circus, she couldn't have been more surprised. "But you just divorced me. Why would I want to go through it again?"

"Because you love me."

Lily shot up off the bench, heart pounding. "How dare you come here and try to manipulate me this way! What happened,

Nico, did you decide you'd made a mistake and now you want us back?"

"Yes." Said without hesitation.

The steam faded from Lily's tirade. She had not the strength to battle him, not anymore. "You pushed us away. You told us to go."

"I have regretted it every moment since. I made a mistake."

Lily shook her head, tears blurring her eyes. "I can't do this, Nico. I can't go through the ups and downs of a life with you."

"The ups and downs can be quite pleasant, yes?"

"I can't do this," she repeated.

His smile faded. He looked grave, as serious as she'd ever seen him. "I want you, Lily. I want Danny. Come back to Montebianco with me. I will protect you both with my life."

She choked down a sob.

"I can't." She clenched her fists together, fought the urge to scream at the top of her lungs. Her entire body trembled with the opposing forces beating at her. "Oh God, it's not fair! I can't stand a life without you, but how can I manage one with you?"

She whirled around, intent on getting away, but he caught her against him before she'd taken the first step, pressed her cheek to his chest while she clutched his jacket. She wanted to push him away, and yet she couldn't. How pitiful was she?

All she could do was cling to his warmth, his strength. He smelled like home to her, like everything she'd ever wanted in her life. She closed her eyes, drank in his scent.

Beneath her cheek, his heart beat nearly as fast as her own. He pushed her a step back suddenly, tilted her head up with his palms on either side of her face. His eyes were as haunted as she felt as he looked down at her.

"I love you, Lily. Do you hear me? I love you."

She felt the tears slip down her cheeks now, faster than

before. "You don't mean it," she said. "You can't love me. You're supposed to love someone like Antonella—"

"*Never.* I love *you*. No other woman compares to you. You are bright and beautiful, and you love me—"

"I didn't say that!"

His smile was tender. "You didn't have to." He grasped her hand, pressed it to his heart. "Do you feel what you do to me? You see the real me, Lily. You are the only one who ever has, the one who owns me body and soul. If you tell me no now, I will respect that. But I will die inside for every day you are not with me—"

"Stop, Nico," she whispered. "I can't take anymore—"

"It is the truth, *tesoro mio.* I adore you, I adore our baby, I want my life to be full again. It will only be so with you in it."

She stared up at him, her heart careening into territory she didn't understand. But her mind was more cautious. "I want it, too, Nico—but how can I be sure you won't change your mind? That you won't tire of a wife and children? I won't accept girl-friends or royal mistresses or whatever you want to call them."

"Lily, for God's sake, didn't you hear me? I love *you*. Only you. I want no one else. I cannot imagine being with anyone else." He took her by the shoulders, looked her square in the eye. "You told me that you never wanted anyone but me. How can you imagine that I don't know my own heart like you know yours?"

"That's fair," she whispered, her throat aching.

"Tell me you love me, Lily. Tell me you will marry me."

But she couldn't do it just yet. "It's been six days, Nico."

"I was on my way within hours after you left, but my father had a mild heart attack—"

"Oh no! I'm sorry."

"He is well, *cara*. It was very mild, and the drugs dis-solved the clot instantly. But I had to return and remain as regent while he was on bed rest."

"Duty called," she said.

"It will often do so. I cannot lie to you about that. Sometimes, I will have to obey the dictates of duty. But I will never do so when your happiness is at stake. Never, *Mi Principessa*."

She toyed with one of the strings on his jacket. "I understand, Nico. And it's one of the things I admire most about you. Your dedication to doing what is right, I mean."

"It has taken me a very long while to get this right." He dropped to one knee, and her breath caught. "Marry me, Liliana. Have babies with me. Make me smile, make me crazy, but most of all, say yes and make me happy."

She blinked down at him. He meant it—oh God, he *meant* it.

"Shouldn't you have a ring?" she teased, joy beginning to bubble inside her soul.

He grinned, fishing something from his pocket. "I do. It is most gaudy and ostentatious, but I have learned my lesson, I assure you. This," he said, slipping the correctly sized blue diamond onto her shaking ring finger, "is merely temporary. Until we can go to the jeweler's and pick out a proper ring together."

Lily clutched the diamond to her. "No, this one is perfect. It's the one you gave me when I said yes to your proposal. I couldn't dream of trading it."

"So you agree to marry me?"

She wrapped her arms around his neck. "I do," she said, then bent to kiss him.

When she finally stopped, he stood and swept her into his arms, twirling her around until she giggled.

Then he set her down and pulled her in close, his hands on her hips. She couldn't mistake that he wanted her when their bodies came into contact.

"I am crazy for you, Lily. *Crazy*." He kissed her thoroughly, groaning when she pressed in against him. But her body ached, too. If she could get him back to the hotel, send Signora Cosimo and Danny down to dinner…

"I have a room," he murmured. "Do you want to come back to it?"

"I would love to."

They hurried through the streets until he pulled up short in front of a building that housed an inexpensive hotel. Lily gaped at him. "It's the same place."

He grinned. "The same room, too."

And then they were inside, tearing at each other's clothes, mouths and bodies desperate to connect again. They never made it to the bed. Nico backed her into the wall and lifted her, then thrust inside her while she wrapped her legs around his waist. Their lovemaking was urgent, intense, and she quickly spiraled to the heights of pleasure, then splintered apart while he relentlessly drove her over the edge.

When it was finished, they slid down the wall to the floor, breathing hard. Lily let her gaze slide over the room. The rose wallpaper was about forty years out-of-date, the furnishings were neat and clean, though slightly scarred and threadbare, and the floor creaked.

"I'm surprised you remembered which room," she said.

He looked indignant. "This place is very special, *cara*. The future king of Montebianco was conceived here."

"And maybe, if we're lucky, a brother or sister."

Nico kissed her and grinned. "I will do my part, Lily. As many times as you deem necessary."

"I'm sure one night won't be enough. We will need to keep trying again and again…."

His smile widened. "And again and again."

"Now you've got the idea." *Men.* Thank God.

Nico laughed. "Until I die of exhaustion, *Mi Principessa*, I live to serve you in all ways."

Lily traced her finger along his beautiful, lush mouth. How had she ever gotten so lucky? *This* was right, so right.

"I love you, Nico Cavelli. Even if you are a prince."

EPILOGUE

THEY WERE MARRIED AGAIN in Montebianco, a big state wedding with television crews and world media coverage. Princess Antonella caught the bouquet, and Donna Morgan looked very elegant and respectable as the mother of the bride. She wasn't finished with her rehabilitation, but she was making progress every day. Lily actually enjoyed spending time with her, and Donna seemed to take the pageantry and protocol of having a royal daughter in stride.

Lily had even managed to recruit the local reporters into her way of thinking. The coverage wasn't always glorious, and falsehoods most definitely made it into the European tabloids, but Lily established a public relations office where she interacted with media representatives for a few minutes each week. She'd quickly become their darling, and she was determined to maintain as much control over her image, and her family's, as possible. She enjoyed meeting with reporters now, and she always felt satisfaction at a job well-done. Public relations, it seemed, was her true calling.

When Nico asked where Lily wanted to honeymoon, she answered without hesitation: the house on the coast. The days were spent making love, playing on the beach with Danny and simply enjoying each other's company. They even returned to the cave, this time with a picnic and a nice blanket, and finished what they'd started the last time.

Lily emerged from the shower after a particularly delightful afternoon in bed with her husband to find him sitting on the floor with their son. He often went and got Danny and brought him into their room while Lily dressed.

Danny stood across from Nico, his little face very serious as he held out his blue dinosaur and said something. Nico's brows drew together, but he smiled and said something back.

Danny shook his head and said it again.

Nico looked up when she walked in. "Help."

"I don't know, Nico."

Danny swung his gaze to Lily, but turned back to Nico. Then he toddled over and threw his arms around Nico's neck. "Baba," he said. "Baba."

And then he set his dinosaur in Nico's lap and walked away.

Nico's eyes were shining as he looked at her. "Did he just say…?"

Lily pressed her hand to her mouth. "Yes."

"Don't cry, Lily," he said, getting up to come and hold her close.

"Same to you."

"Princes don't cry," he said very seriously, even though his eyes were suspiciously wet.

"Of course not," Lily agreed, squeezing him tight.

Then he tilted her head back and kissed her. And in spite of the fact they'd just made love, she wanted him again with a fierceness that always took her breath away.

"You are my happiness," he said, pressing his lips to her forehead. "My soul. Both of you."

"Three of us," she corrected.

He searched her face. "This is true? You are pregnant?"

"I think so, but I will need to be tested."

"Get in bed," he ordered.

"Nico, we just got out of bed."

"No, *you* get in bed. Immediately. I will bring you dinner and—"

She put her hand over his mouth. "We're not living in the Middle Ages. I think I can safely walk around the house, perhaps even swim a bit. Who knows, maybe I can even make love…."

"Very well," he said with a long-suffering sigh. "But no more motorcycle riding."

Lily laughed. "I'm sure I can agree to *that*."

* * * * *

Prince of Montéz, Pregnant Mistress

SABRINA PHILIPS

Sabrina Philips discovered Mills & Boon® romances one Saturday afternoon in her early teens at her first job in a charity shop. Sorting through a stack of preloved books, she came across a cover featuring a glamorous heroine and a tall, dark, handsome hero. She started reading under the counter that instant—and has never looked back!

A lover of both reading and writing, Sabrina went on to study English with classical studies at Reading University. She adores all literature but finds there's nothing else quite like the indulgent thrill of a romance novel.

After graduating, Sabrina began to write in her spare time, but it wasn't until she attended a course run by author Sharon Kendrick in a pink castle in Scotland that she realized if she wanted to be published badly enough, she had to make time. She wrote anywhere and everywhere and thankfully, it all paid off—a decade after reading her very first Mills & Boon® novel, her first submission—*Valenti's One-Month Mistress*—was accepted for publication in 2008. She is absolutely delighted to have become a published author and to have the opportunity to create infuriatingly sexy heroes of her own she defies both her heroines—and her readers—to resist!

Sabrina continues to live in Guildford with her husband, who first swept her off her feet when they were both sixteen and poring over a copy of *Much Ado About Nothing*. She loves traveling to exotic destinations and spending time with her family. When she isn't writing or doing one of the above, she works as deputy registrar of civil marriages, which she describes as a fantastic source of romantic inspiration and a great deal of fun. For more information please visit www.sabrinaphilips. com.

With thanks to Penny, for her art expertise
and her much-valued friendship.
And to Phil, whose enduring patience
continues to astound me.

CHAPTER ONE

HER heart was beating so loudly in her chest that Cally Greenway was convinced the whole auction room could hear it. Drawing in a deep breath, she uncrossed then recrossed her legs for the umpteenth time and tried to dismiss it as a flurry of anticipation.

After all, tonight *was* the night she had been waiting for. She looked at her watch. In less than ten minutes, the dream she'd worked so hard for would finally be a reality.

So why did it feel like her whole body was going into meltdown?

Cally closed her eyes and trawled her mind for a legitimate explanation as the penultimate lot, a heavily sought-after Monet, reached astronomical heights. Yes, that was it. She might be a restorer of art, but the art world— epitomised by nights like this, where beauty and expression became about money and possession—left her feeling out of her depth. She didn't belong at Crawford's auction house at the most prestigious art auction in their calendar, she belonged in overalls in her studio.

That was why she couldn't concentrate, she argued inwardly as she tried to encourage the hem of the silky black dress she'd borrowed from her sister back towards her knee. It absolutely, categorically, had nothing to do with the fact that *he* was here.

Cally castigated herself for even having noticed him arrive, let alone entertaining the idea that he had anything to do with the physical symptoms that were assailing her. There was no way any man could have that kind of effect on her, least of all one she'd never met before.

Well, technically. She had seen him once before, when she'd attended the sale preview two days ago, but she hadn't actually *met* him. 'Met' implied that there had been some interaction between them, which of course there hadn't been. He was classically handsome, and the expensive cut of his clothes—along with his very presence at an event like this—suggested he was filthy rich. He probably had some meaningless title like 'duke', or 'count', which altogether added up to him being the kind of man who wouldn't give a woman like her a second glance. Which was absolutely fine, because she had no desire to meet someone that arrogant and conceited anyway. One man like that had been enough to last her a lifetime; she had no desire to meet another.

So why was it she hadn't been able to drive the intensity of his deep blue eyes from her thoughts, ever since she'd walked into that sale room and had seen him standing there like Michelangelo's famous statue come to life? And why was it taking all her willpower not to steal another glance over her shoulder to the second row in the back right-hand corner of the room? Not that she had plotted the layout on an imaginary piece of graph paper and knew his exact co-ordinates, or anything. Why would she? *Because every time you look round he slants you an irresistible, one-sided smile which sends the most extraordinary shiver down your spine?* an unfamiliar and thoroughly unwelcome voice inside her replied, but immediately she silenced it.

'And finally we come to lot fifty. A pair of paintings by the nineteenth-century master Jacques Rénard, entitled *Mon Amour par la Mer* from the estate of the late Hector Wolsey. Whilst the paintings are in need of some specialist restoration in order to return them to their original glory, they are undoubtedly the two most iconic pieces Rénard ever painted.'

Cally drew in a deep breath as the auctioneer's words confirmed that the moment she had been waiting for was finally here. She closed her eyes again, trying to visualise the air travelling up her nostrils and blowing her errant thoughts aside. When she opened them, the wall panel to the right of the bespectacled auctioneer was rotating in a spectacular one-hundred-and-eighty-degree turn to reveal the stunning paintings, and the breath caught in her throat in awe.

She remembered the first time she'd ever seen them, or rather a print of them. Not long after she'd started secondary school, her art teacher, Mrs McLellan, had held them up as an example of how Rénard dared to push the boundaries set by his contemporaries by having a real woman as his subject rather than a goddess. The rest of the class had been lost in a fit of giggles; between the two paintings, Rénard's *Love by the Sea* went from fully clothed to completely naked. But for Cally it had been a defining moment in her life. To her the pictures spoke of beauty and truth, of the two sides of every story—of herself. From that moment on, she had known unequivocally that her future lay in art. A certainty matched only by her horror when she had discovered that the original paintings were shut away on the country estate of a pompous aristocrat getting damp and gathering cigar smoke, rather than being on public display for everyone to enjoy.

Until now. Because now they were owned by Hector Wolsey junior, whose horse-racing habit had caused him to demand that Crawford's auction house sell his late father's paintings immediately, before they'd even had the chance to say 'in-house restoration team'. Which meant the London City Gallery had been frantically trying to raise enough money to buy them, and had been lining up a specialist conservator to undo the years of damage. To Cally's delight, her enthusiasm, impressive CV and her expert knowledge on Rénard had eventually convinced the gallery team that she was the right person for the job. The job she had wanted for as long as she could remember, and the break in her career she desperately needed.

Cally glanced around the room as the bids took off, starting reassuringly with Gina, the gallery's agent, who was seated just along from her. There was a low hubbub of hushed, excited voices in every row of seats. Telephonists packed around the edges of the room were shaking their heads and relaying bids to eager collectors the world over. Within seconds, the bids exceeded the estimate in the sale catalogue, so much so that Cally was tempted to use her own catalogue as a makeshift fan to combat her soaring temperature—but she refrained, partly because she was rooted to her seat in anticipation, and partly in fear that it might inadvertently be taken for a bid. The moment was tense enough.

Unless you were Mr Drop-dead Gorgeous, Cally observed, her pulse reaching an unprecedented pace as she stole another look in his direction and caught him leaning back with a casual expression, his body utterly at ease beneath the blue-grey suit. She could do with a bit of that—composure, that was. Because, whilst she saw Gina raise her hand in between every figure the auctioneer repeated at speed, it did little to ease her nerves. Even if the gallery had promised her it was a dead cert.

But no doubt that was what Wolsley's son said about the races, she thought, caught between recalling the dangers of trusting anything too blindly and willing herself to relax. No, however convinced the gallery team had been that they had secured enough funds, the only time you could truly relax in a situation like this was if you had nothing riding on it—as *he* clearly didn't, she justified to herself. So what was he doing here when he hadn't bid on any of the previous eleven paintings since he'd entered the room at lot thirty-eight? Just as Cally was about to make a list of possibilities in her mind, something happened.

'That's an increase of—wait—ten *million* on the phones,' the auctioneer said uncharacteristically slowly, taking off his glasses in astonishment as he looked from the gallery of telephonists back to the floor. 'That's seventy million against you, madam. Do I have seventy-one?'

The rest of the auction room went ominously still. Cally felt her heart thump madly in her chest and her stomach begin to churn. Who the hell were they bidding against? According to the gallery team every serious collector with their eye on the Rénards should have been sitting in this room. Gina's horrified expression said it all. Cally watched on tenterhooks as she looked discomposedly at the paper-work in her lap. Eventually, Gina inclined her head.

'Seventy-one million,' the auctioneer acknowledged, replacing his spectacles and looking back to the phones.

'Do I have seventy-two? Yes.' He moved his head back and forth like a tennis umpire. 'There, do I have seventy-three?'

Gina gave a single, reluctant nod.

'Any advance on seventy-three?' He looked up to the gallery.

'We have eighty on the phones.'

Eighty?

'Any takers at eighty-one?'

Nothing. Cally squeezed her eyes tightly shut.

'Last chance at eighty-one—no?'

Cally stared helplessly at Gina, who shook her head apologetically.

'Closing then, at eighty million pounds.'

The sound of the hammer, and the auctioneer's cry of 'Sold,' echoed through her body like a seismic tremor.

The London City Gallery had lost the Rénards.

Horror ripped through her gut. The paintings she loved were to be shipped off to God knew where. Her hopes of restoring them were dead, and the door to the career she'd been on the cusp of walking through slammed in her face. The wall panel revolved another one hundred and eighty degrees and the paintings disappeared.

There *was* no such thing as a dead cert. It was over.

As the people began to gather their things and make their way out into the anonymity of the London streets, Cally remained in her chair, staring blindly at the empty wall. She didn't see the way that Mr Drop-dead Gorgeous lingered behind, and barely even noticed Gina's whispered apology as she crept away. She understood; the gallery's funds were not limitless. Even if they could have raised enough retrospectively, they had to weigh up their expenditure against the draw of the public. At a few million over the estimate, the paintings were such a prolific attraction they'd considered them still worthwhile. But almost double? She knew Gina had been taking a risk to go as high as she'd gone.

So, someone else had wanted the Rénards more. Who? The thought snapped her out of her paralysis. Surely whichever gallery it was planned to get someone to restore them? She knew it broke every unwritten rule of auction-room decorum there was, but suddenly finding out was her only hope. Launching herself from her seat, she rushed over to the back of the room where the row of telephonists was filing away.

'Please,' she cried out to the man who had taken the call. 'Tell me who bought the Rénards.'

He stopped and turned to look at her along with several of his colleagues, their faces a mixture of curiosity and censure.

'I do not know, madam. It is strictly confidential between the buyer and the cashier.'

Cally stared at him in desperation.

The telephonist shook his head. 'He said only that he was bidding on behalf of a private collector.'

Cally stumbled backwards and sat down in one of the empty chairs, resting her head in her hands and fighting back her tears. A private collector. The thought made her blood boil. The chances were they would never be seen by anyone again until *he* died of over-excess.

She shook her head. For the first time since David she'd actually dared to believe her life was going somewhere. But her only ticket out had just been torn into a million pieces. Which left her with what? A night in the cheapest London hotel she'd been able to find, and then back to the cramped town house-cum-studio in Cambridge. Another year of sporadic restorations which would barely cover her mortgage, because on the rare occasions a career-altering piece like this came up it only ever seemed to matter who you knew and never what you knew.

'You look like you could use a drink.'

The accented voice was French, and to her surprise it sent an even more disturbing tremor through her body than the sound of the auctioneer's hammer. Perhaps because she knew immediately who the voice belonged to. Though she had told herself that if he came near the alarming effect he had on her would inevitably diminish, the reality was that it seemed to double in strength. She ran her hands through her hair as if she'd really just been fixing it all along and turned around to face him.

'I'm fine, thank you.'

Fine? Cally laughed inwardly at her own words. Even if she'd been asked to restore every painting in the auction she doubted it would have been possible to describe her mental state as 'fine', with all six-foot-two-inches of him stood before her, filling her body with sensations she barely even recognised and which she certainly had no desire to confront.

'I'm not convinced,' he said, looking at her altogether too closely.

'And who are you, Crawford's post-auction psychologist?' Cally replied, unnerved by his scrutiny. 'Brought in during the final ten lots ready to mop up the disappointed punters after the show?'

A wry and thoroughly disarming smile crossed his lips. 'So you did notice me as soon as I walked in.'

'You didn't answer my question,' Cally retorted, colouring.

'So I didn't.'

Cally scowled. There was only one thing she hated more than people who oozed wealth, and that was people who were selective with the truth. She picked up her handbag and zipped it shut.

'Thank you for your concern, but I have to get back to my hotel.' She turned to walk towards the open doors at the back of the room.

'I'm not,' he countered. 'A psychologist, that is.'

She turned, no doubt just as he'd known she would. It was arrogant, but at least it was honest. 'Then who are you?'

'I'm Leon,' he replied, stepping forward and extending his hand.

'And?'

'I'm here in connection with my university.'

So, he was a uni lecturer? Her first and utterly shameful thought was that she should have done her degree in France. The art professors she'd known had all been pushing sixty, and had looked like they hadn't seen a razor, and smelled like they hadn't used a can of deodorant, for just as long. Her second was pure astonishment; he seemed to exude too much wealth and sophistication. But then all Frenchmen were known for being stylish, weren't they? And it did explain why he'd simply been observing, not buying. She castigated herself for being too quick to judge.

'Cally,' she said, extending her hand in return, then wondered what the hell she'd been thinking when the touch of his fingers made her inhale so sharply that speech deserted her.

'And *are* you a disappointed punter?' He raised one eyebrow doubtfully.

'You think I'm not the type?' she rebounded defensively, finding her voice again, though she didn't know why she was arguing with him when as a lecturer he was no more likely to have the spare cash to buy a priceless painting than she was.

'I think you didn't make a single bid.'

'So, you noticed me right back?' Cally replied with more pleasure than she ought to have felt. He hadn't given her a second glance two days ago, when she'd been wearing her usual work clothes instead of dolled up as tonight's occasion demanded. Besides, why should it matter if he had noticed her? It would only be a matter of time before he noticed someone else.

He nodded. 'Indeed. And, since you haven't answered my question about whether or not you are a disappointed punter, it seems we're even.'

She stared at the wall where the paintings had been only moments before and was hit by a renewed sense of failure. 'It's complicated. Let's just say tonight should have changed my life for the better. It didn't.'

'The night is young,' he drawled with a supremely confident grin.

Cally dragged her eyes away from his lips and made a show of looking at her watch, horrified to find that she was almost tempted to find out what he meant. Ten-fifteen. 'Like I said, I have to get back to my hotel.'

She turned to walk towards the door.

'Do you have a better offer waiting at your final destination, or are you just the kind of woman who is scared of saying yes?'

Cally froze, not turning round.

'No. I'm the kind of woman who is well aware that asking someone you've only just met out for a drink is really asking for something else entirely, and I'm not interested.'

Leon whistled through his teeth. 'So you prefer a man to cut to the chase? Detail exactly what he has in mind before you agree?'

She blushed. 'I would prefer it if a drink only meant a *drink.*'

'So you *are* thirsty, *chérie?*'

Cally swallowed, her mouth going inconveniently dry. Was she the kind of woman who was scared of saying yes? she wondered, suddenly both horrified and aggrieved that he might actually be right. No, she justified, she wasn't afraid—she'd just learned from experience that *that* kind of yes inevitably led to disappointment. Which was why—unlike other girls she knew, who invariably spent their evenings making out with random guys in clubs—she'd spent the last seven years sitting at her desk into the early hours of every morning memorising the chemical make-up of conservation treatments, practising each and every technique for the sake of her precious career. But look where it had got her now! Precisely nowhere.

Cally took a deep breath. 'Yes' might very well lead to disappointment, but right now it didn't get much more disappointing than the thought of returning to her hotel with nothing but her misery and the overpriced minibar for company. At least accepting the offer of one drink with a perfectly normal man for once in her life would take her mind off what had just happened.

'On one condition, then…' she began confidently, but the instant she raised her eyes she caught sight of his devastating smile, and remembered too late that there was absolutely nothing remotely normal about the way he made her feel. If anything, that was what she should be afraid of. 'The topic of work is off the agenda.'

'Done,' he answered decisively.

'Right.' Cally's head began to spin. 'Then…where did you have in mind?'

CHAPTER TWO

LEON didn't have anywhere in mind. He hadn't had anything on his mind for two full days—except her. He'd come to Crawford's to view the pre-auction exhibition of the paintings the world wanted to get their hands on, and had found himself wanting to get his hands on something else entirely: the narrow waist and shapely hips of the woman with lustrous red-bronze hair, who'd been transfixed by the paintings he'd suddenly forgotten he'd come here to see. The wave of desire had come out of nowhere, for it was certainly unprovoked. Though the luscious curves of her figure were obvious, she couldn't have been dressed any less provocatively, in a drab, crinkled blouse and olive-green skirt that reached her ankles. He'd wanted to dispose of them both there and then.

And he would have done, if he'd known who she was and that she could be trusted to be discreet. But he hadn't. Standing there, all misty-eyed before the paintings, she'd looked—most inconveniently—like exactly the kind of woman who would cloud everything with emotion and make discretion an impossibility. But the knot of heat in his groin had demanded he find out for certain. How fortuitous, then, that when he'd asked a few discreet questions of his own it turned out that she was the London City Gallery's choice to restore the Rénards. For once in his life, a twist of fate had amused him. She would have to be fully vetted anyway. Suddenly it made perfect sense for him to stay on for the auction and undertake the investigation personally.

Leon watched her as she walked beside him, oblivious to the sound of taxicabs and buses that filled the tepid June evening. To his pleasure, she looked a world away from the olive-green drabness of just over forty-eight hours before; she was luminescent in black silk, the halter neck revealing an ample cleavage, and her striking hair, which had previously been tied back, now fell over her shoulders in waves. Tonight she looked exactly like the sort of woman capable of the kind of short and mutually satisfying affair he had in mind.

'Lady's choice,' he said, realising they had reached the end of the street, and he still hadn't answered her question as to where they were headed.

Cally, whose nerve was evaporating by the second, looked around the street and decided that the sooner this was over the better. 'The next bar we come to will be fine, I'm sure. After all, its only requirement is that it serve drinks, is it not?'

Leon nodded. *'D'accord.'*

As they turned the corner of the street, Cally heard a low, insistent drumbeat and saw a neon sign illuminating darkness: the Road to Nowhere.

'Perfect,' Cally proclaimed defiantly. It might look a little insalubrious, but at least it was too brash and too noisy for there to be any danger of lingering conversation over an intimate table for two.

Leon looked up, to see a young couple tumble out of the

door and begin devouring each other up against the window, and he stifled a grin.

'It looks good to me.'

Cally did a double take, doubting he was serious. Then she wished she hadn't, because the sight of his impossibly handsome face beneath the soft glow of the street lights made her whole body start with that ridiculous tingling again.

'Fabulous. And my hotel is only two streets away,' she said, as much to convince herself that after one drink she could return to the safety of her room as to remind him.

'What could be better?' he drawled, the look in his eyes explicit.

She swallowed down a lump in her throat as they passed the couple, who were yet to come up for air, and entered the bar.

It was dark inside, the sultry vocals of a female singer stirring the air whilst couples absorbed in one another moved slowly together on the dance floor. *Oh yes, great idea, Cally. This is much safer ground than a quiet bar.*

'So what will it be, a Screaming Orgasm or a Pineapple Thrust?'

'I beg your pardon?' Cally swung round and was only partially relieved to see that Leon was reading from a cocktail menu he'd picked up from the bar.

'I'll just have a mineral water, thanks.' Leon raised his eyebrows in disapproval before the words were even out of her mouth. 'OK, fine,' she retracted, briefly running her eyes down the menu. 'I'll have a...Cactus Venom.'

When was the last time she'd had a drink? A glass of wine at her nephew's christening in January. God, she really did need to get out more.

Leon slipped off his jacket and ordered two of the same,

somehow managing, she noticed, to look exactly like he fitted in. She, on the other hand, crossed her arms awkwardly across her chest, feeling horribly overdressed and self-conscious.

'So, don't tell me—you come here all the time.' Cally said, marvelling at how quickly he seemed to have got the waitress's attention, although on second thoughts she could guess why.

'Well, you know, I would, but I live in France. What's your excuse?'

She laughed, relaxing a fraction as they found themselves a table and sat down. 'I live in Cambridge.'

'You mean you didn't know that the Road to Nowhere was waiting just around the next corner?'

'No, I didn't.' Cally shook her head, remembering the auction and thinking that the bar's name was altogether too apt.

Leon seemed to sense her despondency and raised his glass. 'So, what shall we drink to?'

Cally thought for a moment. 'To discovering hard work doesn't pay off in the end, so why bother?'

Something about his company, the atmosphere, made her realise that maybe she did need to talk about it after all. She hoped it was that, and not that she couldn't go five minutes without mentioning work.

'Sorry,' she added, suddenly aware of how discourteous that sounded. 'To...the Road to Nowhere.'

Leon chinked his cocktail glass against hers and they both took a sip of the yellow-green liquid, smarting at the sour taste.

'So, tonight didn't exactly go to plan for you?' Leon ventured.

'You could say that. The London City Gallery promised me the restoration job on the Rénards if they won them. They didn't.'

'Maybe you should offer your services to whoever did.'

'According to the guy manning the phone, it was an anonymous private collector.' Her voice rang with resentment.

'Who's to say a private collector won't commission you to complete the restorations?'

'Experience. Even if I could find out who he or she is, they'll either choose someone they know or the team who can get it done fastest. The rich treat art like a new Ferrari or a penthouse in Dubai—an acquisition to boast about, instead of something everyone deserves to enjoy.'

Leon went very still. 'So if you *were* approached, your morals would stop you from working on them?'

Cally turned away, emotion pricking at the backs of her eyes. 'No, it wouldn't stop me.'

She was aware how unprincipled that sounded—or more accurately how unprincipled that actually *was*—but it wasn't just because of the opportunities that working on them was bound to lead to. It was because she could never turn down the opportunity to work on the paintings that had determined the direction of her entire life, even if that life now seemed to be one big road to nowhere. She shook her head, too mortified to admit as much.

'I'd be a fool to turn it down if I ever got the opportunity. If I worked on the Rénards, I'd be known across the world.'

Leon gave a single nod. So, whatever impression she'd given at the pre-auction, what she wanted was renown. But of course, he thought cynically, what woman didn't? And, going by her protestations that she didn't want to talk about work, followed by her emotional outpouring on the subject, she didn't seem any more capable of sticking to her word than the rest of her sex. Well, there was one way to be sure.

He leaned back in his chair. 'So, was the pre-sale the first time you'd seen *Mon Amour par la Mer?*'

Cally shivered. 'I…I didn't think you'd noticed me that day.'

He waited for her eyes to lift and meet his. 'On the contrary, that was when I decided that I wanted to make love to you. In fact, that was why I came back to the auction.'

Cally gawped in shock at his nerve, whilst at the same time a treacherous thrill zipped up her spine, which surprised her even more than his words. Words which told her that, unbelievably, he had wanted her when she'd been dressed like *Cally,* not just tonight when she felt like she was playing dress-up to fit in with the art world. The world which, contrary to her initial impression, he wasn't a part of either. He who had only been there tonight because of her. How was that possible? Wasn't it obvious that she lacked that sexual gene, or whatever that thing was that most other women had? She didn't know, but suddenly all the reasons she'd amassed for loathing him toppled over, taking her defences with them.

'I ought to walk out of here right now.'

'So walk.'

'I…I haven't finished my drink.'

'And do you always do exactly what you say you are going to do, Cally?'

She was sure he turned up his accent when he said her name on purpose, sure he knew it made her stomach flip. Even surer that she didn't have the strength to walk away.

'I hate people who go back on their word.'

'As do I.' He looked at her sharply. 'However, there were some parts of this agreement we didn't specify—like whether this drink included a dance, for instance?'

Cally drew in a sharp breath as she looked to the grinding mass of bodies on the dance floor, now slowing to a more languorous pace as the soloist with the heavy eye-liner and the husky voice began a rendition of *Black Velvet*.

'You're not serious?'

'Why not? Isn't seizing the moment one of life's beauties that art celebrates?'

Art, Cally thought. It was a celebration of life. But when was the last time she'd actually stopped to remember that and allowed herself to live it? She drank him in—his dark blond hair falling over his forehead, his eyes smouldering with a fire that both terrified and excited her—and for a split second she didn't feel as though she'd lost anything at all tonight.

She offered him her hand and answered him in a voice she didn't recognise as her own. 'You're on.'

As she stood up the alcohol went to her head, and for a second she closed her eyes, breathing deeply. The air felt thick, the heady beat of music vibrating through every cell in her body. She'd loved this song as a teenager. David had hated it. Why had she never played it since?

'Come on.' Leon snaked his hand around her waist and pulled her to him before he had time to consider whether or not this was such a good idea. He wanted her with a hun-griness that unnerved him. He watched her mouthing the words of the song and, unable to drag his eyes away from her full lips, wondered if for once in his life he was going to be incapable of sticking to his own rules.

Always wanting more, he'd leave you longing for...

The lyrics seemed to reach into her soul. *He* seemed to reach into her soul. She had never met anyone like him. She had only known him five minutes and yet—clichéd thought it sounded—it almost felt like he knew her better than she had known herself, about everything she'd been missing out on. Being pressed up against him was intoxicating, the smell of him, the touch of him. She ran her hands up his muscular back, locked them behind his neck and allowed the tension to leave her body as he moved easily, her body following every movement his made.

'Did I tell you how sexy you are?' he whispered in her ear, the warmth of his breath sending an inordinate level of heat flooding through her.

He did this all the time; she was sure he did. Which was why it was crazy. She'd never done anything like this in her life, and she didn't know what she was playing at now. But, though in her head she knew she was probably a fool to continue, right now her body was the only thing she could hear—and it was thrumming with a whole host of new sensations, all clamouring to be explored.

'Did I tell you how sexy *you* are?' she whispered nervously, grateful that she couldn't see his face, hoping he couldn't sense that she was trembling all over.

'No,' he whispered, drawing back to brush his lips just below her ear. 'You most definitely didn't mention that.'

She couldn't bear it. His mouth was playing havoc with the sensitive skin of her neck. She needed to kiss him. Properly. Shakily, she guided his head with her hand until their faces were level, not knowing where her confidence had come from. Had he known if he touched her like that she wouldn't be able to resist him? Probably. But right now she didn't care. She just wanted to kiss him.

His lips brushed hers, painfully slowly, then opened hungrily. He tasted decadent, like dark chocolate and cinnamon. He ran his hand gently down her spine, slowing over the curve of her bottom. It was the kind of kiss that would have been utterly inappropriate in an exclusive little wine bar. To Cally's shock it had a lot more in common with the display of primal need they had witnessed in the street outside, but to her astonishment she wanted more. She told herself it was down to the charge of the music, the distinctive scent of his hypnotic, balmy cologne. But she could blame it on exterior forces all she liked; the truth was that it was kissing *him* that was explosive. Suddenly she forgot everything else—the fact that he was a man she had only just met, the fact that she was bound to disappoint him, that this could only lead to heartache—because her need for him was overwhelming, and he seemed to feel it too.

'You want to get out of here?'

She took a deep breath. 'Yes, I do.'

So, Leon thought, fighting his own desire, there was the concrete proof that her word could not be trusted. That was the rule.

Cally's cheeks were hot and her heart was pounding as he threaded her through the other couples on the dance floor and out onto the pavement, hailing a cab.

He opened the door for her as it rolled up. Then he coolly shut the door behind her and remained standing on the pavement.

She wound down the window, her brows knitted together in bewilderment. 'I thought we were getting out of here?'

His face was grim. 'No, *you* are. One drink was all you wanted, wasn't it, Cally?'

Cally felt a new fire burning in her cheeks as Leon signalled for the driver to go and she suddenly realised what was happening.

'Bastard!' she shouted.

But the driver had already pulled away, and all she could hear was the climax of the song as it poured down the street.

In a flash he was gone. It happened so soon, what could you do?

CHAPTER THREE

AS CALLY rested her head on the window of the train from King's Cross back to Cambridge, the sky-rise landscape shrinking to a patchwork of green, she gave up sifting her memories for debris and concluded that, no, she had never felt more ashamed than she did right now.

She, Cally Greenway, had almost had a one-night stand with a total stranger.

And, what was worse, a tiny part of her almost wished she had.

No, she argued inwardly, of course she didn't. She just wished he hadn't subjected her to that hideous rejection, or at the very least that she'd been able to understand why he had.

Had the earth-shattering heat of their kiss, which she'd thought was mutual, actually been so one-sided that he'd realised she would be useless in bed? Or was it all part of a game he played to prove that he was so drop-dead gorgeous he could make any woman abandon her morals if he chose?

Cally spent the next week wavering between the two theories, subsequently caught between reawakened insecurities and fresh anger. In the end, frustration with herself for even caring made anger prevail. She should be glad that she'd had a lucky escape, and the reason for his insulting behaviour shouldn't even matter when he was no one to her, a no one whom she was never likely to see ever again.

So why, whenever she thought back to that night, did that moment in the taxi hurt even more than losing the commission had done? Cally pressed her lips together in shame, but then released them. It was simply because up until that point she had thought that what she'd lost was her dream job. He had made her see that she'd spent so long with her eye on that goal alone that she'd sacrificed every other aspect of her life in the process. Yes, she thought, unwilling to dwell on the other broken dreams his rejection had resurrected, that was it. Finding herself devastated that she would never have Leon's arms around her again just proved how long it had been since she'd actually got out there and spent any time in the company of anyone but herself, and occasionally her family.

Well, he might have reinforced her belief about the futility of trusting the opposite sex, but she had to acknowledge that maybe it was about time she accepted the odd invitation to go out now and again, instead of always having a well-rehearsed list of things she had to do instead. Particularly since the short list of restorations she had lined up for the next three months was hardly going to claim all of her time, she thought despondently as she booted up her computer to see whether her inbox heralded any new enquiries on that front today. It was all very well, deciding to get a social life whilst she worked out what to do next, but it was hardly feasible if it meant not being able to eat.

Three new mails. The first was a promotional email from the supplier she used for her art materials, which she deleted without opening, knowing she couldn't afford anything above and beyond her regular order. The second was from her sister Jen, who was back from her family holiday in Florida, desperate to know if the little black dress she'd leant her had been as lucky for Cally as it had been for her when she'd worn it to the journalism awards last month and scooped first prize. Cally shook her head, wondering how her sister managed to pull off being a high-flying career woman as well as a wonderful wife and mother, and resolved to reply with the bad news when she felt a little less like a failure in comparison.

The third email was from a sender with a foreign-sounding name she didn't recognise. She clicked on it warily.

Dear Miss Greenway
Your skills as an art conservator have recently been brought to the attention of the Prince of Montéz. As a result, His Royal Highness wishes to discuss a possible restoration. To be considered, you are required to attend the royal palace in person in three days' time. Your tickets will be couriered to you tomorrow unless you wish to decline this generous offer by return.
Yours faithfully, Boyet Durand
On behalf of His Royal Highness, the Prince of Montéz

Cally blinked at the words before her. Her first reaction was disbelief. Here was an email offering a free trip to a luxurious French island, so why wasn't she pinging it straight off to her junk-mail folder, knowing there was a catch? She read it again. Because it wasn't the usual generic trash: *You've won a holiday to Barbados, to claim just call this number....* This sender knew her name and what she did for a living. It was feasible that someone could have seen one of her few restorations that had ended up in smallish galleries and been inspired to visit her website—but a prince?

She read it a third time, and on this occasion the arrogance of it truly sunk in. If it was real, who on earth did the Prince of Montéz think he was to have his advisor summon her as if she was a takeaway meal he'd decide whether or not he wanted once she arrived?

Cally opened a new tab and typed 'Prince of Montéz' into Wikipedia. The information was irritatingly sparse. It didn't even give his name, only stated that in Montéz the prince was the sovereign ruler, and that the current prince had come into power a year ago when his brother Girard had died in an accident aged just forty-three, leaving behind his young wife, Toria, but no children. Cally cast her mind back, roughly recalling the royal-wedding photos which had graced the cover of every magazine the summer she'd graduated, and hearing the news of his tragic death on the radio in her studio some time last year. But there was no further information about the late prince's brother, the man who thought that she, a lowly artist, could drop everything because he commanded it.

Cally was tempted to reply that, attractive though the offer was, the prince was mistaken if he thought she could fit him into her busy schedule at such short notice. But the truth was he *wasn't* mistaken. Hadn't she only just been wishing she had more work lined up, and thinking she ought to start saying yes to something other than Sunday lunch at her parents' house?

Which was why she decided she would let the tickets come. Not that she really believed they would, until the doorbell rang early the following morning, thankfully interrupting a fervid dream about a Frenchman with a disturbingly familiar face.

Nor did she really believe she'd dare to use them until the day after, when she heard the voice of the pilot asking them to please return their seats to the upright position because they were beginning their descent to the island.

The last and only time Cally had been to France was on a day trip to Le Touquet by ferry whilst she'd been at secondary school, most of which had been spent trawling round a rather uninspiring hypermarket. She'd always fancied Paris—the Eiffel Tower and the galleries, of course—but she'd somehow never got round to taking any kind of holiday at all since uni, nor felt she could justify the unnecessary expense. So when she stepped out of first class and was greeted by the most incredible vista of shimmering azure water and glorious tree-covered mountains sprinkled with terracotta roofs, it was no wonder it felt like this was all happening to someone else. For the first time in years she felt the urge to whip out a sketch pad and get to work on a composition of her own.

A desire that only increased when the private car pulled up to the incredible palace. It almost looked like a painting, she thought as the driver opened the door of the vehicle for her to depart.

'Please follow me, *mademoiselle*. The prince will meet you in *la salle de bal.*'

Cally frowned as he led her through the impressive main archway, trying to remember her GCSE French in order to decipher which room he was referring to. He must have caught her perplexed expression.

'You would say "the ballroom", I think?'

Cally nodded and rolled her eyes to herself as they passed through the courtyard and up a creamy white staircase with a deep red carpet running through the centre. There was a very good reason why she hadn't needed to know the word for ballroom for her project on *'ma maison'*.

The thought reminded her just how hypocritical it was to feel impressed by the palace when the man who lived here was guilty of the excess she loathed. She was even more ashamed to look down at her perfectly functional black jacket and skirt, teamed with a white blouse, and wish she had brought something a little more, well, worthy. Why should she be worried what clothes she was wearing to meet the prince? Just because he had a palace and a title didn't mean she ought to act any differently from the way she would with any potential client. Any more than he should judge her on anything but her ability as a restorer, she thought defiantly, hugging her portfolio to her chest.

'Here we are, Mademoiselle Greenway.'

'Thank you,' Cally whispered as the man signalled for her to enter the ballroom, bowed his head and then swiftly departed.

She entered tentatively, preparing to be blown away by the full impact of the magnificent marble floor, the intricately decorated wall panels and the high, sculpted ceiling that she could see from the doorway. But, as Cally turned into the room, the gasp that broke from her throat was not one of artistic appreciation, it was one of complete astonishment.

The Rénards. Hanging, seemingly innocuously, right in the centre of the opposite wall.

Cally rushed to them to get a closer look, momentarily convinced that they must be reproductions, but a quick appraisal told her immediately that they were not. She felt her heart begin to thud insistently in her chest, though she couldn't accurately name the emotion which caused it. Excitement? She had wanted more than anything to discover the identity of the mysterious telephone-bidder, to have the chance to convince them she was the best person to carry out the restoration. Now it seemed that somehow *he* had found *her*.

Or was it horror? For wasn't this exactly the fate of the paintings she had feared—shut away in some gilded palace never to be looked upon again? She closed her eyes and pressed her hands to her temples, trying to make sense of it, but before she could even begin a voice behind her cut through everything.

'See something you recognise?'

A voice which made her eyes fly open, every hair on the back of her neck stand on end and every thought fly from her mind. Every thought, except one.

Leon.

Stop it, she scolded herself. The Prince of Montéz is French, of course he's going to sound a little like him. God, she really did need to get out more if that one meaningless episode had the power to make her lose all grip on reality every time she heard a man with a French accent. The voice belonged to the Prince of Montéz, who had brought her here as his potential employee, so why was she still staring rudely at the wall? She turned sharply to face him.

The sight before her almost made her keel over.

Her imagination hadn't been playing a trick on her at all. It was him. Irritatingly perfect him, his impressive physique all the more striking in a formal navy suit.

Her mind went into overdrive as she attempted to make sense of what was happening. Leon was a university professor; perhaps he'd been invited here to examine the paintings in more detail; perhaps this was just one of life's unfortunate coincidences?

But as she stared at his wry expression—impatient, as if waiting for her tiny mind to catch up—she suddenly understood that this was no coincidence. Her very first appraisal of him in that sale room in London—rich, heartless, titled—had not been wrong. It was everything else that had been a lie. Good God, was Leon even his real name?

'You bastard.'

For a second his easy expression looked shot through with something darker, but just as quickly it was back.

'So you said last time we met, Cally, but now that you know I am your potential employer I thought you'd be a little more courteous.'

Courteous? Cally felt the bile rise in her throat. 'Well, since I can assure you I am not going to be capable of courtesy towards you any time this century, I think I should leave, don't you?'

Leon gritted his teeth. Yes, he did think she should leave, the same way he'd thought he should in London. But after countless hot, frustrated nights, when all his body had cared about was why the hell he hadn't taken her when he'd had the chance, Leon was through with thinking.

He blocked her exit with his arm.

'At least stay for *one drink*.'

'And why the hell would I want to do that?'

'Because, yet again, you look like you need one.'

Had he brought her here purely to humiliate her further, to revel in how much he had got to her? She fixed a bland expression on her face, determined not to play ball. 'I'll have one on my way back to the airport.'

'You have somewhere else to be?' he replied, mock-earnestly.

She knew exactly what he implied—that she had nowhere else to be today any more than when she had protested the need to return to her hotel room that night. It was the same reason he'd known she would come at short notice. And exactly why staying here could only quadruple the humiliation she already felt.

'No, you're absolutely right, I don't. But anywhere is preferable to being on this dead end of an island with some lying product of French inbreeding who has nothing better to do than to toy with random English women he meets for sport.'

'*Woman,*' he corrected. 'There is certainly only one of you, Cally Greenway.'

'And yet there is one of you in every palace and stately home on the planet. It's so predictable, it's boring.'

'I thought that you liked things to turn out exactly the way you expect them to—or perhaps that is simply what you pretend to want?'

'Like I told you, all I want is to leave.'

'It's a shame your body language says otherwise.'

Cally looked down, pleased to discover that if anything she had stepped further away from him, whilst her arms clutched her portfolio protectively to her chest.

'And do you always take a woman's loathing as a come-on?'

'Only when it's born out of sheer sexual frustration,' he drawled, nodding at the gap between them and her self-protective stance.

'In your dreams.'

'Yours too, I don't doubt.' He looked at her with an assessing gaze.

Cally felt her cheeks turn crimson.

'I thought so,' he drawled in amusement. 'But think just how good it will be when we do make love, *chérie.*'

'I might have been stupid enough to consider having sex with you before I knew who you were,' she said, trying not to flinch at the memory of her own wantonness. 'But I can assure you I am in no danger of doing so again.'

'You have a thing for university employees?' he queried, raising one long, lean finger to his lower lip thoughtfully, as if observing an anomalous result in a science experiment. 'Mediterranean princes just not your thing?'

No, men that self-important couldn't be any further from her thing, Cally thought, not that she had 'a thing'. So why in God's name was she unable to take her eyes off his mouth?

'Liars aren't my thing. Men who lie about who they are, who pretend not to be stinking rich and who profess to lend a sympathetic ear when—' Immediately the auction, which had slipped her mind for a moment, came back to her. The auction room. Leon the only one with the nonchalant glance. Not because he had nothing riding on it, but because he was so rich that he'd just instructed one of his minions to make the highest bid by phone on his behalf. That was why he had been there that night, to stand back and watch smugly whilst he blew everyone else out of the water. It had had nothing to do with coming back because he wanted her, and suddenly that hurt most of all. 'When all the time you were the one responsible for wrecking my career!'

Leon raised his eyebrows. 'Are you quite finished? Good. Firstly, I told you my name. You didn't ask what my surname was, nor did you give me yours. All I said was that I was in England in connection with my university. I was. The new University of Montéz has just been built at my say-so, and I was there to purchase some pieces for the art department. Since you chose where we should go, I can hardly be blamed if the bar you selected gave no indication of my wealth. Which brings me to your accusation that I offered to lend a sympathetic ear with regards to your career—on the contrary, it was you who insisted we should *not* discuss work. You simply chose to, I did not.'

'You consider being a prince a career choice?'

'Not a choice,' he said gravely. 'But my work, yes.'

'How convenient, rather like arguing that omitting the truth does not constitute a lie. If you and I were married—' Cally hesitated, belatedly aware that she couldn't have thought of a more preposterous example if she'd tried '—and you happened to be sleeping with another woman but just didn't mention it, would such an omission be tolerable?'

Leon's mouth hardened. Hadn't he just known that she was one of those women who had marriage on the brain?

'Tolerable? Marrying anyone would never be a tolerable scenario for me, Cally, so I'm afraid your analogy is lost.'

'What a surprise,' Cally muttered. 'When it proves that I'm absolutely right.' How utterly typical that he wasn't the marrying kind, she thought irritably, though she wasn't sure why she should care when she'd lost her belief in happy-ever-afters a long time ago.

'But surely a welcome surprise?' Leon seized the moment. 'For, rather than being the one responsible for wrecking your career, I think you'll find yourself eternally indebted to me for beginning it. What an accolade for your CV to be employed to restore two of the most famous paintings the world has ever known?'

Indebted to him; the thought horrified her. Yet he was also offering exactly what she had always wanted—well, almost. 'You said you were in London to purchase some pieces for the university's art department. Do you mean that once the Rénards are restored they will go on public display there?'

Leon lifted his arm sharply, the motion drawing back the sleeve of his shirt to reveal a striking Cartier watch. 'I would love to discuss the details now, but I'm afraid I have a meeting to attend with the principal of the university, as it happens. Much as I'm sure that, given your predilection for university staff, you'd find meeting Professor Lefevre *stimulating,* it is something I need to do alone. You and I can continue this discussion over breakfast.'

'I beg your pardon?'

'Breakfast. *Petit déjeuner.* The first meal of the day, *oui?*' He stared at her face, which was aghast. 'It is also a painting by Renoir, I believe—but, of course, you're the expert.'

Could he have any more of a cheek? 'I am well aware of the concept of breakfast, thank you. Just as I am well aware that I will be eating mine back in Cambridge tomorrow morning. You invited me here to discuss this *today.*'

'And I subsequently discovered that unfortunately today is the only day Professor Lefevre can have this meeting. But since you have nowhere else to be this can wait until tomorrow, *oui?*'

Cally seethed. 'I have a plane to catch. Home.'

'But how can you make the most important decision of your career without knowing all the facts?'

There was nothing to decide, was there? How could she even contemplate working for a man who had humiliated and lied to her? Because the job was everything she'd strived for, she thought ruefully. She recalled the hideous boss she'd once had at the gallery gift shop who'd paid her a pittance for running the place single-handedly, how she'd ignored him and had just knuckled down. She could do it again for her dream commission, couldn't she? But somehow she wasn't sure that ignoring Leon would be so easy. Unless she could do the restoration without his interference. Rent a studio by the seafront and work on the paintings there, only return here when she'd completed them. The idea seemed almost idyllic without the threat of his presence.

'If I stay for—for *breakfast,*' she repeated, the concept still ludicrous to her. 'You'll be open to discussion about how I would wish such a project to be completed?'

'Discussion? Of course.'

Cally did a mental calculation of whether she could afford one night in a French guesthouse, having presumed that she'd be back on a plane out of here this afternoon. She supposed that she *had* left that hotel in London a night earlier than planned...

'What time would you have me return?'

'I would have you here ready and waiting,' he said, beckoning for her to keep up with his brusque steps out of the ballroom and into the hallway, where the man who had driven her here was waiting compliantly, head bowed. 'This is Boyet. He will show you to your room and bring you dinner.'

And before she could argue the prince was gone.

CHAPTER FOUR

CALLY picked up her mobile phone from the bedside cabinet and stared at its neon display through the darkness. 2:48 a.m., and still awake. She had tried everything: lying on her back, on her front, and rather awkwardly on her side; shutting the window to block out the sound of the ocean in order to pretend that she was in her bed at home; opening the window in the hope that the ebb and flow of the sea would act as a natural lullaby. Finally she had tried to fool herself into sleep by pretending she didn't care whether she was awake or not. But still the minutes ticked by. And, the more the minutes ticked by, the more questions heaped up in her brain.

Why had she even come here? Life wasn't some fairy tale where princes were valiant men who did noble deeds. She, more than anyone, should know that a man who had been born into privilege was bound to be selfish and dishonest, and, if she'd forgotten, his arrogant email should have acted as a reminder. Perhaps it was because she'd been confident that he was *just* selfish and dishonest, and had thought she could deal with that. What she hadn't known was that the prince would also happen to be *him*. Yet how was that possible when she'd even tried to look him up? Especially as a couple of years ago, she hadn't been able to avoid photos of his late brother and his wife.

Cally took a deep breath and to her chagrin found herself wondering how Girard's death must have affected Leon, how terrible it must have been to lose a brother and to gain such responsibility in the same moment. But that presupposed he had a heart somewhere within his perfectly honed chest, she thought bitterly, and nothing about the way he had treated her suggested that he did. Had he chosen not to reveal who he was in London simply for his own amusement?

Probably. Just like he probably thought that a night in his opulent palace would make her feel like she owed him one. *As if.* The thought of being indebted to him in any way whatsoever made her feel sick. Which was why, despite feeling famished, she had rejected Boyet's offer of dinner last night. Which was why she had got into bed without using a single thing in the pale apricot bedroom, with its beautiful white furniture, including the array of luxurious toiletries laid out for her. Instead she had used the mishmash of bits and pieces she'd thrown in her handbag for freshening up on the flight—even if she hadn't been able to resist removing the lids of the eye-catching bottles and smelling each one in turn...

When Cally's alarm went off four hours later, she felt like an animal who had been disturbed from hibernation three months early. Thankfully with the morning came rational thought: that there was only one question that mattered, and that was whether or not he planned to offer her the job of working on her dream commission.

Which meant she had to treat this breakfast—however unwelcome the concept was to her—like a job interview.

A job interview she wished she could attend in something other than yesterday's crumpled suit, she thought uneasily as she walked towards the veranda where Boyet had told her she would find Leon at eight-twenty. At least she'd had the foresight to pack a change of underwear and a clean top.

Now that it was daylight, she noticed for the first time that this side of the palace had the most fantastic view of the bay below, the ocean so blue it reminded her of a glittering jewel. As she stepped onto the cream tiles of the patio, she was forced to admit that Leon gave the landscape a run for its money. He was sitting on a wrought-iron chair, one leg crossed over the other whilst he leafed through the day's *La Tribune*, looking more like a male model than a prince in his cool white linen shirt which had far less buttons done up than most other men could have got away with. On him, she thought shamefully, it seemed criminal not to be unbuttoned any more.

'You like the view?' he drawled, closing the paper.

Cally turned back to the horizon, all too aware that he had caught her out. 'I suppose it's on a par with the British coastline.' She shrugged, determined to remain indifferent to everything even remotely connected to him.

'Oh yes, this is England—just without rain,' he replied dryly as he motioned to the chair.

Cally sat, resting her portfolio on her knee, her back rigid and eyes lowered. The exact opposite of his languorous pose.

He ran his eyes openly over her face. 'You look terrible. Didn't you sleep?'

The insult cut her to the quick. She ought to be glad that he was through with faking desire where she was concerned, but it only made her feel worse. She could just imagine the kind of woman he was used to having breakfast with—perfectly made-up, top-to-toe designer. Just like Portia had been the morning she'd answered David's door sporting that enormous pink diamond.

'I'm afraid this is the way a woman who isn't plastered in make-up tends to look in the morning, Leon.'

He shook his head irritably. 'You are not the kind of woman who requires any make-up. I simply meant that you look a little—drained.'

The compliment caught her off guard, and she didn't know what to do with it. 'Actually, I could count the number of hours' sleep I've had on one hand. Without the use of my thumb.'

Leon stifled a smile and made a show of furrowing his brow as he poured her a strong black coffee without asking whether she wanted any. 'That suite has just been refurnished. I was assured that particular mattress was the best on the market. I will have to see that it is changed.'

How typical that he thought every problem in life could be solved by material goods, she thought irritably, trying to ignore the delicious scent of the coffee wafting invitingly up her nostrils. 'There was nothing wrong with the bed, save for the fact that it was under your roof.'

'Large houses have a few too many dark corners for you?' he suggested with feigned concern as Boyet appeared with a tray overflowing with food: spiced bread, honey, fruit with natural yogurt, freshly squeezed orange in two different jugs—one with pulp and one without. Cally's mouth watered, and she could feel her ravenous stomach start to rumble, but she cleared her throat to disguise it.

'Whilst you are right that it does have an unnecessarily large number of rooms, it had nothing to do with that. Believe it or not, I simply have no desire to be anywhere near you.'

'Yet you are still here.'

'Like you said, whatever my personal feelings, I would be foolish not to make this important decision in my career without discussing the facts.'

'Over breakfast.' He nodded as if her career was immaterial. 'But you are yet to have a sip of coffee or a morsel of any food. So, eat.'

It was tempting to say she wasn't hungry, but the tantalising aroma of nutmeg and sultanas was too enticing, and she succumbed to a piece of bread.

Leon watched her, thinking it was the most erotic thing he'd ever seen as she bit into it hungrily before twisting her rosebud of a mouth back into a look of disapproval.

'No woman I've ever invited to breakfast has ever tried so hard to look unhappy about it as you.'

Thinking about the different women who might have sat in this self-same seat before her for a second time made Cally fidget uncomfortably, and do up another button on her suit jacket despite the rising heat of the early-morning sunshine.

'Emotions are irrelevant, aren't they?' She slid her portfolio from her side of the table to his, telling herself to ignore his casual attire and the holiday setting and treat this in exactly the same way as she had treated her interview at the London City Gallery. 'This contains photographs of all my major restorations, as well as details of my qualifications. I specialised in Rénard for the theory side of my post-grad.'

He opened it casually, flicking to the first page and briefly reading through her CV as he sipped his coffee.

'You began studying for a fine-art degree in London,' he said thoughtfully, raising his head. 'But you didn't finish?'

Trust him to notice that first. She remembered the owner

of the London City Gallery getting to the same question at her second interview—remembered how, after all the years of hard work, she had finally felt able to answer it with confidence and integrity. So why did she feel so ashamed when *he* asked?

'No, I didn't complete it.' She drew in a deep breath. 'And it was a mistake not to. But for two years afterwards I worked a full-time job, and painted and studied in every spare moment I had. The Cambridge Institute then accepted me on their diploma in conservation based on my aptitude and commitment.'

'So why didn't you finish it?' Leon flicked her portfolio shut without looking at another page. 'Did you fall in love with a university professor and drop out in a fit of unrequited love?'

'I don't think that's relevant, do you?'

Leon saw a flash of something in her eyes which told him he had hit a raw nerve. He was tempted to probe deeper, but at the same time the thought of her having past lovers, let alone hearing about them, irritated him. Which was preposterous, because the women he slept with always matched him in experience.

He looked her straight in the eye. 'Actually, I happen to think the way someone behaves in personal relationships is indicative of the way they are likely to behave as an employee.'

Suddenly, the penny dropped in Cally's mind. So *that* was what London had been about. She felt herself grow even hotter beneath the fabric of her dark jacket as she realised what that meant. It had all been an underhand investigation into whether he considered her fit for the job, and she could only imagine what his conclusion had been!

Wasn't it just typical that the one night she had acted completely out of character was the one night that, unbeknown to her, she'd needed to be herself most of all? But what gave him the right to make such a judgement based on her behaviour, anyway? Just because he was a prince didn't give him permission to play at being some moral magistrate!

She challenged him right back with her gaze. 'Then you don't want to know what your behaviour indicates about you, *Your Highness.*'

'Since you are the one who wants to work on my paintings, my behaviour is irrelevant. Yours, on the other hand...'

'So why bother bringing me here if I've already failed your pathetic little personality test?'

His voice was slow and deliberate, 'Because, *chérie,* although you showed that your word cannot be trusted and that you are only interested in these paintings because you think they will bring you renown...' He paused, as if to revel in her horror. 'After extensive research into your abilities over the past week I happen to believe you are the best person for the job.'

Cally was so taken aback by the damning insult and high praise all delivered in one succinct sentence that she didn't know what to say—but before she had the chance to utter anything Leon continued. 'As a result, I wish to employ you. On one condition. There will be no *renown.* You may detail the commission in your portfolio, but that is it. On this island it is already forbidden for the press to print anything about me and my employees except in reference to the public work I carry out. It is a policy I do my best to ensure is reflected throughout the world, and which I expect all current and former staff to ensure is upheld. Indefinitely.'

Well, that explained the lack of information on the Web, Cally thought, perplexed that he seemed to think that that one condition might be her only bone of contention with his offer of employment, and at the same time wanting to ask if he'd ever heard of three little words known as 'freedom of press'.

She frowned. 'Yesterday you suggested that the Rénards were purchased for the university. Aren't they therefore part of your public work anyway?'

Leon raked a hand through his hair in irritation. Didn't he just know that she would try and twist it any way she could? 'No. The Rénards are for my private collection. I purchased a small Goya at the same auction for the university. Thankfully, it needs no restoration.'

Cally exploded. 'So the Rénards *are* to be treated like some trophy enjoyed by no one but you?'

He took a sip of coffee. 'If that is the way you choose to view my decision, *oui*. How fitting, then, that the two paintings themselves are a celebration of difference.'

Cally felt her temper flare, as much because his crude analysis matched her own studied interpretation of the paintings as at the discovery that he would be keeping them to himself.

'So you lied to me yet again.'

'I didn't lie, I just postponed the truth.' He shrugged nonchalantly. 'Are you going to pretend it makes a difference?'

'Of course it does!'

'Really? As I recall it, you told me that despite your oh-so-ethical principles nothing would stop you working on the paintings. Unless...'

'Unless what?'

'Unless you are going to go back on your word. Again.'

His eyes met hers in smouldering challenge. He was baiting her, she knew he was, and every instinct within her screamed *walk away*. He *had* bought the paintings for no other reason than as an acquisition to boast about. He *was* a damned liar. And she had never felt so humiliated by any other man in her life. *Or so alive.*

But just what would she be walking away to—a blank diary and a pile of bills? Only now it would be worse, because she would know that she had walked away from her dream restoration for the sake of what boiled down to her pride. And, worse, though she hated to admit she gave a damn about what he thought, he would believe that she *was* incapable of sticking to her word, of seeing things through. The very trait that, after that one mistake, she'd spent years proving was not part of her character.

If she turned him down, the only person who would lose out was her. Leon would simply employ someone else to do the work, and a man with more money than morals would have thwarted her dreams for the second time in her life. The thought set free a deep-rooted ball of fury inside her. So what if he and his plans for the paintings were the antithesis of everything she believed in? For once in her life, why the hell shouldn't she turn that to her advantage?

'Do you wish me to begin work straight away?'

'That depends. Will you sign a contract which states that your employment will terminate if you break the condition?'

'I see no reason why not.'

'Then this afternoon suits me.'

Cally smiled a sickly smile, determined to make this difficult. 'In which case, I will require some payment up front in order to rent somewhere to stay, and—'

'Somewhere to *rent?*' he said with unconcealed disgust.

She nodded.

'And why on earth would that be necessary when, as you have already pointed out, the palace has an excess of rooms?'

'Because…because I hardly think living as well as working here is appropriate, under the circumstances.'

His raised his eyebrow. 'Circumstances?'

She felt a whole new level of heat wash over her and wished she had never opened her mouth. 'You know what I mean.'

'If we had slept together I would see your point, *ma belle,* but since you were so vehement that we should not there is no problem, *d'accord?'*

Yes, there is a bloody great problem, Cally thought, *and its despicably handsome face is staring right at me.*

'Fine. So I shall stay here and work here. But I'll need my conservation equipment.' She looked down at her suit and back up at him. 'And, as I thought I was only going to be here for a matter of hours, I'll need my clothes sent from home as well. Surely you can't deny that I shall be needing those for the duration of my stay?' she spat out, before she had time to realise that such a statement was just asking to be twisted.

'Only time will tell, Cally,' he purred. The way the two syllables of her name dropped from his tongue reminded her of hot, liquid chocolate, and she felt a bead of sweat trickle down between her breasts. 'But there will be no need to send for anything,' he drawled, as if her suggestion was utterly ridiculous. 'I will have everything you could possibly need brought over from Paris, a new wardrobe included.'

'I don't need a new wardrobe!'

He ran his eyes over her suit critically. 'Oh, but I think you do.'

Cally's cheeks burned at his insult, her body temperature continuing to rocket. 'Well, then, it's lucky I don't care what you think, isn't it?'

'Lucky? I'd say irrelevant is more accurate,' he said, draining his cup of coffee.

'But…!' Cally glared at him, her whole body teeming with frustration, but he simply ignored her and carried on.

'In the meantime, I presume you will wish to examine the *paintings.*' He emphasised it insultingly, as if she was the one getting sidetracked. 'Make a list of all the materials you will require and pass it on to Boyet by the end of the day. He will see that they are ordered immediately.' He ran his eyes over her figure as he stood up. 'And although it will be tomorrow before the clothes arrive from Paris I'm sure it wouldn't kill you to remove that jacket sometime before then. You look like you're about to pass out.'

Leon got to his feet and Cally stumbled to do the same, determined that this meeting would not end up with him walking away from her. 'You may be used to women fainting in your presence, Leon, but I can assure you that you leave me completely cold.'

'Well, if this is cold, *chérie,* I can't wait to see you fired up,' he mocked, and before she could even attempt to beat him away from the table he was halfway back to the palace, so that to her consternation it simply looked as though she had been standing ceremoniously for his exit.

'Then I hope you're a very patient man,' she yelled back, and, seeing that he had already entered the glass doors, allowed herself to drop back into her chair and tear off the blasted jacket.

'I'm not sure patience will be necessary,' he drawled as he pulled back the inside blind and dropped his eyes to her blouse. 'Are you?'

CHAPTER FIVE

'WOULD you have me carry these to your room now, Mademoiselle Greenway?'

Cally gawped in disbelief as she descended the stairs the following morning to find Boyet surrounded by countless bags and boxes. It reminded her of the sea of gifts that had spilled out from beneath the ten-foot pine at David's house that Christmas eight years ago, and his subsequent withering expression when she'd taken him back to meet her parents and he'd seen their sparse equivalent. It immediately soured her mood.

'I suppose there must be something suitable for work hidden in one of them, Boyet, thank you. Here, let me give you a hand.'

Despite his protests, Cally helped Boyet carry the fifty-four bags and boxes upstairs, but after peeling back enough tissue paper to completely bury the bedroom carpet she discovered that her supposition had been wrong. Yes, in amongst the high-heeled shoes, cocktail dresses and a disturbing amount of lingerie there was the odd pair of fine linen trousers and a single pair of diamanté designer jeans, but there was nothing she would have considered even remotely suitable for getting covered in paint. In fact it was the kind of wardrobe that would better befit a mistress than a woman he'd employed to do a job that could be both mentally and physically exhausting.

Maybe that was because it *was* a mistress's wardrobe, Cally thought cynically as she recalled Leon's comment yesterday which had implied just how frequently women joined him for breakfast. He probably had the whole lot on standby and simply ordered a new batch whenever he chose someone new to warm his bed. Well, she thought bitterly, her purpose here was not to dress for his pleasure. Not that she supposed for one minute that she was in any danger of that; whatever attraction he'd feigned towards her in London had simply been an elaborate plan to test her suitability for this job, hadn't it? She didn't know why that got to her most of all, when the real reason why she was angry was that he obviously had no concept of a woman needing clothes to work in. Well, she thought, grabbing for the designer jeans and rooting around in her handbag, she would soon see to that.

Cally doubted that her nail scissors would ever be fit for their intended purpose again, but twenty minutes later she felt rebelliously gleeful as she redescended the stairs and headed to the studio wearing the freshly cut-off, diamanté-less jeans, which now ended mid-thigh, and a royal blue silk blouse knotted at her waist.

The studio was triple the size of the room she used for restorations back home in Cambridge, but compared to everything she had encountered in the palace so far it was surprisingly understated. Aside from the tall glass doors which faced the sea and let in an ideal abundance of natural light, the room contained very little save for a row of cupboards, a sink, a comfy-looking sofa covered with a red throw and a CD player in the corner.

And of course the Rénards, which now dominated the space. She had been sitting alone on the veranda after breakfast yesterday, her jacket still tossed aside in frustration, when Boyet had approached to inform her that the paintings were being set up on easels in here for her to begin her assessment. Relieved to be able to concentrate on practicalities, her mood had instantly turned to one of resolve. When she had taken Boyet the list of materials she anticipated she would need for the duration of the restoration later that afternoon, she had been even more relieved to hear that Leon had gone out on royal business and would not be back until after dark.

However, though Leon seemed to be leaving her to it this morning as well, Cally was perplexed to find that she was not consumed by the single-mindedness she usually felt when confronted with a new commission, and which she had expected to have in spades when it came to the Rénards.

She pulled up her stool before the masterpieces and drew in a deep breath, forcing herself to block out everything else, but her mind was still running riot. Perhaps it was too quiet. She was used to the buzz of traffic outside her window back home. She went over to the CD player and ran her fingers along the shelf of jewelled cases, surprised to find there was more than one rock album amongst his collection. She hesitated over one of them. Tempting though it was to put it on, she knew it would only serve to remind her of *that* night, and that was bound to skew her thoughts completely. So she put on some contemporary jazz, told herself a prince didn't buy his own CDs anyway, and sat down again.

Being able to focus was her speciality; it always had been. She cast her mind back to her conservation course in Cambridge. There had been plenty of students with more natural talent than she had, but, to quote the words of her tutor, no one who applied themselves in quite the same way that she did. Whilst other students had partied till dawn, and only started thinking about their assignments on the day of a deadline, Cally would be finished with weeks to spare, already working on the next. Maybe it was because she had fought so hard for a second chance. Or maybe it was because since that moment in Mrs McLellan's class all those years before her passion for art had surpassed everything.

Even though her epiphany had initially taken the form of wanting to be an artist in the traditional sense, Cally admitted, unsure why that thought was accompanied by a deep pang of regret today when usually she could view her change of vocation objectively. It was probably because, if she had been able to bring herself to paint any of her paltry compositions after her split with David, even they would have had more chance of appearing in a public gallery than the two most impressive nineteenth-century paintings in existence. Cally balled her hands into fists. How was it possible that a man who was opening a university which encouraged learning about art could keep these incredible paintings for his eyes only? The university was just a princely duty, she supposed, a role which was separate from his own sentiments. Which was exactly how she needed to view this job.

'Before shots, that's where I should start,' Cally said aloud, as if talking to herself might drown out her tumultuous thoughts and help with her focus. She reached into her bag and found her battered camera, then took a step backwards, lining up the lens.

'Thinking of your precious portfolio, *chérie?*'

At the sound of his voice she dropped her hand guiltily. As soon as she did, she realised how ridiculous that was, but by then her hand was too unsteady to continue.

Only because he had made her jump, Cally reasoned. How had he snuck in without her hearing? She was annoyed that she had no way of knowing how long he'd been standing there watching her, and made a mental note to lower the volume on the CD player in future, though the music was far from loud.

'Having a record of their initial appearance for reference is an essential part of the process,' she said defensively, turning to face him. The sight caught her off guard. He was perched on the arm of the sofa in a pair of faded light blue jeans that moulded his thighs, and a white T-shirt that revealed the taut plane of his stomach, the casual attire doing nothing to belittle the power he seemed to exude naturally. She swallowed slowly, her mouth suddenly feeling parched. 'Was there something you wanted?'

'I just came to check you hadn't been attacked by the palace lawnmower,' he drawled, producing two pieces of hacked-off denim. 'Stéphanie was a little concerned to find these whilst cleaning your room.'

Cally's mouth twitched into a smile. 'Well, as you can see, I'm absolutely fine.'

'It's a shame I can't say the same for the jeans.'

'What's a shame is that you didn't allow me to have my own clothes sent from home. How am I supposed to do my job wearing some skintight, dry-clean-only designer outfit?

You're lucky I didn't decide to do a Julie Andrews and take to your curtains instead.'

'Sorry?' Her words shook Leon out of his state of semi-arousal. Ever since he'd entered the room he'd been trans-fixed by her pert little bottom and her long, shapely legs in her makeshift shorts. Until she'd just revealed that her outing with the scissors had all been a protest because he hadn't let her have her own way.

'You know—Julie Andrews in *The Sound of Music*—where she makes clothes for all the children out of the curtains. Didn't you ever see it?'

'I can't say that I did.'

Cally looked at him with new eyes, truly comprehend-ing for the first time that he wasn't just Mr Drop-dead Gorgeous with whom she'd shared one earth-shattering kiss before he'd humiliated and lied to her. He was royalty, the sole ruler of a Mediterranean island. Whilst she'd spent the school holidays watching old movies with her sister whilst her parents were out at work, what must he have been doing—opening the odd university here, making a state visit there?

Yet, even though he owned this luxurious palace, had the title and the sense of self-importance to match, she still found it somehow difficult to imagine. Maybe it was because he'd described his role here as if it was just a job. But that was ridiculous, because being royal wasn't an occupation, it was who he was. So how was it that he had seemed to fit right into that bar in London when he ought to have stuck out like a Van Gogh in a public toilet?

Cally quickly returned her camera to her bag and moved back to her seat, appalled to realise that she had been inadvertently giving him the once-over. 'Don't you have royal duties this morning?'

Leon had never been so glad that someone had elected to sit on a stool rather than a chair as he watched the waist-band of her shorts come tantalisingly close to revealing the top of the perfect globes of her bottom. 'Not until my meeting later with the president of France.'

'Oh.' It took all Cally's powers of concentration to transfer a bottle of distilled water into a small beaker without pouring it all over her lap. 'Then I'm sure you must have a lot to prepare.'

'If it's not distracting, I thought I might watch you quietly.'

It wasn't really even a question, and if it was then he had asked it so airily it was impossible to answer that, actually, she felt seriously in danger of putting the cotton bud through the canvas if he stayed. She'd worked in front of people heaps of times before—students, enthusiastic clients—and, for goodness' sake, the first step of the process was only removing the dirt and grime. All it required was a little focus.

'As you wish.'

Leon witnessed her hesitation and smiled to himself. 'You can begin without the supplies from Paris?'

Cally felt herself marginally relax, glad to talk about work. 'The cleaning, yes. It's more a case of time and patience than apparatus in the early stages.'

'Like so many things,' he said, deliberately slowly.

She told herself she was imagining his suggestive tone. 'I had a tutor who used to say that half the work is in the diagnosis. Each painting is like a patient. The symptoms might be similar, but working out the treatment is unique to every one.'

An image of Cally wearing a nurse's uniform and tending to him in bed popped into Leon's head, and the erection which had begun at the sight of her legs in those shorts grew even harder.

'So, did you always want to restore art?'

As Cally returned to her seat she felt the muscles in her shoulders go taut. 'I started out wanting to be an artist in the traditional sense, but things changed. I don't do my own work anymore.'

She waited for the snide comment, the probing questions, but was surprised to find they didn't come.

'Our lives don't always follow the course we expect, *non?*'

'No,' she said, somehow finding the courage to begin in the top corner of the first painting. 'They don't.'

He must be referring to his brother's death, Cally thought, for it occurred to her that, if Girard had lived, then Leon might never have become prince. She wanted to ask him about it, but at the same time felt bound to show him the same quiet respect.

He broke the momentary silence. 'But providence works in mysterious ways, wouldn't you say?'

'I'd say that view of the world is a little romantic for me.'

She heard him move and saw on the periphery of her vision that he was leaning up against the cupboards to her left, contemplating her profile.

'You mean you do not believe in romance, *ma belle?*'

She dipped the cotton bud back in the distilled water and deflected the question. 'Why, do you?'

'I am a Frenchman, Cally.' He laughed a low, throaty laugh. 'It's in my blood.'

'How curious, when only yesterday you were telling me that you find the idea of marriage intolerable.'

He eyed her sceptically. 'What amazing powers of recollection you have for someone who professed to have no interest in the subject.'

'A good memory is essential for my job,' she replied a little too quickly. 'In order to recall the mixes of different chemicals.'

'Of course.' He stroked a hand across his chin with mock sincerity. 'Your job. That is what we were discussing, after all. So, tell me, is it coincidence that you chose to start with the fully clothed portrait before moving on to the nude, or is the significance intentional?'

Cally's hand was poised in mid-air an inch away from the canvas. 'I'm sorry?'

'Is it deliberate that you have begun on the work which has the least damage first?'

She pursed her lips, knowing that he hadn't been implying anything so innocuous.

'Yes. It allows me to get accustomed to the necessary techniques before moving on to the larger areas of damage.'

'The patient requiring the most intensive treatment.' He nodded seriously, startling her with the evidence that he had been listening thoroughly to her earlier explanation.

He saw her falter a second time and stifled a grin. 'I am sorry. I promised to watch quietly. I will leave you to carry on in peace, if you'll just excuse me whilst I just pick up a couple of things?'

Cally inclined her head, thinking how impeccable his manners could be when he wanted. She did not really take in what he was saying until she saw him move to the cupboard at the front of the room and remove a towel.

'I thought they were all empty, ready for the paint supplies,' she commented.

'They are, except for these few. I've got rid of the majority of my equipment now I have so few chances to use it.'

'Equipment?'

'Diving equipment,' he explained, before catching sight of the intense curiosity on her face which told him that it had not been clarification enough. He supposed no harm could come from telling her. 'Before it became necessary for me to rule the island, I worked as a diver for the Marine Nationale.'

Cally tried to hide the astonishment she felt. 'The French Navy?' As an admiral or a captain she could well imagine, but a diver? She swallowed as he hooked his thumbs under the corner of his T-shirt. It certainly explained his incredible physique—in which she had absolutely no interest, of course. It was just that she'd been trained to admire things that were aesthetically pleasing.

'This room is closest to the sea. I used to train out of here before I signed up full-time.'

Cally watched, her whole body besieged by a frightening and unfamiliar paralysis as he revealed his taut, muscular chest and exceptionally broad shoulders. He had a scar, she noticed, running from just below his belly button to somewhere below the waistband of his jeans. The mark of his fallibility fascinated her. How had he got it? How would it feel to trace its pale crease with her fingertips and find out where it led—and, more to the point, why was she even wondering? Her pulse skittered madly. Good God, now he was unbuttoning his flies! She moved her face closer to the painting, pretending to look at it closely, willing herself to concentrate on Rénard's artistic genius. But the live work of nature before her was suddenly a whole lot more impressive.

When she raised her head to look again he was wearing pale blue swimming trunks, and she found herself inexplicably frustrated that she had no way of knowing whether he had been wearing them underneath his jeans all along or not.

'We haven't had a day this hot for weeks.' His mouth twitched in amusement as he walked over to the small fridge by the sink and took a long swig from a bottle of water. *Try years,* Cally thought, her mouth growing dry at the sight. They ought to use him to advertise mineral water. Or on second thoughts perhaps not; it would probably cause a drought.

'It's definitely even warmer than yesterday,' she replied weakly.

'So join me.' He nodded at the inviting blue glitter of sea outside the window.

Join him? She followed his gaze and imagined plunging into its cooling depths. Then she turned her attention back to the tanned, muscular profile. Far, far too dangerous.

'Thanks, but it could be detrimental not to complete this part of the process now I've started.'

'Of course,' he said slowly. 'Just don't get too hot in here all by yourself.'

And with that he opened the glass doors, strolled the short distance to the cliff and dived in.

Several minutes passed before Cally realised she was still staring at the empty space where he had been, her cotton bud poised inanely in mid-air. Racked with irritation that the ability to apply herself to her work was now even further from her grasp, she dropped the bud back into the container of water and stood up, hoping that stretching her legs and turning off the CD player would allow her to regroup her thoughts. But before she could stop herself she was stretching her legs back across the room to the wide glass doors.

Cally touched a hand to her hair and looked behind her guiltily as she got closer to the threshold between inside and out. Which was ridiculous, because she was perfectly entitled to get up and look at the view, and it wasn't as though anyone could see her anyway. She peered over the cliff edge and down into the expanse of blue below, then across the bay, out at the horizon and back again. It was so still there was hardly a wave. So where was he? She tried to pretend she didn't care, that she was taking in the amazingly cloudless sky as her eyes frantically skimmed the water. Until—thank goodness—there he was, returning to the surface.

However much she wanted to argue to some invisible jury that she was just admiring the glorious landscape, the sight of him held her transfixed. His muscular shoulders were stretched tight, his strong arms slicing rhythmically through the water; he was so focussed that she was not only mesmerised but envious. He dipped beneath the surface, sometimes for so long that she almost did herself an injury as she strained to see below the water, each reappearance causing a clammy wash of relief across her shoulders and down her back.

Shockingly, half of her—like the woman in the paintings—felt the unprecedented impulse to brazenly remove her clothes and follow him into the sea. Her more sensible half told her that that was not only inexcusable, because she was his employee, but that she had to be deranged if she thought she had anything in common with the siren in Rénard's painting. So why as she watched him was she unable to stop herself running her hands over the silk of her blouse as if to check it hadn't disappeared of its own accord? And why did she feel the urge to close her eyes and explore the unfamiliar ache pooling between her thighs as her hand lingered over her breasts?

Because you're a fool, Cally, a voice inside her screamed at the exact moment that the memory of his kiss on the dark and crowded dance floor flew into her mind, and she suddenly remembered the auction. Remembered that he had lied to her from the moment she had met him, and that even if he hadn't, thinking about him that way could only lead to disappointment. So why was she standing here allowing herself to feel this way—no matter that they were feelings she could never recall ever feeling before—when she was supposed to be working on her dream commission?

It was because the thrill of getting this job had been diminished by the way in which it had come about, she thought pragmatically, knotting her hands behind her and walking back towards the paintings. It was discovering that her employer was not only the epitome of everything she loathed, but that he was also the man who had dented her pride on the first occasion in years when she had actually dared to live a little. If the London City Gallery had won the paintings the night of the auction, everything would have been different; she would have rung her family, euphoria would have hit and single-minded focus would have followed. Yes, Cally thought, what she needed was to be reminded of the enormity of this opportunity, to talk to someone who would know how much it meant to her.

She bent down and rifled through her handbag in search of her paint-smattered mobile, scrolling through the shortlist of contacts until she found her sister's number.

Jen answered amidst the usual sea of background noise

which seemed to follow her around; if it wasn't the sound of Dylan and Josh using each other as climbing frames, then it was the hustle and bustle of a breaking news story. This time it sounded like the latter.

'Cally? Are you OK?'

'Hi, Jen, I'm fine,' Cally replied, unsure why her sister's voice was loaded with concern. Although she'd wanted to talk about it, she hadn't told Jen anything about Montéz. Last time they'd spoken she'd been ninety percent sure that the email was a hoax, and, when the tickets had arrived, she'd decided it would be prudent to wait and see if it actually yielded a job first, rather than have to report back with another story of rejection if it didn't. 'Is it a bad time to talk?'

'No, not at all—I'm outside Number Ten waiting for the prime minister to emerge, but I could be here for hours. It's just that I left a message on your answer phone inviting you to dinner on Sunday and you haven't replied.'

'When was that?'

'Last night.'

Last night? She hadn't replied in less than twenty-four hours and that automatically made her sister think something was up? Cally pulled at a loose thread on her shorts and frowned. She'd always thought her swiftness to reply to people was a positive thing—she was the first one to send out thank-yous after Christmas, always RSVP-ing on time to invitations to weddings and parties, even if it was to decline them. Only now did she realise how much it screamed 'I need to get out more'.

'Thanks, but I'm afraid I can't come. I'm in Montéz.'

'Montéz?' The utter disbelief in her sister's voice bugged her. 'Good for you. It's about time you had a holiday.'

'I'm not on holiday. I'm working on the Rénards.'

'Cally, that's fantastic! How? Tell me everything. You found out who bought them?'

'The buyer found me.'

'That's because you're the best person for the job. Didn't I tell you that was a possibility? So, who is it?'

Cally hesitated, not having foreseen that this discussion would inevitably end up being about the very person she was trying to put out of her mind. 'He's the prince here.'

There was a shocked pause. 'Oh my God—don't tell me you're working for Leon Montallier?'

Cally almost dropped the phone. 'How on earth do *you* know his name?'

Jen whistled through her teeth. 'Everyone who works for a paper knows his name. We're just not allowed to print anything about him. Not that anybody knows anything— he's too much of an enigma.'

'Too much of a bastard,' Cally corrected, turning to pace in the other direction as she realised that during the conversation she'd walked herself dangerously close to the glass doors once more. 'There's nothing else worth knowing.'

'Hang on a minute. Hasn't he just given you your dream job?'

'Yes, he has,' Cally admitted, trying to sound enthused as she recalled that this was the whole purpose for her call. 'And the chance to infill for a master like Rénard is incredible but—'

'But what? Oh, don't tell me that because he's royalty he thought that gave him the right to try it on?'

The frankness Jen had developed from her years reporting on the wealthy and powerful usually amused Cally, but today its accuracy—or rather its inaccuracy—only succeeded in making her feel more wretched.

'But he doesn't plan to display the pictures in a gallery, that's what. They're nothing more than a symbol of his nauseating wealth.'

'Well, I can't say I'm surprised about that, I'm afraid,' Jen said, unaware how close her initial remark had been to the bone. 'But that doesn't mean you can't share your restoration process with the public, does it?'

'Sorry?'

'The paper could run a story. Our arts specialist, Julian, would kill to do a piece on it!'

'I *wish*. But he's so anti-press that it's written into my contract that I can't even— Jen?'

The volume of the background noise suddenly doubled, and Cally could hear the clash of a thousand cameras and the sound of bodies jostling forward.

'Jen, can you hear me?'

'Sorry, sis, gotta go!'

''Course—look, just forget I even mentioned him, OK?'

Leon's mouth curved in amusement as he approached the studio doors to find her concentrating hard on facing the wall as she finished her call. She was making a show of trying to stick to her word, he'd give her that. But, if it was for his benefit, she needn't bother. Didn't she know that he had seen her from the water? And didn't she know that it made no difference whether he witnessed it or not?

Her desire for him was written into every move her delectable body made. It had been from the very first moment she had looked at him with those expressive green eyes. He wondered how much longer she would keep fighting it, pretending that what mattered to her were the paintings. Had she forgotten how clear she had made it in that insalubrious bar in London? Had she forgotten that she had told him she was only interested in this job to gain renown? Since he had made sure *that* wasn't an option, her reason for accepting was obvious—him. But, then, he was well aware that women were experts at pretending to be driven by their careers in order to entice a man. Women who claimed to have moved on from their nineteenth-century counterparts, who learned a handful of accomplishments to try and coerce a man into marrying them, but who really hadn't changed at all. They had simply got more devious.

Not that Cally was claiming to want *marriage,* he thought dryly. But he didn't doubt that those wistful looks into jewellers' windows would inevitably come if he kept her in his bed for too long.

'Someone special?'

Cally jumped and swung round to see him crossing the studio as the deep timbre of his voice reverberated through her body. How the hell hadn't she heard him come in this time? She looked down, convinced he mustn't be wearing shoes. She was right, but for her gaze to have alighted on the bareness of his toes was a mistake. Not only did she notice that even his feet were impossibly sexy, but it only encouraged her to sweep her eyes upwards over the damp hairs clinging to his legs, to the towel slung about his waist and his mouth-watering chest.

'Sorry?'

'The phone call. It must have been someone special, to interrupt what you were doing when you seemed so reluctant to stop.'

'I—I'd finished the section I was on. I'm just about to start on the next.' She sat back down in the chair and made to pick up a fresh cotton bud.

He looked at her with amusement dancing in his eyes. 'I wasn't talking about the paintings.'

Cally froze and felt herself blush redder than her hair as she realised what he meant. Wanting to die of embarrassment, she clutched around in her mind for some feasible excuse as to why she had been looking out to sea with her hands on her body, but it didn't come.

He broke into a wry smile and continued. 'But, much as I would like to watch you continue, I'm afraid I cannot keep the French president waiting.' Cally swallowed as he removed the towel from around his waist and laid it around his shoulders. 'I will be back tomorrow evening, when the Sheikh of Qwasir and his new fiancée will be coming for dinner. I thought perhaps you might like to join us, show them what you're working on.'

Cally stared at him, her embarrassment turning to astonishment. Firstly that he had even asked her, and secondly that, despite his own rebuttal of the press, he socialised with two people who could not have had a higher media profile.

'You mean the couple who are on the front of every newspaper in the world?'

Leon tensed and gave a single nod.

'And you wish me to show them the paintings?' Even though she hated the idea of private buyers wanting famous artwork for no other reason than to impress their friends, she couldn't help feeling both excited and honoured at the prospect of getting to share them with anyone.

'That is what I said,' Leon ground out, only now aware that, whilst he had envisioned a night with her beside him wearing one of those figure-hugging dresses he had selected, she saw it only as an opportunity to get herself known amongst the rich and famous.

'Thank you—then I'm delighted to accept.'

'Of course you are,' he drawled, before walking over to the table and handing her the cotton bud she was still yet to pick up. 'In the meantime, I'm sure you'll want to get on with what you came here to do.'

CHAPTER SIX

GET ON with what you came here to do. Leon's sarcastic words were still reverberating through Cally's mind as she tramped upstairs twenty-four hours later. If only she could. More than anything that was what she wanted, but to her horror another day had passed unproductively. Even though the supplies she needed had arrived that morning, even though she'd had the palace to herself, she hadn't been able to stop herself from gazing up at the glass doors, imagining him rising half-naked from the sea.

Allowing herself to get distracted in any way at all was completely unlike her, she thought as she entered the bedroom, never mind by thoughts of that nature. Everything she ever took on she always committed to one hundred and ten per cent until it was complete. Except her fine-art degree, she admitted ruefully. Was that it then— every time she met a man she found remotely attractive she was reduced to a mess of distraction which robbed her of all her artistic focus?

Cally cast her mind back to the summer she had met David, when she had taken a job as a waitress at the tearoom in the grounds of his father's stately home. Had she been so bowled over by his charms that it had rendered her completely incapable of holding a brush? No, she thought frankly, actually, she hadn't. She'd been flattered by the unexpected attention he'd bestowed upon her, naively impressed by the upper-class world in which he lived, but she certainly hadn't felt this kind of paralysis. That was not what had made her throw in her studies, it was that she'd foolishly believed him when he'd said she would never become a great artist spending all her time working towards a degree. Only later had she discovered that, just like his chauvinistic father, the idea of a woman going to university had appalled him, particularly one whose father was just a postman.

So why the hell was it this way with Leon? Cally wondered as she opened her wardrobe to find it had been miraculously filled with the contents of the fifty-four bags and boxes whilst she had been working—and to her amusement some additional T-shirts and casual cut-offs too. And why was she so tempted to wear one of the glamorous dresses now, when she loathed the excess they represented? Because his guests were an esteemed desert ruler and a model, which meant such an outfit was appropriate for this element of her work in the same way her sister's black dress had been necessary for the auction, Cally justified, feeling both apprehensive and thrilled at the prospect of talking about the paintings. Even if talking about them was all she was able to do at the moment.

In the end she selected a beautiful jade dress with an asymmetric hem that felt so good swishing around her legs as she came down the stairs that, when she reached the grand dining room, it took her a minute to process that the table was completely bare. She looked at the antique clock on the wall, wondering if she had got the time wrong. Noting she hadn't, she decided she must have been mistaken about the place. Heaven knew, the palace was big enough, and Leon could hold the soirée in any number of rooms.

'Boyet!' Cally caught sight of him just as he was about to turn the corner of the inner stairs. 'I was supposed to meet His Highness in the dining room for the royal dinner at eight. Is it to be held elsewhere?'

'I believe there has been a change of plan altogether, mademoiselle.' He looked at the floor, evidently embarrassed that he was in possession of information that she was not. 'The last time I saw His Royal Highness, he was headed outside, as if he intended to go diving.'

'In *this*?' Cally gasped, concern furrowing her brow as she looked out across the hallway and through the high windows towards the inky blue sky, the rising wind beginning to whip against the glass.

'Thank you, Boyet,' she replied with a quick but earnest nod, turning on her three-inch heels in matching jade and hastening to the studio with none of the ladylike elegance with which she had just descended the stairs.

The room was bathed in darkness, and her pace slowed as she approached the glass doors; she was almost afraid of coming upon the view of the sea too quickly for fear of what she might see. Eventually she reached the handle and, finding it locked, began fumbling around in search of a key.

'Looking for something?'

Cally turned sharply to find Leon sitting absolutely still on the sofa, bathed in shadows. The look of accusation in his eyes matched the warning tone of his voice.

'Boyet said you were out in this.' She raised one hand out towards the blackness of the ocean, as if the concept was the most preposterous thing she had ever heard, choosing to overlook his equally sinister mood. As far as she could see, she was the only one who had a reason to be angry.

'I was,' he said abruptly as she turned on the lamp next to the paintings, softly illuminating the room.

He was dressed in jeans and a T-shirt that clung to his body in such a way that she could see his skin beneath was still damp. His hair was dark and heavy with moisture. If she hadn't been so determined not to think it, she would have admitted it was the most alluring thing she had ever seen in her life.

'Are you insane?'

'Insane to risk being late for our high-profile dinner engagement?' he drawled, eyeing her so critically that all the joy she'd felt in wearing the jade dress evaporated.

'To go diving tonight, when the ocean is so restless,' Cally corrected, wondering how he wasn't shivering with cold when just thinking about being in the water had her arms breaking out in goose bumps. 'Isn't one scar enough?'

Leon's mouth twitched into a sardonic smile. 'Though your observational skills are as touching as your concern, I can assure you that swimming in the cove outside my back door is hardly a risk in comparison to defusing a mine one hundred metres below sea level. I'll admit it's been a while, but—'

'Fine.' Cally blushed furiously. 'So, what about dinner? Boyet said there had been a change of plan.'

'There has. Unfortunately Kaliq and Tamara are unable to join us. Exhaustion after their journey here, I believe.'

'And you didn't think it polite to tell me before I went to the trouble of getting dressed up?'

'Given your track record, I had no idea you would go to so much trouble.' He stared at her legs, remembering where her shorts had been. 'But, then, I suppose I should have known, shouldn't I?'

'Known what?' Cally swiped, growing increasingly frustrated at his unaccountably bad mood.

'That everything's different when you're presented with the chance of renown.'

'Renown?' She turned to him blankly.

'God, you really are good, aren't you?' His mouth twisted in disgust.

'Good at what, Leon? At least tell me what the hell I've done so I can *try* and defend myself.'

He had flung it before she'd even finished speaking. It narrowly missed the first painting, hitting the lamp, which crashed to the floor, by luck avoiding the easel of the second painting by less than an inch. It was only after she'd thrown herself in front of both Rénards as if to shield them from further attack that she realised that it was a rolled-up newspaper.

'What the hell do you think you're playing at?'

'I was about to ask you the same question.'

'What?' she cried in exasperation. 'You're the one who just nearly destroyed an eighty-million-pound work of art!'

'*My* eighty-million-pound work of art,' he replied smoothly. 'Which I was nowhere near. It's a shame I can't say the same for you and the press.'

Grasping that there was something she was missing, Cally was already on the floor, unrolling the paper, cringing as she saw the teaser at the top of the page.

THE WORLD TODAY
Restoring our interest: Rénard's masterpieces since *that* auction.

Art conservator Cally Greenway shares her eighty-million-pound secret!

Cally's eyes widened in horror. She'd told her sister that running an article was out of the question, hadn't she? Cally's cheeks coloured as she fought to remember the details, details which were hazy because at the time she'd been so distracted by the thought of *him*. Yes, she most definitely had, and she knew there was no way that Jen would run a story regardless. Unless…unless in all the commotion on the other end of the line her sister hadn't heard her properly.

'There's been a mistake,' Cally cried helplessly. 'I told her not to print anything.'

'*Her?*'

'My sister Jen's a journalist.'

'Oh, fantastic.'

Cally's voice became defensive. 'I only called her because I wanted to share the fact that I'd got the job I thought I'd lost.' His expression was utterly remorseless. 'In the same way *she* calls *me* about what's going on in her life. She happened to mention that an article about restoring the Rénards would be a great way of sharing them with the public. I agreed that it *would* be, but I told her there was no way you'd allow it. But…but we got cut off, and she must have misunderstood what I'd said.'

'How convenient for you.'

'Are you calling me a liar?'

Leon looked at her patronisingly. 'I'm saying that, if you think I have forgotten that night in London, then you are even more foolish than I thought.'

Cally coloured instantly. 'What has this got to do with London?'

'You mean you have forgotten, *chérie?*' he drawled, his eyes lingering on her lips. 'You told me your reason for wanting to work on the Rénards. It was so that your name would be known across the world, was it not? So how can you possibly expect me to believe that this exposure is an accident?'

'I told you! Jen must have misunderstood. Let me call her, get to the bottom of it—'

'I think calling her once has done enough damage, don't you?'

Cally let out a frustrated sigh. 'And for that I'm sorry, but…' She scanned her eyes down the article, and noticed that the 'secret' the headline referred to was nothing more than the fact that she was restoring the paintings for a private collector in France. 'Look.' She pointed to the text. 'You're not even mentioned. Yes, that the article exists is a mistake. But everyone makes mistakes now and again—' she hesitated '—even you.'

'But this isn't about me.' He paused, and then the tone of his voice suddenly turned. 'Unless, of course, what you are really trying to tell me is that I'm *precisely* what this is all about.'

'Please don't talk in riddles, Leon.'

'Well, if I'm to believe that you didn't do this on purpose, that fame wasn't top of your agenda when you agreed to work for me, then what else could possibly have induced you to say yes?' His eyes licked over her.

'I just told you. I'm passionate about the Rénards. I have been since I was a child.' She avoided his gaze, knowing it was only designed to humiliate her further. 'Is that so hard for you to believe?'

When she looked up he was staring at her with an intensity which told her there was nowhere to hide. 'It is when I know that for every minute you spend working on them you spend thirty thinking about me.'

Cally felt horror tear through every tissue in her body, not only because, to her shame, he was right and he knew it, but because she was terrified that what he implied was true. Had she accepted this job because the feelings he evoked in her obliterated everything else? No, she'd accepted it for the sake of her career, the Rénards.

'You're wrong, Leon.' Her voice was a husky whisper.

'Am I? Then how would *you* explain the symptoms. Dilated pupils, shallow breathing, the way you can't stop yourself from running your tongue over your lower lip every time you look at me? For someone who's supposed to be an expert on diagnosis and protection, I would have thought it was obvious.'

'I don't need protection,' Cally shot out determinedly, not noticing the look that flared in his eyes at her words.

'No, I didn't suppose for one minute that you would.'

But before she had time to process what he meant he slid his hand across her back and drew her to him, until their bodies were pressed so closely together that in the half light it would have been impossible for an onlooker to discern where she ended and where he began.

She froze, wanting to push him away, but unable to muster the strength. 'Leon, don't.'

He held perfectly still, save for his thumb tracing the base of her spine with an affectionate intimacy that made her want to cry out. 'Why not, *chérie,* when we both know it is what you want?'

Cally shook her head wretchedly. 'Be-because you don't want to.'

At her words even his thumb stopped moving and he regarded her with a faint look of surprise. 'Is it not obvious that I want you so much I have lost the ability to think straight?'

'But in London…'

He trailed his hand up her back and rested his fingers on the pulse beating wildly in her neck. 'It seems we were both a little guilty of saying one thing and meaning another in London.'

Her head fell back to look into his eyes, her own eyes widening as she realised that his were completely unflinching. He meant it. Though that ought to have changed nothing, to Cally it changed everything. He *did* desire her. Much as she'd been convinced that was impossible, much as she'd never dreamed she could ever feel such fervent need in return, suddenly it consumed her so overwhelmingly that she didn't even feel like the same Cally she had been two weeks ago. And, although she knew the safest option would be to button down her feelings as if they were nothing but awning caught in a disobedient wind, although she had never felt more terrified in her life, above all she understood that she would never know what it truly was to live unless she let it fly. Now.

'Leon, I—'

'Want me to kiss you again?' he ventured, moving his face so close to hers that his lips were only millimetres away.

The small sound that escaped from her throat said it all. It was unconscious, automatic, and with it he closed the gap between their mouths and gave an equally primal groan.

His kiss was exactly as she'd remembered but completely different at the same time. Not only did it feel like he was slowly turning every cell in her body to liquid with each masterful stroke of his tongue, but now there was no languid music deciding their tempo, his hunger set the pace and dared her to match it. Not only did he smell of that distinctive musk she knew she would never fully be able to drive from her mind, it was now mixed with the smell of the sea—salty, damp and agonisingly erotic. So potent that she had to cling on to him to stop her knees from buckling. As she did, they stumbled forward a little, the heel of her shoe catching something other than floor.

Her eyes flew open to find it was the foot of an easel, and suddenly she remembered where they were and froze. 'The paintings!'

'Forget the damned paintings,' he drawled, steadying the fully clothed *Amour* with unconcerned ease. 'Let's go upstairs.'

The thought of the royal bedroom terrified Cally. Down here she could almost believe that he wasn't the prince, that she hadn't completely taken leave of her senses. She bit her lip for a moment, knowing that suggesting the alternative required a boldness she wasn't sure she possessed. But then she looked at him; his eyes were so hungry for her that it was almost possible to forget that she lacked anything at all. She swallowed down the excess of saliva that had formed in her mouth and imagined her fear disappearing with it. 'Actually, do you…do you mind if we stay here?'

The thought of taking her here and now made Leon harder than he had ever been in his entire life.

'Mind?' he breathed, doing nothing to disguise the roughness of his voice. 'The only thing I mind is that you are still wearing that dress.'

Cally's moment of relief was replaced by a new army of nerves. 'It does seem a little formal,' she whispered hesitantly as his hand trailed down her neck and swept around the circle of her breast. Instinctively she arched her back to encourage his hand upwards to the unbearable tightness of her nipple, but instead his fingers moved behind her, releasing the zip of her dress with ease and peeling the straps from her shoulders.

It was then that she remembered with horror the jade green basque and panties she was wearing underneath. She had put it on in that insane moment earlier when she'd been filled with delight at the thought of wearing the dress, followed by the girlish longing to try on the beautiful matching lingerie, the likes of which she had never worn in her life. It had felt so good, and, never supposing for a minute that anyone would see it, she'd seen no harm in keeping it on. Suddenly she felt ridiculous. What must he think of her, standing before him in lingerie that made her look like a courtesan at the Moulin Rouge, when she was nothing but an art restorer from Cambridge who hadn't had sex for almost a decade, and had never been good at it even then?

But when he peeled her dress down to her ankles and stepped back the pleasure on his face was so palpable—as if this was exactly how he had expected her to look, how she should look—that he made her feel like a butterfly emerging from a chrysalis. So much so that it was easy to forget how many other more beautiful, more experienced women than her must have stood before him like this. Easy to forget her old insecurities, to think only about how much he seemed to want her, how much she wanted him.

Cally reached forward with new-found boldness to encourage his T-shirt from his jeans.

'Allow me,' Leon interrupted, deftly removing both so that he was standing before her in nothing but his silky dark

boxers, every inch of hard muscle illuminated in the refracted light from the lamp still lying on the floor like
some piece of modern art.

He pulled her to him with renewed urgency, and she
bucked in pleasure as at last his thumb brushed over her
nipple through the lace of the bodice, making her whole
body tremble.

'I hope you're not cold?' he asked, the corner of his
mouth quirking into a smile as he circled the taut peak.

'No.' She shook her head, her breathing ragged. 'Not *cold.*'

'Good,' he rasped, raising his arms and moving behind
her to slowly unlace the basque.

'Are you?' Cally whispered.

'Am I what?' he whispered distractedly as he kissed the
delicious hollow between her neck and her shoulder.

'Are you cold?'

'What do you think?' he ground out as the basque fell
to the floor and he spun her round to face him, revelling in
the sight of her.

Slowly, tentatively, she daringly reached out her hand
to touch him through the thin, silky fabric. 'You feel pretty
warmed up to me.'

Leon closed his eyes and groaned as she gradually
tugged down his boxers. When he opened them again her
eyes were fixed on him, her whole body momentarily still.

'What are you thinking?' he asked choppily.

Cally forced herself to blink, stunned by her own
boldness, by the size of him, by the way his scar led into
the mass of thick, dark curls. 'Your ego is big enough as it
is,' she breathed, suddenly nervous again.

'So, show me,' he teased in delight.

Cally looked into the depths of his eyes, her mind filling

with a host of unfamiliar and erotic images that she was convinced he must somehow be transmitting to her. Images which excited her even more than they surprised her, made her forget that she wasn't the kind of woman who instinctively understood the art of love, made her think quite the opposite. Slowly, slowly, with her breath caught nervously in her throat, she began to feather light kisses from beneath his belly button to the tip of his arousal.

Leon watched. Her breasts grazed the shafts of his thighs as she took him in her mouth. It was almost too much for him to bear. He guided her upwards and towards the sofa.

'I want to be inside you.'

Cally wanted him inside of her too, irrationally, inexplicably. In that instant she understood, however astonishing, that was what she had wanted from the very first moment she'd laid eyes on him. Now he was sitting on the sofa, guiding her legs to either side of him, his middle finger rushing up her inner thigh, finding the most intimate part of her, moist, open, *ready.*

She heard herself gasp in shock as he lowered her down onto him. Not in pain, she thought in amazement, but in pleasure. He was so warm, so thick, and it felt so right that Cally wondered how on earth she'd never known it could be like this before. Before she had time to examine what that meant, her thoughts faded like a watercolour in the rain as he began to rock her slowly back and forward.

'Now you,' he breathed hotly, slowing his pace and encouraging her to set the speed. Cally hesitated and then slowly began to move, heat rising through her. Leon placed his hands on her bottom, watching her.

'Close your eyes.'

Cally felt her breathing grow faster as she increased

pace, Leon suckling her breasts. An uncontrollable groan of pleasure broke from her throat. The sound shocked her into opening her eyes, and she slowed the pace fractionally.

'Let go,' he commanded.

'No, I...I don't know... I can't.'

'Yes, you can,' he replied forcefully, and she felt him shift slightly beneath her, reaching even deeper inside her, so deep, she felt her muscles contract around the hard length of him and the beginning of a new sensation that was so frighteningly powerful—like teetering on the edge of an unfamiliar precipice—that she didn't know what to do; she was afraid to let go.

'Now,' he urged, but still her eyes were squeezed tight. 'Damn you, I can't hold on!'

Cally felt his climax rip through him, saw the tendons in his neck go taut, felt his seed spill deep inside her, and...

It was only then, as she had been on the cusp of her very first orgasm, that she realised they hadn't used a condom.

CHAPTER SEVEN

HALF-WRAPPED in the maroon throw that covered the sofa, Cally felt instantly cold. No, cold was an understatement. She felt sub-zero, as though if she went anywhere near a thermometer the mercury would shrink in on itself and disappear altogether.

They hadn't used a condom.

She stared at the black restless sea outside the window, and then across at Leon, who lay by her side in a state of repose, thick-lashed eyes closed. How could they have been so stupid? They weren't a couple of naive teenagers, they were grown adults, for goodness' sake. He was a prince, for whom such basics had to be even more important than they were to the average male, and she was ordinarily so sensible that she never left the house without an umbrella and a packet of plasters. So why on earth hadn't either of them given a second thought to the small matter of protection?

Cally opened her mouth to share the burden of their irresponsibility, but just as she was about to speak a warning siren went off in her brain. *Protection.* She screwed up her eyes, their earlier conversation dropping back into her mind like bad news through a letterbox, her own words echoing back at her: *I don't need protection.*

Oh, dear God, he hadn't actually assumed that she'd meant the contraceptive kind, had he? No, he couldn't have. Perhaps Montéz was a pioneer of the male Pill and he hadn't thought to mention it. Or maybe, since he never intended to get married, he'd had the snip. Oh, who the hell was she trying to kid? She'd inadvertently led the most virile man she'd ever met to believe that she was protected, and it was a lie. And now there was every chance that his seed was already firmly rooted inside her.

Don't be so ridiculous, Cally, she reprimanded herself. *Whatever the movies would have you believe, the chances of getting pregnant after only one night are miniscule. Look at Jen—it took over a year of trying to get both Dylan and Josh. You're just a natural born worrier trying to punish yourself because for once in your life you acted a little recklessly.* Her eyes returned to Leon; his whole body was at ease in the aftermath of their lovemaking. What would be the good in telling him that he'd misinterpreted what she'd said? He'd probably laugh at her for being the faintest bit concerned. Either that, or he'd think she'd done it on purpose because she wanted to have his baby.

Cally untangled her legs and swung them over the edge of the sofa, horrified at the thought. Then she froze again. On some unconscious level, did she want his baby? Suddenly an idyllic image popped into her brain: Leon and her in the water teaching two children how to swim, a boy with dark blond hair like his father's, a girl with little red pigtails. Quickly, she forced herself to snap out of it. She didn't even like the man, and he no doubt took the same view of children as he did of marriage. Which was perfect, because she'd known for years that she was neither wife nor mother material, and that suited her just fine—even if at this precise moment she couldn't for the life of her remember why.

Because it allowed her to focus on her career, she recalled despondently, staring up at the paintings and then down at the rolled-up newspaper below them, remembering she had a whole other set of worries to occupy her mind on that front. Worries that were far more palatable than why she had never known making love could be that good until now, or why she wanted to crawl back into his embrace and stay there for as long as he'd have her.

Worries like whether she even still had a job, she thought, abruptly realising that she was still *sans* clothes, and that if she didn't think fast she was not only in serious danger of being fired but of being fired in the nude. The horrifying thought spurred her into action, and she quickly slipped from the sofa to locate her clothes, not noticing the way Leon's nostrils flared in arousal as he watched her dismiss the complicated hooks and ribbons of her underwear and throw on the dress without it.

Cally tiptoed across to where the newspaper lay pitifully beside the fallen lamp and picked it up. She took one more look at the offending page and then folded it away, trying not to think about how much she still wanted to scream at him for being so unreasonable. She understood now that it would do her no good.

Leon watched through heavy-lidded eyes as she reacquainted the light with its shade. Her hair was mussed from their lovemaking, her expression so misty-eyed that he was reminded of the first time he had seen her at the pre-auction. It seemed strange that he should be reminded of the moment he had suspected her of being the kind of woman to cloud things with emotion, when she had come to him dressed to seduce. It was perfectly obvious that it had all been an act, that what she really wanted was the kind of no-strings affair she was no doubt accustomed to. After all, why else would she be on the Pill, or have casually got up to retrieve her dress, instead of trying to embrace him afterwards, the way emotional women always did?

It didn't please him as much as it ought to have done. Instead it made him wonder, irrationally, how many men she had gone to like that, straddled and used the sum of her obvious feminine wiles to get her own way with? Yet she hadn't climaxed. For the first time in his life he was struck by a momentary fear of sexual inadequacy, but he dismissed it just as quickly. She had been about to come, and she had fought it on purpose. In some attempt to show him that she was in control? he wondered angrily, irritated that he hadn't been able to hold off his own orgasm.

'I will speak to Jen first thing in the morning, make sure she understands the paintings should never have been mentioned,' Cally said quietly, feeling his eyes upon her. 'And you have my word that I will never find myself in danger of breaking your law again.'

A shadow darkened his face at the note of disapproval in her voice. 'It's not *my* law. The royal family of Montéz has always been forbidden territory to the press. And with good reason. Being followed around like the stars in some hideous reality TV show can only interfere with our work on the island.'

'But your brother—'

'My brother upheld exactly the same law until he met Toria.'

Cally raised her eyebrows and looked directly into his eyes for the first time since she had moved away from the sofa, disturbed as much by the discovery that a reasonable principle lay behind the law as by his glorious nudity. 'She got him to change it?'

'In a word, yes.' It didn't cure the look of curiosity on Cally's face. Leon drew in a short, frustrated breath, not sure why he felt so impelled to explain. 'Toria came to Montéz to star in a low-budget movie one summer when I was serving in the Marine Nationale. She had no talent, but she was desperate for fame and incredibly attractive. When she heard that the Crown Prince favoured a low profile over celebrity status, she thought it was preposterous and decided to seek him out. Girard was fifteen years her senior, lonely and flattered.'

He made a pattern with his fingernail on the arm of the sofa, not looking up. 'By the time of my next visit home, she had convinced him to marry her, and by the time of the wedding she had persuaded him that the media exposure was vital to her career. Which wouldn't have been so detestable if she had accepted even one role after he had given her the exposure she craved. She told him she was waiting for the right part, whilst all the time dragging him to photo shoots for magazines, movie premieres, A-list parties. All the time Montéz was suffering, and Girard was growing more and more exhausted. Eventually it came to a head.' Leon's expression turned as dark and foreboding as the night outside the window. 'They had been invited to a high-profile awards ceremony in New York on the same day as the private memorial service held annually to mark the anniversary of our mother's death. Toria demanded he go with her.' He looked stricken with guilt. 'I told him I would never forgive him if he did.'

'He went with her,' Cally breathed, recalling that the tragedy had taken place in the States.

'No. He decided to try and do both.' Leon gritted his teeth, remembering that, for all his faults, Girard's peace-keeping skills had been second to none. 'Toria went ahead without him. He stayed for the memorial, vowing to meet her at the awards ceremony as soon as he could. And he would have made it—but he fell asleep at the wheel on the stretch between JFK airport and the auditorium.' Leon's eyes glazed with pain. 'When Toria called to give me the news, all she could ask was why he hadn't been using a chauffeur.'

'I'm sorry,' Cally whispered, wanting to tell him not to blame himself, seeing in his eyes that he did. 'I had no idea.'

'Very few people did. Toria adored the press, and the press adored her. After his death everyone wanted to interview the poor, grieving widow.' He gave a bitter, broken laugh. 'It was the best performance of her career.'

Cally could only imagine what it must have been like to deal with that in every newspaper and on every news channel, having just lost his brother and been thrust into the role of prince. 'So you reinstated the law?'

She saw him hesitate, and instantly his expression became shuttered. 'It was around that time, yes.'

'And Toria?'

'Never forgave me for denying her the media circus here in Montéz. So she moved to New York. She still turns up occasionally with a mouthful of idle threats.'

'I'm sorry,' Cally repeated, understanding now why he had automatically assumed that she wanted to use her work here to feed off his fame, that she had planned the article. Somehow, the revelation made her feel even closer to him than she had done when they'd been making love. She looked down at the newspaper she was still holding and clutched it tighter. 'And I meant it when I said that nothing like this will ever happen again.'

She didn't see Leon's gaze drop to her hand, the look of distaste which shaped his mouth, as if he was a soldier who'd just realised he was inadvertently fraternising with the enemy. 'Good,' he replied, reaching for his jeans. 'Because as my mistress I require your absolute discretion.'

Cally's head jerked up in disbelief. 'Your *what?*'

'My mistress,' he said in a clipped tone which suggested he found having to repeat himself an inconvenience.

She stared at him in horror, suddenly feeling like a trapeze artist who thought she'd caught the bar in her hands but was suddenly plummeting towards the ground. 'And when exactly did I agree to be that?'

Leon shook his head. She *had* to be kidding. Surely she didn't expect him to buy the holier-than-thou charade now? 'I rather think your actions did the talking, don't you? Unless you're going to tell me that that little outfit and those moves are all part of some new and innovative conservation technique.' He dropped his head to one side. 'Although, it was certainly revitalizing, I'll give you that.'

The rant she'd been preparing collapsed under the weight of hurt and shame. 'No wonder you insist on never being quoted in the press. You're so crude, your people would question your royal blood.'

For a second an acute sharpness, almost a wince, cut across his face—but then as fast as it had come it was gone.

'I thought you liked your men to tell it like it is. Don't tell me sex has made you sentimental?'

'Hardly.' Cally turned away, fighting the tears that pricked behind her eyes.

'Then I suggest you spare me the lecture and come and have something to eat.'

'I'm not hungry.'

'Really?' he goaded. 'Or is it simply that you can't swallow that I was right all along?'

'Right about what?'

'That you only accepted this job because you wanted to go to bed with me.'

Cally's hurt caught fire, transforming into white-hot fury. 'Is your ego so gigantic that you can't accept that after years studying art restoration, and months of preparing to work on the paintings before we even met, that maybe *they* were the reason?'

'Of course I can accept that, *chérie*. All women who forge a career do so with gusto until they get whatever it is they really want. Fame, sex, whatever. Now you have sex, you may drop the pretence.'

'So, because your brother's wife was a manipulative bitch who wasn't interested in having a career once she'd seduced your brother, in your eyes the entire female population is guilty of the same crime?'

Leon raised one derogatory eyebrow at her hackneyed analysis. 'On the contrary, I've based my assumptions entirely on you. You'd barely touched the paintings before this little—how would you like me to phrase it delicately for you?—episode. And I hardly think touching *them* is your top priority now.'

Cally averted her eyes as he looked down at his body, as if he was remembering where she had trailed her hands, her lips. Why the hell had he still not put on his flaming T-shirt? 'They *are* my only priority, they always have been. Every job takes a while to settle into. You employed me because I am the best person to do it, and I still am. I'm not some virgin priestess who's lost her gift because I've lain with a man!'

'Oh, I think we both know you're not that, Cally, don't you?' he said silkily, his gaze raking over her with renewed desire. 'Just like I think we both know that your being capable of the job is only half the reason I employed you.'

'What?' Cally felt her whole body tense.

With a look of unconcern, Leon reached for his T-shirt. 'Don't sound so surprised, Cally. Do you suppose I employed you, despite the fact that you proved yourself indiscreet in London, purely because of your skills? I employed you for the same reason that you accepted— because we both knew that the sex between us would be *incroyable.*'

Cally wouldn't have thought it possible that her body could wind itself any tighter, but it did, so tight she felt faint. Clamminess broke out at the nape of her neck, between her breasts, behind her knees, heat pouring over her in a wave. It *had* been incredible, and it was incredible that he thought so too. But after everything she had worked for, fought for, clung to... He had only given her the job because he wanted to have sex with her? Cally felt sick. She had supposed there was no greater blow than the gallery losing the paintings that night at the auction, believed there was nothing more mortifying than his subsequent rejection, then discovering that he had lied. But this was even worse.

'I hate you.'

For a second Leon looked slightly taken aback. Only for a second. 'And yet you still desire me.' He shook his head condescendingly. 'Reason is always at such a disadvantage when paired with that.'

'Not any more,' she answered, willing it to be true. 'We shared an attraction, and we saw it through to its natural conclusion, but—'

'So that was the euphemism you were looking for.' He nodded slowly, as if she were one of a new species whose peculiar habits he was coming to learn. 'Attraction, natural conclusion...'

'But now it's over,' she concluded abruptly, catching sight of the Rénards. 'So, if you will just kindly confirm whether I may continue with my work...?'

'Do you really suppose that our shared *attraction* is something that has ceased to exist because we have given into it once?' He stalked across to where she was standing. 'Desire is an animal. We set it free, it cannot be tied up again.'

It can be, Cally thought. *It has to be.* She bit her lip, her mind traitorously filling with the erotic image of Leon tied up.

'Well, I'm sorry to disappoint you, but I think the animal has run off,' she said, so loudly that she gave herself away.

Leon laughed, the sound so deep and low it sent a vibration through her body. 'You still want to pretend you don't feel it, *chérie?* Be my guest, continue with your *work.* I give you a week at most before you're begging me to take you again, because if I don't you'll die of longing.' He stopped at the door, one eyebrow cocked. 'Unless, of course, you want to be done with the whole pretence and join me for dinner right now?'

'Like I said, I'm not hungry.'

'Of course you're not,' he mocked. 'Just like you weren't thirsty that night in London.' And with that he turned on his heel and left her once more.

* * *

Over the next few days Cally did everything she could to forget how it had felt to make love to Leon Montallier. She tried to excuse away that night as a single moment of recklessness she had simply been due for a while, like last February, when she'd got a sore throat and had conceded that she couldn't go any longer without succumbing to a winter cold. She relabelled her desire for him as nothing more than curiosity about his body which had now been satisfied. But, no matter how hard she tried, it was impossible not to think about the incredible way he'd made her feel, about the sensations which she'd never experienced before in all of her twenty-six years.

Which ought to have been crazy, because she wasn't a virgin. Yes, she might have only ever slept with one other man, but sex was sex, wasn't it? No, Cally thought, apparently it wasn't. What she'd just experienced with Leon had felt like exactly the kind of lovemaking she'd read about, whereas with David… Well, from the very first day he had talked her into it, she'd never really enjoyed their forays in the bedroom department. They had been rushed, uncomfortable, and had always left her feeling somehow inadequate—not least on the night when she had finally plucked up the courage to ask him if they could try kissing a bit more first, because she wasn't sure it felt exactly the way it was supposed to for her. He had told her not to be so absurd, and that if she didn't like it as it was then she was obviously just lacking the right gene.

In her naivety, she had always supposed she did lack something. Now she understood that she had simply been lacking the right sexual partner. But 'right' only in *that* sense, she thought grimly; Leon might have altered her perception on sex, but he'd confirmed that Prince Charming only existed in fairy tales. Which was why she had to forget him and get on with the paintings.

It felt a little like trying to push rocks through a sieve—never more so than during the hours in which he insisted on silently watching her work, as if it was an endurance test he was waiting for her to fail—but slowly, slowly, she began to make progress. In fact, after she had completed the cleaning of the first painting and begun work on the infill, she almost felt her old focus return. Almost, because to her surprise she found that, on the few occasions she became completely absorbed in the paint work, she would find herself drifting off into thoughts about two things in particular, neither of which were things she might have expected to find herself thinking about.

The first was that she was repeatedly and inexplicably struck with a burning desire to begin working on a painting of her own, to the extent that one afternoon, when she'd known she had the palace to herself, she had begun sketching the remarkable view from the studio window onto a piece of spare canvas. She didn't have the faintest idea why, because she hadn't painted anything of her own since her split from David, and it seemed incomprehensible that she should do so now when she was finding even her conservation work a struggle, but something impelled her to.

The second distraction was Leon, but not in the sexual way that haunted her whenever she closed her eyes. When she was busy on the paintings what she'd catch herself thinking about most frequently was the conversation they'd had immediately after their lovemaking, when he had told her about his brother. And to Cally that seemed even harder to forget. Aside from Leon revealing that his insistence against media attention wasn't just a dictatorial whim, she couldn't help wondering if it was significant that he, the man who insisted on such confidentiality, had told her something so private about his family. But, just as quickly as such thoughts came, she would dismiss them. After all, he had followed it up with the assumption that she would become his mistress, for goodness' sake, and it didn't come much more meaningless than that. Besides, even if they had been in some parallel universe and his *doppelgänger* had declared it was significant, she'd walk away anyway. Wouldn't she?

Cally's eyelids fluttered down to meet her cheeks in a moment of mortification as she envisioned turning back and walking willingly into his arms. But that was just because in the parallel universe he'd be the complete opposite of who he was, not a heartless prince, not a lying bastard, she told herself at the exact moment he entered the room, sending a shiver of awareness down her spine.

'I'm actually on a really tricky bit. Do you mind not watching today?' she said quickly without turning around.

'You mean I'm in danger of distracting you?' he drawled.

'Not specifically you—anyone,' Cally lied, only hoping he hadn't guessed that when he watched her it felt like every movement she made was being magnified and projected on the wall for his scrutiny.

'If you say so. As it happens, I've only come to tell you that Kaliq and his fiancée will be joining us for dinner this evening, so you'll need to be ready by eight.'

Cally blanched. When they had been unable to make it on Saturday she'd known he planned to reschedule, but it hadn't occurred to her again since… Since he'd made it clear that asking her to join them last time had had nothing to do with her expertise and everything to do with wanting her to become his mistress.

'Actually, I planned to begin work on the nude this evening. I'm almost finished on this one.' They both turned to the first painting, as surprised as each another to see that the restoration work was almost complete, and the difference it made was breathtaking.

'Well, then, it seems the perfect place to stop, does it not?'

'All the same, I'd rather not join you for dinner.'

'Then it's a good job it's not optional, then, isn't it?'

Cally glowered at him. 'Since I declined the generous offer of becoming your mistress, I rather think it is up to me when and with whom I dine.'

'Not if it is a requirement of your job, which, for your information, is the capacity in which I require you to be there.'

'Really? Since my job is only to restore and conserve art, am I to assume that the prince is bringing a painting with him that you'd like me to take a look at between courses, perhaps?'

'Kaliq does not share my passion for art,' he growled.

'Then how can my joining you for dinner possibly be in the capacity of work?'

'The meeting is part business, part pleasure.'

'Well, then, why do you need me when you're the expert on combining the two?'

A cloud settled over his features. 'Kaliq and I have a trading treaty to discuss, but I also wish to toast my acquisition of the paintings.'

'Like a new Ferrari or a penthouse in Dubai,' she said sarcastically. 'So I can't understand why you'd want me there to lower the tone.'

'That's because you have no idea how good you look

in that green ensemble,' he ground out beneath his breath. 'But luckily your comprehension isn't a requirement. I am your employer, and I consider your presence tonight a necessary part of your work. And, since I am not asking you to do anything more unpalatable than have a world-class meal in more than amicable company, I cannot comprehend *your* objection. Unless, of course, you are worried that you might not be able to keep your desire tied up when you see me in a dinner suit.'

'God, you're arrogant!'

'So you *do* think you can keep it tied up?'

'Of course I—I have no desire for you!'

'Then we don't have a problem, do we? I will see you at eight. Oh, and wear the green dress, won't you?'

'Over my dead body.'

'Why, does it bring back too many memories?' He raised his eyebrows, daring her to say no.

She stared back, mute, furious.

'Good. Eight it is, then.'

CHAPTER EIGHT

RESISTING the urge to storm into her room and find out why the hell she wasn't ready yet, Leon paced the forecourt of the palace and turned his thoughts to his guests, whom Boyet had gone to collect from Kaliq's villa. After years of failing to convince his oldest friend to bring a female companion to Montéz, he could scarcely believe that tonight Kaliq would be accompanied by his future bride. Leon shook his head. Despite the law of Kaliq's homeland, which stated he had to marry in order to inherit the throne, Leon had never really believed that the cool and cynical sheikh would settle down. In fact, when he had first received word of his engagement, Leon had dismissed it as rumour. Then, when Boyet had confirmed it, he had supposed that in the wake of his father's ill health duty must have forced Kaliq to find a docile Qwasirian bride. So discovering that his choice was in fact a British model had filled Leon with both surprise and concern. A concern which on second thoughts was unnecessary, because Leon knew that Kaliq, unlike Girard, was an astute judge of character and would never marry a woman who wouldn't make a perfect queen and mother to his children.

Leon stopped pacing, wondering if the concern in his

chest might therefore really be for himself, for Montéz. No doubt before long Kaliq would have an heir to his throne. He drew in a deep breath, wondering how long he could go on ignoring his own duty—the duty which should never have been his, he thought grimly. What happened if Toria's body clock started ticking in the meantime? No, he thought, pacing the floor and wishing he had time to tear off his clothes and obliterate those thoughts in the ocean. She didn't have a maternal instinct in her body. It wouldn't happen, and he was only allowing it to bother him because for the past three days he'd been driven wild by her red-haired equivalent.

Cally. Leon's body tightened beneath the tailored fabric of his suit at the thought of her. The rational part of his brain warned him that she was every bit as conniving as his sister-in-law—and ought to be just as unappealing. Except in his mind they couldn't be further apart. Toria had offered herself to him on a plate more times since Girard's death than he cared to remember, but he found the thought of her about as desirable as walking into the web of a black widow spider. Yet Cally...

How many times over the past few days had he gone into that studio and had to leave because if he'd stayed a moment longer he would have ripped the damned paint-brush out of her hand and kissed her until she begged him to make love to her again? So many times he wished he could forget. Was it some kind of elaborate game to ensure his surrender to her was total, helpless? If it was, then it was futile. No matter how many cold showers it took to keep his permanent state of semi-arousal at bay, he would be patient, and he would have her on *his* terms. It was only a matter of time until she came to him again and admitted that he was what she had wanted all along. And, if her resistance to this evening's meal had been anything to go by, it would be soon.

'Sheikh A'zam and Miss Weston are here, Your Highness,' Boyet announced, heading towards him.

'Thank you. Right on time.'

It was a shame he couldn't say the same about Cally, Leon thought, his nostrils flaring.

Cally stared at the jade green dress hanging on her wardrobe door. He had her cornered. If she didn't go to dinner, not only would she miss the opportunity to share her work on the paintings, and be placing her job in jeopardy for a second time, but he would also deduce it was because she thought herself incapable of resisting him. The dilemma with the dress was just as bad. Wear something else, and he'd know it meant something to her. Wear it as he'd demanded, and she might just as well have agreed to become his mistress. But then he'd chosen everything in her wardrobe anyway, she thought sullenly.

Aware that she had been cutting it fine when she'd left the studio at seven-thirty, and that she'd now been staring at the dress for what felt like an age, Cally glanced at her watch. Seven fifty-five. She tried to ignore the usual sense of horror she felt at the prospect of making anyone wait on the rare occasions she was late. So what if she was late for him? He could hardly get annoyed that she had been working late to finish the restoration of the first painting for his guests to see. But it would be mortifying to make *them* wait, Cally thought suddenly, grasping for the dress. After all, they were what this whole evening was about. He wasn't even part of the equation. All she had to do was remember it.

* * *

'Ah, Cally.' Leon turned to watch her descend the stairs with a sardonic expression. 'You decided to join us.'

'I wasn't aware I had a choice,' Cally hissed under her breath, before smiling broadly at his guests, grateful to have an excuse to take her eyes off of the disarming sight of him in his navy dinner suit.

'May I introduce His Royal Highness Sheikh Al-Zahir A'zam, and his fiancée, Miss Tamara Weston. Kaliq, Tamara, this is Cally Greenway.'

'It's a pleasure to meet you,' Cally said genuinely as she shook their hands, grateful that, although the sheikh was just as regal as she had imagined, and Tamara was stunning in an evening gown of mesmerising coral, they weren't the least bit disparaging towards her.

'Do you live here on Montéz?' Tamara asked her amiably as they took their seats at the antique dining table.

'I am just working on the island at the moment—'

'Cally is living here at the palace,' Leon interrupted. 'One of her many talents is restoring fine art. She is working on some paintings I purchased in London.' He looked directly at Kaliq. 'Rénard's *Mon Amour par la Mer.*'

Cally stared at him, so incredulous that he had cut her off that she didn't notice the significant look which Kaliq gave him in return. 'Congratulations, Leon. You must be very pleased.'

'It sounds fascinating. I'd love to see,' Tamara added, too polite to show that she had noticed Leon's rudeness.

'I'd be delighted to show you,' Cally replied, before Leon halted any elaboration on her part by bombarding Tamara with questions about their stay on the island, and cracking open the champagne to celebrate their engagement. And who could blame him? Cally thought as a plethora of palace staff she'd never seen before brought in platters of meats, cheeses, olives and fresh bread. Although Leon spoke to Tamara with appropriate respect, he was no doubt as captivated by her beauty as any man would be.

As captivated as you are by him, Cally thought despondently, unable to stop her eyes from straying to his mouth, or the lance of jealousy which jabbed at her heart.

'You must be used to exploring different countries by yourself?' She made the effort to chip into the conversation as Tamara mentioned that she had visited the university today whilst Kaliq had been working.

She nodded. 'I don't get as much time as I would like to explore when I am on a shoot abroad, but I don't mind travelling alone.'

'It sounds very exciting,' Cally replied with genuine admiration, trying to feel inspired by the possibilities that might await her once she had finished the Rénards. The kind of opportunities she'd spent a lifetime dreaming about but which suddenly seemed to have lost their appeal, she thought bleakly. She wondered how much longer she could go on pretending that was what she wanted when, in spite of all the reasons why she shouldn't, all she really wanted was for Leon to make love to her again more than she had ever wanted anything in her life.

'It can also be very dangerous.' Kaliq cut into the conversation. 'Naturally, once we are married Tamara will give up work, so it shall cease to become a concern.'

Cally registered the triumphant look on Leon's face and hated him for it. She could just imagine him adding Tamara's name to the list in his mind which proved that women only troubled themselves with a career until they secured themselves a position as a mistress or a wife. But he was wrong. She might have only just met them both, but it was obvious that the desert prince had only said that because he cared for Tamara with such a passion he couldn't bear the thought of her being at any kind of risk. And she only had to take one look at Tamara's less-than-impressed expression to know she would never let her future husband stop her if she chose to continue with her career.

What would it be like to be here because she mattered to Leon the way Tamara mattered to Kaliq? Cally thought hopelessly as the conversation moved on to discussing the forthcoming wedding. What would it be like to have a man love you so deeply that he wanted to spend his life with you, and who actually cared, not just about having you in his bed, but about your safety and well-being?

She didn't have a clue, and for the first time since David had quashed her dreams she couldn't think of anything worse than never finding out. But they were just childish dreams, she reminded herself as she pushed the main course of duck around her plate, and that was why she'd given them up. So why did it seem so difficult to go back to accepting that she was destined to be alone, the way she had been before she'd met him?

Because he had made her aware of the gaping hole in her life, she thought wretchedly as she watched him speak animatedly about the international trading treaty with Kaliq, shamefully aware that, though she had spent the past few days telling herself to forget how it had felt to make love to him, tonight she was failing more spectacularly than ever.

She drew in a ragged breath. If she gave in now she may as well toss her self-respect out with the trash. *He wants you as a mistress, nothing more,* she repeated in her mind. *And you don't even like him.* But as she listened to him chatting about his plans for the university, for cutting taxes, for strengthening the links between Montéz and Qwasir, even disliking him was getting more difficult. She had turned up here believing that, like David and the rest of his moneyed family, the ruler of Montéz was a snob who didn't care about anyone but himself. But there was no denying that Leon had his people's best interests at heart and that, palace and paintings aside, he also seemed re-markably frugal for a billionaire. Apart from one cleaner and the additional staff he had called upon tonight, Boyet seemed to be his only aide, and his pleasures, like diving out at sea, were equally simple. So how was she supposed to focus on hating him when the reasons for doing so were getting fewer by the second?

Because, prince among men or not, the stonking great reason remains: he only wants you to warm his bed. And if you give in to your desire now what does that say about you? That you have no pride, she answered inwardly. *Or you're so delusional that, in spite of all the evidence, you've started to believe in the fairy tale again.*

Either way, Cally knew that to give in to her desire would be to set herself up for a fall, but that didn't make it any easier to step away from the edge. Her whole being seemed attuned only to filling the gaping hole he had opened, she realised as she cracked open the hard layer of caramel on her crème brûlée and stole a glance at him. And she was unable to stop herself from wondering whether, when he looked at Kaliq and Tamara, their evident love for one another made him aware of a missing link in his own future too.

'Thank you, Leon, that was delicious.' Tamara's words made Cally snap out of her lust-induced daze.

Leon turned to Tamara. 'I hope you will persuade Kaliq not to leave it so long between visits in future.'

Tamara nodded.

'So long as you promise to visit Qwasir soon so that we can return the favour,' Kaliq added.

'What an excellent idea,' Leon said, eyeing Cally with increased hunger as he imagined making love to her in the sultry climes of the desert. 'Now, you must forgive us, but I find that tonight *I* am now somewhat exhausted.'

Leon, exhausted? Cally had no idea what he was playing at, but she knew that was impossible. She'd seen him get back from a fourteen-hour day of negotiations on the mainland only to dive straight into the ocean. Not that she had been watching out of her window to see when he got back or anything, she argued inwardly, then wondered who on earth she was trying to kid.

'I thought perhaps Sheikh A'zam and Tamara would like to see the paintings before they leave.'

'Well, that will be an additional incentive for them both to return.' Leon smiled through clenched teeth.

'But—'

He signalled over her shoulder for Boyet to bring the car round and shook his head. 'It won't be necessary, Cally, thank you.'

Cally could barely hide her fury as the two princes embraced and all four of them exchanged farewells, before Leon accompanied Kaliq and Tamara down the steps amidst well wishes for their nuptial plans.

When he returned she was standing at the top of the steps, hands on her hips.

'So you're done with even pretending my presence here tonight had to do with work? The boast that the Rénards were yours might have been enough of an ego boost for you, but surely the least you could do was have me show them to your guests? But, no, you bundle them away before it's even eleven o'clock. I'm not sure I've ever met anyone so rude.'

'There will be another time. I don't consider it rude when two people can't keep their hands off each other and clearly want to be alone.'

Cally smarted, forced to concede his insightfulness. 'They did seem very much in love.'

Leon looked her straight in the eye. 'I wasn't talking about them.'

She flushed crimson and broke his gaze. 'Then you have not only acted without manners but you have also misread this situation.'

'Have I?' he breathed, taking a step so disturbingly close that she had to shut her eyes to block out the sight of him. Except she could still sense him there, smell that unmistakable musk, which tonight was mixed with a citrusy cologne.

'Yes, just like you read everything wrong! That look on your face when Kaliq said that Tamara was giving up work—you think it proves your archaic theory about women using their career until they ensnare a man, then giving it up the second they've succeeded, but you're wrong. Kaliq simply cares about her safety.'

'So now you think you know my oldest friend better than me?'

'Don't you think it's possible for two people with their own careers to meet, fall in love and marry?' Cally cried, wondering whether she was asking the question of him or herself.

Leon gritted his teeth. There was that word again:

marriage. The one she allegedly loathed as much as him. *Allegedly*. 'Do you want me to say yes so that you have something to dream about, *chérie?*'

'I just—' Cally exhaled deeply. 'Aren't you ever worried the endless line of women will come to an end? That you'll end up alone?'

His face turned to thunder. 'Alone suits me fine.'

'I know.' She breathed deeply, trying to focus on one of the regal gold buttons on his jacket, and willing her feet to walk her away from him. But as she raised her eyes to his impossibly handsome face, bathed in the soft lights from the palace, her pride somehow felt like an inevitable sacrifice. Her fight had already gone—left at the bottom of her glass in the Road to Nowhere, lost down the back of the sofa in the studio, gone from the palace with Tamara and Kaliq.

Her voice was a whisper. 'I know, and I thought it suited me too. But I don't want to be alone tonight.'

CHAPTER NINE

IT SEEMED that admitting he couldn't bear to be alone even for one night was too much to ask of Leon Montallier. But, though Cally was well aware that her track record for reading the opposite sex was abysmal, she couldn't shake the feeling that his expression said it for him. In fact, if she hadn't known better, she would have sworn from the grim set of his mouth that she'd just stumbled upon his Achilles' heel. But, as he lightly brushed his hand down her side and resolutely scooped her up into his arms, all she knew was that he wanted her body with the same voracious need that she wanted his, and suddenly that felt like the only thing that mattered.

'This time we're going to do this properly,' he instructed her huskily as he carried her back into the palace and up an unfamiliar spiral staircase.

Unfamiliar, because this was the staircase that led to the master bedroom. Where, unlike in the studio, there could be no more pretending that this was somehow to do with the paintings, no more conveniently imagining that he was just an ordinary man, a diver in the Marine Nationale. He was the sovereign prince, and this was his palace. Perhaps it ought to have felt terrifying, yet somehow, as they entered the room with its stained-glass windows and four-poster bed, it felt utterly liberating. It was as if she'd had an internal pair of scales which she had been trying desperately hard to balance ever since she had arrived and finally she had let them tip. But, rather than the disaster she had felt sure would assail her, she felt a great surge of relief.

'I've been wanting to do this all night,' he breathed, lowering his head and releasing her just enough for her feet to touch the gold-and-aquamarine rug, whilst keeping her so tightly pressed to him she could feel the lines of his suit imprinted on her body through the thin fabric of her dress.

'Just all night?' she whispered against his lips, so provocatively that for a moment she wondered whether she was possessed by the spirit of some other woman, a woman who wasn't convinced that any minute now she'd lose her nerve, a woman who was confident—sexy, even. She realised that, without being wholly conscious of it, every time he touched her she became that woman. A woman she didn't recognise, but who she had always wanted to be.

'What do you think?' he bit out raggedly, answering her with an urgent, drugging kiss and reaching behind her, cupping her bottom, then running his hand down the back of her thigh, balling the dress in his hand.

Cally kissed him back with equal need, snaking her arms behind his back, encouraging the jacket from his shoulders until it fell to the floor.

Leon broke away from her momentarily, his eyebrow quirked at the exact same angle it had been the day he'd walked into the studio brandishing the hacked-off fabric of her jeans. 'You know, I've never met a woman who has so little regard for designer clothes.'

'Is that such a bad thing?' she whispered.

'On the contrary,' he answered roughly, 'right now I find it a very good thing.' And before Cally knew what was happening he reached his hands inside the neck of the jade green dress and pulled, tearing the garment in half and leaving her standing there in nothing but her own plain black bra and knickers.

He eyed them with a puzzled expression. 'That's not the underwear I selected.'

'No,' Cally said, her tone cautious but not without a note of defiance. 'It's not.'

Ever since that night she had steered clear of the tempting drawer full of lingeric and had repeatedly laundered her own set of smalls, not only because they were more comfortable to wear during the day but because she'd decided they were far more likely to prevent her thoughts from wandering than the feel of lace against skin. *Wrong again,* a voice chimed inside her head, but as she caught his gaze sliding over her with lust-filled appreciation it couldn't have felt more right.

'Is it a problem?' she asked, slanting him a daring look as she watched his pupils dilate.

'That depends.' Leon took a step back, drinking her in. 'On what?'

'On how good the show is,' he answered huskily, extending his arm, and she realised that his step backwards had put him in reach of a CD player.

Her legs almost buckled as she heard the slow, familiar beat begin to fill the room.

'Mississippi in the middle of a dry spell...'

It couldn't be a coincidence; it was their song. No, that was far too sentimental. It was the song that had happened to be playing that night. But what was it doing on the CD player in his bedroom if it didn't mean something to him too?

'Don't tell me,' she whispered, trying to make her voice sound light, 'you and Kaliq often meet up in dodgy rock bars, and there's one in the centre of Montéz called *La Route à…*'

'*La Route à Nulle Part,*' he said slowly, sexily, a smile tugging at his lips as she attempted the French for Road To Nowhere. 'Almost. Either that, or for some reason I couldn't get the damned song out of my head and I had to hear it again.'

'And did it work?' Cally asked, trying not to tremble as she slowly began to move in time with the music.

Leon's throat went dry as he watched her. 'Did what work?'

'Did it help you get it out of your head?'

'No.'

Cally felt her heart turn over. She wanted to bottle that feeling—the helplessness in his voice, that one syllable which told her she affected him as deeply as he affected her—but she dared not let him see.

'It is a memorable song,' she whispered.

'Very, very memorable.' He nodded as she daringly slipped down one strap of her bra.

'Has anyone—' he cleared his throat, his voice coming out so low it was almost inaudible '—has anyone ever told you how sexy you are?'

'Once,' she smiled, remembering Leon's warm breath in her ear on the dance floor. Tonight she even believed it. So much so that somehow, she—bookish, bad-at-sex Cally—had the confidence to strip in front of him in his royal chamber.

'Then I think you need telling some more. Because you are the sexiest woman I've ever known.'

And I've known a lot, was the unspoken, implicit end

of that sentence. But she didn't care, because his words were so precious to her that tonight it felt like they were the only two people in the world.

'So would you like it if I did this?' she asked innocently, hooking her thumbs into the sides of her knickers.

'Mmm.'

'Or this?' Cally teased, sliding her hands back up her sides and behind her to the catch of her bra. His eyes were transfixed by the sight of her breasts strained against the thin fabric.

'I've changed my mind,' he said in a clipped voice, and for a minute Cally froze, terrified this was going to be a repeat of that moment in the taxi. But her fears vanished as he quickly closed the gap between them. 'I'm through with waiting.'

Without a moment of hesitation he raised one hand behind her and unclasped her bra, tossing it to the floor to join the tatters of her dress. Her knickers went the same way.

'Perfect,' he breathed, his fingers taking the same path up her body as hers had done until he found her full, heavy breasts.

'Not quite!' she cried breathlessly.

'No?' he murmured against her skin, trailing a line of kisses along the base of her throat, his lips a whisper away from taking her nipple in his mouth.

'No! No. I…I want you naked with me.' Her fingers moved to his shirt, fumbling with the buttons.

'*Now* you decide to be more careful, *chérie?*' he scolded.

Cally pulled back, and, comprehending what he inferred, shook her head with a thrill. But, just as she dropped her eyes to his shirt to ponder how, his hands had covered hers and they were ripping open his shirt, buttons flying in all directions until he was naked from the waist up, every inch of his torso revealed in all its golden glory.

Quickly he pulled her back to him so that her breasts were crushed against the hardness of his bare chest, and with equal speed she reached for the waistband of his trousers. In a second he had discarded them and was standing there in nothing but his dark navy boxers, which did nothing to hide his straining excitement.

But, if Cally had thought their mutual urgency was a sign that their lovemaking was to be as frantic as three nights ago, she was mistaken. As he led her towards the bed and slowly laid her down, she understood that when he'd said they were going to do this properly, he hadn't just meant that this time their lovemaking would take place in bed. Because, although she could see that his body was most certainly ready, his expression told her that he fully intended to explore her as if this was the very first time.

And in a way, as she watched him lick across her nipple with his tongue, the lines of his face taut with desire, it felt like it was. Because it was the only time she had ever truly given in to this kind of pleasure. It was as if until this moment her mind had always been a barren wasteland filled only with fears, but now in its place was a lush and tropical garden with no space for anyone but him. Him, the part of her she'd never known was missing, that she needed to complete her, to fill her.

'Leon!' She threw back her head as his fingers reached lower, dipping inside her. She squeezed her eyes tightly shut, riding the rhythmic sensation of his circling, intimate caress, reaching out to stroke her hand along his silky-smooth length, guiding it towards her. So hard, so virile…

Then suddenly her eyes flew open.

'What is it?' he bit out, afraid that she was going to choose this moment to have an attack of conscience.

'I—we need to use protection.'

Leon frowned. 'I thought you were on the Pill.'

Cally looked up at the ceiling, avoiding his gaze. 'I…I was, but…but, as I didn't expect to be here so long, I've run out.'

Leon shrugged, the momentary tension in his upper body released. 'No problem.'

As he reached across to the drawer of the bedside cabinet, Cally felt a hideous sense of shame wash over her. Not only because she had lied, but because his trust in her was so implicit that he hadn't thought to doubt her explanation for a second.

But as she felt the heat of his thighs parting her own, her mind returned to the tropical paradise, and she let go of her guilt. It was a misunderstanding that would have no consequence, an omission of the truth that he of all people would understand if it ever came to light. Which it wouldn't, she assured herself, as her body parted to welcome him.

Cally slid her fingers up his back and lost them in his hair, loving the feel of his body on top of hers as he entered her. She didn't have a clue how many perfect minutes passed as he moved slowly, assuredly, inside her, determined that they should both savour every second. She could see from the muscle in his jaw that he was fighting to keep his excitement on a leash, and she loved that most of all.

'Do you want to change position?' she asked, pretending she couldn't see that he wanted to up the tempo.

'No.' His voice was throaty. 'This time it's going to happen to you, and I want to watch.'

Once Cally might have blushed, tensed, vowed it was impossible—or possibly all three. Not tonight.

'Then take me a little faster,' she whispered.

Leon's eyes flared in pleasure as he did as she commanded. 'Tell me what else you like.'

'You,' she answered without thinking. 'Everywhere.'

Finding the only part of their bodies that wasn't already interlocked, Leon entwined her fingers with his, and if Cally had been clinging to one remaining sliver of control that was the moment she lost it. For with the tenderness of that gesture she gave in to the mounting sense of longing that felt like an intense pain but without any of the hurt, gave in to every exquisite stroke, each one more insistent than the last, like waves against a breakwater about to give way.

She heard a moan escape from her mouth, low, insistent, infused with pleasure. She felt him grow even harder within her at the sound, and then completely withdraw before deliciously filling her with a thrust that was thick and fast.

'Oh God!'

Cally felt the imaginary breakwater give way as every inch of her body was flooded with an exquisite heat, all-consuming, astonishing. The tide drew back and then washed over her again in a flurry of aftershocks as Leon cried out, reaching the height of his own pleasure just seconds after her own.

He'd been holding off, she realised, had wanted her to come first. It could have been to prove his own prowess, or to demonstrate that any restraint on her part was a thing of the past. But right at that moment as she lay locked in the circle of his arms she believed it was simply because he wanted her to know that pleasure. A pleasure she had never dreamed she was capable of reaching. Whatever happened, she would always be grateful for that.

'Thank you,' she whispered, shifting her body to his side, though her arm remained slung across his chest.

'You're welcome,' he smiled. 'I'm glad I managed to persuade you to give in to it.'

She wasn't sure whether he was talking about her desire for him or her orgasm. Perhaps it didn't matter.

'It was my first.'

Leon blinked in astonishment, observed the slash of colour still high on her cheekbones and the faint surprise in her bewitching green eyes, and felt a surge of triumph accompanied by a slow dawning of something unpleasant he couldn't quite put his finger on. So she hadn't been holding back that first time to prove a point; she simply hadn't recognised the sensation or known how to let go. Which meant nothing, he quickly rationalised, refusing to revisit the thought which had momentarily flashed across his mind when he'd seen her modest underwear. Her usual encounters were probably one-night affairs after a quick fondle on a darkened dance floor, that was all.

'It can take time to get to know a sexual partner,' he said, too patronisingly for Cally's liking.

'If you are implying my sexual history consists of one-night stands, then you're mistaken.' She bristled, moving away from him and tugging the sheet around herself so that there was something more substantial than air between them. He was steering the conversation down a road she didn't want to take, but she couldn't bear the thought of him thinking that way about her.

Leon hesitated, as if unable to decide whether asking the question that hovered on the tip of his tongue was really such a good idea. 'Then perhaps you'd care to fill me in with the correct history.'

'Not really.'

'I am a modern man, Cally. The women with whom I choose to share my bed have inevitably had other lovers. It is not something which concerns me.' At least, usually it wasn't.

'Well, then, I'm afraid my sexual CV is going to be unimpressive in comparison,' she said quietly, not wanting to think about his other lovers, and at the same time wishing he did give a damn whether or not she was a complete whore or not. 'There was only one other man before you.'

Leon's eyes widened in shock, and then the blinding satisfaction of the revelation gave way to something far less palatable: the short stab of his conscience as the truth slotted into place. The day he'd seen her at the pre-auction, the plain underwear... She wasn't some practised seductress who had set out to ensnare him, she was as good as innocent. Suddenly he felt consumed with regret for the assumptions he had made, the wrong he had done her.

And, ashamed though he was to admit it, worst of all he supposed he had always known on some level that she was the sentimental kind. He had simply chosen to believe the opposite rather than stick to his own rule. The rule that, in spite of everything, he wanted to break all over again.

'So who was he?' Leon propped himself up on his arm and looked at her. 'A fiancé?' He paused. 'A husband?'

Cally shook her head. 'No, David was never in any danger of finding himself in either of those categories when it came to me.'

'But you hoped so?'

She nodded reluctantly. 'But I should have known from the start that I lacked the right credentials.'

Leon's mouth was a picture of disdain. 'How do you mean?'

'He was the son of an earl. I was working part-time on his father's estate. I don't know why I persisted in thinking that the difference in class between us was irrelevant. My parents, I suppose.' She gave a brittle laugh. 'They always told Jen and me that there were no barriers.' She shook her head. 'They were wrong. It was nothing more to him than an affair with a scullery maid would have been to one of his ancestors. I let him talk me into sleeping with him because he told me he loved me—and, worse, I let him talk me out of continuing with my degree because he said going it alone would make me a better artist. He lied. One of the other girls working there warned me that David shared his father's misogynistic views on women of a certain class trying to better themselves by getting too much education, but I thought she was just jealous. Until I left uni, turned up on his doorstep and found out that he had got himself engaged to an heiress without bothering to tell me.'

Cally looked up and, seeing from the look in his eyes that she was in danger of being at the receiving end of his pity, she continued quickly. 'So, do you always quiz women about their ex-lovers in bed?'

'Only when they tell me I am the first man to make them reach orgasm,' Leon answered, filled with a new and grim understanding.

'To bolster your ego?'

'Because it's a shame, Cally. Fantastic sex is like…art.'

'You mean everyone should enjoy it, like putting a great painting in a public gallery?'

'*Touché.*' He raised one eyebrow sexily. 'No. I mean the more you learn, the more you enjoy it.'

And the more likely you are to see weaknesses in the work of an inexperienced artist, Cally thought dismally, realising that if her lack of sexual expertise hadn't said it for her then her attack of verbal diarrhoea had just given the impression that she only ever slept with men who she saw as potential husbands.

'I was very young then,' Cally added quickly. 'When I thought I wanted to marry David, I mean. Of course, I was upset by what happened, but I realised very quickly that I was not cut out to be anyone's wife.'

Leon eyed her with a degree of scepticism. 'And yet you say you do not wish to be a mistress either. That makes for a very cold life, Cally.' He ran his hand over her bare arm. 'And, if you are planning on pretending that you are a cold person, don't bother, because we both know different.'

She had resigned herself to the fact that her life was destined to be cold, Cally thought, only now aware of how sad that sounded. But that was because she'd never known this kind of passion, a passion she knew she couldn't fight anymore even if it was destined to go nowhere.

She shook her head. 'No, I'm not going to pretend that. But nor do I want to downgrade my role of art restorer to mistress.'

Cally saw a nerve work at his jaw. 'I shall presume that was a slip of the tongue and you meant *up*grade.'

'Don't. I take great pride in working hard to earn my own living, difficult as that might be for *you* to comprehend. I don't want to toss it in so I can be at your beck and call, have you tell me what to wear and when.'

'So what is it you *do* want?'

Leon wondered if he had heard himself correctly. Since when did he conduct affairs where he invited a woman to lay down the ground rules? Never, he thought, looking at her fiery red hair spilling across his pillow. But then never before had he ever experienced a desire which felt like it would render him permanently debilitated unless it was appeased. Or been so conscious that here was the last woman in the world who needed a man riding roughshod over her a second time, he thought ruefully. Maybe it was breaking his own rule, but so long as she meant what she said about not wanting to be anyone's wife there was no problem, was there?

'I want to carry on working here—under the terms we have already agreed—and I want this…' She scrambled around for a word which described whatever 'this' was, and decided that there wasn't one. 'This sex between us to be something entirely separate. That isn't about anything other than mutual pleasure because the opportunity, whilst I am here, exists.'

'Just like I can dive into the sea because it is outside my back door?' Leon ventured.

'Exactly.' Cally nodded, not knowing why that made her heart sink, when having him agree to treat this as a pleasure they both chose to indulge in was far more preferable to being made to feel like a call girl on extended loan.

'Good,' Leon replied abruptly, having heard exactly the answer he needed. 'Then you shall work during the day and share my bed at night.' He made a show of picking up his watch from the bedside table. 'Which, if I'm not mistaken, still gives us another eight and a half hours.'

And with that he tossed aside the sheet and pulled her to him all over again.

CHAPTER TEN

WHEN Leon had compared fantastic sex to art, Cally hadn't considered it as anything other than a boast about his sexual prowess. But in the weeks that followed she couldn't help thinking that there was more to his statement than even he would have given himself credit for. After the physical abandon of that night, she felt fundamentally altered, as if up until that point her life had been the equivalent of a rather dull and dreary still life, and now he had splashed it with vibrant colour.

As bright and vivid as the underwater paradise beneath them, Cally thought happily as she lay flat on the deck of his boat after an hour just spent snorkelling, breathing in the scent of sun cream and feeling the droplets of seawater evaporate off of her skin. Although she had insisted that she would work during the day, and only share his bed at night, Leon tended to leave the palace early in the morning and return just after lunch, and since it suited her to work to a similar pattern their afternoons were invariably spent together.

Of course, they made love, sometimes in the studio, sometimes in his bedroom if they made it that far, sometimes even out on the terrace. But to her surprise Leon hadn't only wanted to indulge in sex. He had taken her across to the opposite hillside to show her the stunning site where Kaliq had chosen to build his villa, and then for a drive along the coast road with its magnificent cliff-top views. He had taken her down to the harbour with its lively market, to the central square with its endearing medieval church, and of course he had brought her out here to the ocean.

And Montéz had unquestionably captured her heart, Cally admitted, ignoring the nagging voice in her head which said *and that's not the only thing*. But, whilst she could get away with claiming that it was the natural beauty of the island which was responsible for inspiring her to work on her own painting whenever she got a spare moment, she couldn't deny that ceasing to fight her sexual appetite was responsible for the return of her much-missed focus on the restorations. In fact, she had made so much progress that after—how many weeks, three?—it wouldn't be many more days before they were completely finished.

But it wasn't until she'd spotted a missed call on her mobile and listened to the answer-phone message that morning that Cally had really faced facts and realised that she ought to start thinking about what she was going to do next—which went for her relationship with Leon too. The prospect shouldn't have felt like trying to remove a limpet from the bottom of his boat—after all, that night in his bedroom she had been heartened by the thought that their lovemaking would reach an enforced conclusion rather than waiting for his desire for her to wear thin—but it did.

Which was probably because in so many ways it didn't feel just like lovemaking anymore. For, even though she had resigned herself to the knowledge that theirs was a passion that was destined to go nowhere, in these past few weeks Leon had really opened up to her of his own accord.

He'd talked to her about his daily work at the university as they shared their evening meal; he'd told her about his time in the Marine Nationale. In turn she'd told him about her family and her degree, and they'd spent hours conversing about art, a subject upon which he had a knowledge more extensive than she would ever have imagined.

In fact, it felt pretty much like a real relationship in every way—except that their relationship was the one thing they didn't discuss, she thought, looking across at his beautiful body sprawled out beside her, his tanned chest glistening in the sunshine. Was it because, as far as he was concerned, it was already decided that the second she put down her paintbrush she'd be picking up her bags and leaving on the first plane home? He had told her himself that romance was in a Frenchman's blood, so perhaps this sex with added sentiment was just what you got with him, she thought dismally. Or was there a possibility that the reason he hadn't brought it up was because he didn't want her to go?

Not that it would change anything, even if he didn't, Cally quickly rationalised, because her career was what mattered first and foremost. So why did the answer-phone message, which ought to have had her jumping for joy, make her feel like she had been rudely awoken from the perfect dream?

'You know, I reckon it won't be much longer before my restorations are complete,' Cally said, trying to make her voice sound as blithe as possible.

Her words interrupted Leon's unruly thoughts. Thoughts which involved him rolling over and peeling down her black bikini top, which in his opinion had been on for far too long this afternoon, particularly now that the wet Lycra was beginning to dry in the coolness of the breeze and he could see the tight buds of her nipples that cried out for his mouth. Although on second thoughts it wasn't so much her words that had made that image vanish from his mind as her tone, which sounded offhand, as if the actual words were nothing but a code she expected him to crack. It was a tone he had never heard Cally use before, but ever since he had witnessed the starry look in her eyes that night Kaliq and Tamara had mentioned their forthcoming nuptials, ever since she had filled him in on her sparse sexual history, he had always feared she was in danger of adopting it. Had known too, that there was no way he was going to allow it to get to him, any more than he had any intention of allowing their lovemaking to come to an end. Yet.

'It hadn't escaped my notice.'

Cally rolled over, leaning on one elbow. 'So, will you be glad when I'm all done?'

His eyes remained closed. 'Of course. I cannot wait to see them both restored to their original glory.'

Cally hesitated. 'Me too. But I have to admit I shall be a little sad not to be working on them anymore, in that studio and—'

'Are you by any chance trying to induce me to ask you to stay on after you have finished, Cally?' Leon opened his eyes and challenged her with his piercing blue gaze. 'Because if you are may I remind you that *you* were the one who insisted that our lovemaking should only last whilst— how was it you delicately put it?—whilst your work on the Rénards placed us in close proximity to one another.'

Cally flushed, the previously pleasant heat of the sun now making her skin prickle uncomfortably. 'No, I— It just occurred to me this morning that I had finished them a little more quickly than I expected, that's all.'

'It's been a month, as you estimated.'

'A month?' Cally stared at him, dumbfounded. 'No, it can't have been.'

'Time flies when you're having fun,' he drawled, sitting up and drying his legs with a towel.

A month? A month in which they had made love pretty much every day, she thought, suddenly realising she hadn't had a period since before she had arrived. The heightened colour drained from Cally's face as she fished around in her mind for an explanation to quash her fears of the unthinkable. Her periods were sometimes irregular, weren't they? And if anything was going to change a woman's cycle it was a different diet, a different climate from usual, wasn't it? Yes, that had to be it. In a couple more days, it was bound to arrive.

'Well, anyway, all I'm trying to say is that I hadn't given much thought to any future projects until I received a phone call from the Galerie de Ville in Paris this morning. They have just purchased a collection of pre-Raphaelite pieces and they are looking for an additional restorer to work with their existing team. The London City Gallery recommended me, and they want to meet to discuss whether I'd be interested.'

'Congratulations,' Leon replied gruffly. 'You should have said earlier. When's the meeting?'

'I don't know yet. As soon as possible, I think. I missed their call yesterday afternoon and I only picked up their answer-phone message this morning.'

'And you haven't called them back yet?'

'Not yet, no.'

Leon's momentary surprise evaporated. 'And why would that be, *chérie?* Because you wanted to ask me whether I thought it a golden career opportunity first? Surely not, for we both know that it is. Therefore you must be wavering because you wish to see whether I will offer you a more attractive alternative, *oui?*'

Cally flew to her feet. 'As if!' she shot out, terrified that was why she had wavered, that she had been willing to jeopardise her career for the sake of a man who felt nothing for her for the second time in her life. 'I suppose I just hoped you might show a little regret that our *affair* is inevitably reaching its end.'

'Inevitably? Why? Montéz is only ninety minutes away from Paris. You will have weekends, will you not?'

Cally's mouth dropped open. 'You mean… You wish it to continue?'

'Just because I do not ever wish to marry does not mean that I am not interested in extending a mutually pleasurable affair.'

He made it sound like their relationship was a library book he wanted to take out on six-week loan instead of three. Yet, wouldn't he end this now if she meant absolutely nothing to him? *Oh, don't be ridiculous, Cally. He'll end it eventually, so what's the difference?* Agreeing to let it continue could only prolong the hurt until the day he decided that he no longer found her satisfying. Which surely, if they were only to see each other at weekends, would be sooner rather than later for a man with a sexual appetite as insatiable as his. Unless, of course, exclusivity was not part of his offer in the first place, she thought with a start, feeling suddenly nauseous.

'And who will you make love to Monday to Friday, Leon?'

Leon's mouth twisted in disgust. 'You have my word that you will be the only woman sharing my bed.'

She stared at him, wanting to believe him, wanting to believe that it was possible to have a relationship and the career she loved, wondering if she even dared try. 'But why?'

Leon ran his eyes over her face. Her pale skin was flecked with light freckles brought out by the sunshine, the faint mark from her snorkelling mask was still visible on the bridge of her nose and her red hair was matted with seawater. It would have been easy to think to himself that her vulnerability was the reason, that she didn't deserve to be let down for the second time in her life, but the truth was that he had quite simply never seen anything so alluring and he didn't *want* her to go. Was it because she was the first woman who had come out on his boat like this? he wondered, trawling his mind for a logical explanation. No, there had been others, he recalled, surprised to find that his ex-lovers all blended into one faceless, nameless and frankly dull mass. But they had either demanded that he sail them across to St Tropez for lunch at a restaurant followed by an afternoon in the boutiques, or after a few minutes in the water had spent two hours below deck re-trowelling their make-up and ironing their hair. Yes, it had to be because he had never met anyone quite so appealingly *uninhibited* as she was.

'Because I've never wanted anyone as much as I want you,' he breathed, sensing her capitulation as he reached out his arm and dragged her towards him. 'And I'm not ready for this to end.'

Neither was she, she thought, forgetting all the reasons why this was a bad idea when he looked at her like that. And maybe, just maybe, if they both learned to trust, neither one of them ever would be.

'Then I hope you are not prone to dizziness, Leon,' she whispered.

'And why is that?'

'Because the first thing I want you to show me when you come and visit me in Paris is the Eiffel Tower.'

Leon paused. 'Maybe the second thing, *chérie,*' he said with a wicked gleam in his eye, before lowering his head to plunder her mouth.

Cally completed the restoration of the Rénards at lunchtime three days later. Standing back to admire them, she was overcome with a feeling quite unlike any other she'd experienced in her life. It always gave her a thrill to see a work of art restored exactly the way an artist had intended, but this transcended that; it was almost as if a part of her own personal destiny had been fulfilled.

She couldn't wait to show Leon. She looked at her watch. Twelve-thirty. He'd be back at two if not before. Which meant for the first time since that afternoon on the boat she had an hour alone to spare. Since there was still no sign of her period, she decided she really ought to take herself off to the pharmacy she'd spotted in the nearby village just to be sure it was just late and nothing more. That way, when she went to Paris to speak to the gallery tomorrow, at least she could go without any niggling concerns.

Unless of course the niggling concern turned out to be a full-blown worry-fest, she thought. She was still convinced she couldn't be pregnant when she felt absolutely no different from normal, aside from a little tiredness, which was probably due to the amount of time she spent making love to Leon or swimming in the sea. But what if she was? A slow and thoroughly unexpected warmth crept through Cally's body. She didn't know whether it was her buoyant mood or too much sun, but for some reason it didn't feel like something that would be a worry at all; it felt like it would be the most natural thing in the world.

Hearing footsteps approaching the studio door made a wide smile break out on her face. He was back early.

'Finished,' she said triumphantly. 'What *am* I going to do— Oh.'

Cally stopped mid-sentence as she turned round to discover the footsteps were not Leon's. On second thoughts she wasn't surprised, for she so rarely heard him enter, a trait she had come to associate with his natural diver's stealth. The feet belonging to the person who had entered, on the other hand, could not have been less subtle, for they were clad in bright-purple stilettos.

Cally took in the matching purple dress and blue-black hair which reached the woman's waist. A waist which she was sure would have ordinarily been no wider than the span of two hands, if she hadn't looked about five months pregnant.

'Can I help you?' Cally asked, raising her eyes to look at her face for the first time. Suddenly she realised that the woman she was looking at was Toria. Toria, whose face she recognised from the wedding photo that had graced every magazine cover the year she had married Girard. Toria, who, if Leon was to be believed, was nothing but bad news for a list of reasons as long as her hair. But he hadn't mentioned that she was expecting.

'I'm looking for Leo,' she purred, a look of disdain on her wide, painted mouth.

Cally flinched. 'You must be Toria.'

'And you must be his latest conquest.' Toria ran her eyes critically over Cally's paint-splattered outfit. 'How… charitable of him. Now, where is he, out *there*?' She motioned towards the sea in disgust.

'He's not here at the moment. Actually, I'm alone, and I rather thought all the doors were locked. Do you mind me asking how you got in?'

'Keys,' she said, reaching into her oversized designer handbag and producing a bunch full. 'Don't look so surprised. This *is* my home. Or, should I say, *was*.'

Cally gritted her teeth. 'He's at the university. I have no idea what time he'll be back,' she lied, hoping to make her leave. She had no idea why Toria still had a set of keys, but Leon had said she only ever came back to Montéz to stir up trouble.

'Then I suggest you call him and tell him that I am here with some very important news.'

Cally was tempted to tell her what she could do with her suggestion, but she spotted the opportunity to forewarn Leon that she was here.

'Of course,' Cally replied with artificial sweetness. 'Do take a seat.'

Cally went into his office and dialled his mobile. It rang and rang but there was no answer. Skimming her eyes down a list of numbers on his desk, she found one for the principal's office at the university and tried that instead.

'*Bonjour.*'

Cally hesitated at the sound of the unfamiliar, accented voice. 'Um… *Je voudrais parler à Monsieur Montallier, s'il vous plaît.*'

The man on the other end of the phone clearly recognised her less-than-fluent grasp of French. 'This is Professeur Lefevre. The prince is not here, I am afraid. Can I help?'

'He has already left to return to the palace?' Cally asked hopefully.

'*Non, mademoiselle.* He has not been here today.'

'Oh.' Cally frowned, certain that he had told her he was expected there for the duration of the morning. 'So you haven't seen him at all since yesterday?'

'*Non,* you must be mistaken. I haven't seen him for at least…' Professeur Lefevre gave a considered pause. 'It must be three weeks at least.'

Her breath caught in her throat. 'Then I…I suppose I must have been mistaken. I'm sorry to have disturbed you.'

Cally continued to clutch on to the receiver long after he had hung up, her knuckles white. Leon had told her he had been at the university almost every day for the past month, but he hadn't been. She tried to tell herself it was no big deal. It was probably easier to say he was there than to go into details about his duties. But it grated on her. And now the woman he professed to hate had turned up with her own set of keys to the palace. She took a deep breath, trying to compose herself, remembering that their relationship was never likely to work if she was always so quick to distrust him. Plastering on a smile, she re-entered the studio.

'Men do have a warped idea of beauty,' Toria said, regarding the Rénards with a pinched look as Cally entered.

'Don't they,' Cally replied, looking right at her. 'I'm afraid Leon is otherwise engaged. For all I know, he could be hours.'

'Well,' Toria replied irritably, 'then I suggest, since I cannot be expected to wait around in *my* condition, that you give him a message.'

'Gladly.'

'Tell him I'm pregnant. With the heir to the throne.'

CHAPTER ELEVEN

CALLY stared at Toria aghast, dropping her eyes to the swell of her belly.

Pregnant. *With the heir to the throne.*

Her mind raced as she fought to process the information in some way other than a way which felt like a bullet tearing through her flesh. Toria had to mean that Girard was somehow the father, didn't she? But he had died a year ago, so that was impossible—unless via frozen sperm or IVF? No, she thought, his death had been too unexpected for that.

Cally lifted her eyes to the other woman's face, recalling how Leon had described her as 'incredibly attractive', how she had swung her own set of palace keys from her forefinger, purring his name. Suddenly Cally felt sick.

'Surely you don't mean that Leon...?' Her voice was scratchy, desperate.

Toria hesitated for a moment and then looked at her squarely. 'Yes. Leon is the father.'

Cally blanched and stumbled the short distance to the sofa, her whole body beginning to tremble. 'No. How?'

The other woman gave an acidic laugh. 'How? Surely I do not need to explain that to *you?* Leon Montallier is not an easy man to resist.' She shrugged. 'I made the mistake of believing that because I was his brother's widow he wouldn't set his sights on me unless his intentions were honourable. I was wrong.'

She paused for a moment, and then, seeing that Cally's head was safely buried in her hands, continued unreservedly. 'Afterwards I was so angry that I tried to go to the press, but he got there first. Thanks to his carefully engineered law, his pristine reputation on this island remains intact, just the way he planned it.'

Cally raised her head in horror.

'Oh, don't tell me, he spun *you* that line about reinstating the law to get on with his royal duties without the media circus as well?' Toria clicked her tongue scornfully. 'That was what the last one fell for. If I were you, I'd leave before he knocks you up and throws you out too.'

Cally closed her eyes, missing the malicious smile on the other woman's face.

'I'll bear that in mind,' she choked.

'Good,' Toria said, tossing her dark mane over her shoulder. 'And I trust you'll remember to give him my news. I'll see myself out.'

Cally gazed helplessly at a knot on the wooden floor of the studio. More than anything she had ever wanted in her life, she wanted to believe Toria was lying. She tried to think of her as the witch Leon had made her out to be, of her capacity for deceit. But the more minutes that ticked by the harder that seemed. She recalled the girl she'd worked with at David's father's estate, the one who had warned her about what he was really like, but who she had chosen to ignore. She couldn't help thinking that history was repeating itself—and that she really ought to have learned her lesson.

If Toria and Leon had been living here together after Girard's death, it hardly required a stretch of the imagination to envisage them falling into bed. And if he had romanced Toria the way he had romanced her, particularly under the delicate circumstances, it was no wonder that Toria had mistakenly assumed his intentions were honourable. Most of all it was remarkably easy to imagine his lust turning to disgust the second she'd attempted to sell her story. Cally had witnessed his anger when it came to the press herself.

And, though she knew Toria had taken a warped pleasure in telling her, even that only served to make her story seem all the more plausible. For she had exhibited exactly the kind of behaviour one might expect of a woman returning to an ex-lover with the news that she was carrying his child only to find another woman in her place.

Which could so easily have been her. Cally squeezed her eyes tightly shut, trying not to contemplate the unspeakable possibility that brought to mind.

What if they were both carrying his baby?

She felt the speed of her breathing double, the red of the sofa on which she sat and the blue of the sea outside the window starting to blur before her eyes as though she was spinning around on some garish purple fairground ride. She lay back, curling herself into a ball, threading her fingers through her hair to clutch at her skull, trying to block out everything.

But just as she was about to slip into the oblivion of unconsciousness she heard his voice.

'No wonder you're exhausted.'

It was soft and unbearably tender. Cally blinked and forced her eyes open. He was standing before the paintings, examining the final and most intricate part of her restoration with delight.

'It looks fabulous.'

She didn't move. 'I'm not exhausted.'

'No?' he queried, his eyes never leaving the canvas. 'In that case, how do you feel about celeb—?' He turned round and caught sight of her properly for the first time. 'What on earth's the matter?'

Cally pushed herself up on one arm, the blood rushing to her head. 'Toria was here.'

He visibly stiffened. *'Toria?'*

She nodded.

Leon looked incensed. 'What did she want?'

Cally took a deep breath. She was aware that she should probably tell him to take a seat, do this slowly. Aware, too, that it should never have been her news to tell. But above all, selfish though it was, she just wanted to get it out so that she could see his reaction—because she knew that alone would tell her everything she needed to know.

'She came to tell you that she's pregnant with your child.'

To her disbelief, he laughed. 'She has resorted to lies before to try and scare away any woman she sees as a threat, but this takes it to a whole new level. After everything I told you, I thought you'd know better than to believe a single word that comes out of her mouth.'

'It wasn't her words that convinced me,' Cally whispered brokenly. 'It was her sizeable bump.'

When she saw the look that came over Leon's face then, she would have given anything to have his cynical humour back. The blood shrank from his cheeks and his expression grew so taut that it looked as if his skin had been removed and stretched in order to cover the bones of his face. For the first time since they had met, she witnessed every last glimmer of sardonic amusement vanish from his eyes until there was nothing there but emptiness. It was the look which confirmed that everything she'd feared was true, and which banished Cally's last remaining shred of hope.

And that was the moment Cally knew that, if she had even one ounce of self-respect, she had to leave now. If nothing else, the entire stance of his body told her that the prospect of being a father was on a par to him with being told he had some horrible, degenerative disease. With it she understood that whatever she had started to believe about him opening up to her, human commitment of any form would always be unpalatable to him. She had to make sure *she* was not in danger of carrying his baby, and then she had to get on that plane to Paris and forget she had ever made love with the Prince of Montéz.

Slowly, on legs which felt like their muscles had disintegrated, she found the strength to stand.

'Where are you going?'

So she wasn't completely invisible. 'To Paris.'

'Your flight doesn't leave until tomorrow.'

She stared at him aghast. Surely he didn't actually expect her to stay? 'Under the circumstances, I hardly think—'

'Oh, but of course,' he said, snapping out of his temporary trance. 'Just because *she* says I'm the father, it *must* be true.'

So now that the initial shock had passed he had decided it was in his interests to deny it, Cally thought bitterly. She shook her head. 'Why would she lie?'

'Because she's a bitch, Cally, a cold-hearted, evil bitch.'

'So after Girard's death, when you were both living here, you're telling me you never went near her?'

Leon's mouth soured as if he resented having to explain himself to her. 'No, *I* never went near *her*.'

'What does that mean?'

'It means she lost no time in attempting to seduce me. What she wanted above all else was to be the wife of a prince, regardless of who the prince was. But I made it perfectly clear to her that I would rather stick pins in my eyes than go anywhere near her, and informed her of my intention to reintroduce the law against the press. She left the island almost immediately.'

'You never mentioned that when you told me about her.'

Leon shrugged. 'Compared to the rest of her sins, it's nothing.'

'So how come she still has keys to the palace?'

'Unfortunately for me, as she's Girard's widow there are some rights to which she is still entitled. Access to the palace is one of them.'

Cally closed her eyes, breathing deeply, feeling like she had been presented with the prosecution and defence in a trial for which she would face the punishment however she judged it, wishing she could be handed a simple picture which depicted the truth.

'Toria tells it very differently.'

'So you choose to believe her word over mine?' he bellowed incredulously. 'Why? Because the first time we met I neglected to mention my title? I thought we were past that.'

'We were.' Cally felt tears begin to prick behind her eyes and swallowed hard. 'That's why as soon as she arrived I tried to warn you by calling the university. But you weren't there, were you? You haven't been there for weeks, and yet you've been telling me you have!'

'I—'

'No. Let me finish. I told myself there had to be some logical explanation for that, and then I tried as hard as I could to believe that Toria wasn't telling the truth. That's why I waited to hear your side of the story. But that look of utter horror on your face when I told you she was pregnant told me everything I needed to know.'

Leon paused, and for a moment he actually contemplated telling her, but the thought of saying the words aloud was so agonising that he crossed his arms and turned away. 'I'm just horrified by the prospect of that witch bringing a child into this world.'

'How gallant of you to be so concerned about the life of an unborn baby.'

'It's an insult to the memory of my brother.'

'The merry widow doesn't fit into one of your neat little boxes for characterising women?' she shot out sarcastically.

'Like the giant box labelled "liar" that you have reserved for all men?'

'So, what, you're telling me that you were at the university all along?'

Leon scowled, wondering how the hell the one woman he had broken his rule for wasn't even capable of trusting him in return. 'Yes. Not at the main campus, but at another building off-site.'

'So why did the principal of the university know nothing about it?'

'Because I haven't shown it to him yet.'

Cally looked at him disbelievingly. 'So, show *me*.'

It was then that the room went ominously silent and Leon looked down at her with an expression that was even more crushing than the one she had read there when she had announced Toria's pregnancy. It was a withering look which told her she had just made the unforgivable mistake of assuming that he had to prove anything to her. And with it she saw with agonising lucidity that it really made little difference whether he was telling the truth or not, because she didn't mean anything to him, and she never would.

'And what if I did show you, Cally? Would you demand Toria has a paternity test before we can continue with our affair? Because we could, but something tells me even that wouldn't be enough. You were envious, were you not, when you met Kaliq and Tamara, so newly engaged? And now Toria claims to be having my child and you are practically inconsolable. Are you sure that you aren't so upset because what you *really* want is for me to propose we get married and start making babies of our own?'

Cally tried her best to steady her breathing as the colours of the room threatened to blur before her eyes again. 'No, Leon, what I want is to leave. I want to get on the plane to Paris, and I want to get on with my career.'

'Like hell you do, Cally Greenway.' He raked his eyes mercilessly over her body sending a renewed yearning hurtling through her bloodstream. 'Why cut off your nose to spite your face?'

Because if I don't stem my desire I'll lose my heart, Cally thought. 'Whatever is between us is over.'

'Over?' Leon laughed a low, impertinent laugh that seemed to reverberate around the whole room. 'This thing will never be over between us, *chérie.* It's too damned hot.'

She should have been quicker, but Leon was one step ahead, catching the top of her arm with his fingers and spinning her round easily to plant his lips on hers. His kiss was a kiss of possession, hot, furious and undeniably physical; it felt like he had poured his whole body into it, though only their lips were touching. She knew what he was doing as her treacherous body responded with predictable arousal thrumming through her veins, her nipples hard, longing for the press of his chest. Oh yes, he was waiting for her to succumb to him, to draw herself to him and clasp her arms around his back with all the wild abandon which she always did.

Not anymore. Abandoning her senses had got her into this mess, and it certainly wasn't going to get her out of it. She needed to escape now, while she at least had the promise of the career she had worked so hard for. Even if it seemed to have lost all its meaning.

But it had more meaning than his kiss ever would, a voice inside her cried, and somehow it gave her the strength to push herself away from him and she stumbled backwards, desperate to put as much distance between them as possible.

'Like I said,' he breathed, his chest rising and falling in double-quick time, his lips as swollen as hers felt. 'Too damned hot.'

No, she thought desolately as she drank in the sight of him against the backdrop of the ocean for one final time, *too damned cold.*

CHAPTER TWELVE

Four months later

CALLY wanted to like Paris. There were plenty of reasons why she should. For a start, professionally speaking, she could finally say that all the years of hard work and study had been worthwhile. The head of the conservation team at the Galerie de Ville had gladly employed her, and had done so based on her merits alone. The work was stimulating and the paintings prolific; last week they had showcased an early Rossetti that she and the rest of the team had restored, and it had been extremely well-received. The other conservationists were dedicated and friendly, the studio state-of-the-art. And, where once her lunch breaks had consisted of a dash down to the rather lacklustre local shops on the outskirts of Cambridge, now she could take a walk along the Seine, wander through the endless rooms of the Louvre, or, as had been her preference of late, sit in a café in Montmartre and watch the world go by.

When she was not at work, she returned to a small but pleasant apartment near the Eiffel Tower which she was renting from a dear old woman by the name of Marie-Ange who was also giving her French lessons, and with the help of Jen back home she had even arranged to get tenants into her house so that she wasn't out of pocket. What with her earnings from the Rénards, deposited in her account within a day of leaving Montéz, her bank balance looked positively healthy.

Oh yes, Cally thought, on the surface everything looked just dandy, that business with the Prince of Montéz far behind her. All except for a couple of minor details. Like the excruciating pain of finding herself in the most romantic city in the world with a broken heart. And the fact that she was pregnant with his baby.

Cally ran her hand protectively over her stomach as she looked across at the higgledy-piggledy rows of umbrellas and easels of the Place du Tertre and cast her mind back to the day she had left. She'd rushed into the pharmacy at Montéz airport as soon as Boyet had dropped her off, desperate to put her mind at rest before catching her flight. And then she had taken the test. Or rather she'd taken three tests, because each time she'd seen the positive result she had scuttled out of the toilet to buy another, convinced that the previous one had to be faulty. Until the sympathetic look of the pretty girl on the till had said it all, and she'd had to acknowledge that the evidence was irrefutable.

That was also the moment she'd realised that sympathetic looks were categorically not what she wanted. She might initially have been in denial about the possibility of being pregnant because of the less-than-perfect circumstances, but accepting that their lovemaking had created a new life growing inside her brought with it an innate joy that was as profound as it was unexpected. So much so that her first instinct had been to turn around and get a taxi straight back to the palace to share the magic of it with

Leon. But in her heart she had known that he would hate her for it. He'd probably have accused her of having planned it all along in some attempt to trap him into marriage, and then that look of utter horror would have come over his face the way it had when she'd told him about Toria. Toria, who for all Cally knew could be carrying her baby's older half-brother or half-sister.

That thought had had her running back to the airport toilets once more—this time with a violent nausea—and was what had convinced her to get on the first plane off the island. Of course, the most obvious final destination would have been England, and her nice, ordered life in Cambridge where she could have sat down and worked out how to go about this whole thing sensibly. But in a moment of hideous clarity she'd seen what would happen if that was what she did. Yes, she probably would have worked out a way to scrimp and save and continue with the bland restorations she'd survived on to date whilst raising a child. But then what? She would have grown into an old spinster, bitter that all those years of hard work and study had counted for nothing, that her only work of note was the Rénards, and that she'd only got to work on those because they happened to have been bought by a man who had wanted to bed her. And, worst of all, she would have remembered those weeks in Montéz as the highest point in her life because nothing in England was ever likely to eclipse them.

So, although it was the most unsuitable time to take a new job in an unfamiliar city, to Cally the possibility of a temporary contract with the Galerie de Ville offered her the chance to prove to herself that she had felt so alive on the island because of the creative challenge, the change of scene. Living in the French capital was bound to equal her experiences in Montéz, if not exceed them, and she would be placated by the knowledge that in years to come, as well as having achieved her dream of working as a restorer in one of the world's most prestigious galleries, she could look back on that time in her life much more rationally and be better prepared to face the challenges ahead.

But Cally had failed to take into account one very important variable.

Leon Montallier was not in Paris.

And, though she was loath to admit it as she dug into the delicious crêpe that the waiter had just placed in front of her, that was the reason she wasn't even close to the feeling of happiness she'd felt in Montéz. However perfect Paris was on paper, in reality it simply made her realise that everything she had always thought she wanted wasn't what she wanted at all. Even the new restorations which she was supposed to be enjoying were only vaguely satisfying in the sense that she was using her skills, filling her time. Creatively, the only thing she found herself wanting to do was create another composition of her own. But every time she sat down before a blank canvas she just couldn't bring herself to begin; it was as if the vast expanse of emptiness represented the contents of her heart.

It was probably for the best, she thought miserably. Yes, she'd thought that landscape she'd done at the palace had been all right at the time, but she was sure if she ever saw it again without the rose-tinted glasses of back then she'd know it was dire. She should have tossed it into the sea before she'd left, she thought, suddenly hideously embarrassed by the thought that by now Leon had doubtless come across it, vaguely recalled the conversation in which

she'd told him she never painted her own stuff and concluded there was a good reason why. He'd probably tossed
it into the sea himself.

And, as for supposing that once she was on her own the
gaping hole he'd opened would close again, she couldn't
have been more wrong. It was irrational, it was hopeless,
but the truth was she was in love with him, and there could
be no more denying it. Paris had only magnified the very
feelings for him which she had come here to try and dispel.
Feelings which, as the first few weeks went by, she had
hoped would be diminished by the passing of time, but
which remained stubbornly unchanged.

Unchanged, all except one thing. Last week she had been
practising her French translation by listening to a gossipy
radio station when suddenly she'd heard Toria's name.
Apparently she was celebrating the birth of her baby boy—
a beautiful, mixed-race baby boy—with her partner, a professional footballer, with whom she was now living in Milan.

It was, of course, an enormous relief to Cally to know that
she wasn't in the running for some hideous Oprah Winfrey
show entitled *I'm pregnant with the prince's baby… Me too!*
But in some ways it made coming to terms with her own
actions even harder. For whatever reason—maybe purely to
stir up trouble for the man who had curbed her fame—Toria
had been the one spinning the lies, and Leon had been telling
the truth. Except about where he had been all those mornings,
she thought in a bid to continue to think ill of him, but now
that just seemed petty. That was hardly a crime—unlike not
telling someone they were going to become a parent.

Of course, she'd thought about it ever since. The instant
she'd heard the news on the radio she'd seriously toyed
with the idea of phoning him, or catching a flight out to

Montéz. But every time she imagined his respônse she lost her nerve. Discovering he was not the father of Toria's baby only changed things from her perspective, she thought as the waiter cleared her plate. Maybe she could trust him, but it didn't alter the fact that Leon did not want a child, and that if it hadn't been for her lust-induced idiocy Leon would not be having a child. So why should he have to feel some burden of responsibility to her and their baby for the rest of his life because of her mistake? She couldn't bear the thought of that. If he had wanted any further part in her life he would have come looking for her, but he hadn't.

'Mind if I join you?'

At the sound of a voice which sounded uncannily like his, Cally's head flew up so fast she saw spots and knocked her cup flying, the dregs of her coffee heading straight for him across the glossy red-and-white-checked tablecloth. She was just about to jump up and catch it, when he reached forward and stopped it with a napkin that he seemed to produce out of thin air and dropped into the chair opposite in one fluid movement.

'Leon.' Her voice came out altogether too breathlessly, part shock at seeing him here, part horror at the realisation that if she had jumped up, he would have seen the evidence of her pregnancy. 'What are you doing here?'

She shifted underneath the table, suddenly grateful for the cover it offered.

'One of your colleagues at the gallery told me I might find you here.'

'Who?' Cally asked, praying he'd spoken to Michel and not Céline, who was bound to have mentioned that Callie had been coming here every day since she'd developed a peculiar craving for spinach-and-gorgonzola crêpes.

'A man. I didn't catch his name.'

'Michel.' Cally smiled and breathed a temporary sigh of relief, not noticing the look of displeasure that flitted across Leon's mouth. 'Anyway, that wasn't what I meant. What are you doing here, in Paris?'

Her mind rewound to what she had been thinking about seconds before he'd appeared out of nowhere. *If he had wanted any further part in your life, he would have come looking for you...* Was it possible? She examined his face, the face that was etched so clearly in her mind that it was there even when she closed her eyes. It was even more devastating than she remembered, but, if it were possible, even more shuttered too.

'Why do you *think* I'm in Paris, *chérie?*' His look was depreciating, and for a second she was terrified he knew. No, he couldn't.

'You're here on business?' she ventured.

He chuckled, running his finger down the menu. 'Partly. What are you having?'

Partly. What the hell did that mean? It meant business and pleasure were always inseparable to him, she supposed, that maybe whenever his princely duties took him within a cab journey of an old flame he looked them up out of curiosity. Yes, Leon was the kind of man who would think it was possible to be friends afterwards, because he was never the one who got hurt. 'Nothing, thank you.'

'Then why don't you let me walk you back to the gallery?'

'Actually,' Cally backtracked, remembering the benefit of the table, 'I ought to have something or I'll be hungry later on.'

Leon gritted his teeth as she pretended to study the menu. The menu from which he had watched her order an enormous lunch less than twenty minutes earlier, and consume with a rapidity that would have made him think she wasn't earning enough money to feed herself properly if he hadn't known the truth. The truth that had stared him in the face from the newspaper article Boyet had left for his attention three days ago—the one about the new Rossetti the Galerie de Ville had on display, returned to its original glory by their team of restorers. With photographs.

At first he had been beside himself with fury. She was pregnant, and he knew the child had to be his—for he could accuse her of many things, but looseness was not one of them. Yet she had kept it from him, after all the accusations she had thrown at him about dishonesty and omitting the truth!

But, alongside his burning rage, he had realised that not only had she neglected to tell him, but she had not gone to the papers or come running back to him either. And that puzzled him. Yes, he had come to believe that maybe she wasn't the kind of woman who would sell her story for her fifteen minutes of fame as he had once believed, but he would have put money on her coming back to try and wangle a marriage proposal out of him. Hell, he had been convinced she would come back for the sex alone, just as soon as her desire for him threatened to consume her the way his desire for her had threatened to consume him so frequently in the weeks since her graceless departure, but to his infinite frustration she hadn't. So why hadn't she, even though she now had the perfect leverage?

The discovery that he did not have an answer to that question was the moment that it had occurred to him that, if he was capable of quelling his anger, then maybe, just maybe, she could be the perfect solution to the unpalatable problem which had been plaguing him ever since he'd heard about Toria. Along with the problem of the unbearable ache in his groin which had only increased at the sight of her newly voluptuous curves, he thought, observing her keenly through narrowed eyes and deciding it was time to find out if she really did suppose he was too stupid to notice.

'I think I'll have an almond *friand*,' Cally said, hoping it was the smallest thing on the menu. 'How about you?'

'I don't know. How about some answers?'

'Sorry?'

She tried to avoid his gaze but she felt his eyes bore into her. 'Some answers,' he repeated. 'Like why you haven't told me that you're having my baby.'

Cally felt a surge of panic knot itself around her heart. 'How—how did you find out?' she asked hopelessly.

'Not the way I deserved to.'

Her eyelids fluttered down to her cheeks and she nodded shamefully. 'I should have told you.'

'So why didn't you?'

She shook her head and fiddled with the menu, unable to look at him. 'Because I knew you didn't want a child, and it's my fault that you're having one.'

Leon frowned, not knowing what she meant, but certain he wasn't going to like what was coming next.

'That first time—when I said I didn't need protection— I thought we were talking figuratively. I didn't realise that… It wasn't until afterwards that I realised that you were talking about contraception.'

'So after that you just lived the lie, whilst accusing *me* of deceit at every opportunity?'

She hung her head.

Leon felt a white-hot anger blaze within him but he forced himself to bite his tongue. If she had come to him with that excuse he never would have believed her, he would have known that it was all part of an elaborate ploy to get him to waltz her down the aisle from the start. But she hadn't. The fact remained that she'd had the perfect reason to throw in her career and get everything he'd thought she wanted but she hadn't used it. Which was why, even though he was livid that she'd lied, it was almost possible that this could work.

'It was an easy mistake to make,' he forced out, biting his lip.

Cally raised her head in utter disbelief. Understanding. From Leon Montallier.

'Yes, it was.'

'And yet you planned to see the consequences through.'

'Just because it was unexpected does not mean I even thought for a moment about not having this baby,' she shot back, a fierce and thoroughly arousing maternal protectiveness glowing in her eyes.

'So what you are saying is since discovering you are to become a mother, your feelings towards the idea of becoming a parent have changed?'

'Yes.'

'Did it not occur to you that if you had told me I was to become a father my feelings might have altered also?'

Cally watched as the lines of his face softened and her eyes widened in disbelief. 'I—I suppose I expected you to react in the same way that you did when I told you that Toria was pregnant,' she said guiltily. 'But I know now that had nothing to do with you.'

Leon nodded gravely, determined not to invite questions

about the real reason for his horrified reaction that day, but Cally was too lost in her own thoughts to notice.

'So, have they changed?' she whispered. 'Your feelings, I mean?'

Leon paused, knowing his answer demanded the utmost consideration, and took a deep breath. 'You are right that I did not expressly want a child, Cally. Not because of any aversion to the prospect, but because I believe that a child is best brought up by a mother and father who are married. Since I have always been disinclined on that front, by default the prospect seemed unlikely. But life is never quite that— neat.' He shook his head and turned away the waiter who had approached the table. 'You *are* carrying my child.' He ran his eyes over her face, surprised to find that the words were ready on the tip of his tongue without any of the resistance he had expected. 'But, even before I knew that, for the past four months I have found myself aching for you in a way that is completely unprecedented—not only to have you back in my bed, but to have you by my side.'

The heavy lashes that shadowed her cheeks lifted in disbelief.

'I therefore find that my inclination has changed. I wish to marry you, Cally. As soon as possible.'

Cally had to pinch her leg under the table to check that she wasn't dreaming. Leon Montallier—*Prince* Leon Montallier, the man who had told her that he found the institution of matrimony categorically intolerable—hadn't *really* just said aloud that he wished to marry her, had he?

Yes, she thought. He had. And, impossible though it seemed, he'd said it in such a way that it sounded like the sincerest thing he'd ever uttered. It hadn't been some overblown, rehearsed proposal that befitted the romantic reputation of his countrymen; it had been a statement, simple and unadorned. It said that, no, this hadn't been the way he had expected things to go, but now that they had he wanted to take this chance because he felt what they had already shared could continue to grow. It said that he trusted her, and he was asking her to place her trust in him right back.

Could she? she wondered. Could she really dare to believe in things that she had spent years, and in particular the last four months, forbidding herself to even dream about? Like sleeping with the man she loved every night and waking up beside him every morning. Taking breakfast at the table on the terrace, a table laid for three, maybe one day even four. Cally closed her eyes to stop the visions overwhelming her. Surely those kinds of dreams were too big? Like he said, life wasn't neat. Even if they could tidy it now, what happened when the swell of unexpected feelings that had hit him with the discovery that he was to be a father diminished, and he remembered that he had never been cut out for family or fidelity after all? Wouldn't she be doing them both a wrong not to be more cautious?

'Don't you think that maybe getting married is a little too *rash?*' she replied hesitantly, focussing on the caricaturist and the small crowd of onlookers on the opposite side of the street, afraid that if she caught his eye he would know that talking him out of this was the last thing she really wanted.

'No,' he replied, his voice gentle but firm. 'And I'm not sure that you do either.'

Cally felt her breath catch in her throat, taken aback to discover that he didn't need to look in her eyes to know exactly what she was thinking. To know that she was looking for a reason to say no because it felt safer, because that was the answer that her nice, ordered life had got her into the habit of. And she understood that even if they'd been in a proper relationship for a year and had already had a conversation about what they'd call their children one day, saying yes would still feel just as scary because it involved her placing her trust in another human being. Rash was just an excuse.

'Perhaps you're right,' she admitted. 'But I just don't want either of us to look back and think this was a mistake.'

'No one can know what the future holds,' he said with all the gravity of a man who had experienced the arbitrariness of fate. 'But surely it could never be a mistake to try and raise our child together?'

He had her there, Cally thought, for how could she ever regret raising their baby with him in Montéz when the alternative was going it alone in her damp two-up two-down in Cambridge? However much she'd once hated the concept of privilege, she couldn't think of any better start in life for their child than growing up at the palace. Besides, she realised with a start, he or she would be first in line to the throne; how could they grow up anywhere else and be prepared for what lay ahead?

Leon hadn't even mentioned that, and suddenly she loved him all the more for it. Of course it would be important to him that his heir be raised on the island, yet he hadn't pushed it, just like he hadn't stressed that her acceptance would mean an official role for her too. But it would, she thought anxiously, wondering whether saying yes would mean kissing everything in her old life goodbye.

'As well as raising our child, I had hoped to continue working, Leon.'

'Of course,' he replied with none of the sarcasm she might once have expected. 'Perhaps you can freelance out of the studio.'

Cally almost couldn't believe her ears. He wasn't asking her to give up the work she loved, he wasn't assuming that that was what she wanted. Yes, there were so many unknowns, so much to overcome, but surely if they were both willing to try...? 'Perhaps I could.' She nodded tentatively.

'Are you by any chance thinking that you wouldn't be averse to the idea of marrying me either, *chérie?*'

'Yes, Leon, I think I am.'

'Good,' he said, leaning across the table and whispering in her ear. 'Because I've already booked the church for this time next week.'

'This time *next week?*'

Leon nodded.

It was arrogant. Maybe it was overly romantic too. But the joy in her heart overtook her exasperation and in an instant she was on her feet and closing the short distance between them. But just as she pressed her body into his and raised her hands to tangle them in his hair he placed one hand on her elbow and stopped her.

'What is it?'

Cally followed his eyes, which had dropped to her pregnant stomach.

'I just—' It was the first time it had really occurred to him that his child was growing inside her womb, and he was shocked by the feelings of both helplessness and strength that swelled within him. 'Can I touch it?'

'Of course you can!' Cally grinned, breathing a sigh of relief and grabbing his hand to place it on her belly. She was equally unprepared for the weight of her own emotions as he stroked her protectively.

'I'm sorry,' she whispered, drawing in a deep breath as the magnitude of what she had denied him truly hit home. As she did, her agitation caused the baby to give a tiny kick. He jumped back and looked at her in awe.

'I'm sorry I didn't tell you,' she repeated.

Leon felt a muscle tighten at his jaw but he forced himself to let it go.

'My twenty-week scan—it's booked in at the hospital here in three days. Come with me?'

He nodded with a conviction that told her he wouldn't miss it for the world. 'And then to Montéz.'

CHAPTER THIRTEEN

'How about Jacques?' Leon grinned as they drove over the hilltop and the palace came into view. It was even more resplendent than she remembered in the low November sunshine.

Cally looked down at her lap. She was holding their marriage licence which they had just collected from the town hall in one hand, and the ultrasound photo of their baby boy in the other. If she had had a third hand she would have pinched herself again.

'Inspired by Jacques Rénard?' she asked, studying the photo as only an expectant mother could, ignoring the fuzzy patches of light and shade and trying to discern whether their son might look like a Jacques. She turned back to Leon and her smile widened in approval. 'I love it.'

They had both wanted to know the sex. Maybe it was because having a baby in the first place had been surprise enough, or maybe it was because they had both wanted to discover one thing about this pregnancy together, but either way they were delighted.

'Remind me again of your nephews' names?'

'Dylan and Josh. Dylan's the eldest.'

It continued to amaze her that Leon had not only insisted

her family be invited to their wedding in four days' time, but that he seemed genuinely interested in them too—even Jen, despite her being a journalist, which she knew deep down he viewed as a heinous crime. However, Cally's amazement couldn't be greater than her sister's had been when she'd called her yesterday.

'Married? To the Prince of Montéz?' Jen had cried when she'd finally stopped apologising for the hundredth time for only hearing 'I wish' and 'Don't mention him' during that telephone conversation when she'd suggested running the article. 'But… I thought you said he was a complete bastard?'

'He has his moments.' Cally had laughed. 'But I've fallen in love with him, Jen, and, well… We're expecting a baby in March.'

Her sister had been even more flabbergasted then. But she decided that no one could be more amazed than she already was herself as she drew up outside the palace and she saw Boyet descending the steps, ready to unload the car of the few bits and pieces she'd brought with her to begin their new life together. Like the beautiful cot that had been a farewell gift from Michel, Céline and the rest of the gallery team, and enough knitted babygrows from Marie-Ange to clothe the entire maternity ward—she had been beside herself to discover that she had been renting a room to a future princess and heir of Montéz.

Yes, she would always recall the friends she had made in Paris with affection, but leaving the capital had been a million times easier than it had ever been to leave here, she thought as they walked through the courtyard and up the creamy white staircase. Montéz felt like home. And, whilst living in a palace was going to take some getting used to, she couldn't help believing her parents had actually been right when they had once told her that wealth and class could be irrelevant. She couldn't help hoping she'd been wrong to stop believing in happy-ever-after too.

Even if there had been a few moments in the past few days when the look in Leon's eyes had been so unfathomable it was like he had momentarily shut her out in the cold. But she told herself it was to be expected, that it was just going to take time for two people who weren't used to sharing their lives to learn to live with one another. She tried to repress the nagging fear that he'd always be closed to her, the realisation that he hadn't once asked how *she* actually felt about *him*. Was it because he didn't want to make her say things that he thought she might not be ready to say? Or because those things would never matter to him?

'*Bonjour, mademoiselle.*'

Cally shook herself and smiled warmly as Boyet opened the car door for her. '*Bonjour, Boyet, ça va?*'

'*Oui, ça va bien, merci.*' He grinned, clearly impressed with her improved accent, and then turned to Leon. 'I alighted upon a newspaper article that may be of some interest, Your Highness. The daily papers are out on the terrace as usual.'

He nodded '*Merci,* Boyet.'

Cally and Leon entered the hallway together, and whilst she popped to the bathroom Leon continued through to the terrace. He was standing above the wrought-iron table when she entered the drawing room, and she observed him as she walked towards the glass doors; his forehead was deeply lined.

'What is it?' she asked anxiously, stepping outside to join him. He raised his eyes casually from the article he was reading, but the second they met with hers he froze. For one long moment he seemed to look at her as if he was seeing her for the first time, and then his frown disappeared altogether and his whole face seemed to lighten.

'It's nothing, *chérie,*' he said, folding up the sheaf of paper and placing it in the top pocket of his shirt. 'Nothing at all. But I'm afraid there are some documents which urgently await my signature at the Treasury.' His eyes dropped to her hand that was still clutching their marriage licence and he smiled. 'I can drop our papers in with Father Maurice on the way. It's been a long day. Why don't you get some rest?'

Why don't you tell me what the article is about, if it's nothing? Cally wanted to retort, but she knew that she was probably just being paranoid, and making him aware of it was hardly going to encourage him to open up. 'You're probably right.'

Leon ran his finger tenderly down her arm and took the papers from her hand. 'I know I am.' He grinned. 'I'll be back in an hour or two, and if you're up to it we can take a stroll along the beach before dinner. It's not quite as warm at this time of year, but the sunset is always spectacular.'

She nodded as he kissed her lightly on the mouth. 'I'd like that.'

Cally tried to nap, but failed. Her mind was too full of all that had happened over the last few days and, if she was honest, too troubled by old insecurities. Which was ridiculous; she was lying on the royal bed, carrying his son, with their wedding just days away.

It was probably just coming back to the palace and trying to get her head around actually living here, she reasoned. For, though she had resided here for that month, it had been as nothing more than his lover and his employee, and as a result she hadn't really ventured beyond his bedroom or the studio. Cally sat up and swung her legs over the edge of the bed, feeling the luxurious rug beneath her toes. If she was to embrace her new life and feel comfortable raising their son here, then it shouldn't feel like the palace was just a sea of closed doors without any idea what lay behind them. *Like Leon,* she thought bleakly, and then scolded herself. It was going to take time. And, since he'd only just been saying that they should choose a room for the nursery, opening a few doors—literally—seemed like the perfect place to start.

Cally exited the master bedroom and turned right. There had to be at least eight other rooms she'd never entered just in this wing, never mind in all the other wings on the other floors. But she couldn't imagine choosing a room for their son's nursery—Jacques' nursery—more than a few steps away from their bedroom.

The first door she entered, opposite the master bedroom, revealed a large room with an oak ceiling and a view of the inner courtyard. It would have fulfilled its function more than adequately, but it didn't feel in any way cosy, and it seemed a shame to Cally for their son's room not to face out to sea when that was the part of Montéz that she most associated with Leon. The second room she entered was to the right of their own, and couldn't have been more different. It was a moderate size with a fabulous view of the bay, a long window seat and lemon walls bathed in late-afternoon sunlight. She could just imagine the cot in here. A rocking horse, piles of play bricks. She smiled, running one hand over her belly, and felt her heart settle. All it needed was some brightly coloured paintings, she thought, catching sight of a large frame propped face down against the wall and wondering if she could make use of it.

Cally walked towards it and wiped the dust from the edge of the frame with her finger. Leaning it back against her body to discern whether or not it was empty, she saw that behind the glass was an enormous royal-family tree. Fascinated, she carefully manoeuvred the frame so that it was propped against the wall face up and sank to her knees to survey it.

Leon so rarely spoke about his family. Not that she could blame him for that, for she had gathered that both his parents were dead and the pain of losing Girard was still very raw. But she couldn't help being curious about the royal dynasty that, incredibly, she found herself about to marry into, that her son was going to be a part of. She ran her eyes along row after row of unfamiliar names, sovereign princes past, their wives, their children. Then she dropped her eyes to the bottom of the picture, desperate to find Leon's name, to trace the branches she knew and to locate the spot where two new ones would soon be added. But the second she saw the swirling typescript of his name she dropped her hand as if she had been burned, shocked to discover that the existing branches around him didn't even begin to lead where she'd expected.

Rapidly, she tried to make sense of what she was seeing. Leon's mother Odette had married Arnaud Montallier, the Sovereign Prince of Montéz, and together they'd had one son—Girard. Seventeen years later, Girard was crowned Prince—the same year, quite logically, that his father had passed away. But it wasn't until the *following* year that Odette had given birth to her second son, Leon. Whose father was not listed as a prince at all, but as a man named Raoul Rénard.

Cally stared in disbelief. No wonder Leon had implied that his title was a fate that should never have befallen him. It was not simply because Girard had died unexpectedly, but because the royal bloodline—if it was like any other she'd ever read about—had technically died out with him. Which meant that Leon had inherited the throne simply because his mother had been the sovereign's widow.

Cally felt an icy fear begin to grip her as all that that meant slowly began to hit home. Her eyes rested on the branch between Girard and Toria. Toria, who was the former sovereign's widow just as Odette had once been. Toria, who had also given birth to a son. A son who—if Leon was an example of what happened in such circumstances—could inherit the throne one day. Unless Leon married and had a child of his own.

Suddenly, Toria's words that afternoon in the studio echoed through her mind with new and devastating clarity: *Tell him I'm pregnant. With the heir to the throne.* That was why the expression on Leon's face had been one of such unmitigated dread. She'd been so convinced she understood it, but she had actually read it as wrongly as she always did. It wasn't because he was the father of her child; oh no, Cally understood now that Toria had simply alighted on that lie as a way of hurting her. It was because the woman he loathed was carrying a child who had the potential to inherit everything.

And, with that realisation, the trust that Cally Greenway had dared to place in Leon Montallier came crashing down around her shoulders, taking her fragile heart with it. He hadn't come to Paris because he had missed her, hadn't proposed because he thought they had a shot at happiness, or even because he thought it was the best thing to do for their child. He had simply discovered that she was pregnant, and that making their child his legitimate heir was preferable to the thought of Toria's child being first in line to the throne. Hell, he'd even waited until he had accompanied her to the scan before they had gone to get their marriage licence. Fit, healthy and a boy; no wonder he'd proceeded with such enthusiasm!

Cally felt a tortured moan escape her lips and sank back on her heels, head raised as if appealing to some invisible god for mercy. Could she have been any more foolish? How easily she had fallen for his honeyed words and feigned understanding! She'd even supposed that he hadn't mentioned the small matter of their child's legitimacy because he didn't consider that to be the most important thing! Why the hell hadn't she learned that with Leon the important thing was always the thing that he *didn't* mention? Like the fact that he was a prince, that he had bought the paintings for himself, that he had only employed her because he wanted to take her to bed. He had lied to her from the day she had met him, and all this time she had been stupid enough to go on believing what she wanted to believe, thinking he simply needed time to open up.

Unable to bear the evidence of his lies in black and white before her, Cally backed away from the family tree and stumbled out into the corridor. Suddenly the whole palace felt like a conspirator in his betrayal. Tearing down the stairs and out into the grounds, she found herself on the grass verge overlooking the magnificent bay. The bay where Leon had planned to take her for a walk before dinner, that had been the subject of the picture he had inspired her to paint after so many years of believing that part of her was dead. Now every part of her felt dead, oblivious to everything except the sobs which began deep inside her chest and took her over. She couldn't remember the last time she had succumbed to such irrepressible tears, but she did know that her practised mechanism of swallowing hard and blinking repeatedly would do her no good, for her eyes were already sore, and her throat was so constricted it was all she could do not to choke on her own sobs.

She didn't even stop as she sensed him come up behind her. Looming. Blurred. She wanted to lunge at him, pound her fists against his chest, but she didn't have the strength.

He swooped down to her level. 'What the hell's the matter, are you in pain? The baby?'

'No, Leon,' she gasped, her words punctuated by sobs. 'The heir to the throne is perfectly safe.'

His brows descended into a dark V, and he ran his eyes over her as if checking all her limbs were intact. 'If not the baby, then what?'

'What else is there?' she swiped.

'Well, clearly there's something the matter with you, and I think I have a right to know.'

'A right to know?' Cally cried hysterically. 'You mean like I had a right to know that the only reason you wanted to marry me was because you couldn't bear a child of Toria's to be first in line to the throne?'

Leon went very still. 'Has she been here again?'

A ridiculous part of her had been waiting for him to deny it all. His response only drove the knife in deeper. 'No, Leon. Toria has not been here. Your pathetic little fiancée worked it all out by herself, from the family tree.'

Leon clenched his teeth. The family tree in his old nursery. The one his mother had given him as a child to try and help him come to terms with the truth, but which had only succeeded in making him feel more different.

'What were you doing, poking around in there?'

'Poking around?' she rasped despairingly. 'I thought this was to be my home, Leon, our son's home?'

'And so it will be.'

'No, Leon.' Cally shook her head. 'How can this ever become my home if there are parts of it I am forbidden to enter? Unless all you want is a wife in name only…' She looked out at the horizon, still trying to come to terms with her discovery. 'Yes. I suppose that *is* all you want.'

'I do not want you as my wife in name only!' he protested—too loudly, she thought, as he raised back up to his full height and began to pace.

'But unless you're prepared to be honest,' she whispered brokenly, 'how could I ever be anything else?'

Leon stilled, and, lowering his eyes, he caught sight of a single tear rolling down her cheek. As it splashed onto her pregnant belly, something unbearable began to invade every organ in his body. Shame? Regret? Fear? No, all three. That afternoon, when she'd left here for Paris, all he had wanted was her trust, to believe that her hysterics weren't some attempt to weasel something out of him. Now he realised that in agreeing to become his wife she had put her trust in him unquestionably, but he'd been so bloody single-minded—so driven by the solution she presented, by his own libido—that he'd trampled all over the one thing he had wanted to protect.

He dropped to the grass beside her, knowing it was too late, but that more than anything she deserved to know the truth, however shameful. 'How I became the prince isn't exactly something I'm proud of.'

Cally read the look of agony on his face. 'Well, you should be,' she said grudgingly. 'Whatever else is true, giving up a career you were passionate about because your country needed you is admirable.'

'It was my duty. It's complicated how that came to be the case, but it was.' He took a deep and ragged breath, his eyes fixed on the horizon. 'My mother's marriage to Arnaud was arranged by her social-climbing parents. It was an entirely loveless match, but she provided him with the son he desired and stayed loyal to him until he passed away. A few months after that, when she was still only in her late thirties, a sailor ran into trouble in the bay and she offered him shelter inside the palace whilst he repaired the engine on his boat. His name was Raoul Rénard.' Leon paused over his name, a tortured expression in his eyes, and suddenly its significance dawned on Cally. 'According to my mother, he was a descendent of the great artist Jacques Rénard. She fell deeply in love with him, and within weeks she was pregnant.'

Cally looked at him in wonder. That was why he had been willing to pay any sum for the paintings, and why he'd done so anonymously too: Jacques Rénard was one of his ancestors! She immediately felt guilty, for all the accusations she'd thrown at him about wanting them purely to boast about, and for how quickly she had jumped to the wrong conclusions about him. But they hadn't been all wrong, she thought, wiping the stream of tears from her eyes with the sleeve of her cardigan. Even if he did have a deep attachment to the paintings, he still had no real attachment to her. If he did, he would have told her sooner, would have understood that her own passion for the Rénards ran just as deep. And he would have proposed because he loved her, she thought, stifling a renewed sob, not just because he needed a son.

'And did he love her?' Cally asked, wondering why, in spite of everything she had always known about true love being the stuff of legend, not history, she wanted to hear that he had.

'Yes.' Leon nodded gravely. 'I believe he did. But my mother's moment of happiness was short-lived. The next time my father returned to sea, the boat's engine caught fire and he was killed.' His eyes clouded as he recalled that the twist of fate which had been responsible for the start of his life had also led to his father's death. 'The shock sent my mother into labour early, and as a result the people of Montéz simply presumed that Arnaud was my father. My mother's closest advisors suggested that was for the best. And, besides, I was the next in line regardless.'

Cally frowned. 'But…how?'

Leon replied in a voice that seemed to come from a long way off, and Cally realised that the guard she had been wanting him to drop ever since that night in London was slowly coming down before her eyes. But only now did she see that she had been wrong to assume that behind that closed door would be the proof that he loved her; the reality was that he felt nothing for her at all. Which probably ought to have fuelled her anger, but all she could think about was how much he'd had to deal with, how much she wanted to hold him.

'The royal bloodline in Montéz differs from that of other countries, or at least it has since the turn of the sixteenth century,' Leon continued, watching the breeze blow wisps of her hair out of her ponytail, wishing he had the right to smooth them away from her face, hating that he didn't.

'At that time, the king of the island, who had subjected the islanders to a long reign of oppression, was overthrown by a hero amongst the people named Sébastien. He was the tyrannical king's illegitimate half brother—the son of the old king's widow and one of the palace advisors. Sébastien declared that the royal family should be abolished and that Montéz should become a democracy. The people were overjoyed, but they clamoured for him to become the king. He was reluctant, but eventually he agreed, on one condition: that he and his future successors should only ever be known as Sovereign Prince, not King, as a reminder that the greatest power should always remain with the people.'

At what point had he lost sight of what mattered? Leon wondered, and what made him even think that his son would be the worthiest successor to the throne with *him* as a role model? He shook his head and continued. 'But the rest of France was reluctant to accept Sébastien as the new sovereign, because he couldn't prove that he was royal. The citizens of Montéz were outraged, and so, to grant him legitimate status, they voted for a change to the law. It states that any widow of the sovereign retains her royal status after his death, and thus any child she bears afterwards inherits that status and a claim to the throne, so long as she never marries again. Therefore, they argued, Sébastien's mother had passed her royal status on to him.' Leon took a deep breath. 'As my mother did to me.'

Cally stared at him in amazement as all he had said sunk in, and the knock-on effects of the ancient and remarkable law began to crystallise in her mind. No wonder he had always spoken of his title as if it was something that didn't really belong to him, but a job that he had reluctantly taken on. And no wonder he had always found the concept of marriage so intolerable. For when the sovereign of Montéz took a bride, he had to trust her to honour him not only during his lifetime but even after his death.

Which meant he had been willing to place that trust in you, a voice inside her whispered, but she ignored it, for what good was that if she couldn't trust *him?* And what good had it done her to think this was just about feelings like trust or love, when he was a prince for whom marriage and children would always mean something more? Or was it really something less? she wondered sorrowfully.

'So, there you have it,' Leon concluded uneasily. 'I am the prince, but only because of an ancient technicality. In terms of the usual rules of patrilineal descent, I do not have a drop of royal blood.'

Cally's heart filled with empathy. 'Do you really suppose it matters whose blood runs through your veins, Leon?' she answered croakily, conscious that not so long ago she had been guilty of pigeonholing anyone with a title. 'Why should it matter who your father was, whether you inherited the throne because of a technicality or because of biology? What matters is that the prince has the best interests of his country at heart. That was why the people supported Sébastien all those years ago, the same way your people would support you.'

'Perhaps.' Leon turned back to her, his eyes searching her face in wonder, wishing he hadn't allowed the shame he felt for a past over which he had no control jeopardise his future with the only woman he had ever met who hadn't cared who he was, who had cared only whether he was a decent man. Well, he thought grimly, he had proved that he wasn't that all by himself. 'Not long after Girard passed away, the truth began to gnaw at me so badly that I almost made up my mind to find out. But I realised it would not only cause enormous unrest during an already turbulent time, but it would become common knowledge that any man who got Toria pregnant would be the father of the next Prince of Montéz, the consequences of which could have been catastrophic.'

'But Toria herself has always known?' Cally replied, her mind returning to the agonising present.

'Girard explained the intricacies of the law when they married, but it wasn't until after his death that she saw the opportunity to use what she had once seen as some boring old decree to benefit herself. When I resisted her advances, she realised that if she went to the papers with it it would ensure her a permanent following. That was what finally convinced me to reinstate the law against the press.'

'So the only way left for her to take revenge on you was by actually getting pregnant?' Cally stared agog, horrified that any woman could possibly use their potential for motherhood in such a despicable way.

'At the time I thought so, but now I believe that angering me, attempting to drive a wedge between you and me, was a convenient by-product of an accidental pregnancy.'

'Just like the solution to that problem was a convenient by-product of mine,' Cally said despondently, tugging on a piece of grass.

'I can't pretend that isn't partly true.' Leon's eyes were hooded, self-condemning. 'But it isn't that simple. I was always adamant that I never wanted to marry.'

She could understand that now, Cally thought, if not because of the peculiarities of the law then because of the loveless marriage his mother had endured, the union of misplaced trust his brother had fallen into.

He continued. 'I've always been adamant that I didn't want to marry, but once I met you I had to keep inventing new reasons why that was the case, because you kept proving all the old ones wrong. Like thinking all you wanted was fame or sex. By the time you went to Paris there weren't any reasons left.'

'Even if that is true—' Cally shook her head '—you still didn't do anything about it until you discovered that it was in the interests of your kingdom to act. And maybe I would have understood that too if you'd told me. But you didn't.'

Leon nodded remorsefully. 'I suppose I was still reluctant to admit it to myself, too scared you'd walk away if you knew and… And then it stopped having anything to do with my kingdom anyway.'

'What?' Cally searched his face as he reached into his pocket and unfolded the newspaper article he had put there that morning, the one he had refused to show her, and placed it down on the grass.

At the centre was a wedding photo, Toria's wedding photo, taken yesterday. Cally ran her eyes over the frothy white dress, the groom's garish white suit and their baby son dressed like a cherub as she tried to process what it meant. Leon's words rang through her mind: *Any widow of the sovereign retains her royal status after his death, and thus any child she bears afterwards inherits that status and a claim to the throne,* so long as she never marries again…

What it meant was that the second that Toria had got her figure back marrying a high-profile footballer had appealed to her more than revenge. It meant that Toria's son was no longer in line to the throne. And that meant, as of a few hours ago, Leon had had every reason to call their wedding off.

But he hadn't, because he'd taken their marriage

licences to the priest after that. She looked up into his face, her eyes enormous. 'You mean you don't *need* to marry me, but you were going to anyway?'

CHAPTER FOURTEEN

LEON nodded slowly, and part of Cally's heart felt like it was about to explode with unmitigated joy.

He doesn't need to, but he wants to marry you anyway, she repeated to herself.

Yet the other portion of her heart knew that whatever his reasons for wanting her to be his wife now, love couldn't possibly be one of them. If he had loved her, he would have told her the truth about his past months ago, or a week ago, or even this morning. He would have wanted to be open with her and to find out how she felt about him. But he hadn't, and he'd only told her now because she had accidentally stumbled upon his family tree.

'I understand why you were reluctant to tell me,' she said hopelessly. 'I even admire the whole host of practical reasons you had for proposing. But when I agreed to marry *you…*' She shook her head, knowing that now was the time for honesty on her part too, however futile. 'It was because I was in love with you. I think I was from the first moment I laid eyes on you in London, and because of that I thought I could marry you even if you never loved me. But I can't.'

As Leon listened, he felt something deep within him

shift. Once he'd believed that women only used words like 'love' as a means to an end, but Cally meant everything and wanted nothing. And that was the blinding moment when he realised that her love was everything he wanted, but the last thing that he deserved. Which was why, though the three little words hovered on his lips to say right back, he knew they weren't enough.

He took a deep breath, wondering if he was capable of even half her integrity. 'Let me show you something.'

'What?'

'Let me show you something.' Leon rose to his feet, tentatively reaching out his hand to lead her somewhere—to the car parked on the driveway, by the looks of things—but not daring to touch her. He was probably afraid her emotion was contagious. So, the *L* word really did mean nothing to him, she thought. Was he just going to pretend she hadn't mentioned it at all?

'Now?' she asked disbelievingly.

'Yes, now.' His brows creased with concern as he eyed her bump. 'If you can.'

Cally was too emotionally exhausted to argue. So she let him help her into the passenger seat of the car. The plain and perfectly ordinary black car, she noticed dismally as he pulled away, wishing it could have been some ridiculous sports model so that she could loathe its excess. That would have been easier. Easier than thinking about the real reason he had spent a fortune on those paintings, or why he had always been happiest out in the ocean. Things that reminded her that he was not just a billionaire prince with an overly complex family tree, but a man, a man who she admired more than she'd ever thought possible.

Eventually, after what felt like an age of twisting and

turning along the coast road—Cally staring helplessly at her puffy eyes and red cheeks in the wing mirror—he rolled the car to a standstill outside a modern white building just on the outskirts of the main town.

'Where are we?'

Leon unfolded his lithe frame from the seat beside her and walked round to open her door. 'That day when you called the university and I wasn't there—I was here.'

Cally sighed. Four months ago, she had wanted nothing more than for him to show her where he had been all those mornings. Now it just seemed too little, too late. 'You don't need to show me.'

'Yes, I do.'

Reluctantly, Cally followed him round to the front of the elegant building. He swiped a card and led them inside. It smelled of fresh paint, and there were workmen's tools scattered on the floor.

'This part should be finished by the end of the week,' he said. 'The rest is complete.'

Stepping over plastic sheeting, he led her through to an enormous atrium, and that was when she saw them. There, on the wall in front of her, were the Rénards, flanked by enormous windows which looked out over the Mediterranean.

Cally immediately hurried closer, her mind suddenly oblivious to everything except the ingenious way in which they'd been displayed. 'His love by the sea,' she whispered in disbelief, her eyes darting between the paintings and the view, then falling to the beautifully presented accompanying details which gave information on their composition and credited her with the restoration work. 'When, how— What is this place?'

'Ever since my mother told me I was descended from a

great painter, it occurred to me that Montéz was lacking its own art gallery.' Leon shrugged, as if it had ceased to matter now. 'Once I started working with Professeur Lefevre, I realised that the students at the university were going to need somewhere to showcase their own work too. So I started to have this place built. I just hadn't planned to tell anyone until it was completely finished.'

'It's perfect,' Cally said slowly, the genius of it running through her mind. 'The big names will draw hundreds of visitors, and the students' work will immediately be in the public eye.' She shook her head in wonder. 'Do you mean to tell me that you planned to display the Rénards here all along?'

Leon ran a hand over his forearm uncomfortably. 'Much as I would like to say yes, that was not my intention initially. I bought that Goya in London, amongst others, to display here. But I bought the Rénards for myself. I suppose I wanted a little of *my* father's history inside the palace.' His eyes lifted to meet hers. 'Until you made me realise that if I kept them there I would have more in common with that tyrannical sixteenth-century king than with my own ancestors.'

'If I had known why you wanted them I would never have been so tactless,' she said regretfully.

'But, like you said, the blood that runs through my veins ought to be irrelevant. They deserve to be enjoyed by everyone. Besides, when it came down to it, they were not as hard to part with as something else.' Leon nodded to the wall behind her and she turned.

'My painting!' Cally cried, utterly overwhelmed, and yet also wholly embarrassed to see her landscape, beautifully framed, hanging just a few feet away from the

Rénards. An enormous lump rose in her throat that she had a job to swallow. 'I—I thought if you found it you'd throw it in the sea.'

Leon shook his head. 'It's brilliant, Cally.'

'Hardly.'

Leon raised his eyebrows. She looked at it again, and was forced to concede that it didn't look as dire as she had imagined it might. Not that she had ever expected to see it again.

'I thought you didn't do your own work.'

'I hadn't done.' She shook her head. 'Ever since David. But then I met you.'

She could admit that now—that her inspiration, which had disappeared in Paris, hadn't risen again in Montéz because she'd been in a new and exciting part of the world but because being with the man she loved had been stimulating in every way there was. And constantly surprising, she thought, as seeds of hope dared to take root in her mind.

He nodded and looked up at it. 'I mean it when I say it's brilliant. When I look at it, it's like I can actually feel the passion you felt when you painted it.'

Cally blushed. 'There's probably a reason for that'.

Leon shook his head. 'No, I don't just mean *that*. It's like it's alive with your excitement for the strokes themselves, the colours, the sheer joy of painting.'

Cally drew in a sharp breath and felt the most acutely powerful tears she had ever known prick behind her eyes. He hadn't laughed or tossed it out to sea, wasn't suggesting that her love of painting buried an ulterior motive, nor had he once even implied that a girl like her should never harbour dreams about becoming an artist. He'd framed it, treasured it and hung it in a gallery beside the paintings which had fired her love of art in the first place. 'Thank you,' she said suddenly, her emotions threatening to overwhelm her. 'For understanding what it means to me. I thought—'

'That I'd always presume your career was just something to fill your time until you married? I know,' he said flinchingly. 'You'd think that with everything you endured in order to work on the Rénards I ought to have realised earlier.'

Cally drew in a very deep breath, and for a moment it felt like the world had stopped spinning. All this time she'd been convinced that he saw no need to let her in because he had no desire to understand her… And all the while he had understood her better than anyone she had ever met. She stared at him in utter amazement. 'It wasn't as hard to endure as you might think,' she whispered.

Leon didn't seem to hear her. 'I should have brought you here earlier,' he said hopelessly. 'There are a lot of things I should have done earlier. But this I had planned to tell you…at our wedding. I was just waiting for Jen to let me know whether she could make the date I'd fixed for the grand opening.'

Cally stared at him, dumbfounded by this new information. 'Jen?' Her *sister* Jen?

'I've invited her to cover the story. I'd planned to invite Kaliq and Tamara too,' he continued with immense effort. 'Maybe it isn't the only thing I should think about revealing to the public.'

As she looked up into his face, lined as it was with anguish, full of strength, that was the moment when she knew that everything was going to be OK. Because she suddenly understood that he hadn't just chosen to keep his guard up when he was around *her,* but that ever since childhood he had been forced to keep the truth a secret from everyone. But he was trying to change, and it was because of her.

'That's fantastic,' she whispered, her heartbeat beginning to pound in her ears.

Leon shrugged, his whole pose listless. 'I know that displaying the paintings can't undo all the wrong I've done you, but I just… I need you to understand that you have shaped the way I feel about everything. There were a hundred practical reasons that I held responsible for my proposal to you, but the truth is that I would have dismissed them all if you hadn't changed the way I feel about marriage altogether. That month we spent here together— it was the best of my life.'

He took a deep breath. 'I know I can't ask that of you now, but, if you meant it when you said that you loved me, then please let me learn how to love you properly, how to love our son properly.'

Cally felt a warm glow begin to flow through her, like a diver catching sight of the mast of a sunken ship he had given up hope of ever finding. For those were the words which confirmed that unearthing the rest of Leon's heart was going to be the easy part. 'Something tells me that now you've set your mind to it you're going to be a fast learner.' She smiled.

Leon looked at her in awe, feeling the tension in his shoulders begin to seep away, wondering if he dared let it. 'I don't care how long it takes.'

Cally squeezed his hand and fleetingly she thought she saw him blink back a tear. It was a gesture which confirmed that he understood how close they had both come to losing something so precious, that he was happy to take things slowly, and above all that she could trust him. With it, she was struck by the most phenomenal moment of fulfilment she had ever known.

Well, emotionally speaking, Cally thought with a grin, as she ran her eyes over his impossibly handsome face and athletic body, as drop-dead gorgeous today as he had been that night in London…and every night since.

'As long as it takes,' she repeated thoughtfully. 'But, you know, you have taught me the benefits of acting impulsively, giving in to what *feels* right.' Her eyes gleamed wickedly.

Leon took a cautious step towards her, his tone husky. 'What are you saying, *ma belle?*'

'The church is booked for four days from now, is it not?'

He looked at her in amazement and shook his head in joyous disbelief. 'You mean you want to go ahead with the wedding, just as we planned?'

Cally beamed, thinking how far he had come, how far they had both come. 'Unless you think that is a little *too* rash?'

Leon shook his head commandingly and pulled her close. *'Non, mon amour par la mer,'* he whispered. 'I think that would make me the happiest man alive.'

* * * * *

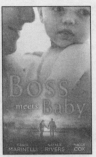